Also by Kristen Heitzmann in Large Print:

Halos
Twilight
The Rose Legacy
Sweet Boundless
A Rush of Wings
Secrets
The Tender Vine

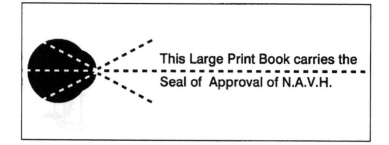

Unforgotten

Kristen Heitzmann

Thorndike Press • Waterville, Maine

L.TE.
Heitzman

Published in 2006 by arrangement with Bethany House Publishers.

Thorndike Press® Large Print Christian Fiction.

The tree indicium is a trademark of Thorndike Press.

The text of this Large Print edition is unabridged.
Other aspects of the book may vary from the original edition.

Set in 16 pt. Plantin by Carleen Stearns.

Printed in the United States on permanent paper.

Library of Congress Cataloging-in-Publication Data

Heitzmann, Kristen.
    Unforgotten : a novel / by Kristen Heitzmann.
      p. cm. — (Thorndike Press large print Christian fiction)
    ISBN 0-7862-8311-4 (lg. print : hc : alk. paper)
    ISBN 1-59415-126-1 (lg. print : sc : alk. paper)
    1. Triangles (Interpersonal relations) — Fiction.
2. Large type books. I. Title. II. Thorndike Press large print Christian fiction series.
PS3558.E468U54 2006
   813′.54—dc22   2005029152

To Jim, always

I have given them the glory that you gave me, that they may be one as we are one: I in them and you in me.

John 17:22–23

National Association for Visually Handicapped
---------------------- *serving the partially seeing*

As the Founder/CEO of NAVH, the only national health agency solely devoted to those who, although not totally blind, have an eye disease which could lead to serious visual impairment, I am pleased to recognize Thorndike Press* as one of the leading publishers in the large print field.

Founded in 1954 in San Francisco to prepare large print textbooks for partially seeing children, NAVH became the pioneer and standard setting agency in the preparation of large type.

Today, those publishers who meet our standards carry the prestigious "Seal of Approval" indicating high quality large print. We are delighted that Thorndike Press is one of the publishers whose titles meet these standards. We are also pleased to recognize the significant contribution Thorndike Press is making in this important and growing field.

Lorraine H. Marchi, L.H.D.
Founder/CEO
NAVH

* Thorndike Press encompasses the following imprints: Thorndike, Wheeler, Walker and Large Print Press.

This book would have been impossible without the generous assistance of both my new and my tried and true friends.

From the Belmont neighborhood in the Bronx:
Robert Lupo, Dominick D'Auria, John DeAngelos, Ida at the candy store, the two Vinnies, the shop owners and residents who made our treks through your streets a true pleasure. To all of you, *grazie molto.*

To Ken and Carolyn for your memories, my gratitude.

To my Bronx stomping partner, Kelly — way too much fun.

To Karen — awesome prayer support and friendship.

To Betty, Kelly, Theresa, Mary, and Doug for reading.

Kati, Romona, and all my sisters and brothers in the Lord.

To my editor Karen Schurrer for attention to detail and all the relevant questions. To all the people at Bethany House whose partnership I so appreciate, my thanks and respect.

For the praise and glory of His name. Thy kingdom come.

Prologue
1931

A moonless night invites deceit, empty sky glutting the stars with self-importance.

The scritch of my fountain pen stills as I raise my eyes to the chill night slipping through my window. I wait; I listen. No tones of Kate Smith from Nonno's radio, only the raspy yowls of two cats tangling and the throbbing crickets' refrain. Only the quickened pulse of the night.

I should curl up and sleep, ignore the feeling inside of something creeping just beyond my thoughts, but there is a bitter tang in my mouth like sorrow. And Papa's words haunt me. *"Take Nonno and hide if trouble comes."* What trouble, Papa? But I know its name.

Arthur Tremaine Jackson. Eyes with no depth, like pewter plates, that look as though he knows everything and has a right to know it. Papa didn't argue when I said that. He merely answered, "Some people want too much."

I don't want too much, only what I have. But lately I find myself looking at a vine bursting with blossoms that will become grapes, at a path I have walked a thousand times, at Papa especially, and I feel a seizing sense of loss. Nonna Carina called it angel sight, my knowing things before I should. *"You have a gift, Antonia. Do not fear it."*

But I fear it now as the little hairs rise on my neck, as my hands grow cold with speculation. The sides of my mouth are dry as chalk. The only other time it was this strong was when Momma died and I felt the angel of death pass down the hall. My hands clench with remembrance.

At a sound outside, I spring to my feet. Tires on the drive and the hum of an engine. I snatch up my diary — no prying eyes will see it — turn off the lamp and hurry to a front window. A car is coming, but not Papa's Ford. It skims the side of the drive and slinks in among the trees lining it. The engine stops; the lamps go off.

But I know the shape of that Packard convertible coupe. Someone gets out the far side. Though I can't see his face, I see him move with stealthy purpose, keeping to the shadows. The driver climbs out, nearly invisible in the trees, but with the flicker of a match cupped near his mouth, I see the glint of Arthur Jackson's hair, his sharp features. Red ash glowing, he leans on the fender and looks up. Though I cannot be seen in the darkened window, his metal gaze pierces me.

Does he want us to know he's here? This could be planned; a meeting with Papa maybe. Or will Papa be caught by surprise? My heart clutches. I have to warn him!

But his instructions were clear. *"If trouble comes . . ."* Is this trouble? It feels like trouble.

I shove the diary into the waist of my skirt and run downstairs, praying with each step, then into the room off the kitchen that is Nonno's place. I shake him awake, the words trembling on my lips. "Come, Nonno. Hurry. There's trouble."

His eyes jerk open, confusion swimming in their gray depths. "Trouble?"

My heart lodges in my throat at the furtive rattling of the front door. "Someone's here. We have to hide. Quickly." I'll see Nonno safe, then think what to do about Papa.

Nonno brings his limbs over, but slowly, so slowly to the floor. I search for his cane as he slides his feet into his shoes, but there's no time. I sling his arm over my shoulders. Leaning on each other, we pass

11

through the kitchen, still smelling of warm bread and garlic.

The front door wrenches open.

"Hurry, Nonno!" I help him into the pantry and shut the door behind us, hardly breathing. Together, we grope past jarred tomatoes, jams, vinegary peppers, wheels of cheese, and sausages hanging from the ceiling. At the back wall, I feel my way down the shelves. There. My fingers slip into the hole, find the lever and release the catch that opens the wall.

I'll see Nonno safely into the cellar. But Papa will come, and when he does . . .

My heart lurches at the sound of footsteps in the kitchen, steps of stealth and malice. I close the wall panel behind us, leaving only a pantry. But in the blackness of the other side, I lean and listen. Either he, too, waits and listens, or the prowler has moved on. He'll find the house empty, report it to Arthur Jackson. *Then go away! Go away before Papa comes home.*

There's no gas or electricity in the cellar, so I light the kerosene lamp hanging on a hook and look down to where Papa said to hide. I promised, but how can I hide when he might come home to a trap? I swallow the lump in my throat. First things first.

Nonno is too old to run, too unsteady to fight. I grab a metal rod from the corner and stick one end into the gears, then

12

wedge the other end into the wall, pressing, then banging with my palms. No one will reach Nonno through this door.

With the lamp in one hand and Nonno leaning heavily, I start down into the cellar that holds racks of red Cabernet and Pinot Grigio. The DiGratia vines yield fruit regardless of Prohibition, and Nonno will not allow their waste. Our last bottlings we've sold for sacramental use, but Papa and Nonno argued over this year's vintage, blessed by extra weeks of sunshine, no frost, no moldering damp.

And so the wine waits. Papa will not let it go cheap; Nonno refuses to consider an illegal sale. He says the government will soon see its folly. Papa tells him governments gorge on folly and there is no glut in sight.

Is this the trouble he meant? Did the banker Arthur Jackson promise Papa a more lucrative market for our wine? I wouldn't doubt it, but if he was there to take delivery, Papa would not have said to hide in the cellar, and someone would not have broken into our house to lie in wait.

. . . *Don't think it. Bad thoughts bring bad luck.*

We reach the bottom of the stairs. "Come, Non—"

My words break at a sound overhead like marbles spilled on tile, a spattering of

13

sharp, angry snaps. *Papa!* I spin, but Nonno's grip tightens. On his face a look of pain. "Nonno, it's Papa. It must be." Sobs climb my throat.

Shaking his head, he draws me on through the cellar, limping and staggering. *Papa* . . . Grief floods my eyes. I have to know, but Nonno won't let go. In the canting light we grope into the arched tunnel at the end of the cellar, and I guess his intention. We'll go out this way and —

"Nonno?"

He seizes his chest and falls against the wall, clutching his arm, then sinking to his knees.

"Nonno, what's wrong!" I clank down the lamp and grab onto him. "Nonno, hold on. Hold on, I'll get help."

He clings to me and rasps, "No, Antonia. You must not be found."

Not be found? What . . . Gunshots. Arthur Jackson. Reality crushes me.

"Antonia." He works too hard for words. "Under . . ." He sags.

"Nonno?" I cradle his head, feeling each of his ragged breaths in the feeble rise and fall of his chest. His eyelids flutter like the slow beat of tattered butterfly wings, then close.

Upstairs something horrible has happened, and in my arms it continues.

14

Nonno! Papa! But there is only the scent of fear and grief as I rock on my knees, silently keening.

There is no time in the darkness of the cellar, only the pulsing of my grief. But slowly my name penetrates, not hollered, but whispered with urgency.

Nonno? His head is cold in my lap.

The whisper comes again, and someone steps into the lamp's glow. Relief and confusion swirl. "Marco? What are you . . . ?"

"Shh." He drops beside me, touches Nonno Quillan's throat to learn what I know already, then meets my tear-filled gaze. "We have to go."

"Go? I can't leave —"

He grabs hold of my shoulders, dark eyes intense in his grim face. "There's nothing more you can do for him."

Where are the laughing eyes, the ardent mouth? Marco, the carefree beau. What is he doing here? "How did you get in? How did you know?" The cellar is my family's secret. He would not just find it.

"Vittorio told me."

Papa told Marco?

He slides Nonno's head from my lap, folds the arms across his chest.

No. Leave him alone. Don't pose him like a dead man. I suck in a sob. "Papa's been shot. I heard it."

He pulls me to my feet. "Let's go."

15

"I have to stay."

"You can't."

My hand stings with the slap. "Don't tell me I can't."

He takes hold of my arm, but I swing again. Marco ducks, grabs hold of me hard, trapping my arms and hissing, "He'll guess you saw and heard."

"I did see!" I thrash. "Arthur Jackson —"

He plants his hand over my mouth. "Don't say it. Don't tell anyone what you know." I kick and squirm, but he forces me along the tunnel to the intruder gate he has left open. I have never felt such fury.

The diary digs into my ribs as I fight. Marco tightens his arms and pushes me through the gate that closes behind us. How has he gotten so strong, so cruel? I jerk my face free and sink my teeth into his wrist, wanting to hurt him more than I have ever wanted anything before.

Sucking in a breath, he eases his flesh out of my teeth. "Believe me, *cara*. There's no other way."

Believe him? I don't know him, have never seen this man who grabs hold and forces me to leave behind the ones I love. What if Papa didn't tell him? Was it Marco in the kitchen?

Panic infuses my struggle. Exasperated, he hoists me over his shoulder, trapping my kicking legs with a bear-like grip. The diary bites into my belly as he climbs the stairs, emerging into the garage. My inverted view passes over timbers that once formed stabling partitions, tools and pails and mechanical items. Then Marco lowers me to the floor.

The moment my feet touch, I haul back and kick his knee. "How dare you!"

Wincing, he grips his leg, and I shove him hard. Arms flung wide, he falls to his back.

"Get out of my sight." I clench my hands, wishing he couldn't see me shaking.

Marco rolls to his feet as the door opens and Joseph Martino slips inside. Joseph won't expect me to leave when Nonno . . . But he looks from me to Marco, and something passes between them, a slight shake of Joseph's head.

"What?" What did they communicate with a head shake?

Marco limps toward me. "We have to get out of here."

I turn to Joseph. "Nonno Quillan is dead."

Joseph's face twists with pain. "Quillan?"

I point to the hatch. "His heart . . ." My words break on a sob. Joseph will understand my pain. He will share it. And there are tears in his eyes, tears in mine. But now I see blood on Joseph's hand.

My gaze jerks to the house. "Papa?"

Joseph blocks the door. "He's gone,

Antonia. And Marco's right. You have to get out of here."

A moan passes through me. They'll find Papa and investigate. But what about Nonno? If they find the cellar with the wine, they'll think Papa did something wrong, that he deserved to die.

But Nonno . . . My head spins. I couldn't save him. The pain is suffocating, but suddenly I know. I couldn't save his life, but I can keep his secret. "I have to bury Nonno."

"Don't be crazy," Marco barks, reaching for my arm.

Shoving his hand away, I search the garage, snagging my glance on the timbers. I've blocked the pantry door, and that leaves only one other way in. If I block it . . . "The cellar will be his tomb."

"Antonia . . ."

Glowering at Marco, I grab a board, haul it to the hatch and wedge it between the stairs and the underside of the floor. I turn back, but Joseph is beside me already with more. Back and forth, until the three of us press the last boards into the tangle. Sweat glistens on Marco's forehead. I press the hatch shut, and even though the square pavers fit snugly with the rest of the floor, I'm not satisfied. "Now dirt. So no one sees the hatch." Like a tomb lost in desert sands.

Marco grips my arm, hissing, "We don't have time."

Joseph takes my other hand. "Please, Antonia. Go now." He turns and grabs a shovel. "I'll cover the floor. No one will disturb him." I can smell his fear.

I squeeze his hand. "Promise."

He presses our hands to his heart. "With the loyalty I owe your Nonno Quillan, I promise I will hide and guard his resting place until you return."

My eyes stream with tears as I stop resisting Marco's pull. His Studebaker is directly outside the door, engine running, a great, growling beast swallowing me up as Marco presses me into the passenger seat, runs around and gets behind the wheel.

"Where are you taking me?" My voice has died with the ones I'm leaving behind.

"As far away as I can get you." He hooks his arm over the seat and spins the car back and around.

As we hurl down the drive and away from the only home I've ever known, I clutch my stomach and feel the empty skirt. No diary. Marco will not turn back, I know. I must have lost it in our struggle. I press my fingers to my forehead. What difference does it make? That life is gone, that Antonia dead. As dead and gone as everything I love.

Chapter One

They say lightning never strikes twice, but Lance hoped there was enough of the first jolt to keep things going with the woman perched stiffly in the taxi beside him. He hoped it enough to bring her home to his family, to show his underbelly; the place, the people who had formed him — and still left him vulnerable. People he loved and needed. He looked at Rese. Love and need, risky business.

As they left LaGuardia, he marveled that she had blocked out an unreserved week from the inn to accompany him, but mostly that she would accompany him at all. She'd given him a second chance, but second chance meant get it right this time or fagedda-bout-it. And what were the odds of that?

He had begun his mission alone and in secret, at the urging of Nonna Antonia. If that had remained his focus, he would have gone home without Rese, but he'd made her part of it — or she'd made him. One way or another they were in it together now. And no more secrets. This time he'd

20

keep everything up front and do it right — or as close as he could get it. Shaky ground, but he was standing. Story of his life.

Rese stared out the window as they drove through Queens, then crossed the Triborough Bridge into the Bronx, where the scene waxed less than lovely. After living in swanky Sausalito, working only in the most elite neighborhoods in San Francisco, and purchasing her own piece of wine country Sonoma real estate, the view was no doubt a disappointment.

His Belmont neighborhood had shrunk to a quaint attraction as progeny went to college, found professional positions, and moved out to the suburbs. Not many third-generation Italian-Americans stayed close and called it home, as he had, until Nonna's request sent him across the country to Rese's inn. Now, although this looked like coming home, it wasn't.

He'd found his place in Sonoma, with Rese . . . if he got it right this time. He'd only known her three months, but that was long compared to his folks, who had met on the dance floor where Pop proposed that same night with the memorable words, "So, I think we should get married; whatchu think?"

Proceeding through the Bronx past Pelham Parkway to Fordham Road and on into the hood, Lance glanced at Rese, who was now studying the architecture of Belmont Avenue and then Hughes, as they progressed along 186th to the four-story building his family owned. No barred windows, no graffiti, and the brick and stonework were nice, especially along the roof.

Rese was noting it all with her trained eye, but he couldn't read her thoughts. Did she see that his family took care of the building they'd owned since the thirties? Or did she see a broken-down neighborhood clinging to its past?

The cab pulled to the curb and the driver popped the trunk. Lance stepped onto the sidewalk that had borne his chalk, his cherry bombs, and for a while, his cigarette butts. More than that, it was the spot where he and his friends had sung when they'd been sent outside to bother someone else.

"Ay, Lance."

He turned at the call.

Frankie Cavallo hung out the window of the Mr. Softee truck, playing the music-box ditty that was the piper's call to children far and near. "Whatchu doin' in a cab? Where's that bike what drowns out my music?"

Lance grinned. If that tune didn't have such good memories attached, it would be pure torture. You had to admire a guy who could hear it all day and still call it music. Probably had no ear at all.

When Rese climbed out, Frankie raised his ridge of eyebrows. "So that's how it is." He winked and crawled on along the block, enticing the children with soft-serve pleasure they would never outgrow.

But the damage had been done, and Lance couldn't help thinking of his Harley back in Rese's workshop. He sighed. "We should have taken the bike. The road stretched out before us, the wind in our hair —"

"Wind in your hair; I wear a helmet."

Lance hauled her duffle out and set it on the curb. "Baxter in my arms. . . ."

"Animal endangerment."

His backpack next. "Did you see his face when we left him behind?"

"It was buried in Michelle's hand."

"She bribed him." Poor dog. Lance felt for the animal with all his heart.

"It would have taken too long to drive. I have responsibilities." Rese folded her arms across her chest.

They had responsibilities. Though he was not surprised she didn't say that. Rese looked as though she might jump back into the cab and leave him wondering if his time in Sonoma had been no more than a dream — the kind of dream that wakes you in a heart-pounding sweat, gasping *Gesù, Maria, e Giuseppe*, then plunging your

23

head into cold water for the clean, painful shock of it. He had fallen in love with a woman who might never trust him again. That she needed his expertise was the only thing he had going.

He leaned in and paid the driver, then turned to find the strained look on Rese that brought his gaze straight to her mouth. He could soften that mouth, but when Michelle had stopped his kissing Rese in the inn's driveway by proffering his grandmother's lost diary, he had seen very clearly the Lord's warning hand. He was not getting away with anything this time.

Rese gripped her duffle and slung the strap over her shoulder. He could carry it for her, but she wasn't that kind of girl. Here in his warmly expressive neighborhood, with her marble features and stoic stance, she was as incongruous as soprasatta on rye. It had seemed right to bring her, but that presumed a facility with good decision-making and a heart that didn't leap before his head could ask how far.

And since most everything he'd done since meeting Rese had been wrong, he was in the hole already. He hadn't meant to hurt her, but the nature of his quest had set them at odds. Amazing how you could blind yourself when you needed something so badly it left a taste like metal in your mouth.

24

And he had hurt her, because he hadn't known how to get out of what he'd started. One of these days, he'd learn what trouble looked like from the front side instead of dead center.

The strap of her duffle dug into her shoulder, and Rese imagined steel rods connecting her head to her spine. Why had she agreed to this? Hadn't she learned that listening to Lance took her directions she never intended to go?

"I have to show Nonna Antonia what I've found, put her mind at rest. But it involves you, too, Rese. I want her to see you, to know what you're doing with the place, what the plan is." As always, his idea had implanted, and now she was on the opposite end of the country with a man she knew better than to trust, yet couldn't seem to resist.

When would she learn to say no? It had never been an issue until the dark-eyed spellbinder strode into her inn with a gilded tongue full of ideas that turned her simple plans upside down. And the worst part was, she'd let him — as she had now, and probably would again.

This was not her normal mode. This was the havoc of Lance Michelli. She shifted the bag and looked up at the red-brick building — circa 1935 judging by the Art

Deco motifs: white brick arches over the highest windows with a prominent keystone that hinted of Mayan and Egyptian influences emerging from the Paris Exposition of 1925.

The same white-brick motif formed a linear design beneath the top story and decorated the edges of the middle two stories. The lower windows were crowned with a boat-shaped header with the same elongated keystone for continuity. Somehow the metal fire escape running down the front didn't ruin the effect.

Hoisting his pack, Lance led her past a storefront with an awning that read Bella Tabella to a metal scrollwork door beside it. He unlocked the door, and she followed him down a bike-strewn hallway, cracking where the walls met the high ceiling that bore a painted pipe along its length — a plumbing addition or repair done in the most cost-effective and least aesthetic way. Rese's fingers twitched. The old place deserved better.

Still, there were some nice features. The marble staircase at the back had geometric designs on the newel post, in keeping with the period, and the Beaumont-glass light fixtures appeared to be original. With some TLC, it could be brought into prime condition.

But what was she thinking? She was out

of renovation, into hospitality, which was why she needed Lance, why she'd agreed to speak with his grandmother to clear up any impediments. This was about the Wayfaring Inn. She had to keep that foremost in her mind.

They climbed the first flight, walked halfway down the hall to the second door, and Lance inserted another key. So this was his place, the apartment he shared with Chaz and Rico. Though not as grim as some of what they'd driven through, this whole scene was not what she'd pictured for him.

Inside the door, he set his pack in the corner, stacked hers atop, and hollered, "Momma! I have someone for you to meet."

Rese stiffened. *Momma?*

A woman stepped out from a side room into the hall, one hand fluffing her hair as she approached. "What, you don't tell me you're bringing someone? You don't want me to look nice when you bring me someone to meet?"

He leaned in and kissed her cheek. "You look nice, Momma."

More than nice. The woman was shapely in a classic hourglass way, with olive-toned skin and shoulder-length mahogany hair laced with silver. Sophia Loren in a housedress. Rese's throat closed up.

Lance drew her forward by the elbow. "This is Rese Barrett."

"Rese?" His mother's brow puzzled.

"Theresa, but she goes by Rese."

His mother turned to her. "Thérése the little flower, or Teresa of Avila?"

"Just Rese," she managed. They were supposed to be meeting his stroke-ridden grandmother, explaining about the inn, making a business plan. Now his mother had fixed her with the expectant look of a cat on a mousehole.

"You're the secret he's been keeping, ay?"

Death by bludgeoning. Where was a hammer when she needed one? "I'm sorry this is unexpected."

"Ah, well." The woman closed her into a hug and kissed her cheek. Rese stood like wood as she moved to the second cheek, planting kisses on a person she'd never laid eyes on, then turning to her own offspring with a glare. "So I would have had a nice meal planned; I would have gotten dressed."

He grinned, and Rese could see the little boy he'd been, the boy who lied just to see if he could get away with it — and the man who lied to her. Or was it keeping secrets? He hadn't told her anything untrue; he just hadn't told her everything — as he hadn't told his mother they were coming.

28

"How's Nonna? Can I see her?"

"Sleeping. I just left her."

He nodded. "I'm taking Rese upstairs. We'll see you in a while." He hefted his pack, and she snatched her tote and followed him back down the hall to the stairs.

As soon as they reached the next floor she hissed, "You didn't tell her I was coming?"

He set down his pack. "I was saving her."

"What?"

He unlocked another door. "If I told her I was bringing you home, she'd have scoured every inch of the building, had her hair colored, lost five pounds, and bought enough food to feed you for a year."

Rese opened her mouth, but no retort came. She couldn't fathom anyone fussing like that over her. "Well . . . she . . . I don't know her name."

"Doria, but just call her Momma. Everyone does."

Rese glared. "You didn't say I was meeting your mother. You said we were telling —"

"We are. But I could hardly take you upstairs without introducing you. Frankie saw you, so the neighborhood knows, and Momma will have heard eleven different versions within the hour."

Rese frowned. It wasn't so much what he

did as how he did it. There was no time to duck.

He pushed open the door and let her into a narrow room with a high plastered ceiling and linoleum floor. As in the rest of the building, the doors and trim were coated in seventy years of white paint, under which she could sense the wood smothering. A navy couch sat in the center with two ecru chairs and glass tables with steel frames. The eclectic art on the walls looked original but hardly museum quality. Lush red and beige rugs saved the apartment from being hard and cold. And of course, in the corner sat a drum set, keyboard, and other musical paraphernalia.

She stopped her gaze at the end of the room. "Kitchenette? Lance Michelli with a kitchenette?"

He shrugged. "I mostly cook downstairs."

"In your mother's kitchen?" She was getting a strange picture.

"All the way down. Bella Tabella, Nonna's restaurant." He went to the window that looked out over the street. Its twin to the left had an air-conditioner, but it wasn't turned on.

Lance tugged the window open, letting in the scent of traffic and pavement. "Not much happening down there now, but when the restaurant opens for dinner, people line the walk waiting for their tables. It's like a family gathering. From up here you get squabbles and boasts and pretty much everything that's happening to everyone. More than you wanted to know."

Everyone's business shared like the flu.

Lance leaned a hip against the frame. "Still mad?"

"I ought to be." He had obviously not improved in the communication department. With as much as he talked, you'd think he would tell people the important things like *"I'm bringing a guest"* and *"You'll meet my mother the minute you set foot in my neighborhood."* "You should have told us."

He spread his hands expansively. "It's going to get crazy once word spreads. I thought it would be easier for you if the whole troop wasn't waiting at the door, pushing and shoving to kiss you first."

"How bad will it be?"

"About thirty curious people's worth. I thought you'd rather meet them little by little."

She had to recognize the logic. The only alternative would have been to give her all the facts, and that, of course, was beyond him.

"In the meantime, you can settle in." He led her to three doorways at the opposite end of the room; a bedroom that must be for Chaz and Rico, a bath, then another bedroom that might have been his, but was now clearly Star's. Brilliant hand-sized tropical frog sculptures stretched, perched, and dangled from a dozen spots, and piles of flimsy, colorful clothes adorned the rest.

"Looks like Star's in here. You can share with her. I'll sleep on the couch."

She felt suddenly claustrophobic. She'd spent many nights with Star, growing up, but not in confined spaces such as these, with five of them in the same apartment. It had been only Dad and her for a long time in their house, and even at the inn, the guests were upstairs and her first-floor suite was her own private haven.

He looked toward the hallway. "Unless you'd rather try upstairs with one of my sisters, but they're pretty maxed out."

"They live here too? Your whole family?" He might have said that, but she hadn't imagined them all packed under one roof.

"Monica's family splits the top floor with Lucy's. Sofie lives with Nonna across the hall. The two rooms in the back are for Dom and Vinnie. They're not family, but they lost their rent control, so Pop fixed them up." He pointed to a bent woman in a black veil sitting in a lawn chair on the sidewalk. "Stella lives across the street, but she likes the shade on our side better.

Some people call her Strega Stella, but I've never seen her fly, with or without a broom. She just feeds the neighborhood cats."

Rese stared at him. From the moment they'd stepped out of the taxi, he had taken on mannerisms and speech that matched his surroundings and made her question all over again who he was. No wonder he was so good at fooling people.

"Except for Nonna, who keeps watch on her restaurant and everything else that happens on the street, we put the old ones in the back so they can look out on the courtyard. Come on, I'll show you." He took the duffle bag from her shoulder and dumped it in the bedroom, then led her back into the hallway. A child cried upstairs as he took her down the stairs to a back door and turned the two dead bolts to exit.

The courtyard had a tree. Three of them actually, though two were spindly, and none had much in the way of foliage. The yard was a narrow, brick-paved space between the surrounding buildings, and a portion of it had been built up into garden beds similar to those Lance had made in her yard at the inn. She was no expert on growing things, but they looked more like vegetables than flowers. Pigeons bobbed and pecked around a metal bench in one corner near a plastic turtle-shaped sand-box.

Overhead a window opened, and a woman called, "Lance! Say hi to Nicky so he'll stop screaming and let me tie his shoes."

Lance craned his head back and hollered, "Ay, Nick. What's with the noise?"

A little face appeared at the fourth-floor window, and even at that distance Rese could see him beam. "I want to play wif you."

"Then get your shoes on and stop giving your mom a hard time."

The window below that one opened, and a gray-haired man leaned out with a stump of cigar between his teeth. "Now, there's the pot calling the kettle black." Smoke wafted out around his head. "Your mother's a saint."

"That's my job." Lance smiled. "Getting Momma into heaven."

Rese glanced away when the old man saw her watching.

"Who's that?" He gestured with the cigar he pulled from his teeth.

"Rese Barrett. My business partner."

"Business! Whatsa matter? You don't got eyes?"

"I got eyes."

The old man shook his head, jammed the stump back in his teeth, and closed the window. Rese tried not to imagine what the smoke was doing to paint and textiles.

Lance turned. "That was Vinnie, and my sister Monica is on her way down with my nephew. She'll try to ditch him with me and get you off alone for every detail of our relationship."

Which would be a feat, since the details were definitely undefined. Rese met his eyes. "You told Vinnie it was business."

"Want to change that?" He'd assured her he would not be able to respect her professional barriers, but in the two weeks since his reprieve, he'd been acutely appropriate.

"We came to talk to your grandmother." To settle things with the Wayfaring Inn that used to be his grandmother's home but now belonged to her. At least on the deed she held. But of course there was also the deed with his grandmother's name.

"Right." He smiled with only a hint of disappointment, which she was not taking responsibility for.

The door burst open, and the child tore over to strangle Lance's legs, his sneakers neatly tied, but his hair a mess of blond curls. He stepped back and punched Lance's thigh. "I missed you." Then he grabbed hold again and squeezed.

"If you hit him hard enough, maybe he'll stick around." The sister Monica came out, shaking her head.

Lance snatched up the boy and pointed to his own chest. "Give me your best shot."

Nicky punched him again.

"You'll never make it to the ring that way. Better go to college."

He wrestled the boy's head, then blew an ugly noise on his neck. Laughing hard, the child squirmed and jerked until Lance let him down. Then Lance kissed his sister and said, "How you doin'?"

"I'm losing my breakfast every morning and napping longer than Nicky."

"When're you due?"

"Not for seven more months."

"You want me to take Bobby down, tell him quit messing with my sister?"

She laughed, then turned, and Rese got her first good look. Monica was at least a decade older than Lance, and the features that were striking on him were a little hard on her. But her figure was soft and shapely and would obviously be filling out more in the next seven months.

Lance spread his hand. "This is Rese Barrett. Rese, my sister Monica."

Rese held out her hand to shake, but Monica leaned in and kissed her cheeks.

Nicky pressed in between them. "Me now."

Rese thought he wanted his mother's affection, but when Monica picked him up, he lunged away and planted his kisses on the stranger too.

Monica rolled her eyes at Lance. "He's like you, kissing every girl that breathes."

Lance winced. "Thanks." He turned. "You can't believe what people say in this neighborhood. It's all *scherzi*."

"No joke." Monica knuckled his arm. "He kept count on his wall."

"Hey, Nick." Lance chucked the child's chin. "I think Momma wants to dig in the sandbox, ay?"

"No, you." Nicky lunged for Lance and would have tumbled out of his mother's arms if Lance hadn't caught him.

"Sure, you little traitor. Gang up on me." He carried the child off to the sandbox.

Monica watched them for a minute, then said, "Have you set a date?"

Rese turned. "For what?"

"You mean he hasn't proposed yet?"

Proposed? A scene came to mind so vividly it brought a flush to her cheeks, Lance on the side of the road, hands on his hips, hollering, *"Do you want to marry me?"*

"We're business partners. An inn, a bed-and-breakfast in Sonoma."

Monica cocked an eyebrow in just the manner Rese always wished she could master. It showed disbelief, irreverence, and humor all at once.

The scrutiny annoyed her. "That's what we came to talk to your grandmother about. It's complicated."

"I'll bet." Monica turned back to her son and brother playing in the sand.

"Hey, look at that," Lance called as Nicky held up a quarter. "Dig up enough of those and you can go to Ida's candy store for an egg cream."

"He's planting them," Monica said. "He always does. Nicky can't understand why he never finds quarters when Lance isn't here."

Rese considered that. "You could plant them."

"And spoil him? I leave that to Lance." Monica slid her fingers through her hair. "So, how does this partnership work?"

Rese drew her thoughts back to the subject. She hadn't had much time to see how it would work. They had barely established a plan when she learned Lance had come there under false pretenses and ordered him out. They'd been reconciled for two awkward weeks before taking advantage of a gap in reservations to come find closure with his grandmother. "Lance cooks and manages the business."

"What do you do?"

"I renovated it. I own the property."

"So he works for you?"

Rese shook her head. "No. I made him a

partner." Though she was less sure than ever what that meant.

"Keep it out of your mouth, Nicky," Monica called.

"He's just getting his pound of dirt," Lance called back.

"Yeah, you gotta eat a pound of dirt before you die." Monica wagged her finger at him. "You pay his dentist bill when he thinks he can eat rocks."

"I told him people used to bite coins to see if they were gold."

"You find any gold in there, we'll all retire." She turned back. "Do you always wear your hair so short?"

Rese touched the fringe of hair above her ear. It was actually needing a trim. "When you work a construction site you don't want anything getting in your way."

Monica gave her a curious look. "Well, you got the ears for it. They don't stick out."

Rese touched an earlobe that Lance had dared her into piercing. She hadn't really cared how her ears, or anything else, looked with the short haircuts. It was simply practical.

Lance left the toddler in the sandbox and rejoined them. "So did you learn everything you wanted to know?"

"Momma thinks you've brought home a prospective bride."

He tipped his head and traveled Rese with his eyes. "Sure. Why not?"

Rese raised her chin defensively.

He said, "You want to marry me?" His supposed penitence had obviously evaporated on his home turf.

She scowled. "I already answered that."

He turned to Monica and shrugged. "She said fagedda-bout-it."

Monica laughed.

Yeah, great joke. Rese seethed.

Lance touched her elbow. "Let's see if Nonna's awake." He headed for the door and waved her in. She stomped past, but he pulled her aside at the base of the stairs. "Monica's my oldest sister. She takes bossy and conniving to new heights. If she thought I meant it, she would hound us, plotting every scenario to throw us together." In the dimness of the narrow hall, he stroked her with his gaze. "I prefer to make my own time."

He'd wasted no time from the start.

"Besides, third time's a charm. Next time I ask, you'll say yes."

Just like that the air left the building.

Chapter Two

The smell of crushed grapes wafting on night air. Crickets sing from the vines to the fog. Another voice joins in gossamer tones, one heart calling to another.

Antonia woke. She didn't want to. Each dream memory was precious, and becoming more so with every playing. Such a carefree time. What halcyon days and dulcet nights — until the day Marco came walking up the lane dressed like a picture from *Vanity Fair*, complete with cocked fedora, his arched nose cutting the air like a prow. . . .

He moves with the gait of a person who knows his place in life and means to take it, and my interest is capped only by my instant desire to thwart him.

He tips his hat and flashes his smile. "Hello there. I'm looking for Vittorio Shepard. This the place?"

I nudge the porch swing with my heel.

"Vittorio Shepard is my papa. What do you want from him?" I am smug in my rudeness, but then Nonno Quillan comes out the door.

"Where is your hospitality, Antonia? It's hot. Offer the young man a drink."

Young? He is not so young. And lately I have scrutinized Papa's companions with caution. Without rising, I ask, "Would you like something to drink?"

In his arrogance he ignores me, turns to Nonno instead. "Vittorio Shepard?"

"I'm Quillan Shepard. Vittorio is my son." He steadies himself with the silver-headed cane. "He's at work in town, but we expect him soon." A balmy breeze lifts Nonno's full white hair from his shoulders and buoys my heart with love for him.

The man approaches and extends his hand. "I'm Marco Michelli."

Their hands come together under Nonno's careful scrutiny, his gray eyes absorbing details this Marco doesn't realize he surrenders. But then Mr. Michelli turns his gaze on me, and every thought flutters up like quail startled from the brush.

"Something cold would suit nicely." He smiles.

I take my time rising, then go inside to perform my duty. I squeeze lemons and sugar the juice, then pick ice chips and add cool water. I could have just given him water, but I want to show that we are above that. Even a vagabond swaggering up the drive can receive something special from the DiGratia Shepards.

I carry the glass out and hand it over, then return to my place on the swing while Nonno and the stranger discuss the weather, the economy, and the political landscape. "Quillan Shepard." Mr. Michelli snaps his fingers. "The poet?"

Nonno tips his head. I want to ask what this man has read, to make him prove he knows my grandfather's work. But then it would seem I am interested — which I'm not, in spite of the sideways glances I can't resist. What business does he have with my papa?

"Antonia also writes," Nonno says, and I frown because now Mr. Michelli fixes me once again in his sight. "And she's an excellent cook."

"You sound like you're auctioning me off." But that is his way, always deflecting attention from himself — unlike Mr. Michelli, who seems to soak it up like parched ground.

Both Nonno and the stranger laugh, and I have to admit he has a pleasant laugh, no hoot or guffaw. He asks a few polite questions about my writing, which is hardly more than a diary I keep of poems and snippets of thoughts and tales that come into my head.

Mr. Michelli nods. "Talent must run in the family."

"What talent are you pursuing with my father?" A slight shifting of his eyes kindles my suspicions.

He says, "Business."

"Then why don't you see him at the bank?"

Nonno clicks his tongue to scold me, but Mr. Michelli holds me firmly now in his gaze, and I wonder if I imagined that earlier blink. "The entity I represent prefers anonymity."

I scowl. "An underworld figure?"

"Antonia," Nonno chides.

"Would your father be the one to see for that?"

I spring to my feet. "If you need to ask that, you have no business with him. Finish your drink and scram."

He raises his eyebrows but makes no move to either drain the glass or leave the porch. "It was your assumption, Miss Shepard, that I represent an underworld figure. Naturally I would be concerned as to why you assumed that."

I rub my hands on my skirt, thinking lately I've seen Papa with questionable people. And that he's gone into the private world of someone I deeply distrust. But I show none of that to this stranger. "Someone who wants to have legitimate business

with my father would see him at the bank."
I draw myself up as tall as I can.

"And where would someone who wants
to have illegitimate business see your father?"

I expel a hard breath and fist my hands.
"You may leave now."

He raises the glass and drains it, then
holds it out to me. "That was fine, thank
you."

I take it with just the feeling of subservi-
ence he intends, I am sure. "Find someone
else to do your dirty work. My papa can't
be bought."

As Lance tapped the door with his
knuckle, Rese geared herself to meet the
woman whose secrets first sent him to the
villa. Nonna Antonia, his grandmother.
Since he didn't have with him the box containing the things he'd found for her, he
would probably not go into all of that now,
but meeting her would be tense enough.

Lance gently pushed open the door.
"Nonna?"

The woman in the chair had once been
striking; Rese could see that, despite the
disfigurement of the stroke. Her hands
looked frail, but seemingly not arthritic, as
the pale fingers were thin and soft. Her
hair was pulled back into a twist that displayed the length of her nose, defined

cheekbones, and a tapered jaw — features Lance shared, though age and infirmity had sharpened hers.

Her soft blue eyes saw nothing but Lance as he moved close and kissed her, holding on moments too long, as though the feel of his grandmother's arms made him want to crawl into her lap and stay there. Somehow it wasn't unmanly at all. Rese held back, aware that this moment was for them alone, but as soon as he released her, the old woman turned.

"Wh . . . o?"

"Nonna, this is Rese." Lance reached out and drew her over.

"Comé bella."

Rese took the hand that jerked toward her with skin that felt like fallen leaves. She didn't know how to answer because she hadn't understood the greeting but didn't want to make her repeat it.

"That means 'how lovely'," Lance said.

No wonder she hadn't understood. It wasn't English.

The woman reached up her other hand to hold both of Rese's. "L . . . et me s . . . ee you."

Rese tried not to flinch as the pale eyes scrutinized her. Maybe they were weak, because the woman pulled her close, then closer. She brushed her cheeks with her papery lips, then made a cross on her forehead with her thumb and followed that with a kiss too.

Rese drew back slowly, strangely moved by this demonstration and not nearly as awkward as she had been with the others. Maybe she was getting used to it, or else the age and dignity of this shrunken woman imbued a certain relevance to the gesture.

Lance turned. "This is my Nonna Antonia, Rese. It was her grandfather I buried."

Rese nodded. "I'm happy to meet you." This woman had apparently grown up in the villa Rese had just renovated. The woman Lance was willing to lie and cheat for. She shook that thought away. Seeing them together, she glimpsed the bond that had driven him. Glimpsed, but didn't understand.

Or did she? Visions filled her mind of her own mother and the fierce love she'd felt for her. Hadn't she done everything to protect her, even lying to her father? She didn't want to think about any of that. There were decisions to be made about her mother's care, but not now, not here.

The door opened and a young woman came in, slighter and fairer than Monica, but similar enough to guess a family connection. "Non —" She stopped. "Lance!" She set down her briefcase, came over and hugged him tightly, an honest hug with no cheek kissing. They looked close in age, but there was life and intelligence in her face that Rese hadn't seen in Monica.

Lance held her back and studied her. "How you doin'?" There was tenderness in his tone that hadn't been there with his older sister.

She tipped her head and shrugged.

"Sofie, this is Rese."

And suddenly the sister realized she was there. She turned. "Hi. Sorry. I was surprised to see Lance." She held out her hand to shake.

Rese took it firmly. "Nice to meet you."

"Nurse or therapist?"

Rese blinked, but Lance said, "She's with me."

Up went the eyebrows. "Oh." Then came the kisses, one for each cheek. Rese stifled her laugh. So far, Lance was the only one who hadn't. It might have been easier getting it all over with at once. But then, it was kind of nice too.

Sofie bent and kissed Antonia. *"Comé stai?"*

"Bene, cara." She seemed to speak Italian without halting and dragging the words.

"Do you need anything?"

"No, *grazie*."

Sofie straightened. "So tell me everything. Does Momma know?"

Lance laughed. "Don't start making plans."

Sofie turned to her. "He's dragging his feet?"

That was one thing that could never be said about Lance.

"We're in business together," he said.

"Business?"

"Business." He looked her over. "Are you finished with classes for the summer?"

"No, I'm in for the summer. It never ends."

"Sofie's getting her doctorate in behavioral disorders."

Rese nodded. "Wow. Sounds like work." And just the sort of brain exercise she'd never pursued herself, until recently, trying to understand her mother's condition — and possibly her own.

"It's hard." A shadow passed over her features as Sofie slipped her loose blouse off and laid it over the back of a chair, then walked in her sleeveless top to the window. She opened the one that looked out over the street. "What's Momma doing for dinner?"

"Ferragosto."

"*Madonna mia!*" Laughing, Sofie turned to her. "Ferragosto is the Belmont street festival. Opera, folk dancing, clowns, and food, food, food. Momma probably will make something on par with that for you."

49

Then to Lance, "You'd better get down there and help her."

"I'm on vacation."

"Then you can't complain."

"Would I do that?"

Sofie huffed. "Only every day of your life."

Lance jutted his chin toward Rese. "She's not picky."

"That's why she stands you, ay?" Sofie nudged him.

"No doubt."

She picked up her briefcase with a sigh. "Well, it's nice to meet you, Rese. Now I have to study." She headed into a room at the back and closed the door.

Rese glanced back to the grandmother, whose gaze was already, or still, trained on her.

Lance said, "Nonna, we need to talk."

"L . . . ater." She raised and dropped her hand.

He took the hand in his. "Nonna . . ."

"N . . . ot now."

He brought her fingers to his lips. "Okay. Anything I can do for you?"

"You al . . . ready have."

Antonia quivered as the door closed behind them. Why wouldn't Lance leave it alone? She didn't want to answer his questions. It was enough to have Nonno

50

Quillan buried. She had done all she could. All she could. She couldn't change the past. Couldn't . . .

I stare at the note, stunned by his audacity.

Dear Miss Shepard,

I fear we have started off on the wrong foot. As your esteemed grandfather, Quillan Shepard, seems somewhat disposed toward me, I hope you will allow me the opportunity to extend my regrets for my imprudent comments. Will you see me this evening?

Sincerely,
Marco Michelli

Muttering under my breath, I stalk to the escritoire and snatch a small sheet of stationery. With the fine fountain pen Nonno gave me just days ago, I write:

Dear Mr. Michelli,

My nonno is the least of your concerns. He is very forward thinking and accepting. It is my papa you will have to convince, and since he is no less discerning than I, your chances remain bleak.

Most sincerely,
Antonia DiGratia Shepard

51

The young man who brought the first correspondence takes my answer, though Mr. Michelli could have picked up the telephone and received my refusal immediately. Did he think his formal and old-fashioned method would impress me?

But the car returns a short while later, and the youth offers my own note back. I am puzzled, then annoyed to find Marco Michelli's answer penned on the back.

Bella Antonia,
 I am up to the task, I assure you. I will call tonight at eight.

Your ardent admirer,
Marco Michelli

Ardent admirer? He pokes fun at me. I look up to offer a verbal and far less civil reply, but the youth has climbed into the car and is pulling away — no doubt as he's been instructed. Taking the note upstairs, I fume.

Bella Antonia. Ardent admirer. I have not overestimated his opinion of himself. *Bene.* I will see him at eight and balance his perspective. Papa will be home by then, and between us, we will teach Mr. Michelli some humility.

But Papa isn't home by eight o'clock when Marco Michelli arrives in the same olive Studebaker Dictator his messenger drove earlier. I have served Nonno the polenta he loves and seen him to his room since he is less steady as the day wears on and the old injuries in his leg pain him. Now I am alone to face Marco Michelli, and that is better still. No one will make me keep a civil tongue.

But when he gets out of the car with a posy of violets in one hand and his mandolin in the other, I am hard-pressed to remember my ire. He approaches the porch holding out the flowers, which I bring to my nose without thinking. *Sweet violets, sweeter than all the roses . . .* The tune carries in my head and makes me smile. If he'd brought a big showy bouquet, I would have scorned it.

He says, "The gazebo might be a swell place to sit."

I raise my nose from the violets. "How do you know about the gazebo?"

"Your papa suggested it. When he gave permission for me to call." He smiles.

Oh, the nerve of him! But when he holds out his elbow, I take it. "So you transacted your business with Papa?"

"I initiated it."

"At the bank." We head around the house.

"In town."

The tweed of his Norfolk jacket is coarse under my fingers. I should have grabbed a wrap myself. Away from the shelter of the porch the evening is chilly. "Why does it have to be so secret?"

"Not everyone in this country is poor, Miss Shepard. But with so many suffering, some people with a pile of jack prefer to handle it quietly."

I look up at that. "Is it your money, really?"

He tips back his head and laughs. "I don't guess you're a gold-digger, but you better look elsewhere if you are."

"I don't care about your money."

"Or lack of."

The path winds through the herb beds past the garage that was once a carriage house to the gazebo that looks out over the vineyard, now a tenth of the original land. We are blessed to have held on when the uncles and cousins and neighbors have all sold out or turned the land over to the bank and moved to the city. Many work for the cannery; some do jobs for the don who owns it. At least Papa takes no part in that, though he's been invited more than once.

With his hand on my elbow, Marco assists me up the stairs. There is something to be said for a man with a few more years on him than the careless youths who call. Benches fill three sides of the gazebo, but I stand at the rail, facing west over the fields.

Marco takes the mandolin from his back and sets it on a bench, then removes his jacket and puts it over my shoulders. *"Megglio?"*

"Yes, better, thanks." My heart scampers inside my ribs. Though the darkness of his coloring suggests southern *paesano* heritage, he is tall and well-formed with a Roman bearing. I am three-quarters Italian, and when he uses the language I learned at Nonna Carina's knee, it has a devastating impact on my decision to disdain him.

And when he picks up the mandolin and sings "Che Gelida Manina" from Puccini's *La Bohème*, I know the gazebo will never again be wood and nails; it will forever house the notes he sends into the night that bring my heart to his feet, as he knew they would.

Lance closed the door of Nonna's apartment, frustrated. "She gives stubborn a whole new face."

Rese looked up. "How?"

"She won't let me tell her what I have, what I found."

"I thought she wanted you to find it."

He expelled a short breath. "So did I." But he was beginning to suspect a purpose-deficit disorder when it came to knowing what was expected of him.

In the dim hall he inserted the key to

open his apartment. From upstairs came his nieces' and nephews' voices, wild with the start of vacation and making his sisters crazy, no doubt. Below, *Gianni Schicchi*'s "O Mio Babbino Caro" rang out from Momma's stereo. She didn't always listen to opera, only when performing her Italian mother routine, triggered now by his bringing a girl home.

"Is it always this noisy?" Rese said.

"This is nothing." It could get noisier, and in his parents' days, before air-conditioning when all the windows were open, it had been worse still.

He gripped the knob but didn't turn it. Standing there with Puccini's opera coming through the floor, he wanted to take Rese in his arms and kiss the breath from her. Come to think of it, why was he holding back, anyway? *"Comé bella,"* Nonna had said, not just stating the obvious, but approving.

He took in her face — brown, thick-lashed eyes with no mascara; milk-smooth cheek that felt as soft as it looked; strong, determined chin that supported a mouth so . . . He leaned, but a squeal rose from the staircase at the end of the hall, followed seconds later by a rush of pale limbs and rosy spirals. Rese turned to receive Star's hugs.

Lance hooked fingers and tapped fists with Rico. "Hey, man. Good timing." He

56

let them all into the apartment.

Rico whistled as Star dragged Rese into her room. "You've got more lives than a Hindu cat."

"Hardly."

"You're walking on water, 'mano."

Lance glanced toward the bedroom. "If she didn't need me at the inn, I'd be bottom feeding."

Rico laid a book on the table, and Lance caught the title. *Beloved Sonnets*?

Rico read his thoughts. "Star likes Shakespeare. I read to her in the park."

Lance dropped his jaw. "You can read?"

"Funny."

"Still celibate?"

Rico grinned.

"Impossible."

He spread his hands. "I'm a new man."

Lance pictured Star just weeks ago with bruises from the boyfriend who "couldn't let her go." Moments later, she and Rico had started a chaste courtship unlike any of his others. There were issues, Star's especially, but Rico didn't seem to see them. He had taken the admonition not to mess with her as a holy decree, though Lance was just trying to get Star through a bad spot. He hadn't expected Rico — who spent his life in two places, the drum set and the bedroom — to manage it indefinitely.

But who was he to judge? Maybe it was just that Tony wasn't there to do it. Here in the city Tony's absence gaped. The towers had come down too long ago to still feel it so bad. But Lance would have liked to show his big brother the woman he'd brought home. He'd have liked to tell him, *"This one won't get me in trouble; she makes me better."* And that was a feat for anyone, given his propensity to mess up.

His throat tightened as he imagined presenting her to Tony. No other introduction would have meant so much. He imagined Tony's face, his ability to read a person's character. He'd have seen it, that special quality in her that reached in and took hold.

"This is it, Tony. I know it."

"Then don't screw it up."

I won't. A hard wave of desire hit him, not the kind that tempted, but the kind that put a hunger in his soul. As Rese and Star came out of the bedroom, he had to remind himself she had only agreed to a working relationship plus neck rubs. His family would assume more, that he wouldn't have brought her unless she mattered. They would see who she was to him.

And Rese would see who he was. So far she seemed shell-shocked. Though she'd grown up on the construction sites of her dad's renovations and worked her way into partnership with him, they'd been high-class renovations, and Sausalito was not the Bronx.

Star's diaphanous dress clung and fluttered as she flitted over to the small refrigerator, moving through the place as though she'd been there longer than two and a half weeks. But then, she had made herself right at home in the Sonoma villa as well. She took out a soda. There wasn't much else in there since they shopped the local markets and bakeries daily.

He hated to think what all Momma had purchased for tonight. He'd been joking about Ferragosto, but Momma would be cooking something — a lot of something. Unfortunately, quantity had never satisfied his need for quality, as Sofie pointed out — one reason he'd preferred Nonna's kitchen to any other.

Not, as Momma thought, because he'd inherited Nonna's scorn for anything south of Piemonte, but because cuisine from either region could be ruined, and, in their house, the Southern fare more frequently was. Momma was a beautiful dancer and a gifted instructor, but she attacked her kitchen like a member of a chain gang; heavy-handed on the seasonings, maybe to make up for the overthickened sauces, the gummy pastas, and gnocchi that could serve as cement shoes. She just couldn't find the light touch in the kitchen that she perfected on the dance floor.

If Nonna were herself, she'd have closed down the restaurant with a sign in the window: Family Only Tonight. Then she'd have filled the space with the finest aromas and welcomed Rese with copious servings of perfectly prepared *coscia di aguello,* leg of lamb brushed with garlic and olive oil using branches of rosemary tied together, and *coniglio in porchetta,* sausage-stuffed rabbit fragrant with wild fennel. Risotto and polenta to complement but never overwhelm. Nonna's was the only Northern Italian restaurant in the neighborhood, and she had opened it in self-defense.

Now it was closed indefinitely, until someone decided what to do. He leaned on the wall and watched Rese and Star chat, Star effusing and Rese soberly responding. Even knowing what he did about their backgrounds, it amazed him they'd maintained their friendship. He and Rico had their differences but came from the same streets, schools, and religion. He couldn't find the connecting point for Star and Rese, unless it was that they'd both needed someone.

Rico batted his arm. "Handball?"

Lance shrugged, guessing the women might catch up for a while and knowing Rico talked easier in motion. There was a court at the park, but he and Rico went down and played against the wall with the closest thing to an old Spaldeen they could find these days. Back when the rest of the country was discovering Atari, he and Rico had still been out there with sawed-off broom handles for stickball, or chalk to make a game floor for skelly, or nothing but their hands and a ball.

Rico set up to serve. "Juan's back."

It had seemed strange at first when Rico called his father Juan, but the lack of relationship or even time spent under the same roof explained it. This was his family; this was his home. He had recognized that before third grade.

"When did he get out?" Lance returned the serve hard and high to win the rally.

Rico chased the ball down, then tossed it over lightly. "A week, two. Don't really know."

"Parole?"

"Only two conditions with that man. Locked up or paroled."

Lance served. "Have you seen him?"

Though his parents' home was less than two miles away, Rico shook his head. Interesting how judgmental Rico could be after their own close calls, when nothing but Tony's influence had kept them from lockup. But Lance didn't say so. They played hard for the next few minutes. With his sparrow's build Rico was swift and cagey. Though not huge himself, Lance had him in strength and form.

They finished one game, and Rico held the ball. "So whatchu really doing?"

Lance stretched and fisted his hand. "Settling things with Nonna involves Rese. I wanted her here to —" Rico's expression stopped him. "Wha-a-t?" He cocked his head. "I don't need her approved. This isn't Naples."

"May as well be for your Neapolitan family."

"Napolitano, Calabrese, Piemontese, and, as I have recently learned, one part pure American." His great-great-grandfather Quillan Shepard without a lick of Italian.

"And you the dutiful son."

"Tell that to Pop. He thinks I'm the screw-up." He sighed. His purpose was to enlighten Nonna and get her agreement on their plans for the inn. While he hadn't set foot on that property until three months ago, it had drawn him the moment he arrived. He loved this neighborhood, all the family and friends and traditions that made it special. But Nonna's roots were in Sonoma, and it was there his restlessness had stilled.

Chapter Three

How gently on my mind his presence
  rests,
as though belonging there.
It is my heart he traps and bests,
my hope that he lays bare.

The next time Marco comes, I am prepared. I didn't know the first time how difficult it would be to resist, but I know it now, and when he suggests the gazebo, I tell him, "I prefer the porch." I set the swing in motion until he steps close enough that it is either hit his kneecap or stop.

"May I?" Before I can answer he takes his place beside me. The swing protests with a soft creaking voice, but he pays no attention, saying only, "This is a swell spot too."

Hibiscus and wild roses scent the air, with now a hint of his pomade, which he must use with a light touch because the hair is scarcely tamed by it. "Are you always this bold?"

"Don't don the gloves if you can't get in the ring."

I raise my chin. "Is this a fight?"

"Just a form of speech, Antonia. Courting is serious business."

I press back into the swing. "What makes you think we're courting?"

He smiles. I turn away before it can have its full effect. I've dissected his smile in my dreams, considering the strong, white teeth, not so straight as to look fake, the full mauve lips that communicate a wry humor and ardor at once, and the shadow of beard scarcely chased away by the razor.

Papa saves me from comment by joining us on the porch. Now we will see Marco's moxie. He stands and shakes Papa's hand, and I sense a tension between them, but that is natural with suitors and fathers.

"I think if you're going to spend time with my daughter, we should talk."

Marco nods. I decide with whom I spend time, and a word from me now would be a knockout punch before the bell rings. But I watch them down the stairs, then strolling the drive to the Studebaker and past. Papa will like Marco's owning a car. Having things makes a man responsible and respectable in Papa's mind.

I don't need a car because I never want to go far enough that I can't hear the breeze in the vines, the sparrows in the orchard, the whisper of the pale, thin olive leaves. I know the stars that watch over our land, that turn my window into a diamond-studded swatch of black velvet. The smell of the mist at night, the damp earth in the morning. Marco Michelli's car means nothing to me.

It is the dark espresso brown of his eyes, the timbre of his voice. It is the very *vanita* with which he approaches me. He is a man who knows what he wants, not a baby who wants me to tell him what he needs. And no matter how I try to resist, that excites me. This is not the old country; it is not the old times, but if Papa feels better having his talks with Marco, that's all right with me. I can tease later, when Marco is fatted on Papa's acceptance and not expecting it. I know how to savor the moment.

Star's childlike frame quivered as she described singing in the subway tunnel with Rico playing Chaz's steel drum. With her iridescent eye shadow and cherry-flavored lip gloss strong enough to scent the whole apartment, she looked twelve trying to be twenty. Though two months younger, Rese always felt like a big sister. No blood connected them, but Star expected the petting, the comfort, the freedom of a younger sibling.

She gave only what she wanted, everything on her terms. But Rese was glad she was there. Even flighty and erratic, Star was the only constant in her life — except for God. *"When all others fail, He will never fail you."* One time the presence had been so real, it consumed her thoughts and made her fight to stay alive. But that was years ago, and she had only recently chosen to believe it. So far it felt like a decision and nothing more.

"The drum makes these vibrations you can hear forever." Star made a windy sound with her voice. "And then I sing just like it. No words, just harmonious vibrations echoing in the cement tunnels. It is so synergistic."

Harmonious vibrations. Synergistic.

"And people give us money for it, stopping to listen or just dropping it in as they walk by." Star imitated the carefree disbursal of wealth. "It's crazy."

"I thought Rico had an agent. Why are you singing in the subway?"

Star tossed her spirals. "The agent's dragging his feet without Lance. He wanted the whole package, Rico's drum, Lance's lyrics, Chaz and the bazillion instruments he plays."

Would Rico push again to get Lance back in the band? The subway thing didn't sound like Lance's music, but . . .

"Rico's going to record us in the tunnel. He told the agent we've got that Enya sound and thinks the guy might go for it."

"What about your painting?"

"Are you kidding? This is New York. I can do anything." She was even starting to sound like them. It was the most positive she'd seemed in a long time.

Rese leaned back. From what she'd seen out the window, they were a long way from Lincoln Center, but if the agent liked their new sound . . . Star had loved to play Rock Star as a kid, but Rese hadn't realized she really could sing until that time in the attic when she took Lance's mic. "That's great." She smiled.

Why could Star float so easily from one thing to the next? Because she wasn't a rock. She didn't have to be strong and solid for someone else to cling to. Rese got up and walked to the front window that looked out over the urban street. Lance had seemed so cosmopolitan with the diamond in his ear and European chef credentials.

Star came over and stroked her arm. " 'How like a winter hath my absence been from thee.' "

Right. Next thing, Star would be on Broadway. Why not? This was New York. Star could do anything.

"It's only been a few weeks," she said.

Though right now it seemed like a lifetime since Star had left the villa with Chaz and Rico for the Bronx in the maroon van that held their sound equipment. And it had been only hours since Rese boarded the plane with Lance, but already she wished for the villa, the garden between it and the carriage house, the fragrant herb beds and flowering pots, almond and olive trees where Baxter loved to sniff or toss himself down in the shade and loll on his side, tail wagging. She missed the bright open rooms with floor-to-ceiling windows and warm, gleaming woodwork, her own carvings adorning it.

The inn was her business, her project, but also her home. Strangers slept and ate and left. They didn't kiss her cheeks and pepper her with questions. Besides, it was Lance's job to answer their questions — if she could ever get him back to work.

Rese frowned. Lance had said he wanted to discuss the inn with his grandmother, to show the old woman what he'd found and tell her what they planned. But it was obvious he had other intentions as well. He wanted his family to accept her.

He didn't know what he was asking. He hadn't lived with a woman whose behavior was unpredictable and destructive, whose disease genetically predisposed future generations. Lance thought he wanted a future with her. He didn't realize she might have no future. As bad as Star's past was, she could make what she liked of the rest of her life. Rese had been lied to and almost killed, but what happened next might be worse than that.

Lance wanted his family to accept what they didn't know. Of course, she didn't know it, either, wouldn't know until she started having psychotic episodes. Why did she automatically assume she would? That her unemotional self-control, her lack of social skills were symptomatic?

Lance and Rico came in, pearled with sweat and laughing. Lance caught her looking. "All settled in?"

"I guess so." She had unpacked her things into the dresser that was mostly empty since Star didn't bother using it. Several of the drawers held the clothes Lance had left behind when he went to Sonoma on his Harley with only his backpack. Would he bring the rest back with him? Or had Rico convinced him to stay?

He said, "I'll just shower. Then we'll have an hour or so to walk around before the vultures descend."

Rese imagined the scene all too vividly. Ever since her mother made them the focal point of the neighborhood, taking her up to the roof to dance, igniting the neighbor's rosebush, and other things

Rese didn't want to remember, she'd controlled the sort of attention she received. "Wouldn't you rather hop a plane back to Sonoma?"

He smiled. "I'll be just a minute."

When Lance came out smelling fresh and a little musky from his aftershave, she badly wished them at the inn, where she could wield a chisel, or better yet a saw and sander. She needed to get physical with a piece of hardwood.

Lance slipped his keys into his jeans pocket. "Ready?"

"Do I need Mace?"

"Not if you're with me."

She'd expected him to scoff.

"If we were touring Rico's street, I'd arm us both, but this is Little Italy. You'll be fine as long as you can say *ciao* and eat fish on Friday."

She shook her head. "No way I'm passing for Italian."

He grinned. "You don't have to."

The knots in her neck loosened as he took her down the streets, dated and colorful with signs and awnings printed with the names of the shops. The stores themselves were tiny, some selling only one thing, like the D'Auria Brothers pork store with sausages that were mixed and dried right there hanging from the ceiling. Sweet or hot. That was the choice. And the two brothers who ran it had taken over from their father, who opened in 1938.

Her chest clutched at the thought that she had sold her father's renovation business, especially since Brad said the new owners were not living up to Dad's standards, to her own. That business with her dad and hero, Vernon Barrett, had been her life until his accident. Now she had an inn — and a new partner.

She had known what to expect from Dad. No one in the world had been more predictable, more grounded in routine. But even he had surprised her. Lance was a live wire, a short waiting to happen. What should she expect from him? Nothing. She would depend on herself. That was the Rese Barrett she knew; not the stranger wearing earrings and looking too much like her mother.

She returned her focus to the neighborhood Lance wanted her to see. Addeo and Sons sold bread and biscotti. DeLillo's had mini cheesecakes, a rolled cream-filled pastry called cannoli, little cakes and tarts. Egiddio's Pastry was hardly more than a long glass counter of cookies, but nibbling the cookie Lance handed her, she could see why.

"*Ciao*, Lance." Two gray-haired men waved from the sidewalk outside the fish market, beside a portable counter with clams and lemon wedges to buy and eat. They eyed her openly. "Aren't you going to introduce us?"

"The less she knows about you two the better." But Lance turned to her. "Rese, this is Joe and Mario. Gentlemen, Rese Barrett."

Rese shook hands.

Mario squeezed hers. "You settle on this girl, *paesano*. She'sa best one yet."

For a minute she thought he would kiss her, but he let go, and she breathed her relief. Stepping back, she caught sight of something moving — a barrel crawling with she-crabs, according to the label. "They're alive."

"Sure," Mario said. "Taste better that way."

She hoped they didn't eat them alive, but didn't ask. She'd been time-warped and body-snatched into another country, another century.

Joe said, "There was that one with the green eyes."

"A crab?" Mario looked puzzled.

"Not a crab. A girl. That one Lance brought up from the city, the long legs." He motioned down his own. "Ankles like sticks."

"Oh yeah . . ." Mario nodded. "What ever happened to her, Lance?"

"Moving along now." Lance took her elbow and walked her past the laughing pair.

"So long, Rese," Joe called. *"Buona fortuna."*

"That means good luck." Lance drew her around a man hosing down the sidewalk outside his doorway.

She glanced sideways. "Do I need it?"

"Doesn't hurt." A poorly muffled car passed in a cloud of dark exhaust. He drew in a slow breath through his nose. "Ah. Summer in the city." He waved to a compact matron with a pushcart whose face broke into a sea of wrinkles as she called, *"Buona sera."*

No wonder Lance had gotten along with Evvy, Rese mused. Most of the people he knew were over sixty — except the girl from the city.

She cocked her head. "Green eyes, huh? Skinny ankles?"

He smiled, looking straight ahead.

"Blonde or redhead?"

He pondered a moment. "Kind of both."

"Reddish blonde, or a blonde and a redhead?"

He shrugged. "It's hard to keep them straight."

She jutted her chin. "So I guess my crush on Brad doesn't matter."

"That depends." He stopped walking.

"On what?"

"If it's over."

"Hmm."

73

She took a step, but he caught her by the elbow, eased her back against the window of the cheese store, then caged her with his arms.

"He kept things from you too, remember."

Had he taken her seriously? Her crush had ended as soon as she and Brad vied for the second crew that she'd won three years ago. But for the first time she felt the delicious power of jerking his chain. "Brad promised Dad." Promised not to tell that her mother was alive in a mental health facility, a small detail that had now rocked her life.

Lance's gaze deepened. "Then I guess we have a vendetta."

"Vendetta?"

"I'll have to add him to the skeletons in my closet."

She drew herself up. "That's not funny. Especially after the last one." Finding the bones of his great-great-grandfather in the dark tunnel under the carriage house had been one of the worst scares of her life.

"Then you have to swear a blood oath never to mention his name again."

She snorted.

He caught her jaw and raised her face to make his claim, her mouth belonging to his, and it did, and she couldn't help that, but he let go and started walking. "I'll see the *padrone,* tell him —"

"Padrone?" She caught up to him.

"The boss. Tell him there's a feud. My honor is at stake."

Like anyone would feud over her. Even Lance said she was manly; bold and direct, unemotional — until she'd broken down and cried all over him. Again, not the stuff of duels.

What made it more hilarious was picturing Brad, fourteen years older and her dad's friend and confidant. Though he'd hinted at a reciprocal crush, she didn't believe it. He just wanted her woodwork and carvings for his renovations. He wanted her to make him look good.

Lance nudged her with his elbow. "No comment?"

"I think a blood feud works. Brad's got some underhanded tricks of his own, believe me."

His mouth tightened. "I'll have Stella use the evil eye. *Mal occhio.*"

Rese laughed. "She could fly to Sonoma on her broom."

"You think I'm joking. But this is serious. When the woman I love —" His voice caught, and she realized the joke had gone a direction he hadn't intended. He walked on in silence.

They approached a tree-shaded park with a hexagonal stone restroom, two playgrounds filled with children, and some kind of playing courts. It was neither large nor elegant, but provided a nice respite from the hard streets and buildings. The ice cream truck sat still, playing its music-box ditty, the driver's head cocked back against the seat as he snored an accompaniment.

She glanced sideways at Lance. "I was kidding."

"I know." But he didn't say he was.

Chapter Four

What is shadow but darkness longing
  for light;
What is fear but courage looking for
  hope?

Papa's face looks gray in the morning light.
I wonder if he didn't sleep well again. A
finger of fear finds my spine. What is this
premonition, this sense that all is not well
with Papa? His job at the bank is secure,
more so now with the personal work he
does for Arthur Jackson. As much as I dis-
like the man, he is powerful, and he sees
Papa's ability, his diligence. Naturally that
would be rewarded with greater responsibility and confidence.

"Do you feel all right, Papa?"

He looks up from his coffee, a demitasse
of strong espresso. "Sure, fine."

"*Crostata?*"

He shakes his head. "Thank you, no. I
need to get in to the bank."

"Why does he work you so hard? Who

does Arthur Jackson think he is? Having you out so late last night, and early again this morning."

After talking with Marco for the third time in as many weeks, Papa had left and not come home until long after I'd gone to bed.

"Are you in charge of my affairs, *ragazza?*" he says with a smile, but there's an edge.

Maybe not, but who else will say it? Why doesn't Nonno speak up, ask his son where he was so late? But he only nods when Papa stands to begin his day, another long one doing who knows what for Arthur Tremaine Jackson. The man thinks he's a king, thinks he controls Papa's life. It's not banking they do at all hours. What right —

"Are you coming?" Nonno reaches for his cane.

"Of course." It's Wednesday. When have we not visited the grave? As he goes to his room for his journal, I run upstairs for my own, then pack a lunch of bread and cheese, olives and peppers. I help Nonno into the car, then crawl into the back. Papa takes the wheel. No more is said about last night, about the things that worry me, the things that matter.

We stop at the bank and he gets out, pressing the seat forward for me to take over driving. "I'll get myself home." He kisses my cheek, cupping my chin a moment longer than usual to show he is sorry for my concern. "Don't worry about me. Take care of Nonno."

I nod, but he has it wrong. Though Nonno is feeble, his soul is right with God. Is Papa's in peril? I watch him walk away with that certain gait, that purposeful stride that reminds me now of Marco's. I sigh. If Papa is important enough to do business with some anonymous person with "plenty of jack," maybe my fears are ungrounded, and I put them from my mind as I drive.

Nonno's unsteady yet stately gait takes him in among the graves. Nonna's stone stands elegantly in the fenced DiGratia family plot. To its left is Momma's grave, but I don't remember much about her. It was to Nonna's knee I clung in the storms of life. Nonno eases himself onto the stone bench where he rests his cane and sighs. Maybe he worries, too, after all.

"Nonno . . ." I don't want to voice my concerns, to give them substance. I don't want to speak bad luck onto our heads.

Nonna Carina would have understood. She knew about bad luck, but her luck had changed when she found Nonno. I wish I could talk to her. She would not have kept silent when she saw her son going the wrong way. My throat tightens. Is Papa going the wrong way?

"Did I tell you about the day your papa was born?" Nonno's voice is sonorous.

I settle down beside him. "Tell me." In my mind I see Nonna Carina as he first knew her, rippling black hair and dark eyes, with the Northern cheekbones and striking features that made her a true beauty even into the older years that I recall.

"I knew something was wrong. Carina had fussed all morning. Unusual for such a sweet temper, a sweet tongue."

I laugh. Nonna Carina had a fiery spirit that was most often directed at Nonno Quillan. I loved to watch them spar, loved it as much as Nonno, who provoked his wife with just the gentle prods to spark her temper.

"I knew before the pain started. I tried to tell her to rest, to stop scrubbing. But she was afraid. She was afraid because the first one died."

I stare. "The first one?"

Nonno nods. "In Crystal, Colorado. I hadn't known she was pregnant. I was away." He says it with such grief in his voice, I can't press for details. He has never told me there was a child before Papa. Nonna never told me, either, and that kindles a dread curiosity. I thought I knew everything Nonna had to tell.

"I was a freighter. I hauled goods and

dynamite between the camps. Long trips away. Doing my job, but mostly running away. I was afraid to stay in one place. I was afraid to love my wife." Waves of grief spill from him.

I take his hand.

"I didn't know the trouble she had caused with the miners. I didn't know another man, Alex Makepeace, my mining engineer, had allowed her to get involved. I didn't know my child was inside her." He closes his eyes. "They beat her, and the baby was lost."

I scarcely breathe.

Nonno opens his eyes and stares at the grave. "I swore nothing would hurt her again. But when the pains started I was helpless. I would have chopped off my good leg to stop it. But she labored on and on. The doctor had said she might never bear children because of the injury. But neither of us had thought of that in the joy of making life again, watching it grow inside her."

His gaunt throat works, the skin jerking up and dropping. "Hearing her screams, I wished I had never touched her. I wanted to undo it, but there was no going back." His breath escapes on a low sigh. "You know her father was a surgeon, that he saved my leg and my life."

I nod.

"When Carina had no strength left, he took the baby out with a knife. He took his daughter's womb as well. It had hemorrhaged and would not bear another pregnancy. The miracle was that she lived, and my son with her."

So that's why Papa has no siblings. I've wondered, when my grandparents' love was as thick and sweet as honey in a comb.

Nonno stays a long time in that memory, then says, "Knowing he was all we would ever have made him too precious. If I was stern with him, Carina soothed. If she got exasperated, I slipped him a butterscotch. He never knew the sting of my hand, though he deserved it. I could only think that we might have lost him. I might have lost it all." Nonno shakes his head. "It's not good to raise children in fear. He sensed the weakness and fought the bit."

Is that why he won't question Papa? Is he still afraid to lose him?

"We should not have chosen Flavio for his godfather. He filled his head with discontent."

"I thought that was Momma." The beautiful woman Papa married, hair like spun gold, eyes as green-blue as the changing sea, and as unpredictable.

He nods. "Yes, her too. But like finds like. There was a hole inside him, as though he knew there should have been another child to share the weight of our love."

"How can a child be loved too much, Nonno?"

He smiles dimly. "Someday you'll know." His eyes tear as he stares at the stone bearing Carina's name. "Some loves attach to your very soul."

The aroma from the kitchen was actually satisfying, and when Lance stole a peek, he saw why; his sister Lucy had come to Momma's aid. Her eight-year-old twins, Lisa and Lara, were twisting dough into sticks while her toddler, Nina, stuffed pinches into her mouth. His cousins Rita, Marianna, and Gigi chopped fennel and mushrooms, and Momma looked like a movie star in her black sleeveless sweater and a string of pearls. Lance ducked out before they saw him. No sense starting the panic too soon.

Monica's husband, Bobby, stood by the window letting his cigarette smoke out in the draft while he argued with Lucy's husband, Lou. Neither had seen Rese yet, but it was only a matter of time. A half dozen kids sat around a Monopoly board because Momma didn't allow video games, and he could hear his cousins Frank and Franky in the courtyard playing handball.

He brushed Rese's arm with his fingers

to direct her into the room, and Zia Anna zoomed in with her matchmaking sonar, and soon all four aunts had descended. He named them to Rese, "My aunts Anna, Dina, Mimi, and Celestina. This is Rese Barrett." He didn't try the business partner line. It would never fly.

Rese's cheeks rosied with their lipstick kisses, and he strategically placed himself between her and their exuberance, placing his own kisses on their powdered faces. Rese must be ready to deck him.

"Is this the one?" Anna asked with festival eyes. "To make you finally stand still?"

"He's hopeless, Anna. I know." Celestina touched her temple to remind them that her spinster status gave her the second sight in these matters.

Dina shrugged. "Why should he marry when the cow doesn't come with the milk no more?"

"Dina!" Mimi slapped her hands to her cheeks. "She didn't mean that about you, cara."

"Meglio un uovo oggi che una gallina domani." Dina smiled knowingly.

Lance ushered Rese away from their laughter. She was tamped as tight as a stick of dynamite. He'd seen her explode once, bore the bruises on his sides for days. Not from blows, just the grip of her fingers as she'd sobbed.

"I didn't know your family spoke a foreign language."

"Only when they're trying to be clever." Lance considered the possibility of conversation without embarrassment and decided they'd have to leave, and they'd never get away now.

"So what did she say?"

"An old Italian proverb. Better an egg today than a chicken tomorrow." He could guess what she was thinking. "It's all in fun. Meant to humiliate me, mainly. And see what kind of rise they can get out of you." A challenge, considering Rese's temperament.

The door opened, and his pop came in with Gina and the kids. Momma must have told him to pick them up after work. Lance kissed Gina and punched his three nephews. "How you all doin'?" But he knew. The weariness in Gina's eyes told him. Raising three boys alone wasn't easy even with the victims' assistance they'd received. The money kept them in their Manhattan apartment, but her sons had no father.

"Gina, Pop, this is Rese Barrett."

Gina held out her hand, too uptown to kiss her, and Pop looked her over with a nod, too jaded to believe this wasn't yet another hard-luck story his son had fallen for.

"Nice to meet you," Rese said, and he heard the strain in her voice. This couldn't be easy. Not when she naturally shunned crowds and intimacy.

Bobby and Lou left off arguing and came over. "Ay, Lance. Who's this hot number?"

Wouldn't pregnant and nauseated Monica love to hear him say that? "Rese, this is Monica's husband, Bobby." He was sure she would never remember them all. "And Lucy's husband Lou, the two 'Lu's.'" That, she wouldn't forget.

Rese held out her hand, but Bobby wasn't missing his chance. Both cheeks, close enough to the mouth Lance wanted to punch him. Lou's kisses landed closer to the earlobes. Rese might need therapy after this night.

Bobby jerked his thumb at Lance. "You better be quick with this bad boy."

Lance could smell the grappa that made him audacious. "Knock it off, Robert."

"You saying it ain't true? How long you gone with anyone?" He wagged a finger at Rese. "He sips from lots of bottles. He don't drink any to the bottom."

Lou slapped Bobby's arm with a light backhand. "Stop before he kills you."

Bobby shot a scornful glance, but Lou had it right. Lance liked Bobby most of the time, but this wasn't one. Right now, he could break the man's nose with one good shot. He took Rese by the arm. "How about some air?"

They slipped through the window to the black metal fire escape with an unobstructed view of the sidewalk and street. It was only the beginning of the evening, but Rese drew a long breath and released it slowly.

He let go. "You okay?"

She nodded. This had not been a good idea, bringing her home. It showed their differences too starkly. Rese was an island; he was everyone's port in a storm. He pressed the space between his eyebrows and sighed.

She said, "What's the matter?"

He leaned his back to the bricks beside the window and brought up his knee. "I don't want you to hear it."

"Hear what?"

"My life. In detail."

"What Bobby was saying?"

He glanced sidelong. "That's the trouble with people knowing you from birth."

"That's when you started dating?"

He laughed. "Just about. But not the way he made it sound."

She gave him the stare that he had thought stony when they first met, though now he saw all kinds of nuance in it; doubt, concern, annoyance. He wanted her to understand. The problem was, she probably did.

"Growing up, Rico was small and

mouthy, a natural target. Being his friend meant being his guardian. Girls liked that; I liked girls." That was understating it. He was fascinated by their soft skin, their fingernails, the sway of their Catholic school skirts.

"I got a reputation for helping people out. Anyone with a hard-luck story. Tears?" He blew through his lips. "Fagedda-bout-it, I'm a goner."

He got a slow blink, but no comment. He spread his hands. "Italians love tragedy. We know we're in love when it hurts. So I was in love every week." And now she'd think it was that way with her. But he'd sworn off secrets, and everyone else was going to tell it anyway. Teasing sure, but it was also to take her measure, see how committed she was. Any woman who couldn't handle his past didn't deserve his future. Protective family stuff — except for Bobby, who just liked making trouble.

"You kept count on your wall?" Careful indifference in tone and expression.

"Girls I kissed? Yeah." He looked away. "Ever heard of Dion and the Belmonts? Sang doo-wop in the fifties?"

She shook her head. "I don't think so."

"Well, on this block they're saints. They came from here, and they made it big. Now, me and Rico . . . a lot of people thought we were the next big thing. We thought so too. Started playing Greenwich, booked the hot spots. Got lots of attention." He met her eyes. "All kinds of attention."

She held herself straight. "I thought that was against your religion."

He ran a hand through his hair. "Around here religion is like breathing. You do it, but it doesn't always get in your way. You know when you're sinning against God. You know, but you don't always stop, so then you confess it and you're absolved — forgiven — and you're supposed to stop doing that sin because it offends God; it hurts Jesus, who's suffered enough. That's the principle. But then temptation comes, and you fool yourself into thinking there's a way around it all. It might not be right, but you can make up for it later."

He crossed over to the railing. "Then something happens, something so big it'll take the rest of your life to make it right."

"It's not your fault Tony died."

"I know that." His knuckles tightened on the metal. "But it was like God's judgment fell on the wrong son."

"Michelle said Jesus took care of all that."

He half turned. "When did she say that?"

"At Evvy's funeral. Or rather, the party afterward. I guess party isn't the right word."

"Sure it is." He smiled, thinking of Evvy, the cantankerous neighbor who'd cornered him every chance she got. "Did you believe it?"

Rese nodded. No wonder she'd given him a second chance. They hadn't talked much over the past two weeks at the inn. She'd worked in the workshop. He'd done his job and tried not to annoy her. But the strain had been palpable, as it was still.

Rese frowned. "I'm not sure what it means."

"What matters is in here." He pressed his knuckle to his chest. "If doing wrong hurts, then your heart is right with God."

Her face told him nothing. "That Italian thing?"

"The human thing."

Hoisted into her son's arms, Antonia let him carry her down. A party to welcome Lance's girlfriend, though he hadn't called her that. The woman was not warm and fiery like Lance. His opposite maybe, and she knew how the poles of a magnet could bind.

Roman huffed down the stairs, but she could do no more than hold on, her body betraying her, the strength in one leg all but gone. Like Nonno's. It gave her comfort to share an affliction with someone she had loved so deeply. She remembered him sitting on the stone bench at Nonna Carina's grave. Having told her about Papa's birth and the first baby they had lost, he had taken up his journal and sunk into the silence that brought words to the page that would never find his lips.

Even with all the work he had published, he was still very private with his journal. She had been honored that he allowed her to sit beside him and write in her own diary the thoughts that rushed with the images he had given her.

Who would that first baby have been? How had Nonna survived the grief? And the awful birth of Papa! To take a baby with a knife. Yet Nonno called it a miracle.

Antonia sighed, thinking of all the things she'd written on that subject and others. What had become of that diary, the pages that held her innocence? It didn't matter. That was gone and done. This was her life.

Roman propped the door open and carried her through it now into the throng. Her *famiglia*. The fruit of her love. She breathed deeply. "Put m . . . e in the m . . . iddle."

"Sure, Momma. I know." Roman perched her on the couch. He had worked all day and come home to a hive. Dori was probably frantic, inasmuch as she could be, with her lackadaisical ways. Not practical like Roman. A dancer. Nonna smiled with the one side of her mouth that still did its job. Was ever a daughter-in-law good enough for the son? Strange, then, that she should feel favorably disposed to this odd woman Lance had chosen.

Oh, he didn't say it. But she knew. She searched the room, saw them outside on the fire escape. Escaping for sure. Who could face this swarm at once? The children came over, pressing to her knees with little hands and faces. Her great-grandchildren. She listened and petted and tried not to talk because she confused them with her slow words.

When Sofie came in, Antonia noted the tight line of her mouth, the strain between her eyebrows. But it was time to gather at the tables stretched across the living room, and she was delighted to find Rese seated beside her. No doubt Lance had arranged it so the girl would have peace on one side at least. His protective nature would have seen to that.

He tried to take the seat to her left, but Monica wedged in, bossy as always. "I haven't gotten to know her yet. Go around the other side."

The communication between Rese and her grandson's eyes told Nonna what she'd already guessed. This one was more to Lance than the others.

Monica stuffed her napkin in her lap.

92

"So tell me about this inn you and Lance have."

And Antonia grew still, listening to her home described in such detail she found herself once again in its comforting arms. . . .

The porch is dark as a light rain falls, and only the lamplight through the living room window spills out. Marco has called regularly over the past weeks, yet made no advance. I am unsure what to make of that. Is he more serious than the suitors who press their luck, or less interested than he seems?

He leans against the plastered pillar, playing softly on the mandolin. It is only the second time he's brought it, and he doesn't sing along this time, merely studies me with a serious mien.

"What is it?" I whisper.

He shakes himself as though only now realizing how he's been, and it's as though he puts on a mask, a smile as flimsy as cellophane. "You're beautiful in the lamplight."

"That's not what you were thinking."

"Bella Antonia, if a man shared everything he was thinking, he'd have his face slapped too often."

I raise my chin. "That's not what you were thinking either. I don't think you had me on your mind at all."

93

His gaze deepens. "Perceptive, aren't you?"

"Angel sight, my nonna called it."

"It's second sight in my neighborhood."

"Where is your neighborhood?"

He sets the mandolin on the railing. "Manhattan. Mulberry Bend." At my blank look he adds, "In New York — all the way across the country."

"I know where Manhattan is. I wonder why you're all the way out here."

"I told you. Business."

"And that's what you were thinking about?"

"In a way." He comes toward me and sits in the swing.

I don't move to the edge, but leave my knee where it touches his thigh. "Is it over soon, this business you have with Papa?"

"It could be." He is so hard to read, one moment ardent and carefree, the next almost painfully serious.

"And then you'll leave?"

"I don't want to think about it."

"What do you want?" I lean closer, and I can see the natures vie inside him. Contrary to his normal assurance, he seems at a loss to choose.

I lean close, letting my Arpège perfume help his indecision. "I think you should kiss me."

He swallows. "I can't."

"Why not?"

"I promised your father."

Promised Papa? "Papa doesn't decide for me." Not for the last couple years, anyway.

"He asked me not to."

"Because you're leaving?"

He glances away.

I lean closer still. "He didn't ask me not to."

"Antonia . . ."

I touch his cheek for the first time, feel the stubble of his beard, rough and thick. Marco will not be the first person I've kissed. And yet I hesitate as though . . . as though nothing. I draw his face close and breathe a hint of pomade, of mint leaf he chewed from the cheesecake I served him. Our scents mingle as I touch his lips with mine.

His arm comes around. "Cara . . ." And then he kisses me.

"Nonna?"

She jolted. Lance's expression said he must have been waiting awhile for her to respond. "Wh . . . at?"

"In the morning we're going to talk."

What use was there in words? Words that could be lost and mixed and jumbled into nonsense. What was inside was what remained. But Lance would not listen. "*Bene.* W . . . e talk."

★ ★ ★

"What, Momma?" Lance squeezed into the closet-sized pantry with his mother, whose flare for melodrama had not diminished.

"I need to know; where is she sleeping?"

"My room." He couldn't resist the pause. "With Star. I'm on the couch."

"There should not be men and women in the same apartment."

"Well, Star's in there with Chaz and Rico."

"They're not mine. You are my son."

"Ma, I'm almost thirty."

"You get her pregnant, you can't marry in the church."

"That's not true, and anyway I'm not sleeping with Rese." He did not want to have this conversation nose to nose with his mother in the pantry. Especially when she looked so skeptical. He jammed his fingers into his hair. "St. Michael the Archangel strike me dead if I lie. I haven't touched her."

"Why not?"

"What?"

"Because she is too cold?"

He expelled a breath. "She's not cold, Momma."

"You are a man of the heart." She pressed her palm to his chest. "You need a woman in your sheets who can keep you there."

Was he confused or had she just switched sides? "I'm sure if she ever agrees to have me —"

"She refused you?"

The outrage of an Italian mother over an insult, real or imagined, toward her son should never be underestimated. There might be no fury like a woman scorned, but there was no terror like a *madre* insulted.

"I haven't asked in a way she could take seriously." He was still trying to dig out of his hole.

"What's to take seriously? You ask; she says yes. What else is there?"

A little matter of trust, and the fact that she had never said she felt the same way. She might really want nothing more than his partnership at the inn. They were all making a big assumption based on nothing more than her showing up with him. And she was almost certainly regretting that.

"Can we get out of here?" He opened the pantry door and nudged his mother out.

She sniffed. "It's your gallivanting all over the world."

"Digging ditches, building houses for people who live in cardboard boxes."

"And all this mysterious business with Nonna."

That much was true. He and Nonna had

not told Momma or anyone else about the quest that had sent him first to Suar Conchessa in Liguria, then to Rese in Sonoma, about burying Nonna's grandfather or any of the other things he'd found.

Pop came in. "Where's the dessert? The children are getting restless."

Getting restless? Lance heard at least two babies crying, a skirmish of raised voices and bumped furniture and parents hollering exasperated threats. "Why don't you skip dessert and send them all home."

"Skip dessert!" Momma looked wounded.

Annoyed, Pop pushed him toward the living room, a.k.a. Bronx Zoo. "Go make yourself useful. Isn't that what you do these days?"

Yeah, it was what he did. But the naked kids in South America were easier to deal with than his nieces and nephews en masse in his mother's living room. *"Basta!* Everyone under five feet down in the garden. *Spicciatevi!"*

With squeals and screeches they crashed through the door; their thundering feet on the stairs could bring the whole place down. He looked at Tony's oldest son, Jake, who hadn't moved from his place in Pop's corner recliner. "What's wrong with you? Butt glued to the seat?"

Jake almost smiled. "I'm not under five feet."

Lance glanced at Gina, caught the tightness of her expression, then back to his nephew. "Prove it."

With sloth-like languor, Jake rose.

Lance swallowed. When had the kid sprouted those extra inches? He would have to spend some time with Jake before he left. "I'll make an exception."

Jake looked toward the wall, neither answering nor moving.

"Come on. I've loosed the horses of the apocalypse. Someone's gotta control the aftermath." Lance scooped a sniffling tot from Lucy's arms and told Jake, "Let's do it, hotshot."

Jake came to him, glanced up — but not that far — then headed for the door. Lance looked at Rese, but Monica had her ear, so he went down alone to the garden with the rabble.

Chapter Five

Chaz sat curled over his book at the small table in the kitchenette, the lamplight gilding the pages as Rese slipped into the apartment, names and faces jamming her head — voices, questions, squalls. The silence around Chaz gaped, and she was sucked into the amber glow, the peace.

He spread his broad, white smile and stood to hold her chair. Towering in the cramped room like a benevolent giant, he said in his Jamaican intonation, "You've met the family."

"That's not a family; it's a horde."

He laughed the slow rippling laugh she had come to appreciate in his short time with her in Sonoma.

She sank into the chair. "How dazed do I look?"

"Like that first morning without Lance."

The morning after she'd kicked him out and had to manage unappreciative guests who expected Lance's kitchen creations and the evening entertainment her Web site had promised, when Chaz and Rico had stuck by her even though they were

Lance's friends, when Chaz's gentle style and Rico's pancakes and Star's fast-talking had kept her from punching someone.

The scene tonight had been close, panic lodging in her throat like a gob of peanut butter over her windpipe, and Lance too enmeshed in family dynamics to notice. If she had realized what she was agreeing to, she'd have sent him off to grandmother's house without her. She had enough wolves at her door without disapproving mothers, prying sisters, knowing aunts, aggressive brothers-in-law, and so many children her head spun.

"Relax," Chaz said softly.

She pressed her fingers to her temples. "I've never heard anything like it. They're so . . ." She shook her head. "I'm not like them."

"You don't have to be."

"I think I'm supposed to prove something."

"You're a daughter of the King. What is there to prove?"

She lolled her head to the side. "A daughter of the king."

"Absolutely." Chaz flipped pages and stopped. " 'The Spirit himself testifies with our spirit that we are God's children . . . heirs of God and coheirs with Christ.' "

Well, that was fine, but so far she'd been called a cow and an egg and endured conversation in volumes intense to deafening, and if she was any kind of heir, no one seemed to know it but Chaz. She frowned. "Lance told me we were coming to discuss the inn with his grandmother. Why can't he ever give me the whole story?"

"I don't think he sees the whole story. He's a dreamer, a visionary. He sees what he hopes for."

Her skeptical mind turned that thought over. Did Lance really not see, or did he not want her to? At the moment, she was disinclined to give him the benefit of the doubt. "I wouldn't have come if he'd told me."

"You're here now."

"Is there an escape hatch? A trapdoor? I don't even mind a skeleton or two."

Chaz laughed. "You could try the dumbwaiter. But it only goes to the cellar."

"Not far enough."

"Then you must be content in your circumstances."

She sighed. "But how?"

" 'Rejoice in the Lord always. I will say it again: Rejoice.' "

Rese startled. Rejoice always? No matter what? That was as bad as Lance's Scripture that said to boast in affliction that developed character. She'd be stellar by the end of this. "Where do you get all that?"

He tapped his book. "God's Word is my university."

The door opened and Lance came in. "Can I play?" He smiled as he took a chair and rocked it back, squeezing his shoulder blades to stretch his chest.

She had an unmistakable desire to overturn the chair with her foot.

He raised his brows. "Still in one piece?"

"Of course."

"I've lost hair and a pound of flesh, but I've still got my teeth."

"You did get the worst of it out in the yard."

"You saw that?"

"I assume you were the center of the mob." She had snuck a look from the bathroom window, where she'd hidden long enough to give her ears a rest.

"Nice to be loved." Lance rubbed a red mark on his arm.

And that was it, Rese thought. In spite of the bickering, the bantering and squalling, the playful and not so playful scuffling, there was a possessiveness, a cohesion in his family she couldn't help but envy. Lance could hardly draw a breath without someone wanting his attention or showering theirs on him. Only his father had remained aloof. But maybe that was normal for them. Even though she and Dad had been partners, they'd had little relationship outside the work they both loved.

"Don't let it go to your head." Chaz gestured with his elegant fingers. "Better a humble stone than a coveted gem."

Lance eyed him. "Jamaican proverb? Or Chazian?"

Chaz laughed. "A stone is used to build. A gem causes strife."

Rese looked from one to the other, knowing what Chaz meant, but also that Lance hadn't forced or even craved the attention he got. Unlike Bobby, who'd grown increasingly domineering and self-important, Lance had focused on everyone else, as he had with her when they first met, drawing her out as no one had before. Caring, as no one had before.

She didn't want to care back, but how could she stop it? There was something inherently attractive about him, even with his faults. Maybe because of them, if there was anything to that affliction thing proving character. She said, "A gem is a stone. It just depends on what's been done to it."

"That" — Chaz raised a finger — "is an excellent point. The transforming power of adversity." And he gave her a secret smile.

She got the point but didn't like it. Dinner had been torture, and she did not feel better for it. Lance might complain about their knowing him too well, but he'd been energized by the interaction. He was the perfect personality to run the inn. He liked people.

She felt drained. Lance had seemed talkative when they first met, but nothing like the rest of them, at least all together in one place. Nonna Antonia had been silent on her right, but on her left Monica had run on about her kids, her Bobby, her nausea, and everyone else had talked to her from whatever position they were in, hollering questions over the din. How was she supposed to take a bite?

But she had worked the food in somehow. Her stomach was full, though she had no idea what she'd eaten. Rese sent her gaze to the bedroom where, even if she couldn't sleep, it would be quiet and private — no, she was sharing with Star. But then . . . where were Star and Rico?

"Recording in the subway tunnel," Chaz told her when she asked; then as he filled Lance in on their new venture, she escaped to the bedroom. The nights with Dad after a long day on a jobsite, after she'd fed him and he had slipped off to watch TV without even a thank-you, seemed normal now, or at least low-stress. Dynamic discussions they'd had on-site or driving or walking together, scoping out opportunities or just dreaming, dried up the minute they'd gotten home.

It was as though Mom hovered invisible

between them, and neither knew how to be without her. Dad had the secret of Mom's committal lodged in his throat, and she'd kept so many things from him when he'd come home and questioned her as though she were the adult that it was easier to be silent. Whereas tonight she'd probably learned the whole Michelli genealogy in one meal.

She changed into sleep shorts and top, gathered her toiletries and went through the connecting door to the bathroom, then locked the other two. Three entrances into a bathroom that was the length of the bedrooms that flanked it, only narrower. A useful layout made interesting by the black and aqua Art Deco tile and fixtures that she guessed again were original. Lance bathed in a museum piece. Did he know it?

There were cracks along the ceiling and floor, but the building had been moderately preserved. Except for a scatter of Star's things, the room was also clean and in order. Which of the men kept it that way? She'd wager on Chaz over Rico, but her perceptions could be wrong, even though she'd trained herself to judge people's strengths and weaknesses. She hadn't seen Lance coming, and it made her wonder how many others she'd gotten wrong.

She washed and brushed her teeth, ran

damp fingers over her hair, and noted the weariness in her face. Sleep would be great, but she didn't expect it. She now recognized the fear that had kept her awake year after year — fear that she would die if she gave in, fear she'd learned the night she almost did. She believed her life was in God's hands. But knowing the truth didn't change years of habit all at once. The best nights she'd had were when Lance sang or talked her to sleep. But she wasn't going there.

As though on cue, a tap came at the door and Lance asked, "Need anything?"

She could swear the man read her mind. She opened it a crack. "No thanks. I packed adequately."

He tipped his head. "Neck rub?"

Her neck was steel cables, but she glanced behind him at Chaz in his "university" and shook her head. "I'm okay."

"I should have warned you about all this."

"You should have."

"You like to know what's coming."

"That's right."

He leaned on the jamb. "But you survived."

"I'm good at that."

"Strongest woman I've ever known."

She tipped her head. "That's saying a lot."

He winced. "Yeah, well . . ."

"And according to Monica they were not all hard-luck stories."

"What would she know?"

"Some right out of *Glamour* magazine, she said."

"A glamorous woman can't have problems?"

"Monica said you're spoiled. With three big sisters, cousins, aunts, mother, grandmother, all treating you like a prince, how would you ever settle for one girl?"

"Monica's a font of wisdom? Try sisters, cousins, aunts, mother, and grandmother all bossing, scolding, squeezing, kissing. Enough to make me take holy orders."

Rese raised her brows. "Which still gets you out of choosing." She'd been right to resist his charm. He didn't discriminate.

He reached for her hand, twined their fingers. "Sometimes there is no choice. You open your eyes, and it's been made for you."

There was the intense sincerity that only Lance could produce and the devastating impact it had on her insides. But she kept her face wooden. No one made her choices, least of all Lance, who couldn't even tell her the whole story.

She loosed her fingers. "Good night, Lance."

Lance sat down with Chaz and sighed.

"Think I'll ever get it right?"

"You should have told her what to expect."

"She wouldn't have come."

"She deserved the choice."

Chaz was right — as always. Lance leaned back and closed his eyes. "Why do I see it after the fact?"

"You don't look before."

He wanted to argue, but he hadn't told Rese on purpose, because if he'd painted the picture, she would have resisted — no, downright refused. He'd imagined her here with Nonna, sharing their plans, their hopes. He hadn't imagined her with the rest of them. He loved his family, but he'd avoided the thought of them all with Rese.

Dinner had been a gauntlet. He'd argued, but Monica was right that they felt responsible for him. They couldn't turn off their nurture; it was ingrained from his infancy. Another reason to stay in Sonoma. He could grow up there.

He reached for Chaz's Bible, found the passage he wanted. *"When I was a child, I talked like a child, I thought like a child, I reasoned like a child. When I became a man, I put childish ways behind me."*

He ran away when Tony died because he didn't know how to become the man his brother had been. He threw himself into projects to help the world, one cause after

109

another, then moved on before he had a chance to fail. He'd always denied it, but maybe his mother had named him after the knight who fought hard and faithfully, but in the end brought ruin to Camelot.

She should have given him a solid Italian name like Frank or Dominick or Vinnie, or Roman like Pop. Why had she grown whimsical when she clutched his waxy, squirming body? Pop could have put his foot down, but what did he care? He had Tony.

Lance looked up.

Chaz met his gaze. "Find what you need?"

"Am I still the guy who showed up with a hammer at your father's church, thinking I could change the world?"

Chaz formed a slow smile. "Yes and no." He turned the book to see the passage, then said, "You thought your hammer would make things better, and it did. It gave shelter where there was no shelter. You dug ditches and laid pipes for clean water to stop disease. You taught food preparation to minimize the contamination that caused swelling in bellies, sores, and hives. Because you suffered, you eased suffering."

Lance dropped his gaze to the table. He didn't want congratulations, only to know that he had made a difference. And he had.

Pop might not see it. He hadn't grown into the same kind of man as Pop or Tony, but in his wandering he'd found his way. Especially with Nonna's quest. He'd gone in, brash and expectant, and learned that life didn't work like that. But still his heart was expectant. He didn't seem capable of dousing hope. He glanced toward Rese's door. He hoped, but sometimes what happened was out of his hands.

Sitting in her chair the next morning, Antonia sighed. Lance was going to force it. Make her remember what she didn't want to. Make her speak aloud the things that haunted her sleep. He wanted answers, but she had none. Only sadness. Only shame.

Too well she remembered the cat claws up her spine, the nerves pinching and seizing with doubt and apprehension. Papa's dead-of-night escapades, pushing the car to the end of the drive so she wouldn't hear him leave . . .

I tell Nonno my fear, but he says only, "Trust what you know, Antonia," and presses his hand to his chest.

But the love I have for Papa is trapped in fear. Two men have been murdered over the last months, and the police found nothing. Something dark has come to Sonoma. I know inside it's Arthur Jackson.

Why can't Papa just make loans at the bank? Why has he accepted the personal position he now seems to hold?

"I'm afraid, Nonno. I feel it inside."

He nods, standing at the edge of what vineyard we have left. "Everything ends, cara. Life is letting go."

I shake my head. "I don't want to. I won't." I stomp my foot.

He smiles, his eyes in the past. "You're so like her, sometimes I forget you're not."

Though I am fair and she was dark, I know what he sees when he looks at me with those distant eyes. Nonna Carina would not have stayed silent. "If she was here, she would tell Papa to stop it."

"She would tell him, but he wouldn't stop. A man has to make his own way."

"Why? Why can a man do anything, even when it hurts his family?"

Nonno drops his chin. "Vittorio doesn't mean to hurt you, Antonia. You are everything to him."

"If that were true he would listen to me. He wouldn't deceive me."

"Because he doesn't tell you everything doesn't mean he deceives."

I ball my fists. "Sneaking out at night? Pushing the car?"

Nonno smiles. "He doesn't want you to hear and worry."

"Why won't he tell me what he's doing?"

"It's not your business to know."

I huff. "It's not my business. It'll be my business when we lose this." I sweep my arm over the view before us. "When I can no longer hold my head up."

Nonno frowns. "Are you ashamed of your papa, Antonia?"

I draw breath but can't answer.

"Then you don't know him." Nonno turns on his cane and walks slowly away. . . .

Antonia jolted. The rap on the door was soft, but still it set her teeth on edge. *Go away. Leave me to my shame.* "Come."

Lance opened the door, but he had Rese with him. Surely he wouldn't bare her secrets in front of a stranger, no matter what the woman meant to him. Lance would not be so callous, so insensitive. That wasn't his nature. Or was it?

"*Buon giorno,* Nonna." He kissed her cheek. Judas betraying her.

She looked into his face. His eyes were bright in spite of their midnight hue. They'd always had a shine, something alive in their depths as though the zeal with which he looked out could not be dimmed. It hurt to see that he thought what he did now was good and right.

She wanted to lash out, tell him to keep what he knew to himself. Why drag her through it again? But then she noticed what he held. Her eyes fixed on the box, her box from long ago, a stationery set Papa had given her for her fifteenth birthday. It had once held papers and pens and a small lap desk. She had used them to write letters to her cousin Conchessa in Liguria, who sent Lance to Sonoma. All she'd wanted was for him to find Nonno, to give him the burial he deserved.

With the box tucked under his arm, he pulled a chair over for Rese, then one for himself. "Is Sofie here?"

Antonia shook her head.

He laid the box on the table next to his chair, and in spite of her resistance, anticipation soared as he worked the lid open. She'd put nothing in the box that compromised Papa. Maybe there was nothing to fear. . . .

At the angle he propped the lid, she couldn't see inside but waited, hardly breathing, as he reached in. He handed her two photos; her mother and Nonno Quillan. She had not looked at Momma in so long. A beautiful woman with the fashionable blond bob of the time. A woman who turned heads, who turned Papa's head and never stopped turning his heart, but who had not much use for a daughter, as though there was a competition between them from the start.

It was to Nonna Carina she turned when

114

the woes of life put her in need of comfort. It was at Nonna's knee she learned the things she would come to value, a language different from the one she spoke at school, an appreciation for beauty — not the useless trinkets her mother desired — the beauty of song and words and nature, the beauty of love. She learned to speak for herself, to hold her own in any situation.

It was from Nonna she learned the give and take of love. In her grandparents' relationship, Antonia saw what had been lacking in Momma and Papa, and she vowed only to bind her heart to one that surrendered likewise to hers. Bald hatred could not be worse than misaligned desires, two lives constantly tugging. Looking at her momma's picture, she felt no loss, only regret that she hadn't known her, hadn't been known.

Then she turned her gaze to Nonno's photograph, striking with his mane of hair that put Samuel Clemens to shame. Nonno's was a face both noble and fierce. The picture didn't capture the warmth in his eyes, the deep capacity for tenderness, or near the end, the unfathomed grief. Without Nonna Carina, he waited only, ready for death, and found it in more grief.

She closed her eyes, remembering. *Nonno.* His last concern for her. And she had obeyed his wishes. She had not been found, not been destroyed as everything she cherished had. She opened her eyes, and Lance handed her letters she recalled saving in the box.

One letter Nonno had given her from Flavio, accepting his charge as godfather. When they came home from the grave that day, he had handed it to her and said, "Know that every choice you make ripples the lake. My Carina wanted it," he said with a shrug. "Maybe to appease her conscience or to help Flavio find his way. He never married; how could he after loving Carina? So Vittorio was like a son to him. And he never stopped vying with me for his heart. Is it any wonder Vittorio is split?"

Antonia lifted the next, a letter from Papa on her birthday. A warmth spread over her as she read his words. She had never doubted his love, only his — Antonia stifled a sob. It had risen up from nowhere and caught her by surprise. She didn't feel the emotions coming sometimes. They attacked from the shadows of her mind. She set that letter down with a trembling hand.

The last was the note from Marco saying he was up to the task of winning her. A new warmth scented with the bloom of love. She drew a shaky breath and looked at the two young people before her. Rese's presence no longer seemed wrong. She was one with Lance's heart, even if she didn't know it yet.

"You might recognize this." Lance took out a book.

She gasped. "M . . . y di—"

He handed it to her, and she rubbed her palm over the cover. How had he found it? Where? Questions clogged her mind.

"It was kept safe for you with this." He laid a paper atop. "It's a deed to the property that Ralph Martino held in trust for you."

Antonia stared at the deed as tears flooded her eyes. Martino. Ralph must be related to Joseph, dear Joseph, who buried the trapdoor in dirt to hide Nonno's resting spot, the foolish demand of a distraught girl who hadn't seen any other way. He must have found her diary wherever it fell and kept it for her. Had he thought she would return?

"Nonna? Do you know anything about this deed?"

She looked at the paper again and shook her head. Nonno must have given it to Joseph to keep for her. Had he known, after all, that trouble was coming, made provision with a man he trusted more than his son? Why else give Joseph the deed, unless he knew they would flee? But Nonno hadn't gone with her. He had stopped his heart rather than leave the home he had

117

shared with Carina. She swallowed the pain.

Lance said, "Rese bought the property in good faith. She's renovated the villa, restored the damage of age and vandals. She intends to run it as a bed-and-breakfast. None of us knew about your deed, and I don't know which one would stand up in court."

What was he talking about, court? Antonia looked at Rese, a strong face, competent. She looked at the hands, callused and strong, the defined and developed forearms. She had restored the villa? Maybe, but could she begin to know what that place had meant to the young woman forced to flee? How it had symbolized a life lost?

"Nonna." Lance covered her hands with his. "Rese and I are partners in the business. With your blessing, I want to go back to that. Make it work."

Rese startled as though she hadn't expected to hear it, and her calm fractured enough to show the underlying strain. Ah. So her strength lay in disguise, hiding the fear and insecurity. She was not sure of Lance, not sure at all. And who could blame her when he was so unsure of himself?

They wanted to make her home an inn, her sanctuary a dormitory for strangers.

She closed her eyes and pictured the place she and Nonno had treasured. The vines heavy with fruit, the walls steeped in life, love, and laughter. And grief and death. Waves of sorrow washed over her. Was it possible her grandson, the one she loved so well, would reclaim the property lost to her?

If this was all they wanted, maybe they didn't know. Maybe . . . She picked up the deed and pressed it into his hands. Rese might have bought the property through some fluke of fate, but Lance would have this deed from her hands. She laid his other hand atop and said, "Y . . . ours."

Lance met her eyes. "Thank you, Nonna. But technically it belongs to Rese."

Why wouldn't he let that go? He was stubborn, this man. As stubborn as she.

"She paid one point eight million dollars for it. And that was in its ransacked condition. She's put a lot into it since then."

Rese turned. "How do you know what I paid?"

"Public record." He half smiled.

One point eight million dollars? Antonia couldn't comprehend such a sum. But then, she'd never accorded things a monetary value. It was what it meant to her that mattered. And that villa meant youth and innocence, love and pain. Did she wish that on Lance? She looked from his face to

119

Rese Barrett's. Whether she wished it or not, they were in it already.

Antonia took Rese's hand and put it on Lance's holding the deed. "Yours." And if they thought she meant the deed, *bene.* She would give what was no longer hers to give, and they would bless her for it.

Rese said, "Thank you." And there was a hint of tears in her eyes. Eyes that would not tear easily, that kept the world back. Something had wounded her. But then, that was life.

"There's more, Nonna."

Lance's words pulled her spine stiff. *No.* The rest should be left in peace. "No m . . . ore."

"I don't want to buck you."

But he would. He thought he knew what was right, and like David he would fight any giant. Including his feeble nonna, who, he knew well, was not feeble in spirit. She gave him the sharp look that transmitted her displeasure. Even as a small boy he had resisted its sting; now as a man he brushed it aside.

"I know you don't want to talk about this, but I don't understand why." An attempt to cajole.

She glared. "L . . . eave it."

He set the deed on the table and took from the box a bundle of money. "I found a stash of these in the cellar with Nonno

Quillan. Silver certificate bills. They're worth a lot."

Money in the cellar? *"Antonia, under . . ."* Was it Nonno's savings, or had Papa hidden it there for some underhanded purpose?

"I also found these." He took a stack of envelopes from the box and laid them so that she saw the names written on each; some she recognized though she didn't want to, men affiliated with Arthur Jackson, some who'd been taken in as Papa had, others as distasteful as he.

A raging geyser shot up inside. *Stop it! Stop!* Wasn't it enough that Papa was killed? Did he have to be dishonored in her grandson's eyes as well as her own?

Lance sat back. "How come Nonno Marco never said he was a federal agent?"

The geyser died as quickly as it had spouted. Marco a federal agent? "What?"

"I have a letter that says Marco Michelli was a federal agent and your pop, Vittorio, was working undercover with him."

Antonia sank back, weak in every cell. It wasn't possible.

But he took the letter from the box. "I got this from Arthur Jackson's great-granddaughter."

Hearing the name spoken nearly stopped her heart. She refused to take the paper he extended. Nothing tainted by Arthur

Jackson would touch her fingers.

"I think this is why Vittorio was murdered."

Her hands trembled. Her lips shook. Her face hung slack. He knew it all, then. Pain coursed through her.

"Nonna? You okay?"

She could hear him, but she couldn't respond.

"Nonna? Rese, get Momma." Lance took the diary from her lap, chafed her hands. "Talk to me, Nonna. Please. I'm sorry I upset you."

Her vision blurred. Her body felt stiff. Her head was a buzzing hive.

Lance dropped to his knees and took her in his arms. "Please, Nonna. Don't do this. I'm sorry."

She wanted to comfort him, to tell him this hurt had nothing to do with him. That he was her joy. That he made everything she'd lost worth it. But no words would come.

Then Dori hovered over her. "Momma?" Doria, her daughter-in-law who had moved into their world when she married Roman, who now took responsibility for the old woman who was no longer able to feed herself, to dress or move about. How bad would the damage be this time?

If she could wonder, wasn't that good? The last time, she'd awakened to a broken mind and a crippled body. She was not unconscious. Maybe this one wasn't as bad. Maybe.

Lance had jammed his fingers into his hair and stood like a tortured soul in Dante's Inferno, blaming himself. Damning himself.

"M . . . ah." That wasn't the sound she needed.

"Don't try to talk, Momma." Dori soothed her brow with a cool hand.

She had to talk, to tell Lance not to worry, not to blame himself. But the sounds that came scared him worse than before. She stopped making them. Stopped trying. Stopped fighting.

"I've called the doctor."

No. No more doctors. No hospital. She wanted her family, not strangers who would take her away. She used to know the people at Saint Barnabas as well as the cheese maker and the baker and the shoe repairman and the clockmaker. Now there were faces she'd never seen. People who never knew she had once been lovely and bright. They saw only her disfigurement.

She closed her eyes. *Leave me alone. Leave me.*

123

Chapter Six

Lance felt the knife in his gut twist with every breath as he stood in the hall outside Nonna's door. Every time he thought he was getting it right, thought he was in God's will . . . Rese stood beside him, but his mind circled one thought only. *My fault.*

He fought the tightness in his throat. He might have had nothing to do with the towers coming down on Tony, but he was directly responsible for Nonna. He had pushed when she begged him not to. He'd wanted to tell her things she didn't want to know; made her remember things she'd never spoken of. Maybe she hadn't even known her papa was murdered. What was he doing, blurting it out like that?

The doctor emerged, one who made house calls to an aged stroke victim in the neighborhood of the hospital. He'd been making rounds, and six blocks wasn't far out of his way. Better than sending an ambulance, taking up a bed. He knew Antonia Michelli.

He had allowed only Momma into the

room with him, and Lance was glad. He didn't want to see the damage, to know he was to blame. But now in the hall Dr. Stern said, "Mrs. Michelli has had what we call a ministroke. The anti-stroke medication she's taking seems to have minimized the damage."

Lance swallowed. "Is she conscious?"

"Yes. But I don't want her disturbed."

Right. No forcing unwanted information on your enfeebled grandmother.

"One person with her at a time." He knew the rest of the Michellis. "She needs rest and peace. If she can't get it here, I'll have to hospitalize."

"She'll get it." Lance only wanted to tell her how sorry he was, that he would not bother her with any of it again. The business with Marco and Vittorio and Arthur Jackson could remain silent forever. *Basta.* Enough.

After the doctor left, Rese frowned. "I know what you're doing."

"What."

"Blaming yourself."

"She asked me to stop."

"Well, that's not your forte."

Understatement of the year. His cell phone rang, and he told Monica the status and the doctor's stipulations. She had taken all the children out to the park, and they'd have to find ways to keep them oc-

125

cupied for the next few days at least. No swarming Nonna. Only one person at a time. And he wasn't the best choice anymore.

"Pray," he told Monica. And he should too. He hung up and looked at Rese. "Is it okay if we go to the church?"

"Sure." She looked relieved, actually. He must be really grim.

They took the stairs down and out to the street, then walked the few blocks to the church. Mount Carmel had been the center of life in his neighborhood since the basement church was built in 1907. Now the triple-arched entrance between the two rusty-red brick towers embraced him. He and Rese arrived as the *donne anziane,* old women in their black scarves and thick stockings, were descending the pale stone stairs from the midday Italian Mass. Many of them greeted him, and he forced a smile as he led Rese inside.

He lowered his head and settled on the kneeler. How many times had he ended up there, hoping God could fix something he'd messed up? He must have some kind of record for getting it wrong. In Sonoma when everything blew up, he'd tried to give it all to Rese; the deed, the money, tried to let her go, thinking that was God's will. But when she wanted him to stay, it had seemed right to bring it all to Nonna,

126

whose approval mattered as much to him at twenty-eight as it had at eight.

But Nonna had asked for help, not a battle. *Lord.* He deserved the tongue-thrashing only she could deliver. Or could she? How much progress would be lost, and how frustrated would she be? He dropped his face to his hands. *Lord, heal her. I'll leave the past to the past. I don't need answers. Just bring her back.*

He dropped his forehead to his hands and sank down until his backside rested against the pew with his knees still on the kneeler. He could remember Momma scolding him for slacking into that position. *"Keep a straight back for the One whose back was scourged for you."*

He meant no disrespect but drew himself up again anyway, sensing a perpetual incense inside the walls, not from the burning of gray powder, but of prayers raised to heaven in silent anticipation and faith. He could almost hear the murmur of whispers in the rafters and added his own.

Into your heart, into your hand,
All that I am, naked I stand.
Selah, O Lord, Selah. In the silence you
   find me.
Selah, my Lord, Selah. In the stillness
   refine me.

His lyrics. The problem was he couldn't get still, couldn't find the silence. He needed the road. He stood up and motioned Rese out ahead of him, dropping down to genuflect before leaving. God had heard him, he was sure. But he didn't know what the answer would be. And he couldn't stand still to find out.

Lance's stride leaving the church meant trouble. He had obviously not found peace and comfort, even though she'd been amazed by the beauty inside, the adoration it inspired. Rese hadn't expected the wealth of stained glass and marbled pillars, the carved and painted scenes along the walls and ceiling. She hadn't thought to find any of that in a neighborhood church.

But she hadn't expected anything that had happened so far. A quick explanation of their plans, a sincere effort to set things right, a chance for Lance to bring his efforts for his grandmother to conclusion — that was what she'd expected. Now she worked to keep up as they descended the sun-warmed steps.

"Lance?" she puffed.

He didn't respond for two blocks, or when they reached his apartment, or when he searched through the keys by the door and raised a ring wordlessly to Rico, who was practicing a drum riff with Star at his feet. Rico didn't pause, merely nodded.

Back downstairs and out the back this time, Lance used one key to unlock a lean-to in the courtyard, then wheeled out a Kawasaki so stripped it made his Harley look like a luxury cruiser.

Rese's jaw dropped. "What's that?"

"Rico's chopper."

"I thought he had a van, the one he drove to Sonoma with all the gear."

Lance brushed the dust from the seat. "He borrows that when he's got a gig. These are his wheels."

She looked again at the bike, barely making out the word Vulcan on the dented metal. The thing looked as though it had been through reentry. Lance rested it on its stand, leaned back into the enclosure, and brought out a helmet, nowhere near as sleek and nice as the black one he'd bought for her.

"Rico has a helmet?" She would have thought he, like Lance, didn't bother.

"It's an old one of Tony's. We'll cinch it up on you."

"Lance, I'm not —" But when he raised the helmet to her head, she noticed his hands shaking. She'd seen him upset, but not shaking. He needed this. She pulled the helmet down and adjusted the chin strap, but cringed when he started the bike. The exhaust pipe choked up gray spume before the engine settled into an asthmatic growl.

He hollered, "Jump on."

"Lance . . ." She had barely come to trust him with the Harley on quiet Sonoma highways.

"Come on." He jerked his chin toward the spot behind him as the idle choked and wheezed.

She knew what he wanted, but she could not get on that thing. It was an accident waiting to happen. Didn't he hear it? What was it with him and two-wheeled death vehicles?

He looked up and caught her expression. His shoulders slumped. "It's okay. You don't have to." He dug for his house keys and held them out. With his other hand, he brought the engine back from death with a rev.

He would go without her, and wouldn't she rather he did? Not if he was upset enough to shake. "Lance . . . don't . . ." Oh, what was the use? She closed her eyes and straddled the bike, clamping onto his waist. It was a closer fit than the Harley, the seat configuration leaning her down against him. As he accelerated through the alley and into the street, her arms tightened. Rico's bike didn't have the rich roar of the Harley. It needed muffler work to quiet the racket the helmet didn't buffer and surely had other issues that begged a mechanic.

As they maneuvered through the city, it took everything in her not to yell for Lance to take her back — if it would even register. His agitated starts and stops, his impatience with the congestion and lights showed just how wound up he was. She knew what he wanted, open road, speed. She recalled with shocking clarity that first ride in which he had intentionally scared her speechless.

Now as he hit the highway heading north into Connecticut, she sensed not rage in him but a similar ferocity. Wind buffeted her face and drowned her breath. She hated being at the mercy of his reflexes, his decisions, especially when she was not convinced he was making any. Lance in this mood was pure emotion, pure reaction.

She had given up control. It wouldn't be as bad if she thought one of them had it, but she knew he was flying blind. She squeezed his sides and hollered, "Slow down!"

Instead, he leaned them out around the vehicle he'd run up on, into the oncoming lane, then back before a minivan whooshed by the other way. She ducked her head behind his shoulder. She could die . . . or worse.

What was a coma like; paralysis? How

131

badly would it hurt to have every bone in her body broken? How would it feel to break every bone in Lance's? But, having caused his grandmother's relapse, he was probably trying to break them all himself. No one could blame himself like Lance Michelli.

Squinting down at the road flying by underneath, she tried not to imagine being launched with him and having those awful seconds to anticipate macadam imbedding in soft tissue, muscles wrenched and screaming before the mercifully swift snap of her neck. And now she was mad. "Lance, stop it!"

But he didn't. Miles of interstate flew by, wooded landscape, quaint towns, and white-fenced estates. She didn't know if Lance saw any of it. He was doing what he did to cope, as she would get hold of her tools and bury herself in a project, tearing out or building up, every cut perfect, every fit tight, every detail considered and executed. Losing herself. Running, maybe, as Lance was, without the speed and danger.

Danger. A flash of a blood-splattered wall, her dad's screams, the warm, coppery scent of life escaping. She forced slow breaths, angry to be flashing back when it wasn't even triggered by the sound and smell of a saw on wood. Only thoughts of death. Agonizing death. "Lance!"

132

He reached down and gripped her knee, pressing her leg against him. Was it supposed to be reassuring that he now drove with one hand? She wanted to scream, but hollered instead, "We need to stop!"

He'd heard her, she knew by the sudden deceleration, and a moment later he let go of her knee and made the arm signal for a right turn onto the exit. She gulped for breath as the wind stopped pummeling her lungs. His speed dropped dramatically as they entered the small town of Darien. A collage of Victorian, colonial, and Edwardian architecture surrounded her with picturesque shrub-lined cobblestone sidewalks that contrasted starkly with the grim streets of the Bronx.

Her limbs softened as he cruised through the town center and postcard-perfect neighborhood to a beach as lovely in its East Coast way as any she'd seen on the other. Pleasure boats bobbed in the water that lapped at the shore, white gulls winged overhead. The air smelled fresh. . . . Well, okay, there was still the exhaust from Rico's bike, and her anger kicked back in when Lance brought the monster to a stop and climbed off.

She yanked off the helmet and glared. "Wha-a-t?"

"You have to ask?"

"I said you didn't have to come."

"And where would you be now?"

"Farther."

She got off the bike. "That thing is a wreck."

"Just looks like it."

"What about the gray smoke spewing out and its death rattle shutting off?"

Lance patted the grip. "A little rusty. Rico must not be riding much without my Harley to keep up with."

She shook her head. "What is it with you? What does driving hell-bent accomplish?"

He sent his gaze off. "It's the miles, the motion of the road."

"It's running away."

"Maybe." His brow pinched. "I can't really get far enough. I just have to try."

She sighed. "Do you have to do it so fast?"

"It feels faster on a bike."

Possible. Her road experience was in a Chevy 4x4. Lots of steel.

She looked out at the tree-lined beach, the golden sand, the cobalt water. After the noise and smell and film of carbon monoxide in the city, it was incredible. She could almost be glad they'd come. She was definitely glad they'd stopped. "Is that the Atlantic Ocean?"

He looked up as though he only now realized where he was. "Long Island Sound."

Where would they have ended up if she

hadn't gotten through to him? Canada? She had a crazy desire to laugh — probably some hysterical release. She cocked her head and said dryly, "Where's the picnic?" Now that the terror was over, she was starved.

He huffed. "Picnics are dangerous."

"Picnics with me, you mean." She recalled the raging climax of their first attempt when Lance cajoled her onto his Harley packed with wine and cheese to share in the sloping pastureland near Sonoma. She had told him no dates with employees, but did he listen? Did he ever?

He started for the shore. "We could dig for clams."

"No thanks." She started after him. "No slimy shellfish."

"Ever tried it?"

She shook her head. "I love what you cook, but —"

"Say that again."

She punched his arm. "I am not stroking your ego."

"You punch like a man."

"Good."

He stopped at the water's edge with a restless look that made her wonder if he would ever quell that urge for speed and distance. But then, she knew better.

The road wasn't enough. He couldn't

outrun what he'd done to Nonna. It wasn't just about getting it right anymore, it was how many people would he hurt in the process.

He should have stopped pressing, but as Rese said, that wasn't his forte. He'd forced Nonna to hear him. Sure it was gentle, it was coaxing, but he had not given in.

Italian machismo. And he'd thought he missed that gene. It didn't play the same as in Pop and Tony. More sensitive, more attentive, but underneath just as determined and demanding. He stared out over the water.

Another woman would have filled the ache with words, given him something to build an excuse around. Rese stood beside him as solemn as the oaks and maples at his back. Hardwood, strong and lasting.

He felt like the whitened driftwood that came in on the tide. Why did he see things too late? Nonna trusted him, and he had used that trust to break her down.

Rese crouched, resting on her haunches, and fingered the pebbles in the sand. Her silence suggested she understood, but she hadn't experienced the interweaving of lives so intricate every step was a dance on a sticky web. He had shaken Nonna loose, and the fragile gossamer that held her terrified him. *Lord . . .*

But he could not whistle for God and command Him along for the ride. Pride, to think so. And pride to expect it of Rese, of Nonna. Love did not force its own way. *"It is not rude, it is not self-seeking."* He had learned the words from Nonna, sitting at her table with a blackened eye, telling her how he would get back at the bullies who attacked Rico.

"It always protects, raggazzo mio."

"But I was protecting."

They'd been caught by surprise, but he wouldn't be next time.

"Love does not seek revenge."

"Hah!" He'd clenched his fists. *"A curse returned, Nonna."*

"You are a child, you talk like a child. Someday you will be a man."

He groaned. Rese looked up, but neither spoke. He had lain in wait for the meanest of the bunch, found him alone the next day and beaten him soundly. He'd said it was for Rico, but there was no vindication in it, no satisfaction. Was he still trying to strike back? At what?

He rubbed his face. "We should get you something to eat."

Rese stood up. "What about you?"

"I'm not hungry."

"Come on, Lance. You know there's more to food than hunger."

He raised his brows. "Such as?"

137

"Connection, acceptance, relationship."

His own words back at him. But right now he felt like poison. "Maybe we could walk a little."

She stooped down and took off her sandals, dangled them from her fingers, and stepped up to the water's edge.

"You might not want to do that."

"Why not?"

"It's cold."

With her toes, she kicked up a fan of sparkling drops, then plunged her hand in and splashed him.

He sputtered. Another blast of salt water, and when he lunged, Rese took off up the beach. His surprise cost him time, but he tore after her. Her legs were strong and swift, and she reached the trees, caught hold of a silver maple, and swung around its trunk.

"You think that's going to protect you?" He approached, a little winded.

She locked her fingers around it. "I've always had a thing for maple."

He stopped a foot from the tree. "You are so lucky I've got a thing for you."

"Or what?"

"I'd dunk you."

She raised her chin. "Then you'd have my soggy self against you all the way home."

He did not let his mind take that and

run. Neither would he give her the last word. He pressed his palm to the trunk and leaned in. "Just might be worth it." He moved around the trunk and stopped. What was he doing? He closed his eyes. Nonna lay in bed, and he was playing on the beach? He dropped his forehead to hers. "I know what you're doing."

She didn't answer.

He opened his eyes and met her gaze. "It's my fault, Rese. I keep thinking I've got it right, then . . ."

"What would she want?"

"To slap my head."

Rese studied him a long moment, then shrugged. "I could do that."

He stepped back. "Right."

She raised her brows. "You think I can't? Ask Sam and Charlie."

At fourteen she'd handled the jerks who assaulted her. Lance cocked his head. "Okay, give me your best shot." He waited. "Come on. I won't hit back."

She shook her head, then looked away. "I can't."

"Why not?"

"I'm not mad. And it's you."

"Just think of all the ways I've torqued you off big time."

She glared. "I'm not going to hit you, Lance."

"What are you, a girl?"

She turned her fury full on him. "Yes. Got a problem with that?"

He grinned, feeling some of the tension release. "You kiddin'? I like girls."

Rese ran her hand over her hair. "Look, I'm not very good at this."

"This what?"

"I don't know, comfort. Perspective."

He wasn't looking for comfort, and his perspective was clear as glass. He sighed. "I just want to take it back, to undo something so stupid I'd . . . do anything to get one more chance."

"You'll have a chance."

He pressed his hands to his face. "What if I don't? What if I can't tell her how sorry I am?"

Rese took his hands down. "She knows."

"How?"

"She knows you."

He studied her as that small comfort leached in. Nonna would forgive more easily than he could forgive himself. He half smiled. "You're better at this than you think."

She shrugged. "You tend to lose sight of things when you're all fire and emotion."

He leaned his palm to the tree. "Do I?"

She nodded. "You do okay the other one percent of the time though." She pushed off from the tree and started back down the beach.

140

Chapter Seven

Like photographs doubly exposed, scenes overlap; bedposts and white walls gilding with wine country sunshine, the bustle of a crowd, the scent of dust. . . .

A shabby boy picks Nonno's pocket, but Nonno gets him by the nape before he slips away into the crowd. I cannot believe the gentleness in Nonno's eyes as he faces the youth and holds out his palm. Though thin and scrawny, the boy is older, I suspect, than my fourteen years. He would bolt but for the power of Nonno's gaze and the press of people in the Plaza.

His throat works up and down as he slaps the wallet into Nonno's hand, the one not holding a cane to support an old man. This youth must have seen an easy mark in Nonno, but he didn't know Quillan Shepard if he thought that. He squirms a little under Nonno's gaze but seems to realize this man has no vindictive spirit in him.

"What's your name?"

He doesn't want to tell but can't help it. "Joseph Martino."

"Looking for a job?" Nonno's words surprise even me. Times are tight, jobs hard to come by. He offers one to someone who just tried to rob him?

"What you got, old man?" The youth's face isn't as tough as his words.

"Your life," Nonno says, "in my hand."

Again the boy swallows. Someone hardened to crime would have sneered. But few men sneer when confronted by Nonno's kindness. What will Papa say when he sees Nonno has brought home another stray? Others have drifted on, but something passes between these two that makes me wonder. Nonno could have brought the cops on him. Instead he redeemed him.

Maybe Nonno sees himself — a bitter, unloved youth who found his share of trouble. Whatever the case, he says, "Know how to cut grapes?"

The youth shrugs. "I can try anything once."

The scenes run together like a moving picture, season after season, hoeing, pruning, harvesting, Joseph becoming to Nonno as devoted as a son.

And then pain twists his face as I tell him Nonno is dead. Quillan Shepard fallen and left to lie. Joseph Martino stands with a shovel in his hand, promising to make a grave, a tomb for our fallen hero. Then he is gone.

The Studebaker swerves and skids down the drive onto silent streets. People sleeping, unaware of the violence, the grief that throbs in my breast.

Papa! Nonno! Signore, why? I ask, but what good are answers that change nothing? I want it to be different. Maybe Papa wasn't shot. Did I see him? I have only the sound of it and supposition and Marco's assertion. And the awful emptiness. *Papa. Oh, Papa.*

And Nonno. His last words, his last breaths as his great heart gave up. Too many griefs; too much loss. Maybe mine, too, will stop.

I keep my eyes on the road. Though I know Nonno will find his place there, I cannot look up to heaven, cannot stare through the stars to the throne where angels sing praises. This is a night for weeping, for beating my breast and raging against the fates. *Mal occhio.* A curse upon me. The devil has had his way. I press my hands to my eyes and sob.

Rese had hoped for a quiet dinner with Lance, Star and Rico, and Chaz, if he wasn't working, but as soon as Lance pulled in on Rico's deathtrap, his mother motioned to him from the window and called, "You two come up. I'm making spaghetti."

Lance killed the engine. "Need a hand?"

Doria leaned on her palms. "I'm capable of spaghetti."

"I didn't mean you weren't." He sounded weary. The day had taken its toll.

His mother fanned a hand before her nose. "That bike smells like burnt oil."

"Maybe you better check the stove."

She started to argue, then turned and disappeared.

Rese climbed off, and Lance wheeled the bike onto the canvas tarp inside the enclosure. It did stink, though it seemed to have worked out some of its issues on the drive. As Lance had? He'd gone out of his way to be cautious on the way back, but, hooking the helmet over the grip, she was glad to lock the bike up behind them. Lance had it out of his system, and they'd survived.

He cocked an eyebrow. "Spaghetti?"

With pandemonium. "I wish she didn't go to all that trouble." Truly.

He finger-combed his windblown hair and looked up at the empty window. "She'll be deeply offended if we don't accept."

That went without saying. She was obviously touchy. It reminded her of Lance in their first days together, how he'd work up

144

a steam over nothing. Her mouth twitched remembering the times she'd infuriated him without even knowing. His heritage was volatile.

"Of course we accept. Mmm, spaghetti."

He smiled. "You're hungry."

"Starved."

The apartment was empty when they went to wash up, so dining with Star and Rico and Chaz would not have been an option. Dining alone with Lance could have been nice or difficult, depending on his state of mind, and the fact that he'd forgotten to stop for food the whole time they were gone indicated a serious instability. So in the interest of sustenance, she prepared for mayhem.

But only Lance's mother and his sister Sofie were there when they went in. A strong tomato aroma that was not unpleasant filled the air, and a violin played a lilting melody on the stereo. Rese felt as though she'd been braced for an attack that didn't come — but she expected it still.

Lance raised his brows to his mother. "How is she?" Nonna Antonia being the first and only thing on his mind.

Doria shrugged. "Not very coherent. Sleeping mostly."

"Unconscious?"

Doria shook her head. "Not like last time."

Rese accepted the glass of red wine that Sofie, standing at the kitchen counter, handed her. With nothing in her stomach, it should incapacitate her soon enough. But Doria took a tray of thick mushrooms slathered with something green and chunky from the oven. It was hard to imagine anything less appetizing.

"Portobello with pesto." Doria sent Lance a pointed look. "Sofie made the pesto."

"Ma." He took the glass of wine his sister offered and a strip of mushroom. This last he held out, and Rese had no choice but to take it.

The mushroom was rubbery, but surprisingly tasty. Hunger charged in, and she finished the appetizer with only two sips of wine, then accepted a second slice as Lance's father came in.

"Roman, you got the bread?" Doria called.

"I got the bread." He brought a brown paper bag to her, and a warm yeasty aroma wafted from the crusty loaf she pulled out.

Rese thought she might faint.

"Good, it's hot." Doria set it in a basket and folded a cloth over it like a baby.

Sofie carried the basket to the table. She had yet to say a word. Monica was obviously the talker. And Lucy. And all the aunts. And several cousins, uncles, and brothers-in-law, nieces, nephews, and even

Lance. But at the moment, it was quiet enough to think and observe, and what Rese noticed was a sag in the kitchen ceiling that didn't bode well. Was it polite to mention it? Probably not.

"You might check the pasta, Momma." Lance raised his chin toward the steaming pot.

"I know. I'm checking."

Lance winced when she pulled up a wad of spaghetti.

"So a little past al dente."

"Want me to drain it?" He reached for the pot and unloaded its contents into a metal cone in the sink.

"The sauce is perfect." His mother dipped a spoon and held it toward Rese. As Doria had no intention of surrendering the utensil, that left no choice but to lean in and suck it off the spoon.

Rese smiled and nodded. The sauce was pastier than anything Lance had served, but if they could just eat. . . .

A noisy faucet turned off in the bathroom, and Lance's dad emerged. "How much longer?"

"Okay, already. Did you say hi to your children?"

"What, I don't see them every day?"

"You don't see Lance, or his . . . Rese."

Roman shook his head, taking his place at the table.

"Hard day, Pop?" Sofie patted his head.

"Oy." His hands fell open on either side of his plate.

Doria pressed a bowl of meatballs at Rese that she took to the table, debating where to put them. Sofie indicated a spot in front of her dad. Lance brought a platter of spaghetti and a pitcher of sauce.

Doria came behind him with a tossed salad. "Fast enough for you?"

"Sure." Roman tucked his napkin into his shirt.

Doria tugged it out and laid it across his lap. "We have company."

He looked up. "I thought it was our children."

"Our children and our guest."

Under his gaze, Rese slid into the chair Lance held and jerked it awkwardly forward. Lance sat across the table from her. Sofie sat down beside her and Doria at the other end from Roman. This was it? Just the five of them? Joy and terror.

They said Lance's prayer in unison, and chin dropped, Rese moved her lips as though she knew the words. Roman's napkin went back into his shirt, and he spooned three large meatballs onto his noodles, then drowned it all in sauce. Rese took everything that came her way, including a small dish with oil in the bottom.

"For your bread," Sofie told her.

The bread wasn't cut. They tore off chunks as it came to them. Rese took a hunk of her own, then watched Sofie break hers into bite-sized pieces and dip them in the oil.

"Who's with Nonna?" Lance still had only one thing on his mind.

"Celestina. She's staying the night." Doria looked up. "You know who I saw at the store? That funny little man with one leg. Johnny Grope."

Sofie frowned. "Momma, it's not nice to call the handicapped funny."

"But he is funny. He makes jokes about his name, said he might be one leg short, but at least he's got two hands."

"And one cracked skull." Roman took a hefty bite of pasta.

The amount of food on the table exceeded anything they could eat, even hungry as Rese was. And it did go down more like something she might cook than Lance. It didn't taste bad; it was simply dense.

"I got a new student. Four years old and already she's got presence." Doria turned to Sofie. "Just like you at that age, all neck and legs."

"Good for soup stock, not much else." Lance yelped when she kicked his shin under the table.

Doria plopped another meatball on Lance's plate. "Where did you go off to today? Myrna Caravaggio wanted to see you."

"Myrna Caravaggio thinks I'm still six years old. She'd squeeze my face and say how cute I was in my tomato costume."

Rese shot him a glance that he returned with a wink.

"Well, you know she likes seeing you. She only gets back a few times a year, and you were her favorite tomato." Doria laughed.

"Yeah, yeah."

"Have some more bread, Theresa." Doria pressed the basket at her.

The bread was delicious once she got used to dipping it in oil. Rese took more salad too. It was crisp and tasty as long as she avoided the limp brown strips that had to be anchovies. Considering she hadn't eaten since the pastry that morning before seeing Lance's grandmother, it was all just what she'd needed.

She brought her plate to Lance at the sink. "I'm so full."

"Momma's sauce has its own gravity."

"I heard that." Doria came in and set the bowl of meatballs on the counter.

"Sticks to your ribs." Roman gave her a squeeze from behind. "As it should." He bent in and nuzzled her neck.

Rese tried not to stare, but was that normal parental behavior? Lance caught her gaze and grinned.

"Not now." Doria wriggled free.

"What? A man can't hug his wife?"

"Shoo." She laughed. "I have work to do."

Roman surveyed the kitchen. "Looks like it's covered to me."

"Guests don't wash dishes."

Rese froze when Roman turned his gaze on her. "Welcome to the family." He took Doria's hand. "Come on. We're taking a walk."

"I have to —"

"We're taking a walk." He tugged her along with a swagger in his step.

Rese stared after them all the way to the click of the door. Well. Lance was certainly his father's son. He wouldn't meet her gaze when she turned back, just swabbed and rinsed the dishes.

Was Dad's personality as evident in her? Lance said she punched like a man, walked like a man. She certainly worked like a man; she'd done that much to excel in his world. She picked up the dish towel and realized it was hopeful thinking, because if it wasn't Vernon Barrett people saw, it might be her mother.

Sofie held the bottle over her wineglass, offering a refill, but Rese shook her head.

"I won't sleep."

"Wine's supposed to help that. Good for

the heart and all."

"Rese has chronic insomnia." Lance handed her a slippery plate.

"Stress?" Sofie filled her own goblet.

Rese snorted. "What could possibly be stressful?" And then she realized how that might have come across. "I mean . . ."

"You mean us?" Sofie sipped.

"No." Not individually anyway.

Sofie tipped her head. "Have you tried relaxation techniques?"

The only thing that worked was Lance's voice, and that required a more intimate situation than she was willing to repeat. She waved the towel. "It's no big deal."

"You'd be surprised. REM sleep is essential to well-being. And sleep disorders can indicate underlying conditions — or generate them."

Rese stiffened.

"How old are you, if you don't mind me asking? I'm older, anyway." She grimaced. "Thirty last week."

Rese swabbed the plate and set it aside. "I turn twenty-five in July." She did not want to discuss her age, her insomnia, or her predisposition for schizophrenia. "And thirty's hardly old."

"Well, it's one of those years everyone expects you to dread."

Rese nodded. If she made it to thirty without psychotic episodes she'd celebrate.

"Well, let me know if you want some ideas. To help you sleep."

Rese shrugged. "I'm fine."

Sofie put the last dish into the cabinet and Rese draped the towel over the rod to dry. There still seemed a lot of clutter on counters and shelves, but Lance told Sofie good night, and Rese went with him upstairs.

He stopped at Antonia's door, then went in. Though he hadn't said to, Rese waited outside, watching from the hall as he stopped beside the bed. Both Antonia and his aunt Celestina were asleep, Antonia swallowed up in the bed, and Celestina overflowing her chair.

Lance crept in so softly neither stirred. He could have gone up earlier. But she knew he was seeing Antonia when she wouldn't see him, as though the mere sight could cause another stroke. Hadn't he noticed how her eyes changed every time he got near? If he wanted a mirror, he should look in that one.

Antonia stayed asleep, but Lance stood a long time beside her bed. Then he murmured, "Good night, cara mia," with such love it hurt.

Lance's soft good-night tried to penetrate, but she couldn't open her eyes. The scene of that awful night played in her head as it had so many times before. Only now it seemed skewed, something awry in Marco's "finding" her in the tunnel, Papa's "telling" him about it. Not as a suitor, but a conspirator?

It wasn't possible. She could not have spent a lifetime with Marco and not known, not been told. Marco had saved her from Papa's trouble. He could not have been part of it.

He had come to Papa in good faith, unaware of the secret liaisons with Arthur Jackson. *"It was your assumption, Miss Shepard, that I represent an underworld figure."* He had been innocent of Papa's imbroglio, wanting only discretion for his client. How could he know . . . ? How could he be . . . ? But hadn't she wondered? So much of Marco was mystery.

Waves of pain. She would trust nothing that came from an heir of Arthur Jackson. A federal agent? Impossible. That would mean he came there knowing about Papa. Had he courted her to trap Vittorio Shepard?

Could Marco have shot Papa? No! Lance said they were in it together. Undercover. Again, that wasn't possible. Papa would never allow him to court her as a ruse, to use her that way.

"I think you should kiss me."

"Your papa asked me not to."

Papa, who didn't interfere, who trusted her in matters of the heart. Why had he put boundaries on Marco's courting? All their private talks. How could they have so much to say about her? Or had she assumed in her vain naïveté that she was their most pressing matter? She was twenty, enraptured with herself, alive with Marco's attention.

She moaned, in her sleep or not, she couldn't tell. Federal agent. Undercover. The terms twisted and turned in her mind. What had she put into motion? Awakening the curse to torment her last days. Papa. Nonno. Marco. Her heart melted like soft cheese, a heart that had learned to be strong, sinking back to those dark days. . . .

Marco is saying things I won't hear. "Marry you?"

"Your papa's trouble isn't over."

"What trouble? How do you know? What did he tell you?"

Marco shakes his head. "You already know more than you should." He stands tall beside the car, stretching his legs from so many hours' driving. The grass and ferns smell savory in the afternoon sun, crushed down where he has stomped the life back into his legs. "Suffice it to say, you'll be safer with a new name."

Dazed and angry, I glare. "How can I

marry you in mourning?"

"Extenuating circumstances."

My grief, circumstances? "I don't know you."

"Matches have been made from less."

"Not for me; not like this. I want . . ." What does it matter what I want? Fury seizes me. "I hate you."

"Antonia . . ." He takes my hand. "Let me help you."

I jerk away. "I don't care what happens. Let them kill me."

"I won't." His words close around me like dread. "You'll be safe as Mrs. Marco Michelli."

"*Uffa.*" I thumb my chin. "What is it to you?"

"You know what it is." His eyes are unfathomable. What does he think I know?

"What happened? Why won't you tell me?"

"They ambushed your father."

"I know. I saw them come."

"That's why you're in danger."

"I don't care about me."

"I do."

"Why were you there? How did —"

He takes my hands. "Stop asking. The less you know the better."

Why am I trying to understand? I am cursed. The Lord has turned His face from me, and there will be nothing but bad luck

156

and hardship. What Marco says could be truth; it could be lies. What difference does it make?

He puts me back into the car. "Where are we going?"

He squeezes my hand. "Home."

Chapter Eight

Lance woke with his face wedged into the navy leather cushions and a taste of copper in his mouth. His calves and hamstrings ached from slogging through tar up to his knees hour after hour. Reaching down to rub, he realized the leg didn't ache; it was the dream lingering.

He worked himself up on one forearm and wiped the leather sweat from his cheek as the day's reality set in. He had set out to discover the past, to right its wrongs, bring peace and restoration, but one thing had complicated the next until it all stood like a house of cards. His stomach clenched with worry.

Nonna had looked peaceful in sleep, but he knew when she awakened it would not be peaceful. She must be frightened, discouraged, and angry as a cat with its tail in a door. How could he be so thoughtless? He groaned.

Whatever the family had been mixed up in, it was over. Done. When she recovered, there'd be nothing to upset her, to jog unpleasant thoughts. He would never bring it up again. She could keep the box, or better yet he'd tuck it away where she wouldn't see it and be distressed. Whatever secrets it held could fade with time.

He pressed up from the couch and saw Rico soundlessly beating bongos to whatever he had on his headset. Lance checked his watch. Earlier than he'd thought, but still the first time in history he'd outslept his friend. Of course he'd tossed and worried most of the night. Should have had Sofie give him a relaxation technique.

He glanced toward the bedroom, wondering if Rese had slept. She'd been in no mood for aid or assistance last night, couldn't wait to close the door between them. And who could blame her? He was a walking hazard. How to derail your life in one fell swoop.

Rico set one of the earphones behind his ear but didn't pause his hands. "Want to add lyrics?"

Lance stretched and sat up, kicking the blanket free. He cleared his throat. "I'd have to hear it. See what comes."

Rico pulled off the headset and walked it over. "You comfortable there?"

Lance looked down at the couch. "Never buy a couch without sleeping on it." He put the earphones on, sat back, and let the sounds of steel drum, Star's ethereal voice, and occasional bongo rhythm sink in. It was lovelier than he'd expected, with an energy and depth of tone that he hadn't anticipated.

He let his mind wrap around the tones and rhythm, looking for rhyme and verse. But all that came were single words. *Sustenance. Beckoning. Winsome. Lachrymose. Bereft. Mercurial. Possibility.* He spoke them as they came to mind, eyes closed, ears covered. Nothing that really went together. No specific emotion or thought he could attach, just a simple flow of yearning and hope. Was he hearing Star's spirit? Or his own?

He opened his eyes to Rico's face.

"Man, you gotta do it."

Lance removed the headset. "Do what?"

"That. Stream of conscience, or whatever it was."

Lance shook his head. "It'll be different for everyone, Rico. Why should I tell them what to get out of it? Their own consciousness needs to speak."

For once Rico didn't argue immediately, even if it would mean having his participation in their project.

Lance handed back the headset. "It's got power as it is. I think you're onto something. Has Saul heard it?"

He shook his head. "That's the first cut. I wanted your impression."

"My impression is go for it." Rico would

160

know he didn't say that lightly. He'd been their biggest critic growing up and even more so when they got serious. If he thought it was bad, he'd say so.

Rico frowned. "Don't you miss it?"

Lance dropped his gaze to his lap. Music had been a big part of their friendship, their lives. "I miss it."

"But you're not coming back."

A slow shake of his head. "I might do something at the inn if Rese still wants it." If they ever got back there. If Nonna . . . when Nonna was better.

Rico set the bongos aside. "You could go solo, man."

"It's not that." Their harmonies and the energy they built between them was the best part of it all. "It was great working with you. I'm just not there anymore." He wasn't going to preach on the evils of the lifestyle. The truth was, he could do music with Rico *and* clean up his act. As Chaz had said, it was a choice to give in to the temptations or not.

"Maybe you're right, man." Rico shrugged. "Star says a cosmic convergence brought us together to make this sound. I mean, she never even sang before."

Lance didn't know about cosmic convergence, but Star had made a complete turnaround. "Do you know what she did before?"

Rico shrugged. "Renaissance Festivals.

Shakespeare stuff. She's got all these lines in her head."

"I've heard. But what about her art?"

Rico frowned. "What art?"

"Painting." Lance pictured the canvas, now hanging in the carriage house, that Star had worked on obsessively and presented to him. He hadn't exaggerated his reaction to her technique when he called it mind-grabbing. "Seemed she was on the brink of something big before Maury messed things up. Messed her up."

Rico looked toward the bedroom door. "She doesn't talk about that. This is what she wants." He turned back. "What?"

Lance shook his head.

"What?" Rico demanded.

"It seems she's drawing her identity from you now. The way she took it artistically from Maury." And tried to from him, sucking his praise like nectar and then, when that didn't pan out, transferred to Rico. Instantaneously.

Rico started to argue.

Lance spread his hands. "I'm not trying to cause trouble."

"What do you mean, then?"

"It's all playing roles with Star, becoming someone else. She's like a phoenix rising up from the ashes to remake herself over and over, but with someone else's passion."

162

Rico stood up and paced. "I didn't make her sing. She took the mic from you."

That jam session in the attic had surprised them all — Star's great, throaty voice, her stage presence. But he wasn't relinquishing his point. Music was Rico's life, as intrinsic to him as breath. Star had attached to that with parasitic force. "It's a big responsibility, Rico. I just hope you're up for it."

Rico's face darkened. "You know the trouble with you? You think too much."

Lance laughed. "Could you record that for Rese? She's fairly convinced I lack that capacity." The shot at himself defused Rico's defensiveness.

"You've got your hands full too, 'mano."

"I do." It was different though. Rese didn't question who she was; her uncertainty was for him. He stood up and stretched, then crept to the bathroom to wash and dress.

When he emerged, Rico was still the only one awake, sitting on the couch with the headset on, eyes closed. Hands immobile for once, he softly repeated, "Possibility. Responsibility."

Lance left him there. He would slip out to church, then have a quick check on Nonna. He was going to have to face her sometime; he just didn't want to risk upsetting her. But he stepped out to a hornets' nest of aunts and sisters outside Nonna's door. They all turned on him. Even though it was first thing in the morning, he said, "What did I do?"

"Nonna wants you," Monica told him.

Probably to rail him up one side and down the other.

"She won't let anyone else in. Pitches a fit if we step one foot inside the door."

Dina added, "She's beside herself. She's gonna have another stroke."

His heart clutched.

"Call the doctor," Celestina ordered.

"Wait." Lance pushed through to the door.

Momma scowled. "What's going on with you two?"

"Nothing. It's over." He pulled open the door and went inside where Nonna looked like a tempest in bed sheets. "Nonna, what's wrong?"

The second he was close enough, she gripped his arm with her functional hand. The other was curled up against her chest, and the noise that came from her mouth was half moan, half snarl. He could feel her shaking.

He stroked the rippling silver hair back from her face, soothed the distorted features with his fingertips. "I'm sorry I upset you, Nonna, but it's over now. No more."

She let out a shriek, and he jumped in

164

spite of himself. "What?" Her gesticulations were dangerous. "They're going to call the doctor if you don't calm down." And he would order her into the hospital. Nonna had to know that.

Her grip softened. She blinked her understanding, one eyelid more effective than the other. She was far more cognizant than the last time. She might not be able to form words yet, but she was understanding.

He squeezed her hand. "You know I'll do whatever you want. But you have to be calm. Can you do that?"

She used a word as clear as day, a word that would have gotten his ears boxed. But she seemed unaware that she hadn't simply responded in the affirmative.

"So you want to tell me something?"

She growled out a different word that he was certain had never left her lips before. Either she was cussing him out or communicating in a crazy way her brain had found. Two distinct words; maybe two opposite meanings.

"No?"

She growled it again.

"You want me to get something?" As he had the last time, going through her room for anything that might have meaning to her.

The first word again, clear and precise.

Not that he doubted she knew these words, but hearing them from his nonna's mouth, it was all he could do not to grin. And then she would slap him if it took her dying strength.

Last time it had been Conchessa's letter that she wanted, so she could send him to Liguria for the information she couldn't communicate. But she had told him to leave that alone. Nonno was buried; that was all she wanted — except for whatever she wanted now.

"Something in here?" He looked around the room.

She strained toward him, her hand crabbing toward her throat, to the chain holding medals and a cross and, he now saw, a key.

He took hold of the key. "This?"

She used the first word matter-of-factly. *Yes, of course. What do you think?* His relief was tangible. It had taken much longer the last time to learn what she wanted, but now God's purpose stirred as he unfastened the chain from her neck and slid the key free. It was an unusual shape, long and flat with square notches and the head engraved with National Safe Corp and an identification number. Though he'd never had anything valuable enough to need one, he guessed it opened a safety-deposit box.

"You want something from the bank?"

The *yes* word. Had to be.

He guessed there were rules about getting into a box that wasn't his own, but he would move heaven and earth to do it. "Okay." Palming the key, he kissed her withered cheek, breathing the scent of her relief.

She gripped his hand, squeezing the key inside it, then looked to the door where the others crowded and whispered the *no* word. She wanted it kept between them . . . again.

"Okay," he whispered back. "But you behave."

She blinked, and he could swear that was a smile her face tried to make. He didn't want it to be pain or fury or fear.

"T'amo." He kissed her other cheek with reverence.

She closed her eyes.

Now she would rest. Now she would heal. *Please, God.*

Banks and bankers. Distrust and fear. Box. Key. Bank. Bankers. Fear.

I don't believe Papa went to work at the bank to prove Nonno Quillan wrong, but he certainly tries to change his mind. Nonno will not budge. He doesn't believe in borrowing or lending, though he gives with a free hand. And he doesn't believe in putting someone else in charge of his money.

Though he once lost his fortune in a flood and again when his freight wagon burned with all the paper money he had hidden above the axle, he has not changed his mind about banks. He's known too many bankers, he says, and winks at his son. Papa tries again and again to point out the benefits of putting that money to work through investments. As a loan officer in Arthur Jackson's bank, he offers Nonno all the reasons to borrow and pay back over time.

Besides investing in opportunities, they could improve the house, take out the vines and plant other crops. Nonna Carina's brothers and their sons have all sold out or lost their property with the wine market disintegrating, and only Nonno's plot remains. Some of Papa's plans sound good to me, and I wouldn't mind new drapes and carpets. Why not earn some interest on the money if the Sonoma bank is as safe as Papa claims? Wouldn't he know?

The opportunities are now, Papa says, to buy when things are down. His own earnings he carefully invests — except what we need for taxes and expenses. We are much better off than people in the cities. I could hardly look at the men standing in line in San Francisco when Papa had to meet with someone there and took me along. It seemed every face had been weighed down at the chin.

At least Papa has a job, even if Nonno doesn't respect his profession. Papa doesn't think much of poetry. They love each other, but they're so different. I love them both to splitting, but I can't make them see eye to eye. It's better when Papa doesn't push, but when he hears of a great opportunity he tries to persuade Nonno to pitch in his savings. He even quotes the Scripture about the servant who buried his talent in the sand, and that makes me think Nonno has money buried somewhere, but I don't know where.

Nonno says, "All things in time." And Papa hollers, "The time is now." They are too hardheaded. I slip away to the vineyard, thankful Nonno will not tear out the vines. These vines he says are his inheritance, his responsibility. He has explained to me how the root stock proved resistant to the bugs in the soil that were destroying the other varieties, how my great-grandfather Dr. Angelo DiGratia experimented until he found and planted this plot.

I sink down between the rows. I used to imagine they were trees and I was like Alice in Wonderland grown into a giant. Some of the vines are younger, but most are old and produce a potent grape for a rich vintage. I try to imagine corn in their place and fail. Nonno is right about the vines. Is he right about the banks?

Papa says the closings are over, but what I saw in the city makes me wonder. If so many have no work, how can they put money in the bank for the bank to loan out? But Papa insists Arthur Jackson has important depositors. I do not like Arthur Jackson, though I can't say why. A chill crawls my neck, and I shake my head, dropping it back to let the rosy sunshine warm my skin as it sinks to the west.

Warm, red glow . . .

Antonia shuddered with the image in her mind of Arthur Jackson's face aglow with match light. Lurking in the shadows. To watch her papa's murder? Her own? What if Marco had not found her? If Arthur Jackson had? All this . . .

She looked over her room, empty for the moment, but not for long. Her family would be back. Her family . . . She swallowed painfully. She had to face it for them. Lance needed to know. He was still trying to understand. And perhaps God would have the last laugh; for though she had practiced and passed on the faith, she could not quite believe in a just God.

Rese woke with Star's hand across her throat, her shoulder covered with Star's red spirals that were showing blond at the roots, and experienced déjà vu. So many nights Star had climbed into her window and squeezed into her bed, shaking and crying, *"I can't do this life thing."* And Rese had told her she could go on, they would go on together.

It was a strange closeness, based on nothing but raw need. Two little girls with an ache to be loved; Star's need to be safe, Rese to be needed. The responsible one. Solid.

Yawning, she rubbed her eyes and looked at her watch. After ten. She had actually managed to sleep, but it was strange to wake up again to Lance's room, Lance's world — and Lance.

Yesterday had changed things. There would be no simple solution, no immediate return to Sonoma. Even though she had blocked out a week of reservations, she had assumed they might stay only a few days, as long as it took to bring closure, then back again to the inn. Antonia had blessed their business — the purpose of their trip — but Lance could hardly leave now, even if he didn't hold himself responsible. He cared too deeply.

That much had been obvious in his voice last night. Everything Lance felt was obvious in his voice. When he'd walked out of the room, she had wanted to close him into her arms and tell him it would be okay. But that was different than holding onto him for dear life as he sped them down the highway. He would have taken that gesture and run, and she was not prepared for a sprint. She knew what it felt like at the finish line.

So here she was. His grandmother was ill, his family concerned. At least their thoughts would no longer be on her. She'd be irrelevant, thanks to . . . Antonia's stroke? Something flawed in that thought, and she didn't mean it. If she could undo those moments that upset Antonia she would.

There were lots of things she'd undo, but how could she see in advance what might happen? She pressed a hand to her eyes, gripped by should haves. If she'd known the socket was bad she would not have plugged in the work light that exploded, not startled Dad with her cry. The whir of the saw blade; the blood-spattered wall.

Grief punched her in the stomach. Her breath came raggedly. Not now! She conquered the thoughts and images. At least she was gaining some control. She was not helpless against it. Not anymore. Star whistled through her nose as Rese slipped from the covers and went into the bathroom.

Someone had already been in the

shower. Droplets clung to the walls, moisture hung in the air, and the floor was damp. She breathed in Lance's scent. She had no idea what cologne or aftershave he used, only that she would forever connect the smell to him. She'd never been to a perfume counter, never intended to. Clean was good enough for her. But she had to admit his scent was pleasant.

The tile — laid before lawsuits suggested the non-glazed variety — was slick beneath her moist feet. She loved the slippery feel of it, the smooth flawless surface. She remembered her small fingers guided by Dad's thick hand over the beam she had sanded.

"How does it feel?"

"Soft. No, wait. There's a snag, and a bump."

"Keep sanding, Rese. Make that oak soft as velvet."

A good memory. They were there, not completely overshadowed by everything since. She toweled her hair — a short process thanks to its two-inch length — draped the towel, and dressed in jeans and an olive green knit top. She slipped her feet into the sandals Lance had bought the day he'd had her ears pierced. Nothing but a thin strap of white leather between her toes. No protection against falling chunks of wood or pipe or electrical sparks. But in them her feet looked slender and delicate.

Delicate? She held out her hands, spread the fingers and watched the tendons move under the skin, studied her wrist, the ropey forearm. Her arms had worked, yet they were still feminine. No manicured nails, no rings or bracelets, but most definitely a woman's arms.

It didn't disappoint her as it once might have. She had proved what she needed to. She could perform in her field as well as Dad had expected. It just didn't matter without him. She was no longer Barrett Renovation. She was . . . still deciding.

She went into the living room past Rico, silently drumming to the music on his headphones, to join Chaz in the kitchenette — his university. Lance had put faith into words she understood. The world was under renovation. She pictured a gutted frame, painstakingly refurbished, but not perfect because the original had been so badly damaged. To take the metaphor one step further, even though things didn't look right yet, that was okay; the work was in progress. It was just that her future was so uncertain.

She'd dreamed of her mother last night, watched as she tried to find her way out of a labyrinth of stainless steel walls as tall as skyscrapers, and the trapped feeling lingered. It was not even two months since she'd learned Mom was alive, and decisions needed to be made for her care. Dad had found her the best facility available, and his life insurance covered its cost. But the desire nagged to bring Mom home.

Could she be a competent caregiver? Time would tell — and other things. *"Any psychotic episodes?"* The doctor at the mental health center had not been joking when he asked. She had collapsed at Dad's death, hardly functioned for weeks. Shock, they called it. But catatonia was a symptom of schizophrenia. Would it have looked different if they'd known her mother's history?

She sat down and got a soft "Good morning" in Chaz's resonant baritone.

"Chaz, do you know about my mother?"

He raised his chin. "A little."

"Would God want me to be like that? Schizophrenic?"

Chaz scrunched his brow. "What God wants is beyond me. But if I know who He is, then I can accept whatever He wants as right and good."

"What good would I be, seeing people who aren't there and doing stupid, dangerous things to people who are?"

"God chooses the foolish things of the world to confound the wise, the weak to shame the strong."

She had wanted Chaz to tell her God

175

would not allow it to happen, that, because she now believed, there were some magic words or ceremony to ward off the disease. Wouldn't He rather have her willing and functional? She was a hard worker and a skilled perfectionist. She could do a lot if she had the chance.

"Back home there is a man, Ubaiah, who is palsied and blind. He can do nothing for himself. Each day his caregivers lay him at the door of my father's church. Flies collect on his skin."

Rese took that in without showing her revulsion.

Chaz went on in his same even tone. "People who pass by the church touch him like a charm, their load lifted, their problems suddenly lighter."

"Perspective?"

"Perhaps. And perhaps he is a true conduit of grace and healing. The hem of Christ's robe."

Rese sank back in the chair. "Does he know it?"

Chaz shrugged. "He can't say."

But if he had a part to play, could the same be true of Mom? She had confirmed something Star had only imagined in the dark moments when people treated her unspeakably, when she looked up from the crimes against her body and saw fairies. Mom had called her the fairy child and given Star a deeper comfort than Rese ever had. She didn't get the fairy thing exactly, but why couldn't the presence manifest as something beautiful in the face of incomprehensible ugliness?

And if Mom had seen Star's fairies, did she experience some form of God herself? Lance said the Lord would find an open heart. Maybe the mind was not required. Only God knew what it took for Mom to get through one day to the next, and yet her words had touched Star more deeply than anyone imagined.

The foolish things to confound the wise, the weak to shame the strong. Chaz said if she knew who God was, she could accept whatever He wanted as right and good. She straightened.

So then — who *was* God?

Lance came in and saw Chaz and Rese with their heads together, Chaz's long finger to the page, Rese wearing the expression that challenged and amused and endeared her to him. A seizing jealousy gripped.

How lame was that? He'd abdicated the mentor role by losing her trust. What could he tell her now, that wouldn't show him for the hypocrite he'd been, talking about truth when all the time he'd been misleading and withholding?

Chaz was the one who never faltered. Lance frowned. He should leave them to it, but he went and sat down, satisfied when Chaz slid the ribbon into the Bible to mark his place.

"How is she?" Chaz must have heard the commotion in the hall, or maybe he just guessed where he'd been. Though they had only met four years ago and came from vastly different cultures, it sometimes seemed Chaz was his alter ego, his better self.

"Cussing a blue streak. Only she doesn't know it." He told them the words Nonna had adopted for *yes* and *no*. "And she's consistent. It's like a code." He caught Rese's expression. "What?"

"Nothing."

"I'm sprouting tentacles, molting my skin? What?"

She raised her chin. "You said that without mocking. My crew would have yukked it up big time."

"Are you kidding? It took everything I had not to laugh."

"Nothing was stopping you now." She leaned in. "But you told it as though it was just another symptom."

What was her point?

Chaz closed his Bible. "I think I'll shower while it's available." He was giving them privacy, though Lance didn't know

178

what Rese was trying to say. Rico had moved to the drum set and, still wearing the headphones, employed the air brushes now that everyone was up but Star.

Rese frowned. "You don't know what it's like to be the butt of every joke or have people mocking someone you love."

Had she expected him to make fun of Nonna, thought he would take advantage of someone's fragility? Well, he'd hardly shown her his best self.

Rese clasped her hands. "You saw the humor, but you didn't laugh behind her back. Didn't make us laugh."

Now she was making too much of it. "I might have, if I wasn't so worried."

"I know what it looks like, Lance, that mean streak that feeds on weakness."

He wasn't a mocker, or a joker. And he did champion the down-and-outs, had that sensitive spot for unluckies. Didn't mean he needed a medal. "She gave me this." He took the key from his pocket and studied it.

Rese leaned forward. "A safe deposit key?"

"Do you know how they work?"

"If you're not on the signature card, you don't get in."

He frowned. "Any way around it?"

"Maybe if a court orders it."

"That would take too long."

She reached for the key, felt its smooth surface, and read the engraving. "I don't think you can use this without her."

He looked up. "What about with her?"

"What do you mean?"

"What if she tells them to let me in?"

She gave him a slow blink. "Tells them."

"Sure."

"You're going to have her cuss at the bankers."

He spread his hands. "Who's gonna know? It's in Italian."

Chapter Nine

Sorrow and fear are oily water. I cannot hold both in my heart. Despair extinguishes fear, for if you can't care, what is there to lose?

I gasp as Marco skids into a hollow hidden by shrubs and stomps on the brake. "What are you doing?"

He puts a finger to his mouth and motions me to be still. The road is winding enough that it is some time before the vehicle passes. Marco scrutinizes the car, two men inside.

"Who are they?" I whisper.

"I don't know. Maybe no one." But his fingers tighten on the wheel.

We wait in silence, ears straining for the sound of tires, an engine. It comes so softly at first I am not sure if I imagine it, but there is the car coming back slowly, the men leaning and pointing. Marco shoves me down, hissing, "Stay there."

He eases his door open and slowly

cranks down the window, then he slides out and crouches behind it, peering over the edge. The other car draws near, nearer, then is lost behind the shrubbery that hides us. There's only the sound by which to guess. I tense as the engine quiets to an idle and the grind of tires ceases.

My throat is parched, and I glance at Marco, who has drawn a gun. *Oh, God. Signore . . .*

He motions me to silence, but it is shattered by a thundering spray of bullets. Glass bursts and lands on and around me. I smash my hands to my ears as explosions boom beside me — Marco's gun, firing back, single shots. He told the truth; someone wants me dead.

And suddenly it matters, more than I knew. I want to live! Even if I must grieve what I have lost. I drag myself off the seat and crawl out behind Marco. He doesn't move or acknowledge me. He sits frozen, gun poised, muscles tensed.

Branches crunch. Marco lunges up, fires, ducks. No answering bullets, only a crashing of bracken, a thud. I want to see, but the heavy metal door blocks what is happening as surely as my own naïveté blinded me before. I taste dirt, and blood, and the metal of the car I press my face against.

A stick jabs into my calf, but I don't

move. I sense more than hear something behind me, jerk my head and cry out. Marco spins. Two shots ring out. The man falls with a staccato blast as the long gun drops from his hands. He writhes, then lies still. I press my hands to my face, then pull my fingers away, not wanting to look, but unable to stop myself.

Marco grips my shoulder. "Are you hurt?"

Unable to speak, I shake my head. But even as I do, my skin burns with a dozen stings, and I see flecks of blood on my hands.

He raises my chin. "Don't rub. It's glass." He picks three slivers from my face, then pulls me to my feet. Noting the shard-strewn seat, he says, "Can you stand?"

I can stand; I can move; I can breathe — unlike the person behind me. Holding his gun out before him, Marco walks to the man, crouches, and presses his fingers for a pulse — as he had for Nonno's.

I suck in a sob.

He rises and looks up the slope toward the road to another corpse bloodying the ground. This isn't real. People don't do this, don't . . . I thought Marco would check the other man, but he must know he's dead already, and I don't want to think how.

I peel my lips apart. "What do we do now?"

Marco smiles, just a pulling at his lips and a softening of his eyes. "Attagirl." He raises my face. "You got the goods, babe, and I ain't beating my gums."

The breath returns to my lungs, then escapes with a laugh. "What are you talking about?"

His eyes take on a definite sparkle. "You are one darb dame."

"How can you tease at a time like this?" But that's exactly what he's doing, either to shake me or himself out of it. "What are we going to do?"

He pockets the gun. "Get the glass off that seat." He strides into the scrub, stomps a branch, and breaks off the leafy end.

I shake my skirt and realize my stockings are torn and fine lines of blood lace my legs, from when I climbed out, I guess.

Marco goes to work with the branch, brushing the glass to the floor, then as much as he can to the ground. "Watch where you step."

"Will the car run?"

"Most of the bullets went high since we were sitting in the hole. I don't think the engine's damaged, but we'll know soon enough."

"Marco . . ."

He turns at my tone.

"What about them?"

"I'll place a call when we're far enough away."

"To the authorities?"

He nods.

"Will they help us?"

He pulls my door open with a tinkling of glass. "Climb in." He holds my elbow. "Try not to rub your skin; you're covered in slivers."

By the glitter of his hair, he is too.

"We'll wash off when we get somewhere."

I climb gingerly onto the seat, thankful now for his car, for him. And then it strikes me that he has killed two people. It was self-defense, but still he's done it. My stomach heaves with the smell of blood, the shock of seeing men fall, even violent men who want me dead.

My limbs chill. It could have been me, bleeding in the dirt. My life slipping away. If Marco had not — Who is Marco? Why does he have a gun and know how to use it?

As though reading my thoughts, he takes the weapon from his coat and hands it to me. "Load this, will you? The cartridges are under the seat."

With shaking hands, I get the box of cartridges, but I have no idea how to put them in. He instructs me as he drives, and I do what he says.

I set the loaded gun gingerly on the seat between us. "But they're gone now, right?"

"Better not be caught off guard."

"There could be more?"

He hesitates, then, "There could."

"Why do you have a gun? How do you know —"

"For protection." And protect me he had.

"They had machine guns."

"Tommies. Make a man lazy. You get to spraying bullets everywhere when all it takes is one good shot." He replaces the loaded revolver inside his coat.

"Marco . . ."

"I handle a lot of jack for important people. Have to know how to defend myself. And you." His sideways glance. "I told you I'd keep you safe."

"I don't understand. What's happening?"

He is silent long enough to let the question climb in between us.

"Your father got mixed up in something over his head, I guess."

Tears sting. "That doesn't make sense. Papa wouldn't —"

"Stop fooling yourself. You saw it before I came. You said it that first day on the porch."

"I didn't mean —"

"Yes, you did, cara mia. Deny it now, and you can tell it to Sweeney." He slows for an intersection, then hits the gas. "I'm sorry about your pop." His voice thickens, as though he does care. "Listen, babe. It happens all the time. Guy thinks he's got it under control, but he doesn't know what he's dealing with. Or who."

I picture Arthur Jackson, leaning against his car, his face illuminated by match light. "Papa wasn't stupid." *So why, why, why?*

"I don't believe he was."

Tears fill my eyes. "He wouldn't risk —" My voice catches.

"He knew the risk. Why else tell me where to find you?"

Sobs rise and tears run down my cheeks, stinging the cuts. I shake my head. "I don't believe it."

Marco says, "I'm sorry about your nonno too."

From what she could tell by Lance's side of the conversation, the family lawyer was confirming his inability to access the safe deposit box without Antonia and seemed dubious of her limited communication. Having dealt with her father's affairs, Rese had her doubts, as well, but Lance insisted Antonia's intent was obvious, as though convincing the lawyer would make it so.

Lance stuck his hand in his hair as he

talked, gripping as though he might pull it out. She knew his need to make things right when he thought he'd messed up. She'd experienced it in the painstaking recipe cards and instructions he'd sent so she could make the inn's breakfasts without him.

He was just as determined now, but the doctor had insisted Antonia stay quiet and undisturbed for the next few days. Lance might convince the whole neighborhood it would work, but he couldn't take his grandmother anywhere until she was strong enough. Of course, that didn't mean he would stay still. As soon as he hung up, he took her by the elbow and wiggled that ominous set of keys at Rico.

"Be good to it." Rico twirled and caught a brush over his head.

"I'll even gas it," Lance called back.

She was not going to argue. If Lance thought Rico's bike was safe, fine. He could not afford more guilt, and she assumed her death would cause a twinge. She didn't feel quite as brave when he wheeled it out again. Had it looked that bad yesterday?

"I'm sorry I don't have leathers." He handed her the helmet.

"No problem." She pulled it onto her head.

He stood a moment looking at the bike.

"Wish I had my Harley."

Rese waved her hand over the Kawasaki. "And miss out on this dream machine?"

"I liked you better kicking and screaming."

"I bet." His parents' vignette had been informative. She resists; he insists. It lowered Lance's octane to have her willing. She straightened. "Ready?"

She was prepared for yesterday's speed and terror, but his route this time took them down into the city, and they crept along in traffic for much of it. With the choking fumes and Lance's constant revving to keep the engine alive, she almost preferred the death-defying speed of the open road.

He wasn't acting on impulse this time; he was grimly determined, and she guessed their destination before the rectangular crater came into sight. She had known they would visit this place sooner or later. Yesterday was escape; this trip, immersion. Since he couldn't fix it, Lance wanted to wallow in everything that was wrong in his life.

He found a parking place on the street, a feat he seemed to accept as his due, as though God dared not deny him. But he deflated as they walked up to the chain-link fence and looked through while people milled around them. She concentrated on the scene, wanting to see it first without Lance's grief casting a wash over her own impressions.

A gap in the towering buildings, space in a city that had none. Concrete ramps and platforms in place of the rubble that had been imprinted when images of disaster were played and replayed. Where was the devastation? Somehow she'd still expected smoke. This looked clean and orderly and planned. It looked intentional.

"What is all this?" She recognized the inner workings of massive construction but hadn't kept abreast of plans.

"The new complex. Five buildings. Over there" — he pointed to a spot in the construction — "the Freedom Tower will soar 1,776 feet, with a glass spire pointing to heaven. You can see the master plan in the World Financial Building."

She stared at the subterranean levels and layers before her. "It's not what I expected."

"People who come here now see hope, determination. Even triumph." He stared into the hole. "I just see Tony."

She raised her eyes past the hole to an ornate stone building with its façade chunked and blasted, its windows blown out. Next to it stood another tower draped in black netting. All around them, cars drove, pedestrians passed, business happened. The city would never forget. Those with lost loved ones would never forget. But time was moving forward; life continued. She turned. "You have to move on sometime, Lance."

His eyes narrowed. "Has Gina moved on? Her sons?"

"Will you blame her if she does?"

He stared into the hole a long time. "No."

"Then why do you blame yourself?"

He glanced sideways. "For what?"

"For living your life when Tony can't."

He hung his fingers from the chain link. "Maybe if Pop didn't look so disappointed every time I walked in, as though he's still hoping it'll be Tony instead."

"Oh, come on."

"Think about it. Did he say one word to me last night?"

She replayed the dinner. He must have. There'd been no animosity between them, no friction. Had there? But she couldn't recall anything said. For Lance, with all his words, that silence must be deafening.

He swallowed. "The thing is, it should be Tony. Rese, he had three kids, a wife. People depended on him, not just at home. He was decorated for exemplary service to the city of New York. He could have done so much."

"So God messed up?"

He frowned. "No. Yes. I don't know." He sagged a shoulder to the fence, seeing, she guessed, the nightmare that was personal to him in a way it would never be for her.

"It's renovation, Lance. Not new construction."

He stared a long time at the concrete edge below them, studded with steel at regular intervals. Then he said, "I know that. But I also know evil is not indiscriminate. People like to think so, but it's not. He prowls the earth like a roaring lion. He looks for the brightest and the best. And God says, 'Consider my servant Job.'"

She didn't know what he was talking about, but there was an edge to his voice. "You think God singled Tony out?"

Lance cocked his jaw. "I think we're pawns in a match we can't see. The moves are made and pieces sacrificed. We can hate God and despair. Or love God regardless."

She touched his arm. "Which do you choose?"

He answered without looking. "You know which."

"Say it."

He swallowed. "I choose to love and serve God."

"Then you can't despair. You can't have it both ways."

"Maybe." He gripped the fence and stared a long time. "But here is a world where heroes die and screw-ups are left to pick up the pieces."

The foolish things to confound the wise, the weak to shame the strong. She would tell him what Chaz had said, but Lance didn't seem to be talking to her anymore.

"Either I accept that this was His purpose, that He intended to take Tony and leave me and somehow it was right and perfect, or I despair and curse Him." His knuckles whitened. "I resist; I doubt, but without the guts to turn away, because I'd rather love a cruel God than have no God at all."

He didn't say it to shock her. He was professing a loyalty and love for one who seemed undeserving, yet whose service he could not resist. It ought to terrify her, but it didn't. She drew back her shoulders. "So what's next?"

They left Ground Zero but not the city. Gaping up from the bike, Rese relived her dream — only she was in the maze, not Mom. The effect of the towering buildings was stunning and unnerving. And there didn't seem to be room to breathe, every inch of space in use. She was glad Lance suggested the Staten Island ferry just so she could stretch her arms.

As they circled the Statue of Liberty,

193

with the marine-scented breeze in her face, she said, "I did a report on that statue in sixth grade, all about its shipment in pieces that had to be assembled, and the strengths and weaknesses of copper as a construction material."

Leaning on the rail, Lance slid her a look.

"The teacher wondered if I couldn't have focused more appropriately on the statue's symbolism as it related to American history."

He half smiled.

Back in South Ferry, they disembarked and headed up to Greenwich, where Lance and Rico had sung on the sidewalks until they'd been discovered and booked into the clubs. He motioned toward a doorway as they puttered past, the haze of their own exhaust engulfing them. "That's where we had our break."

The club wasn't much to look at, and in the middle of the afternoon, nothing was happening. But she could imagine the two of them setting up as Lance had in the inn's dining room, the excitement they must have felt to be taking their music somewhere. The front side of a dream. Had Lance really put that behind him? Would he be content with the inn?

When their stomachs started sounding like Rico's bike, she ran in for Gray's Pa-

paya hot dogs while Lance circled the block. She didn't have to worry about getting a table. There weren't any. She climbed back onto the bike when Lance came around. He hadn't found a place to park, so he double-parked behind a delivery van. She handed Lance his hot dog and bit into hers. The bun was crisp, the hot dog bursting with flavor even though she'd forgotten to add condiments.

"Like your dogs naked?" Lance glanced over his shoulder.

"I was worried about you circling." And food details were his province. She kept her seat, but he swung his leg over and leaned sideways on his.

He bit into his hot dog and smiled. "Sometimes simple is best."

"What makes it taste so good?"

"Location."

She scrunched her brow.

"Any hot dog you eat in New York will taste better than anywhere else in the world."

She snorted, but there in the street the plain hot dog did taste better than any she'd had. She didn't admit it though. It would only go to his head.

In midtown she studied the architecture: statuary on the buildings, whole figures or just faces, plant motifs on corners and doorways, art rendered in concrete and stone similar to what she did with wood. Many of the buildings had renovation scaffolding, and she couldn't help noting the ones she'd love to get her hands on — if she were still in the business. Like Lance with his music, it wasn't easy to leave it behind. It wasn't easy to keep at it either. Not after the accident, not when the mere sound of a saw blade . . .

Brad had wondered if she still had it, and she supposed she did, since she had accomplished the transformation of the dilapidated villa into a beautiful bed-and-breakfast, but she would not be able to hide the strain from the guys. It was better that she'd let it go. And they deserved their fate with the new owners. She just wished she'd made them change the name. Of course, that was what they were trading on.

The day had slipped away, and under the streetlights, Lance eschewed the Empire State Building with its serpentine horde coiling to the ticket counter and elevators. He took her instead to Saul Samuel's apartment building. The doorman spoke their request over the intercom to the agent Rico had landed and whom Lance seemed to know as well.

After a minute, the uniformed man admitted them into the lobby. "Mr. Samuels said go on up to the roof. He's unlocked it."

No gift shop or observation deck swarming with tourists; Rese walked out to a garden overlooking the city. Potted trees on a rooftop. If that wasn't the difference between Lance's coast and hers, what was? At the waist-high wall she stared down. All the jewels in the world were spilled beneath her. But looking up, she saw only the reddish hue of the expanse spread above her. "No stars?"

Lance rested his palms on the wall. "They've all been wished on and fallen."

Looking down at all the fallen wishes, she asked, "Did they come true?"

"Maybe. Some."

She searched the sky again for even one prick of starlight, one faint glimmer to hang a wish on. But she didn't know what to say anyway. "What would you wish, Lance?"

He stood silent so long she could almost hear the fallen stars sighing from the ground where they'd lighted. Not even one wish between them. How sad was that?

"There's nothing you'd want?"

He swallowed. "Too much."

Of course. Lance wouldn't stand there like her, wondering what she wanted in life, unaccustomed to wishing or hoping, just bracing herself for what would come next, ready to meet it head on. He was the dreamer, greedy with hopes.

The noise of traffic and sirens in the city that never sleeps seemed far away. She hadn't known Lance could be so quiet, yet it wasn't empty silence; it was filled with thoughts and feelings, as though he charged the blank air above them with the wishes he couldn't speak. They would settle like a mist, sparkling drops of dew at the first touch of morning light. Lance's wishing stars.

Lance locked the bike back into the enclosure and turned. He hadn't been very good company, but Rese had taken up the slack. That meant a lot to him. "So how come I didn't get anything pierced? No double rings in both ears, no stud in my nose?"

Her eyebrows shot up. "Wish I'd thought of it."

He laughed. "Good thing you didn't. Pop almost ripped this one out." He tapped the diamond stud in his left earlobe. "He'd take me apart if I came home with more."

"You're twenty-eight years old."

"And he's sixty-three. And if he wants to take me at eighty-three, he will."

"He'd hit you?"

"Call it physical communication."

She frowned. "Dad's worst punishment was silence. All he had to do was withhold

198

comment, and I was frantic to figure out a way to do better."

Lance headed for the door, unlocked and held it open. "I'm harder to get through to."

Rese paused before entering. "Would you hit your kids?"

Lance leaned his hip to the jamb. "First, you don't hit the girls."

Her chin came up as he'd known it would. "They're too weak?"

"Too precious."

She glared. "I thought sons were the preferred offspring."

"Fagedda-bout-it. They're too thick-headed. Gotta knock the sense in."

"Do you have any idea how that sounds?"

He spread his hands. "Wha-at?"

She shoved his arm. "Be serious."

He motioned her inside the dimly lit hall full of family detritus. "I don't know, Rese. I haven't thought about kids. I mean, I have, but . . . not the details." He pulled the door shut behind them. "There's too much at stake with children, their whole lives in your hands. I'm not sure . . ." He turned the dead bolts. "It's too easy to mess it up."

"You think you wouldn't be a good father?"

He didn't answer.

"You're kidding, right? Lance, I saw you with them. With your nephew in the sandbox."

"No risk. You can't mess up someone else's kids."

She frowned. "Why are you doing this?"

"What?"

"Pretending to be something you're not."

"I'm just saying —"

"In Sonoma you had all the answers. There was nothing you couldn't do. You knew exactly what I needed, what Star needed. Even Evvy. Here it's as though you've forgotten it all. Did it ever occur to you your dad could be wrong?"

He stared into her face. "What if he's not?"

"Then deal with it."

Looking into her strong, practical face, he could almost imagine it. Maybe he just needed the right balance, the right person in it with him — for the long haul. The thought seized in his chest. Bobby was right that it was new territory. But with the light behind him making crags in her face, he could almost see them growing old together.

If he asked her for real, would she say yes? After his performance so far? Not a chance. But it didn't stop him wanting. "Rese . . ."

She rubbed the back of her neck. "Thanks for showing me around." She started for the stairs.

"Sure." He climbed the stairs behind her, getting the point. Don't get close and personal. Don't want more than he should. Don't pretend there's even a chance for permanence.

He had to stop reading more into things than there was. After all, she'd said "your kids," not "ours."

Chapter Ten

Terror stalks on padded feet, a death mask alight by the glow of a flame. One tiny match showing what I do not wish to see, can't bear to see. Papa. Papa!

Marco rushes to my side in the dark. "Shh, cara, shh." Dressed in skivvies and trousers, he sits on the bed and holds me to his chest. I sense more than comfort in his embrace. I sense fear that I will draw them to me, to this boardinghouse or the next, assassins bent on my quick and final silence.

My breath comes in jagged gasps. "I can't stop my dreams, Marco." For days I have found glass in my hair, though the cuts have closed up and some of them scabbed. The worst violence is to my dreams. Bloody bodies with Papa's face.

He stares a long moment. "Then scoot over."

Shaking, I make room for him in the saggy bed. In the sweltering heat, he holds me, back to chest, knees nested, yet still a chill hollows my belly.

"If you scream, I'll cover your mouth, but you won't scream now." And his arms are strong and tight around me.

It is the first time we have lain down together, the first time he has held me as a man holds his wife. How will it be to grow old with him in my bed? But he is already old, and I might never be. The chill makes me shake, but he murmurs into my neck. "Shh, Antonia, shh."

The judge this morning seems far away, a scene played on a stage that I watched unbelieving. After the attack, it seemed right and necessary, but after all I'd hoped for? The castles I built in my dreams? Not some rushed wedding to a man I don't know, but who seems able to accomplish anything.

The judge balked at our lack of birth certificates until Marco took him aside and spoke into his ear. A phone call was made; then we stood with two witnesses and said, "I do." But still, I can hardly believe any of this is real.

When morning comes I feel as ragged as my silk Milanese princess petticoat, the lace of which is hopelessly frayed. I washed my skirt and blouse last evening in the small sink at the end of the hall, and they have dried wrinkled, but there's nothing I can do. As we enter the breakfast room, the woman who runs the boardinghouse looks at us askance. No rings on our fingers, circles under our eyes.

"She thinks I beat you last night," Marco murmurs. "She's looking for goose eggs."

I search the faces in the breakfast room. Did they all hear my screams? "I could walk with a limp," I whisper back.

A quick, wicked grin finds Marco's lips. "And moan a little when you sit."

I jut my chin. "You're enjoying the thought."

"Heaven forbid."

But I've seen him with a gun, seen him kill. Might there be a cruel streak as well? "If you ever hit me, you'll be sorry."

He raises his brows. "Would I hit a peach like you?" But again there's amusement in his eyes. He is toying with me, and I won't give him the satisfaction of an answer.

He leads me to the empty end of the long table. "Shall I fill your plate?" He indicates the toast and gravy on the buffet.

I nod, weary in every bone. It should be the other way. He should be sitting with the napkin tucked into his collar, and I placing the dish before him. That's how it will be when . . . The thought spins in my head. I am his wife. How has this happened?

Grief slices through me. *Nonno, where*

are you? Papa? They are the men I know, the men I love. I'd been larking with Marco, enjoying the way my heart lurched and skipped. I enjoyed baiting him, tempting him, but now . . .

He sets my plate before me, nothing like the breakfasts I used to prepare. The country is poor; the food reflects it. How much better it was in Sonoma! I took a quarter to the picture shows every Saturday. My clothes were clean, my sheets sprinkled with lemon water. We had our garden, Nonno's vines. Migrant workers came to us. We put money in their pockets, food in their bellies.

Beggars received at our door. Neither Papa nor Nonno ever stood in a breadline or swarmed an unemployment office. Neither rode the rails looking for work. I've seen too much of that now, the helpless faces. I want Marco to take me home. Who will pick the peppers, harvest the grapes? My eyes fill. My home, the people I love. All gone.

Marco takes his seat beside me. "Cheer up," he whispers. "You're making them stare."

"I don't care." I hate every one of their staring faces.

"People remember. And when others come asking . . ."

Men with guns and evil hearts. There are

worse things than losing my home. I straighten my spine and apologize. *"Io lo fatto."*

"No Italian, darling. And there's nothing to be sorry for." He lifts my hand and kisses the fingers.

A warm rush curls around my belly.

"Just try to look as though you're enjoying your honeymoon."

Another couple comes to sit in the chairs beside us. Marco chats easily, but my throat has closed around the word *honeymoon*.

He says, "No, we're just passing through. Thought we'd have a look at some property in Pennsylvania."

"Got them Amish up there," the other man says. "Beards and all."

Marco smiles. "That right?"

He had not actually lied, since we will pass through Pennsylvania and see lots of property from the windows of his Studebaker, but as the conversation progresses I realize he is carrying on like a swell, nothing in speech or mannerism to clue in the pale Swede with whom he converses that we are on the run, that I have nothing but the clothes on my back.

Why did he say no Italian? If I hadn't heard him sing *La Bohème*, I would not believe him a countryman. I have always treasured my heritage, a culture even

Nonno adopted. Marco has changed like a chameleon into someone I don't know. But I picture the gun in his hand and realize there's no part of him I do know.

When the man asks about his occupation, Marco remains vague, only giving the impression that hard times are not as hard for some. I blush when he refers to me as his young bride, when I only let him into the bed mostly dressed last night to keep from screaming. What if the nightmares continue? What am I going to do?

Back on the road in the car, I ask, "Should we be telling people we're married?"

He slides me a smile. "Sure." He reaches over and pats my knee. "We are married."

Dio, how can I forget?

Rese gave up tossing and slipped out of bed. With no window, it was impossible to gauge the time, and the clock's face was not illuminated. She didn't want to bother anyone, but she was too restless to stay put. At home, she would have gone to her workshop and sanded or planed or hammered. Her muscles longed for the release.

There was none of that here, but she slipped out of the bedroom, tiptoeing so she wouldn't wake Lance on the couch. But he was awake already, with only the dawn light streaming through the window.

He looked up and set his pencil down.

"What are you doing?" she whispered.

"Jotting something down."

"A song?"

He nodded.

"Can I hear it?"

"It's not there yet."

She sat down across from him, a seed of concern growing. "What are you going to do with it?"

"It's not like that." He sat back and stretched. "Sometimes it just comes out."

"Did you wake up with it?"

He nodded.

She wasn't surprised. "I get ideas that way too. Something that's been nagging at me for days will suddenly come clear just as I'm waking up." The energy that followed was always productive.

Lance smiled. "I thought you worked through things in the dead of night with power tools in the workshop."

She pulled one leg up and crossed the other over. "That's different. That's when I know what's wrong and can't fix it."

"Ah." He reached for his guitar. Closing his eyes, he picked softly, mouthing words she couldn't hear, caught up in the creative flow she'd interrupted. She didn't mind. When he was ready, he'd share it.

She'd been agitated, but now it felt okay to sit there without conversation. Lance was funny that way, full of words but capable of silence. Besides, his mind was on his song. Okay, she was curious. He didn't usually keep lyrics to himself, even autobiographical words that revealed so much. And he'd made things up on the spot, not needing it "there" before he shared.

Why was this one private? She jolted. The things he'd kept private in the past had hurt. "Lance?"

"It's about yesterday." There he was, reading her mind again. "Making sense of it all."

His own struggle. None of her business. "Sorry."

"For what?" He sent her a soft glance.

Doubting. Fearing. Assuming it involved her. "Butting in."

One side of his mouth pulled. "You didn't butt."

"Okay."

And now she was content to sit across from him. He didn't seem to mind that much. As the light grew, she picked up and browsed through a photographic history of the Bronx, Lance's world. His hot-dog remark had revealed something. He might leave New York, but it would never entirely leave him. Whole sections of the book recounted the Italian influence and heritage in the boroughs. She mainly read the captions under the pictures, but she got the idea clearly enough.

She had never thought of herself historically, wasn't even sure what her Barrett heritage was and knew even less about Mom's background. There was Aunt Georgie, Dad's sister, but if Mom had any close relatives, she didn't know them. And she seriously doubted there were any books describing her people's contributions. She'd focused on her own accomplishments, and Dad's. But that wasn't much of a lineage.

Lance was part of — She looked up, surprised, when Star came out of the bedroom. "You're up early."

Yawning, Star balled her hair onto her head. "We're singing at the Java Cabana."

Star was off to sing already? Star who spent days, weeks, in bed?

"You should come," Star said. "We're easing people into their day, soothing their jangled auras."

Did she look jangled, or had the tossing and turning clued her in? Rese frowned. She just didn't know what to think or do or want or hope for. This was supposed to be simple, but nothing with Lance was simple. Their whole day-to-day life was only the surface for him, and then there was this ocean of . . . uncertainty.

Rico joined them, his black hair hanging to his shoulders with several strands bound in thread. In his soft billowy shirt and fitted leather pants, he looked like an astral gypsy with his fingers thrumming the bongos under one arm, Chaz's steel drum hung on his back, a melodious turtle shell.

"You ought to come." Star glanced from her to Lance on the couch, picking his guitar with a soft fury.

Rese shook her head. "Another time."

Star let her hair fall down over her bare shoulders and the cropped halter that revealed her sprite's shape and translucent abdomen. Her skirt was blue strips of cotton batik that swished and parted when she walked, revealing her thin legs to the macrame sandals that were more California than Manhattan. Together they looked as otherworldly as their music.

When the door had closed behind them, she said, "Can Rico keep her safe in that getup?"

"Java Cabana's in the theater district. She'll fit in."

Rese wasn't sure if he meant with the actors or the streetwalkers, but didn't ask. Lance stared after them with a pensive look.

"What?"

He narrowed his eyes. "I keep looking for the real Rico."

"Maybe he just needed the blue fairy to make him a real boy."

"No, there's donkey ears in there."

Rese laughed. "Is he watching for yours?"

"Probably." He set the guitar aside with a sigh. "Want to help with breakfast?"

She glanced at the kitchenette. "Okay."

But they headed out and down the stairs to the restaurant.

"You mean breakfast down here? Are you opening for business?"

"The restaurant is on hold. But it's Saturday and I'm in town; the family will expect me to cook." Lance took a massive carton of eggs from a walk-in refrigerator.

Which meant breakfast would be a stampede. She looked longingly at the door. Why hadn't she flitted away with Star? Because she didn't flit. She stood like a stone and faced the next challenge. "So what'll it be? Crepes?" The first thing he had shown her how to make; her first success without him.

"They'll want something more substantial. We'll prep for omelets."

Rese chopped the long red peppers and the brown-capped mushrooms Lance called porcini while he cut paper-thin slices of Parma ham, also known as prosciutto. Then he mixed up the egg batter and sprinkled it with an herb that he rubbed between his fingers, releasing the aroma.

Rese breathed. "What's that?"

"Nipetella, a sort of minty variety of thyme."

He held a sprig to her nose. It smelled woodsy, and she would not have thought of putting it in eggs.

"It enhances the mushrooms."

She liked how he combined words like enhance and mushrooms. Those weeks in the inn's kitchen without him had felt so empty, even with Star and Chaz and Rico and all the guests they were cooking for. The kitchen might be the heart of a home, but Lance was the heart of a kitchen.

She had just started to enjoy herself when Monica crashed in with her family.

"Oh good, you're cooking. Eggs? Nicky eats them plain. Franky's okay with prosciutto, but don't put the peppers in." She pressed a hand to her stomach. "And don't let me smell porcini."

Lance waved her off as he had when Rese told him she didn't like artichokes.

"Mary and Jonny don't like mushrooms either. No cheese in Bobby's. And go light on the pepper."

Lance took his sister by the arms and moved her away from the stove. "Fan your lips that way; the dining room's stuffy."

Monica swung for his head, but he ducked back to the stove and gave Rese a wink. A rush of warmth swept her. She

213

should know better than to get near him in a kitchen.

He worked at the stove, pouring and filling omelet pans set over low flames. But then Lucy's children ran in and grabbed him around the legs, pummeling and raising the noise level several decibels. He hollered, "Take over, Rese, while I clobber these guys."

She was beginning to understand physical communication. It involved fists and tangled limbs and laughter. While they expressed themselves, she turned to the stove. Though she had managed baked frittatas with his instruction at the inn, the operation he had happening here was beyond her. Thankfully, Lucy and Monica came over, and together they folded and removed the omelets to warmed plates Lance had set ready. Rese frowned. Once again it took multiple people to fill his shoes.

Lucy nudged her glasses up with the back of her wrist. "My kids aren't always violent. Lance brings it out in them."

"Who else is going to train them for the streets?" Lance hollered as Monica's youngsters joined the fray.

"Even as a kid he was always fighting, sticking up for someone smaller — or smarter." Lucy laughed.

"Yeah," Monica agreed, "but sometimes he talked his way out. And with those eyes?"

Rese knew the impact of Lance's eyes. It was an unfair advantage.

The cacophony rose again when Bobby came in hollering that he had a headache and could he get some quiet somewhere someday?

Monica rolled her eyes. "Your headache is your own fault, and don't take it out on the kids."

But Lucy shooed them out to the dining room, and Lance came back to the stove.

Bobby opened and slammed cabinets. "Isn't there any aspirin in this place?"

Monica heaved a sigh. "I'll get you aspirin. Watch the kids."

He jacked up the jeans on his narrow hips. "I'll get the aspirin; you watch the kids."

"You should've gone to work," she hollered after him.

Lance said, "Get your kids fed. Full mouths make less noise."

Monica loaded her arms with so many plates it was obvious she'd waited tables, probably in this very restaurant. Rese noted the differences in the omelets Monica took out to the dining room. Lance had prepared them according to her orders in spite of their argument. How had he kept it straight? His mind obviously processed chaos.

Then he was back preparing the next

wave for Lucy and her children. Her husband, Lou, must be at work or still in bed. At least he hadn't shown his face in the kitchen. And Lance's parents had not joined them either.

"Rese, can you set out the fruit trays?" Lance nodded toward the platters on the counter that held assorted sliced melons and berries. When had he done that? Or maybe it was Lucy, who seemed to have a proficiency with food as well.

Rese carried the trays out to the dining room. It was twice the length but narrower than her own inn's, with tables packed in. The old men who had rooms in the back had taken seats at one of the two large tables that had been pulled together and were swarming with kids. She set a tray on each as Bobby came back and plopped down alone at a small table against the wall. If his head was hurting, why didn't he stay upstairs?

She went back to the kitchen and found Lance leaning on the oven handle, head dropped to his chest. She hurried over. "What's the matter?"

He straightened. "Just thinking about Nonna."

In the midst of the pandemonium, his mind was on his grandmother. She was beginning to see how he could have singlemindedly deceived her when Antonia's

216

wishes required it. And that deception lost some of its sting.

The truth was, if he had told her it was his family's villa and he wanted to find something for his ailing grandmother, she'd have told him to take a hike. She had not been in any condition to placate a stranger. She'd been barely holding herself together.

"She'll be okay, Lance."

"It's hard being in here without her." He sent his gaze around the kitchen. "This was my haven. No matter what I'd done, I knew I'd find comfort here."

But Antonia was old. She might never work in this kitchen again. His world was changing, and Lance didn't like change. He was steeped in tradition, in family ways. He wanted a snapshot, but the film kept running. He drew a slow breath and turned back to the stove.

Rese watched him ladle butter into the pans, then a larger ladle of eggs, then sprinkle in the fixings. "Are your parents coming down?"

"Saturdays they breakfast at the market, see all their friends who've moved out to the suburbs but come back to shop."

"Why haven't they moved out?"

He shrugged. "They could sell the building for quite a bit, I guess, but then the family would scatter. Momma couldn't stand that."

"Oh." A mother who liked her children around, who didn't have an invisible friend, Walter, suggesting murder.

"Come here." Lance fitted her in front of him at the stove and put the spatula into her hand. Then he took hold and they folded the next round of omelets, moving together. His scratchy jaw brushed her ear as his breath warmed the side of her neck. She should stop him, but this melding at the stove was so . . .

"Lance, did you — Oh, sorry." Sofie stopped inside the door. Her oak-toned hair was pulled back in a ponytail, emphasizing the striking features she'd gotten from her mother. Though Lance had his dad's darker coloring, he and Sofie had hogged the good looks.

Lance turned. "Whatchu need, Sof?"

"I have to run. I just wondered if you'd made something I could take."

"Give me two seconds."

Rese moved out of the way as he folded one of the omelets with ham, peppers, and mushrooms into a hard roll and wrapped it in white paper for his sister. "Studying?"

"I've got a presentation Monday." Sofie shifted the portfolio. "Still needs work."

Rese recognized that driven expression, that dissatisfaction with anything less than perfect. It was a snapshot of herself.

Lance grabbed a salt shaker and shook it

over his sister's shoulder. *"Al lupo."*

"Grazie." She smiled.

"Prego." He handed the package over with a kiss to his sister's cheek that was embarrassing in its tenderness.

Sofie only said, "Hug Nonna for me."

"I can't go in for a while. She'll get worked up if she sees me and I haven't done something she wants."

"So do it."

"I can't yet."

She studied his face. "Okay."

Again Rese noted Sofie's restraint. She didn't try to pry out more than Lance wanted to say. She respected the boundary — an anomaly in this family.

"Thanks for breakfast."

Rese returned the quick smile sent her way as Sofie left. Lance watched after her a moment longer than he might have. Something was up with Sofie, but Lance didn't say what. He came back and began flipping the omelets onto plates. Rese carried them, precariously, to the dining room where Lucy swooped in to help disperse the servings.

Bobby raised his face from his hands and took the plate Rese handed him. "Thanks."

"You're welcome. Hope your head's better."

"Only thing's gonna help my head is a little peace and quiet."

219

"It'd be quiet at the office," Monica said.

"That's what you think? You think telemarketing is quiet? All day people yelling in my ear, hanging up on me."

"You're used to that; you been doing it fifteen years. Top sales."

"You think I like it? All day people complaining?"

"You'd be right at home."

"Oh, that's funny. That's real funny."

Rese ducked back inside the kitchen. "Are they always that way?"

"Only when Monica's not meeting Bobby's needs. Then he drinks too much and regresses."

Rese raised her brows. "Isn't that their business?"

"Does it sound like they're keeping it that way?"

"Not exactly."

"There aren't many secrets around here."

Unlike Sonoma, where secrets seemed to breed. Rese fingered the hair at the nape of her neck. "There's Sofie."

His brow puckered. "That's different. We don't talk about it because she doesn't."

Rese nodded. "It's not my business anyway."

"Come here."

She went to stand before him.

He raised her chin, his fingertips emitting an energy barely held in check. "It's all your business. I wanted you here, in the middle of it."

"Why?"

"Because I love you."

Rese stared into his face. He'd said he cared, even that he was falling in love — but "I love you"? The last person to say that put her to bed and disabled the furnace.

"Go to sleep, Theresa. In the morning everything will be different. I love you, sugar. You know I love you."

She had blocked those last words, refused to connect her mother's love with the actions of that night. But not anymore. She was facing things now. No more deception, even in her own mind.

Lance's eyes took on a midnight intensity. She knew what he wanted to hear, what came so easily for him, the love and affection that infected every relationship he had. He was in love every week, he'd said. Well, she wasn't, even if her heart was imitating Rico on the bongos.

He let go and turned to the stove. "You ready to eat?"

"If you're cooking." She'd disappointed him, but she couldn't help that. Two and a half months might be long enough for him to decide he was in love, but what mattered to her was stability, longevity, security. What mattered was truth.

"Thought you were the expert in the kitchen now."

She snorted. "I'm no chef."

He expelled a slow breath. How could empty air say so much?

"What?"

"I'm not either."

She stared at him. "What do you mean?"

"I don't have credentials. I learned from Nonna and my second cousin twice removed, Suar Maria Conchessa. But . . . no chef school, no degree, just old-fashioned apprenticeship."

It shouldn't matter. It didn't change his ability. It was only a title, a paper. Had he ever called himself a chef? She had billed him that on the Web site, and he hadn't corrected her. Lance, like everyone else, letting her believe a lie.

Anger flashed. "I'll have to change your billing." She had taken him off the Web site altogether but intended to reinstate him if they ever got back to the inn.

The tendons of his neck flexed. "Maybe you should get someone else."

What? First he loves her, then he's welching on their deal? "I'm not happy you lied to me, and I'm wondering how much more there is, but you're my partner,

Lance." And she'd hold him to it.

He banged the pan down on the stove. "I can't just do the job. I told you that." Emotion rose from him like heat waves on pavement.

"I know you're upset, and everything's up in the air. Let's just —"

He grabbed her by the arms. "I said I love you."

Emotion seeped in, then rushed, then flooded. She slapped up her walls as fast as they tumbled. "You're confusing love and tragedy."

"I'm not confused." His hands softened on her arms. "I am upset."

She nodded. "I know."

"But that doesn't mean I can't tell the difference."

"Lance . . ."

"I want you with me in everything. Here in my crazy family. In our business in Sonoma."

Had he said "our"?

He caught her neck between his hands, braced her chin with his thumbs. "I want to fight with you like Bobby and Monica. I want to know you so well . . ."

She stiffened. "Don't do this."

"You want me to pretend?"

She scowled. Her whole life was the make-believe of someone else's creating. "I'm not ready."

"I'm not either." He slid his hands up to cradle her face, and the muscles of his throat worked. "I never will be."

What?

"I'm not going to get it right. I'll never have it together. But I'm willing to fail with you."

She stared into his face. That was a good thing?

"I'm willing to mess up again and again. To do it wrong and torque you off."

Her throat tightened. When what he wanted most was to find his purpose and do it right?

"I've never kept a relationship long enough for someone to see that I'm a screw-up. I left them wishing for what they thought they saw, left them believing the myth." He let go. "I want to be real with you."

No words could come. She'd been waiting for him to prove himself trustworthy, reliable, constant. Solid like Dad. When Lance Michelli could no more be solid than she could be Star's light and rainbow. He was offering her something else. Reality.

Chapter Eleven

"Come to me, my melancholy baby.
Cuddle up and don't be blue.
All your fears are foolish fancy, maybe.
You know, dear, that I'm in love with
you!"

The song runs through my head as monotonously as the rumble of the engine while my gaze drifts within the space that has defined my life for days. Marco's hands are long and angular, wrapped over the steering wheel, his shirtsleeve creased at the elbow, the navy blue suspender twisted on his shoulder.

He glances over with a smile. "The whole country's gloomy, Antonia. Let's not be."

He's right, but how can I help it? "I'm sorry. It's just . . . ."

"Did I ever tell you about the two-legged dog I had?"

I lower my brows skeptically.

"It's true. He was sort of a brindle mix,

white and brown, fur so wiry you could scrub the kitchen with him."

"Was it his front legs missing or his back?"

"One of each, and luckily opposite sides."

I don't believe him but can't resist. "How did he lose them?"

"Don't know; I found him that way, down by the train yard. His owner must have hopped the line, and the dog couldn't make the jump."

"So you took him home?"

"Sort of. Momma wasn't fond of dogs, and this one being less than pretty would've had a tough row to hoe. I fed him in the alley until he knew he could trust me."

"That's more than many boys would do. How old were you?"

"Oh . . . it was several years back."

I raise my brows. "You were all grown? I mean, a man already?"

He grins. "Yes, I've been grown for some time now."

"How old are you?"

"You're interrupting my story."

I settle back into my seat.

"Pretty soon that dog took to following me around as I made deliveries and such."

"For the people with lots of jack?"

"That came later. These were preliminary positions, so I conducted business on the docks and train yards. In fact, it was at Grand Central that the little dog saved my life."

I sink against the door and give him a truly withering look.

"You don't believe me?"

"How did he walk?"

"Just like you and me. One foot in front of the other. He'd learned to balance and compensate so well he could almost walk a tightrope."

"Marco . . ."

He raises his hand and drops it back to the wheel, then drives in silence so long I give in.

"How did he save your life?"

"Threw himself in front of a train."

I gasp.

"Why do you care, if I'm just making it up?"

"But you're not, are you?"

He reaches over and squeezes my hand. "I'm not. And he didn't get hit by a train."

Relief and exasperation.

"He did tear out the Achilles tendon of a man whose knife was perched against my throat."

"Why?"

"I fed him pretty well."

"No, why did someone have a knife to your throat?" I shove his arm and we

227

swerve a little in the road.

"Oh, that. He wanted my delivery."

I watch his face for clues. "Is that why you have a gun now?"

"Come to think of it, that was about the time."

I laugh in spite of myself. "You're impossible. What happened to the dog?"

"I sold him to the circus."

"Oh!" I throw up my hands.

"I did. They taught him to walk on a ball. He couldn't really manage the tightrope, but he was amazing on that big red ball."

I punch my thighs. "I don't know when to believe you."

"You should always believe me. I hated to lose that little mutt, but I had landed a new position that would take me away too much. With the circus he had plenty to eat, a safe place to sleep, and he got to be special two shows a day."

My brow creases. "How could you part with him?"

He turns his attention back to the road. "That's always the hard part, isn't it?"

Yes, she thought. *Yes.*

A hand on her shoulder brought Antonia to the present. She looked into the plate presented on a tray. Lance had to have cooked the omelet. Though Monica brought it up, she would have overpeppered, and the eggs would be thick and spongy. She cooked like her mother.

This omelet had Lance's trademark nipetella accenting the porcini that were softly sauteed, a thin golden edge and fragrant aroma to tempt her appetite. Monica settled down beside her and dug the fork in without appreciating any of that. But she was kind and willing as she brought the fork up, and Antonia was thankful for little things. She couldn't say so, but she hoped they knew. She hoped they all knew.

Lance pressed his fingers to the strings, hammering and pulling the notes up the neck, then ending with a feather-soft touch to ring the harmonic pure and sweet. As it faded, he started the rhythm, and then the words, thankful they were automatic since he couldn't focus. The morning had started out fine, then ended with him saying more than he'd intended, more than Rese wanted to hear. Her partner; her *business* partner. Why couldn't he get that into his head? Chief cook and bathroom washer.

That was what she'd offered when he tried to sever ties. *"I need a maid, but I'll settle for a partner."* Why did he take that term and run? Partner . . . wife, lover, mother of his children. Right. When she couldn't trust him as far as she could throw.

The attraction had gripped him even with her baggy shirts and construction boots, her short hair that set off the bones of her face, the stony expression he'd learned to see beyond. It wasn't stony anymore but engaging and enigmatic. In the same way he might begin to see the thoughts of a figure carved in marble, he had learned to read her.

He just didn't like what he was reading. If she was a girl from the neighborhood, three months? She'd be his. But Rese was no pushover. She had him pegged with a cement nail. And it was his own fault.

He'd stopped trying to wow her, to be everything she needed. He was letting her inside, showing her the real Lance Michelli. *Here's how I live. Here's how I am. I sweat in my T-shirts; I talk in my sleep. I cried at* Bambi *and Pop smacked my head.*

Maybe Rese was right, that his worry for Nonna had made him want connection this morning. That he'd confused the hurt and guilt over her relapse with the longing he thought was love. Maybe he didn't get it at all.

He tried to focus on jamming with Rico and Chaz, letting the music take him away, but his mind stayed on Nonna, on the things he'd found that she didn't want to talk about and the way he'd forced the issue — as he'd forced his way in with Rese and hurt her too. He missed the cue for his solo, but Chaz filled in on the keyboard.

Rico's suggestion to jam had been a surprise since he and Star were so wrapped up in their new direction. But of course he'd included Star in the ensemble, and that changed the dynamic. Lance watched her sway and hum as he chorded into a minor key.

He liked Star, but he couldn't get a handle on her and Rico. Then again, he couldn't get a handle on himself. All he knew was things had changed. Maybe the days of singing on the street corners with Rico were really gone. None of it mattered as much as it once had. He was making the break, inside himself.

He looked at Rese, cross-legged on the couch, watching. If the music transported or transformed her, it didn't show. Did she worry still that he'd go back to it? That it was what he wanted? He should tell her, but that would move into what he did want, and she didn't want to hear it. She'd made that clear.

He lost the lyrics and improvised a nonsensical line. Chaz and Rico glanced at each other. They'd gone with him before when he took a tangent or two. He rarely succumbed to "La-la-la," but the words that came were not always what he'd put on the page. He reached the chorus and sang with Rico's descant soaring above. But Star brought her voice in and the line didn't hold.

Lance let them take it and worked the guitar, instead. That was one thing about music; it was fluid. Give something here; take something there. He climbed the neck of the guitar with a countermelody. It was good; it was new. He felt a twinge of pride in the gift. So he hadn't eradicated that.

As Rico launched into a riff, Pop came up, looked in the open door, and walked out. It was all in the expression. Lance stopped chording, took the guitar from his neck, and got up. Chaz raised his brows, but Star and Rico simply morphed into a song with no lyrics or guitar. Once again the flow continued. Just that easily, he could disappear.

"Let's get out of here," he muttered to Rese, then swiped some money from the bowl on the bookcase.

Her face was quizzical, but he didn't want to tell her the unspoken message in Pop's face had triggered all the old memories. *"Why don't you get a job? Make something of yourself."* Even when things had looked good and gigs were stacking up, Pop shook his head. *"Who's gonna pay your retirement?"* It didn't enter his head they could make it big enough to pay all their retirements.

"What's the money bowl for?" Rese broke his reverie as she stepped into the hall.

He closed the door behind them. "It's where we pool the extra."

She smiled. "I like your friendship."

He shrugged. They hadn't decided to throw in their cash together. It had evolved. Chaz made good money at the Restaurant Weston, but sent most of it back to Jamaica since he lived cheaply, sharing a room with Rico. Rico had done well off and on, but music was a hard business and sporadic, no matter how good you were.

And Rico was good. Innovative, yet exact as a metronome. He could hold an entire conversation without dropping a beat. But he didn't hold on to his money well, always seemed to be falling short. The bowl had probably come out of his casing the apartment for loose change. Lance got into the habit of emptying his pockets in one place, bills and coins together, just to keep Rico from rooting through his things.

He led Rese down the stairs through the kids playing in the stairwell who tried to ambush, then followed him out to the street. He handed over a few dollars, and they ran off shouting, "Thank you. Thanks, Uncle Lance." He loved that uncle part.

"Are they okay leaving like that?" Rese followed them with her eyes.

He shrugged. "They know to stay close; the candy store, the ice cream truck. The babies are napping, so Lucy and Monica will be glad for the quiet."

"It's hardly quiet." Rese glanced over her shoulder toward the music streaming through the windows.

"That's white noise. Every baby in that building learns to sleep to Rico's drums."

Rese snorted. "Not exactly Brahms' lullaby."

"Better." He grinned. And then he imagined a baby of his own dozing off to the air brush on the cymbal and swallowed. "You want kids, Rese?"

She didn't answer for so long that he tipped his head to catch her expression.

She said, "Not if I'm schizophrenic." Her face showed nothing but candor, but he knew inside it was eating her.

"I don't see that happening."

"Yeah, well, Dad didn't see it, either, but he noticed when Mom curtained the windows with his underwear. It caught his attention when neighbors showed him burnt bushes and lawn furniture."

"How come he left you alone with her?"

Rese shrugged. "I don't think he wanted to admit things were getting worse. It didn't get bad until the last year. Before that, she was normal a lot of the time; not just normal, wonderful."

"Still, you were just a little girl."

"It didn't feel that way. A lot of the time it seemed like I was the parent. Dad even started giving me instructions. 'Don't play on the roof today, okay, honey?' And his 'How was everything?' meant 'Did Mom do anything I need to know about?' "

He didn't want to think of Rese in that position, but it explained her self-sufficiency, her courage and determination. "That must have been hard."

"It was hard being caught in between." She paused at the corner, the wind flipping the fringe of hair up from her forehead. "I didn't want to let Dad down, but I loved her so much."

That was the first time she'd said it, but he'd already glimpsed her loyalty to the mother who had tried to kill her.

Her brow creased. "I think I knew I might not have her forever. Things were so precarious, never certain."

She liked things certain. No surprises. After believing so long that her mother was dead, learning she still lived had come a little hard. He nodded. "Now you have her back."

She turned. "That's not what I expected you to say."

"What did you expect?"

"I don't know: 'You're better off without her.' 'Good thing they locked her up.' "

"Why would I say that?"

"Because most people don't relish a psycho mother-in-law."

The smile caught him unexpectedly. "Did you say mother-in-law?"

She frowned. "Hypothetically."

He caught her hand and raised her fingers to his lips. "I would love to meet your mother." He felt a quiver pass through her.

But she drew herself up, fully Vernon Barrett's daughter. "You don't *meet* my mother, Lance. She might think you're the president or the devil. She might not even know you're there." She tried to pull away.

He kept hold. "I don't care."

"Because you don't know."

"You're right. I haven't lived with her. But everyone's got something, Rese."

"What? What do you have that I wouldn't want with my whole . . ." She yanked her hand free and stalked down the sidewalk, her reflection framed briefly by the window of Borgatti's Pasta that displayed the certificate from Ladder Company 38 thanking the Borgattis for their generosity during the darkest time in the history of the New York Fire Department. Rese passed without noticing.

He took his eyes from the certificate and caught up to her. "So you like crowds, noise, overt displays of affection?"

She didn't answer, just focused on the section of Arthur Avenue that was more authentic than Mulberry Street's Little Italy in Manhattan. Lance knew how it looked, this little enclave of times past and people united by history and traditions. Quaint. Foreign. Amusing.

Lambs' heads at Biancardi's complete with eyes, brains, and teeth. Religious and regional clutter, and every second store peddling food. His place. His people. Was that what Rese saw, what she thought she wanted?

"Everyone knowing your mistakes, every stupid choice told from one kitchen to another. Prejudices ingrained for generations. Expectations you can't ever meet." Pop's blank stare.

Rese slowed her stride.

He matched it. "Want some pizza?"

She shook her head, but they hadn't eaten since breakfast. She was hungry even if she wouldn't admit it.

"Giovanni's is good." He motioned her through the door. "What do you like? Quattro Formaggio? Capriciossa?"

"You're speaking a foreign language."

He ordered two slices from the glass case and carried them to the small, cheesecloth-covered table. The waitress, Anita, brought their drinks with a shy grin that showed her teeth pushed forward like kids crowding the line. Lance thanked her.

Rese lifted the flimsy tip of her slice. "It's so thin."

"No more than a tenth of an inch in the center or it's not Neapolitan." He folded his and raised it to his mouth.

"I thought New York pizza was thick."

"That's the Sicilian version. A bad copy."

"Oh really."

"I should know. Half my family's from Naples, where pizza originated. Anything else is an illegitimate stepchild."

Rese blinked. "Is everything so black-and-white?"

"The Italian flag should have been black-and-white. But then we'd have argued over which color goes first." He bit into the crisp, gooey slice. "Around here, you take a position and defend it to the death. Right or wrong."

"Like the guys on my crew, always had to be the experts, especially Brad. I said maple; he said oak. I said save; he said demolish. I think he notched his belt every time Dad took his suggestion over mine."

"And when Vernon took yours?"

She looked up. "It wasn't about winning. It was about doing it right."

"So maple was right and oak was wrong?"

"If one worked better for the project."
She chugged her iced tea.

"That's not opinion?"

She set down the glass. "He'd have said anything to edge me out."

"If his input wasn't valid, why would your dad go with it?"

"I'm not saying Brad wasn't good. He knew his stuff. He just . . . resented me."

"Why?"

She pushed back in her chair. "Threatened, I guess."

"You are intimidating." Lance smiled. "Brad admitted that much. But he still wants you back."

She sighed. "I don't believe it. He's got an agenda."

"He knows what you can do. He respects it."

She snorted, but Brad had seemed sincere the one conversation Lance had with him. Rese's skill was not in doubt, only her ability to carry on after her dad's fatal accident.

"Your artistry shows, even to an untrained eye. You did an amazing job on my furniture."

"Making your bed and wardrobe didn't trigger flashbacks."

He knew she'd been reliving the accident, but she'd never admitted it right out. "Why do you think that is?"

"Context, I guess." She toyed with the crust of her pizza. "The focus is different."

"You have skill. That's a good way to use it."

She wiped her mouth with the paper napkin. "Why can't anyone else admit that?"

Lance leaned back in his chair. "You want the real reason?"

The pause before she nodded should have warned him, but he plowed on anyway. "You think the worst of people. You make them fight for a fair shake. Then you're so competent, they want to show you up just on principle."

She raised her chin. "In other words, I'm obnoxious."

He grinned. "Basically."

"So . . . because I know what I'll get from people and don't wait for them to prove me right —"

"See, there it is." Lance let the front legs of his chair down. "Assuming the worst and taking it on. The first look you gave me was combative."

"You walked in on me with no warning."

"I knocked twice and called out. Not my fault you were off in your zone."

"Actually . . . Oh, never mind."

"Actually what?"

"I was thinking of Dad. Reliving it." Her brow pinched. "You pulled me out of the memory and . . . I reacted."

That explained a lot. The way she'd sneered at his filling the position of maid and cook. The way she had dissed his earring, and him in general. With her back to the wall, and all her energy focused on renovating the villa without losing it, a witness to a moment of weakness would seem like a threat. It wasn't paranoid or obnoxious. It was understandable.

He leaned on his elbows. "Did I tell you I think you're great?"

"The word was obnoxious."

He laughed. "That was your word."

"You agreed."

"I promised you honesty."

"Then I'll return the favor."

"Go ahead."

"You intentionally provoked me, walking in as though you owned the place, and standing there with that slacked hip and belligerent expression as though trouble simmered right under your skin. Then you talked your way around my better judgment and enjoyed the fact that I couldn't resist taking the risk."

He spread his hands, already forming his defense.

But she went on. "You put the responsibility on everyone else, like, 'Hey, I warned you, but you wanted it anyway.' "

Okay, that was touching home.

"You make people think the worst, but it's all an act."

He raised his brows with a laugh. "Tell that to Pop."

"Well, that's part of it too. You couldn't compete with Tony for favored son, so you took the part of prodigal."

Lance frowned. "I want to be a screw-up?"

"You want to do what's right and good. Like Tony. But as long as Tony was here, your good wasn't good enough. Now Tony's gone, and neither one of you knows how to get past that."

Lance stared into his plate, clenching and releasing his jaw. He hadn't expected her to slice so deeply. "What's Chaz been teaching you?"

"You told me the prodigal son story."

"I don't remember applying it to myself."

"It's obvious."

"Well, I don't see Pop running down the street with rings and robes." And it wouldn't happen anytime in this life, no matter what he did or didn't do. How could he explain it? "Around here it's practically decided who you are when you're born. I mean, they held me up and said, 'Just look at those eyes. This one's trouble.' "

She nodded. "They're deadly eyes all right."

He leaned in. "Are you flirting with me?"

"It's bad if you have to ask." She flushed.

Had he ever seen her blush? Maybe when she'd wanted to take his head off with a shovel, but never because she'd overstepped, left herself vulnerable.

She huffed. "I can't imagine what they said when I was born."

"I'll tell you. 'This one doesn't want to cry; she hides who she is. But anyone with eyes will see the beauty, the courage, the strength of her.' " He closed her hand in his. " 'And the man who holds on to her will have done the one right thing in his life.' "

Chapter Twelve

Rese hadn't expected to say any of that. Talking to Lance was like passing too close to a black hole; the void sucked in words she couldn't ever get back. It had started the moment he walked in her door.

She'd been so rude, he would have hit the road if he hadn't needed access to the inn for Antonia. He must have clamped a lid on tight, shown a restraint she hadn't believed he possessed. "So . . . how badly did you want to deck me that first day?"

"I don't believe in hitting women." He kept his focus straight ahead as they left Giovanni's and strolled the street.

"On a scale of one to ten."

"Which end's high?"

She laughed. "I wish I'd known how hard you were working."

He turned. "So you could have amped it up?"

"Exactly."

"Ah." He nodded slowly. "What I thought compulsive competitiveness is really intent to torture."

"*You* were not being honest. You deserved to suffer."

"You just wish it had been worse."

She drew breath to answer but couldn't continue the tease. Picturing him in her driveway, ready to give up everything, the pain obvious in every word, every motion, she stopped walking. "I don't want to hurt you, Lance." That was the most personal thing she'd ever told anyone, and her heart rushed with insecurity. Where was the woman the crew called a stone goddess?

He faced her, taking her hands. "It's inevitable."

She started to shake her head.

But he nodded his argument. "Life hurts. Put any two people together and you'll have strife." He brought her hands to his lips. "But making up . . ."

There he went again, taking the little she'd offered and running as though she'd passed the baton. She pulled away.

An orange-haired woman passed with a smile corrugated by too many cigarettes. Lance waved, then sobered as he watched her canting gait. "Wonder how Nonna's doing."

Rese was surprised how long he'd managed to go without voicing it. "Is your mom with her?"

He looked at his watch. "Pop or one of the aunts. Mom's teaching."

"What does she teach?"

"Dance."

"Really?" But she could see that; the graceful way she moved, the flair, the figure.

"Pop took a dance lesson just to meet her. Asked her to marry him that night."

"You Michellis don't waste any time."

"We don't get turned down either. You've made history." He half smiled. "Gina married Tony after three dates."

"So you're comparing?"

"Bad habit."

"I don't want you to be Tony."

"You didn't know him."

"I know you."

He seized her with a probing stare. "Yeah?"

"Almost three months' worth." She backpedaled before he could make more of that than she intended.

"Gina knew Tony all her life."

"Unfair advantage."

Lance traveled her with his eyes, but his thoughts seemed far away.

"What?"

"Wonder what Tony would make of you." But before she could answer, his gaze jerked away. "Uh-oh."

She followed his gaze to two old men across the street hollering at each other. Lance rushed across and got there just as

246

they came to blows. Others came out of the social club, a couple still holding pool cues. She thought they would break up the fight as she hurried across the street, but most of them joined in, pushing and hollering. Lance put himself between the combatants, who seemed as willing to hit him as each other as he got hold of one of the old guys and yanked him out of the tussle.

Though blood gushed from the old man's nose, he kept hollering insults and balling his fists. Lance dragged him away from the mob, who were still pushing but had mostly stopped swinging.

"Porca miseria!" the old man hollered as Lance pulled his own shirt off and pressed it to the bleeding nose.

"You're gonna hurt yourself, Carmine, you keep this up." He eased the old man onto the curb beside a hydrant, and Rese caught a dark shape on the back of Lance's shoulder. A bruise? She leaned, but he shifted position.

"Whatta you thinking, old man?" bawled a thick sausage-shaped woman in a black skirt, sweater, and scarf. She came down the sidewalk with a passel of dogs and two other women in black.

Carmine raised his fist. "Next time, I take outta hissa eyes."

"He no gotta eyes. He's as blind as you."

Lance stepped back as the women engulfed his charge. He swiped the sweat from his cheek with his arm, but he'd left his shirt with Carmine's nose. Rese reached him as he thumbed the blood from his lip. At least one shot had found his face.

"Are you all right?"

He rubbed the blood into his palm. "Yeah."

"Why were they fighting?"

"Sal and Carmine? They hate each other. It's lucky they're too old to do any real damage."

"What are they fighting about?"

"I'm not sure they remember. Probably a woman. It's usually a woman."

She thought of the black sausage woman and barked a laugh. "Are you serious?"

He grinned. "You better believe it."

"That's ridiculous."

"It's a vendetta."

He'd used that word before, but it conjured gangster movies and underworld figures as different from those old men as she was. "Be serious."

"I am." He tongued the split in his lip. "People think vendetta is a bad thing." He looked at the women raising Carmine to his feet, shaking their fists at Sal and the others at the club. "But what it really means is, you take care of things yourself. Families band together. If someone is wronged, there's a duty to right it."

She searched his face, waiting for him to elaborate, but he turned away from the crowd and started down the sidewalk.

Again she glimpsed something, then leaned over for a better view. A cross and crown of thorns on his left shoulder blade. "You have a tattoo?"

"Sorry, you don't get one."

"Me!"

He pulled a wry mouth. "I've got to draw the line somewhere."

She brought her hands to her hips. "I wouldn't even have pierced ears if you —"

"Come on." He took hold of her arm. "I don't want to make a spectacle."

She looked back at the still grumbling contenders, the barking dogs and scolding women. "Brawling on the sidewalk isn't a spectacle?"

"Nah. But standing around without my shirt is." And by the stares coming their way, she believed it.

Her eyes went to the tattoo again. A three-inch cross, the crown of thorns like a wreath at its connecting point. "Why get a tattoo, then hide it?"

He reached over and rubbed the shoulder. "It's personal."

"Personal how?"

"I carry His cross on my back to remember what He did, and be ready to carry my own."

And his dad thought him the prodigal? Either Tony was perfect, or there was some serious misunderstanding. Fresh blood leaked from his lip.

"Does it hurt?"

"Nah." He tongued it away, then touched a scar on his side. "This one hurt."

"What happened?"

"Knife."

"You've been knifed?"

He slipped his arm around her shoulders. "It happens."

"It happens?"

"When you're a friend of Rico's."

Friend had a new meaning when applied to Lance and Rico. Fiercely devoted. Interconnected. One man's battle becoming the other's. Lance had told her enough from their childhood to get that much. But she hadn't realized the altercations had been life threatening.

She slid her gaze to Lance, who seemed energized by this new altercation. Not, she guessed, that he had wanted to fight, but more what Lucy had said, risking himself for someone weaker. When she looked at him now, she saw him carrying Christ's cross on his back. What kind of man embedded that reminder in his skin?

The music had ceased altogether, but

long before that, Antonia knew when Lance left. The magic had drifted away. They were all talented, but Lance and Rico together made the very air tingle. Since they were little boys — Rico's hands never still, Lance with rhymes for everything — what they did together had been special.

Yes, they could get raucous, but even in the harder songs, she felt the power. And when they blended their voices, bringing life to one of Lance's ballads, something happened between them that was almost sacred. Rico had rhythm in his bones, but it was her grandson's gift that transcended. He was a true bard, even if his lute was plugged in and distorted. She almost smiled, but her mouth wouldn't do it. She was glad no one had seen her try.

Anna was snoring in the chair, the afternoon and the chamomile tea they had shared lulling her daughter now that the noise across the hall had ceased. It wasn't noise to her, but Anna didn't know the hearts of the young people as she did. She hadn't watched Lance's fingers grow strong on the strings of one guitar after another.

Antonia sank back to days in the kitchen when he rushed in to show her a new chord pattern, a melody line to fit his lyrical thoughts. While she chopped the tear-inducing onions and fragrant fennel, he'd sit right there and work it out, and sometimes she would reword a phrase for him, Nonno Quillan's poetry in her blood as well.

She sank back again to golden light in the gazebo, and Nonno alive and strong in spite of the silver-headed cane she had never seen him without. . . .

"Why did you become a poet, Nonno?"

He looks at me, gray eyes deep with emotion, and I know he will tell me truly. "Because some experience can't be expressed in common speech."

"Is it all your own experience?"

"Mine and those around and those before me."

"Like Wolf's pictures?"

He nods, seeing, I know, the paintings his father made on the walls of a cave high in the Rocky Mountains. A child captive of the Sioux, Wolf had expressed his life on those walls, and Nonno Quillan had remembered them with his remarkable visual recall.

I am part of them. The thought swells inside me.

Antonia carried the feeling into her waking, almost seeing Nonno still. *You are reborn in Lance, Nonno. Your tender heart, your yearning spirit. Your experience and his, expressed in uncommon speech.* She could not deny the connectedness, and as her thoughts went to

252

Papa, she knew that piece also must be woven in. Her heart clutched. Why didn't Lance bring what she'd asked for? And could she bear it when he did?

Smoke haloed the hooded lights, big-band music emanating from the background system. Rese stood back watching Lance shoot pool. She suspected he'd gone down after supper to the social club to make good with the guys he'd sided against that afternoon — though he hadn't thrown any punches himself. Now the same men who had snarled and cursed and shoved when he pulled Carmine out of their grip, laughed and schmoozed him like one of their own.

Sal wrapped an arm around his waist and grabbed his jaw in an avuncular grip with just a hint of intimidation. "You make this shot now, and we get double."

But it was no ordinary pool they were playing. It was trick shots, balls set out and lined up that had to go into the pockets in some kind of order as the cue ball ricocheted around the table. Lance had earlier explained that the social club was more than a pool hall, including a back room for activities not endorsed by the State of New York. It was about numbers, bets, and money.

He and Sal were up a hundred and ten

dollars, and he could double it with a successful shot. People bet on pool games, she knew, putting their ten dollars at the end of the table, winner gets it. But this worked a little differently, and the stakes were certainly higher.

Lance left Sal's grip and went around the table, setting up the balls as delicately as birds' eggs, nudging one imperceptibly closer to another, bending low to eye the alignments. He blew on his hands and rubbed them together, gave her a wink, then chalked his cue and leveled it with the table.

Rese held her breath as he slid the cue between his fingers back and forth no more than half an inch. Then, almost faster than she could see, he struck, and the balls scattered, running for their pockets like frightened rabbits. All but the yellow number one that tottered on the edge, then rested without dropping. Lance's shoulders sagged.

The room exploded with cheers and invectives. Lance bore the back pounding and good-natured jeers, Sal's tongue-lashing and grudging admission that it was closer than he'd have gotten. They hadn't doubled, but he and Sal pocketed their fifty-five bucks, and Lance refused to get sucked into another bet, saying, "Sorry, Tino. It's past my bedtime."

She didn't think he'd meant it that way,

but every eye turned to her and the loud off-color comments started.

"Get outta here." Lance waved them off, hooked her shoulders, and sauntered out, carrying his bravado to the street. "So, I got fifty bucks burning a hole in my pocket. Wanna spend it?"

"I thought it was past your bedtime."

"That's a throwback to when I started playing with them. Had to be home by twelve or face Momma's wrath."

"How old were you?"

"Eleven."

"And she let you out till midnight?"

"On the weekends. She knew one of them would see me home."

The neighborhood family.

He cupped her shoulder as he walked. "I'd been shooting pool since I could reach the table, but the gang in there wouldn't let me play until I proved myself."

"How could you, if they wouldn't let you play?"

"I challenged them. Put my money where my mouth was. A hundred bucks for the privilege of losing it."

"Smart."

He smiled. "I didn't always lose. Sal and Tino adopted me. Taught me how to set up, how to put the English on. Sal was a lot sharper in those days. He's lost some power."

"Where did you get the hundred dollars?"

"Tips clearing tables at the restaurant, running errands for everyone, beating the other kids at everything." He shrugged. "I saved up the whole summer, then went in and made my play. They figured if I was old enough to lose big, I was good enough to learn."

She knew the pressure of proving herself. She'd done it at an early age too. But Lance had earned respect, not resentment. What was it about him that made everyone cut him slack? Everyone but the one who mattered. Had he set out to win over these older men to show his dad? Or had he filled the need with them instead?

Maybe she'd worked so hard to prove herself to Brad and the others because she needed so badly to hold Dad's attention. He'd respected her skill, her eye for detail and relentless perfectionism. But she was never sure there was more to it than that. Now she suspected he'd resented her for forcing his hand with Mom, necessitating his wife's confinement, even though she'd known nothing about it. She'd only been the one sucking carbon monoxide. Lance was right about children; it was too easy to mess things up.

His hand slid from her shoulder to the back of her neck and rubbed the tension evident there. "Is it something I said?"

She shook her head.

"Something I did?"

She slid him a glance. "It's not always about you."

"I hate that line."

"Because you want it to be."

He winced. "When did you find out?"

"When you walked in my door."

"Ouch."

She laughed, relaxing a little. "It's past midnight. Is your mom waiting up?"

"Probably."

Rese shook her head. "Will she think it's my fault?"

"Nah. She's onto me." He slowed as they approached a darkened corner where three people clustered, their voices just discernible over the sounds of the city. Lance closed his hand over her elbow and stepped into the street, glancing only enough to register oncoming traffic. The street was clear, so they crossed mid-block and continued toward home. She started to look back where they'd been, but he blocked her view.

"What is it?" She dropped her voice instinctively. "What are they doing?"

"Better not to know."

"Something illegal?"

He didn't answer, just directed her around the next corner.

"Drugs?"

"Maybe bingo. I think they were playing bingo."

She huffed. "So everyone just plays dumb?"

"See, there are people like Tony whose job it is to find out. Then there are people like us whose job it is to live through the night."

"I don't understand, Lance. If you know something's wrong . . ."

"And you care about the person you're with . . ." He dug his keys from his jeans.

"So you'll call and report them?"

"They're long gone."

She paused under the light of his family's entrance. "So we don't do anything?"

"We did something. We got back here without bloodshed."

She swallowed. "I can't tell when you're serious."

"I'm serious. If they'd jumped you, I'd have fought to the death. If it's not my fight, I leave it alone."

"It wasn't your fight today."

He let them in and led her down the hall. "That's different."

"Why?"

"Someone could have been hurt."

She climbed the stairs behind him. "You could have been hurt."

He scratched the back of his neck. "It's a judgment call."

Her breath sharpened as they climbed. "That from the man who's been knifed?"

"You choose your battles. You don't always win them." He followed the hallway back to the front and inserted the key to his apartment.

She came up next to him. "Are you going to look in on Antonia?"

He glanced at the door across the hall and shook his head. "I have to get through the weekend. If she's strong enough Monday, we'll try the bank. But I don't want to explain it beforehand, or she'll stew herself into a state."

"Doesn't she know you can't access the box without her?"

He shrugged. "I think she handed over the key because she thought I could get in. I'm guessing she hopes I'll take care of it without her. She's funny about banks."

Rese frowned. "Funny how?"

He leaned a shoulder to the jamb. "Just . . . reluctant, I guess. Pop does her banking for her."

"Then why wouldn't she ask him?"

Lance looked back at the door across the hall and shook his head. "I don't know. Some things . . . they're just between us." He turned the key and opened the door.

Star and Rico sat in the dark with the TV images lighting their faces and a bowl of sesame sticks between them. Star turned. "Come in and close the door. Edward Scissorhands is doing his first haircut. They're just gonna love him."

Edward Scissorhands, Star's favorite misunderstood, maligned, and subnormal character. Johnny Depp at his weirdest.

Rese yawned. Maybe she'd actually sleep. The TV audio coming through the wall would be what Lance called white noise. She glanced over. By his worried expression, she guessed his thoughts were still with Antonia. He didn't seem impressed by the flash and speed of Edward's scissor hands, though no hairdresser on earth compared.

He caught her glance and pulled out of his funk. "Tired?"

She nodded. Another long day, charged with emotion, violence, and unreported crime. Maybe Lance was right about choosing battles. Right now she just wanted to curl up and . . . . listen to him sing?

"Before you get settled, I need to grab a couple things." He ducked into the bedroom and scrounged through a drawer.

Rese waited in the doorway. "They're near the beginning of the movie. What'll you do?"

Lance glanced past her. "I'll take Rico's bed. He can have the couch."

She thought of all the beds lying empty

at the inn, of the kitchen stocked and waiting, the online reservation requests she needed to check. But it all seemed so far away. She was trapped by the friends and family that embraced Lance like a net. It was starting to feel normal to come and go from the apartment, across to grandma, down to mom, up to sisters and nieces and nephews. . . . Okay, it wasn't normal. It was intimidating. But she was nothing if not adaptable. She was the queen of adaptation. She could . . . delude herself. Hey, it ran in the family.

With a couple fresh shirts and boxers tucked under one arm, Lance joined her in the doorway. She looked into his face, saw there a worry and fatigue that once again made her want to hold him — Not what the trip was about. Or was she trying to compartmentalize things in a way that just didn't work? At least with Lance Michelli.

To Lance everything was immediate, interconnected, and essential. He had said he wanted her in the middle of it all. He'd said he loved her, and she believed it. He loved everything and everyone. He loved until it hurt, then kept loving.

And she had no idea what to do with that, so she moved from the doorway into the bedroom — his cue to evacuate. And he got it. Didn't try to kiss her or prolong the moment, just said, "Do you need anything?"

A flight home? "I'm fine."

He touched his fingers to her cheek. "Good night, then."

She swallowed. "Good night, Lance." When he didn't move out of the doorway, she rested a palm to the jamb and raised her brows.

He straightened reluctantly and moved out. "Sweet dreams."

She sighed. "I'm hoping for none." Just deep, solid stupor.

Chapter Thirteen

Rese had never seen anything like the congregations of Latinos, Jamaicans, Cubans, Asians, Albanians, and other Northern Europeans who attended the church in the heart of the neighborhood. The man who'd greeted them at the door had pointed out people to her and included their country of origin or, if they were countrymen, he'd identified their region of Italy down to the village their family had left generations back.

During her first visit to the church, she had marveled at the beautiful architecture. Now she was intrigued by the different accents, shades of skin and hair, and the complete age spectrum represented. She saw nothing pretentious or affluent in the people around her, though money went into the basket that was passed, even if it was only change.

In comparison, her experience growing up seemed diluted somehow. Homogenized. People prosperously removed from their roots. Dad at the top of his trade, their generously compensated crews, and more than that, the people whose historic homes they had restored, whose weekend homes could have housed Lance's extended family. What need had any of them for a supernatural presence telling them to hang on for dear life?

She looked at the cross, the paintings portraying Christ's life, and felt enveloped by wonder. How had God found one little girl in the midst of all that and given her breath to stay alive? Lance reached down and squeezed her hand — reading her thoughts? Or just connecting.

Seated between him with his diamond stud earring and Rico with his double hoops and threaded hair, she felt plain and innocuous, especially compared to the adornments in the rows around them — chains and hoops and studs and hair in every twist and configuration. Star would have fit in, but she didn't do church. Not even Evvy's funeral had induced her to cross the threshold of a house of worship.

This service was different than any she had attended, more structured, what Lance called liturgical, an ancient rite practiced for ages. Studying the faces around her, she sensed the power of this gathering, this sharing of faith. Its reverence embraced her, but it was one more tentacle of Lance's life, like the reminder he wore under his white dress shirt, in his very skin, of not just a debt but an obligation.

A tremor passed through her. She believed God had saved her life and her soul. But did she want to carry His cross? What if she had to bear something so awful it crushed her with its weight? It was one thing to take care of Mom, another altogether to become her.

And there was nothing she could do, no decision she could make, no skill she could develop or power of will that could change a reality that might strike in one weak moment and define the rest of her life. Fear rippled through her as the people dispersed and she and Lance walked the few blocks back.

Rico and most of Lance's family had stayed behind with groups of friends, but Lance was going ahead to prepare food — basically opening the restaurant. From the sounds of it, most of the neighborhood would be there, everyone the Michellis knew and loved, and how could she hide the fear building inside with volcanic force?

Overly perceptive, Lance paused at the outer door. "What's the matter?"

"Nothing."

He cupped her elbow. "You don't want to cook breakfast? Too much noise?"

"Stop trying to read my mind." Her panic surged. "You might not like what you find there."

His gaze bore into her thoughts and left them bare. "If we have to deal with that, we will."

"We? What we?" He wasn't the one with the genetic predisposition.

"You think no one else is affected? That's not how it works. When one person hurts everyone suffers."

She could not put her mind around that. Too many years of insuring that no one knew her thoughts, hurts, and struggles made the idea of communal comfort impossible.

"If it happens . . ." His grip tightened. "I will be there."

She knew better. Aunt Georgie said it broke his heart, but Dad had committed Mom. He and the court with all its witnesses. He'd made the decision he had to. And locked away with Walter, Mom's hair had turned white.

Rese jerked away. Her throat closed up so tightly she could hardly breathe. She could walk scaffolding, roofs, and ridgepoles, take every kind of ribbing, snakes and mice in her lunchbox, and never flinch, but she now looked into the one thing she couldn't bear — helplessness.

She had chafed at Star's calling her a rock, resented her belief that nothing could shake Rese Barrett. But she wanted it to be true. Sweat dampened her forehead; she

266

felt clammy, as though the sun no longer had power to warm her. People who couldn't take care of themselves got put away, forgotten. Her heart sped; her breath shortened.

"Rese." Lance gripped her arm and drew her off the street, into the narrow hall of their building. She tried to pull away, but he closed her into his arms and took control of her mouth. Her resistance shattered as he made his point until she wondered how she had doubted the possibility of connection, because in those moments she could hardly tell where Lance left off and she started. With dizzying comprehension, she experienced the sharing of her burden and wasn't sure she could grab it back if she wanted to.

Pressed against the wall with Lance enclosing her, she hardly heard the door open or the jingle of keys until his dad was upon them. He took them in with a stare, then passed on down the hall. Rese sagged. Of all the impressions to make.

His mother followed immediately with another woman who moved with a smooth liquidity. She tapped Lance's shoulder as she passed, her ebony limbs longer than his and an amiable expression on her face. "Nice to see you, Lance, and whoever you've got in your coils."

He smiled. "You too, Alelia. It's Rese

Barrett, my business partner."

Rese silently groaned.

The two old men who lived in the back passed with a waft of stale cigar smoke. "Business partner," one of them muttered. "Get outta here."

Rese stiffened, but Lance looked amused. "Guess we blew our cover."

"You blew our cover."

He loosened his hold. "You okay?"

The panic seemed to have vanished, but she clenched her hands. "I just wish I knew when it was coming, so I could stop it." If she couldn't even control the thought, how would she handle the reality?

"At least we found a cure." He looked ready to administer it again.

How aggravating was that? "I'd rather handle it myself."

"Yeah, well, you're human." His expression was vexingly vindicated.

She raised her chin. "Not bulletproof?"

He laughed. "Let's not find out." Then he grabbed her hand and dragged her to the kitchen.

The clamor issuing from the restaurant could mean only one thing — Lance was cooking. Too shaky to reach the open window and look down into the street, Antonia nonetheless heard the voices coming and going through the doors propped open be-

268

neath. It would be mostly family, she guessed, some neighbors and friends. Lance wouldn't charge anything, since the place wasn't open in an official capacity, but people might pass a hat, a little something for the cook. They knew how good they had it when he was home. She sighed.

It wouldn't last. He loved them all, she knew. But he'd been born with a restless spirit, as though there was too much of him for any one place. As a child he'd chafed against his boundaries, resisting Doria's grasp until she afforded him more freedom than any of the others. He found his way into circles of every age, every background. But even that wasn't enough. Getting his motorcycle had given him wings he hadn't hesitated to use. No hopping around the nest, testing the wind. He had leaped headfirst, not caring if he fell. And then the world was his limit. Maybe someday he'd find a way out of that.

Sofie peeked in, as unobtrusive as a shadow. "Lance is cooking, Nonna. Want Pop to come up for you?"

Antonia shook her head. Not like this, bent and mute, words jumbled in her mind, her mouth twisted and drooling. One person at a time, she could stand, but not a blur of conversations and too many heartfelt wishes and sympathetic glances. Uffa! Sofie should understand that; she who avoided the limelight but knew well enough the weight of sympathy and judgment.

With what passed for a smile, Antonia waved her out, then tried to rise up in the bed, pushing slowly with her functioning arm. She didn't have to be there to picture the scene. All the men but Lance would congregate and wait to be served. Anna and Dina would beg off helping with a litany of ailments, plunking themselves down to chat. Celestina would be manipulating the groupings while Doria gathered and nurtured her brood, both trying to control the uncontrollable.

It hit her hard. The sound of gunshots. Papa dying alone while Nonno collapsed in her arms. The fear and fury and helplessness. *"Take Nonno and hide if trouble comes."* As though there was any escape when even her own mind turned on her, becoming a bramble entrapping her speech, her thoughts, the basic motions of life, yet leaving bare all the things she had hidden. . . .

Was there something I could have done, more I could have said? The nightmare images plague me even in the daylight now. The moment my thoughts drift, I am seized by the sudden smell of blood, the thought of Papa. "Marco, did you see him, see Papa? Do you know —"

"Yes, Antonia." He doesn't appreciate the reminder. "I tried to get to him, but I was too late." The car rumbles over the rough road.

My chest clenches and I can't breathe. I remember the shots and knowing it was Papa killed and Nonno clutching my hand, Nonno falling. But what if . . . "What if Nonno wasn't dead? What if I buried him alive?"

Marco swerves the car to the side and stops. He pulls me into his arms and holds me tight. "They're gone, cara. And it's not your fault."

Not my fault. Not my fault.

She jolted back to reality with tears streaming from her eyes. Then whose fault was it?

Seeing the glazed look in Rese's eyes, Lance left the cleanup for Momma and anyone else who would pitch in. He had to get through another twenty-four hours at least before he could get Nonna what she needed from the bank and take Rese home. Hopefully there'd be no lasting trauma — for either of them. Having demonstrated his affection in the hall for all suspecting minds, they were in for an assault, but he didn't care because it had felt so good to crash through the boundaries they had both established.

Momma, however, was probably planning their first baby shower. As if she didn't have enough grandkids. But he had yet to produce his share, and in her mind time was running out. She might think Rese cold and unfeeling, but if she was his choice then they should get married and move in where she could oversee everything.

She was mistaken on both counts. He was not staying, and Rese was anything but unfeeling. It was her tenderness that made her work so hard to be tough. She just ran deeper than most people wanted to look. And he loved that about her.

"Come on." He ushered her out the door as Rico passed by with Star. They had eaten and mingled but now were headed somewhere on foot without drums or costumes. Lance tapped Rico's arm. "Where are you going?"

"The park."

"Reading Shakespeare?"

"Listening to the birds sing, man."

Star giggled.

Lance shook his head. "You're whacked."

"Hey." Rico pressed a hand to his chest. "I can appreciate the little things."

Lance laughed. "Hoops?" Something hard and physical sounded better than birds.

"Have to swipe a ball."

"Swiping isn't nice." Lance motioned Rese ahead of him past a tourist couple going the other way. "We'll let the kids play too."

"Ah man." Rico hung his head back.

They'd have no trouble finding takers, Lance knew. He played a fair shortstop, tough handball, and wicked pool, but neither he nor Rico had the size or the spring for hoops. And since the makeup of the neighborhood had shifted to giants more along Chaz's line, the kids would eat them alive.

The game in progress was not maxed out, and their overture was accepted as he's expected. Tall, rangy Lawon Johnson gave Rese the eye and said, "You playin'?"

She shrugged. "Why not?"

Hands on his hips, Lance stared when she joined the other team. He hadn't thought to ask Rese, but he didn't have time to sweat it. The ball had gotten loose in a scramble. He snagged it, passed low to Rico on the bounce, but Lawon got between, spun, and shot.

Ignacio took the rebound and sent it back to Luis. As Lance ran, he glimpsed Star, who had slipped off when they joined teams and was at the playground, leading a hopping, twirling retinue of ragamuffins, fingers splayed, heads thrown back. The Pied Piper of illusion.

"Lance." Rico passed him the ball.

He caught it hard in the chest, then dribbled in and made the shot. He hooked fingers with Rico, but Rese had taken the rebound and sent a sharp bouncing pass to Lawon who dribbled down, then sent it back to her when Ignacio blocked him. It was over before he and Rico reached the other end of the court.

Lance panted in close. "I didn't know you could shoot." He blocked her path as Rico and Ignacio raced the ball down, then missed the rim shot.

"You didn't ask."

"We should put a hoop on the workshop."

She half smiled. "Are you distracting me?"

He took her waist in his hands. "Would I do that?"

She snorted, ducked around him, and rushed down for a pass. Rese Barrett played basketball. There were probably a thousand other things he didn't know. It felt strange, when most of the people he knew were like the back of his hand, Rico a second skin.

From the day they'd met, when Rico's lunch got kicked into the gutter and Lance shared the meatball sub in his own, Rico had stuck closer than a tick. Lance saw right off that he didn't stand a chance, even in his own family. Seven kids fighting over what little they had of food, belongings — and affection.

It was pathetic how Rico had worked for his father's attention — the biggest thing he and Lance had in common. But two years after they met, Juan went to prison for knifing an opposing gang member. He did six years, and when he came back Rico didn't need his attention anymore, which was good since Juan was locked up again seven months later.

Lance took the pass from Rico and turned into Lawon's chest. He ducked under the armpit and bounced the ball at Ignacio, but Rese intercepted, took off down the court, and made the lay-up. Rico couldn't stop her. He gave it all he had, but in spite of quick reflexes and coordination, basketball would never be his game.

Rese high-fived Lawon, and Lance reconsidered the hoop on the workshop. Wouldn't match the decor. They went back and forth, and when Rese got too confident, Rico stole the ball, heaved it at Lance, and he swooshed. They grinned like fed tigers.

One of the younger kids complained that Rese and Lawon were hogging the action, and Lance took the moment to catch his breath.

"Your woman's hot," Ignacio said, beside him.

"Yeah, and don't even think of moving in on her."

The kid grinned.

Four hours at the park — playing ball, watching Star's impromptu skit with a handful of future thespians, talking with Chaz and his friends who joined them — took his mind off the safe deposit box and what it might hold. It almost distracted him from Nonna's relapse and the stress and confusion she must be experiencing.

He didn't want to explain that she had to come with him to the bank. If she wouldn't come down for breakfast, she must not want to be seen in public until she had recovered, and that wasn't likely anytime soon.

Elliot Dobbs had assured him there was no way into the box without her, not without a court order that might be granted only by proving her incompetent. No way. Nonna was perfectly competent, even if she couldn't voice things correctly. She knew what she meant by those words, even if others didn't. But he had no control over other people's reactions. It could be humiliating and aggravating — exactly what she didn't need.

A surge of protectiveness overwhelmed him. Why hadn't she let it go? He had released it all. Why did God keep returning what he surrendered?

Chapter Fourteen

In the bedroom, surrounded by Star's frog sculptures that all seemed to be smirking, Rese frowned. "It's not funny. It was awful." Star had gone out with Rico after the park, and Rese had hoped to join them, but she and Lance were invited to dinner with Monica's family. While the numbers were fewer, the noise didn't reflect it, Monica alone reaching decibels that threatened the eardrum when she shouted her kids down. And then there was the scrutiny, the delving and drilling. Rese felt like a tooth, hollowed and de-nerved and stuffed to insensitivity. "I don't pry into other people's lives; why do they have to know every detail of mine?"

Star pulled a clip from her hair and let it fall down around her shoulders. "You haven't learned the art of deflection."

Rese shook her head. Lance had been right when he warned her that the minute his sister suspected a romantic interest she would give them no peace. Bobby hadn't been much better with his ribbing Lance, though he'd toned it down in front of the children . . . *all* the children. They couldn't all be theirs. She suspected they'd picked up a few of Lucy's and maybe some off the street as well.

Rese pressed her fingers to her forehead. She enjoyed them individually, especially Nicky, whose angelic face hid a naughty streak that reminded her of Lance. But gathered at the table with Bobby's pontifications, Monica's staccato questions — answers interrupted midsentence by admonitions to the kids — and the kids' constant arguing, she had almost craved a cell in an asylum.

" 'Sweet are the uses of adversity, which, like the toad, ugly and venomous, wears yet a precious jewel in his head.' "

Rese frowned. She did not want that message again, especially from Star. Why would she need more adversity? She groaned. "I don't know why I'm here."

"Cosmic convergence." Star threaded her fingers in and scratched her scalp, then slid them out until the coils sprang free. "It was meant to be, all of us here together for this moment in time."

"Right." Rese tugged the comforter back on the bed. "You came to be with Rico. I came to settle business."

Star giggled. "And Lance?"

"What do you think? It's his business." She tossed the pillow up to fluff and set it into place.

"You are so funny."

"It's true. All that business in Sonoma, Star — the skeleton, for heaven's sake. He's trying to finish what he started, and he wanted me here to discuss our plans with Antonia. It's just . . . with Lance nothing goes the way I expect."

Star spun around and laughed. "Because you don't know what you expect."

"I know exactly what I expect. But Lance . . ." She couldn't even blame him this time. How could he know Antonia would get so upset, relapse, and need him yet again?

Star fixed her with a piercing blue gaze. "Lance is your other self."

Rese huffed. "I'm not saying he doesn't matter to me. Just . . . that's not why I'm here."

Star laughed again. " 'Thou art bewitched with the rogue's company.' "

Rese swept Star's clothes from the floor and folded them into a drawer. "So now that you're here by cosmic decree, are you going to stay?"

Star looked startled. "I never think that way." She dropped her head back, the bones of her slender neck forming a delicate ridge. "I am a free bird, sailing the winds of life."

"Don't you ever want a plan?"

Her head came up. "We can't change the

279

forces. I'm just glad they've cast us here now." And the poignant brilliance of her china blue eyes left Rese breathless as Star sprang forward and clasped their hands in a patty-cake position.

"Would you ever have come here with me, Rese? Would you have left that old place at all?"

Rese frowned. Entrenched was probably a fair description. "Maybe."

Star tossed her head and laughed. "Never. I couldn't believe it when I saw you in the hall. Planets must have re-aligned." She let go and spun, her arms in ballet position. "Don't you see? This was all meant to be. Rico and me and you and Lance."

"Star —"

" 'We are bound together, you and I.' " Star's face turned grave, her voice ominous. " 'Two sides of the same magic.' "

Recognizing the lines from *The Last Unicorn*, which Star had devoured as a child, Rese said grimly, "That makes me the harpy."

Star doubled over with laughter. "You can't resist the fates. 'There is a tide in the affairs of men, which, taken at the flood, leads to fortune; omitted, all the voyage of their life is bound in shallows and in miseries.' "

"I'm only here to —"

"Stop." Star put a hand to her lips. "Tempt not capricious gods. The tide is here at flood."

Rese sighed. "Well, I have news for you. There's only one capricious God." Who might not merely allow her to follow her mother's path, but, in fact, ordain it.

Star grew still except for the slight chronic palsy that made her seem ephemeral. "That's one too many."

Rese sighed. "I didn't like the idea either. But I've found it inescapable."

"You're not serious."

"Star, do you remember the night I went to the hospital?"

Star stalked to the other side of the room.

"I should have died that night. Dad wasn't home in time."

"He carried you free; you didn't die. And here you are."

Rese sat down on the edge of the bed. "You know how you saw fairies when things were bad?"

"I cannot believe you saw them too." She clutched herself in her arms. "Rese Barrett does not see fairies."

"I saw nothing." Why was she telling it now, when she'd gone all these years with Star never asking how she got through that awful night? "But there was something there."

" 'A walking shadow, a poor player that struts upon the stage and then is heard no more.' "

"I think it was God."

The energy seemed to leach from Star. Her hand went to her throat. "God was in your bedroom?"

"Not in a bad way, Star. It was a presence that —"

"Don't say it." Star's voice hardened. "Personally, I've had too much of old almighty men in my bedroom."

Lance tapped the door to tell Rese and Star good night. It had been a rollercoaster day, but hopefully the morning would bring some resolution. The door flew open, and Star stared at him with a haunted look, then kissed him square on the mouth. " 'Tis an affliction not without cure. One must merely learn to bleed." Then she swept past and out into the night.

Slack-jawed, he turned to Rese. "Did I . . ."

"You didn't do anything." Rese passed into the living room, then stopped, arms crossed, with her back to him. "I tried to tell her about that night, about the presence in my room."

Something so personal would not have passed easily from Rese to Star. He joined her and began rubbing the ropes of her neck and shoulders. "She didn't believe you?"

"She wouldn't even hear it."

"Why?"

"She'd have to admit I've had bad things in my life."

"She knows you have."

"No, Lance. She thinks that night was my deliverance." Rese bent her head down as he rubbed. "All my adversity is sweet and useful, and only her bad stuff counts."

Star had hurt her, though she cloaked it with frustration. He worked his thumbs into the knots. "Not very equitable."

Rese snorted. "Now she's off again, who knows where or for how long. But she'll come back and expect me to pick up my life where she left it."

He used the heels of his palms along her shoulders.

She groaned a little under the pressure. "I just wanted her to see there could be order in things. That she didn't have to be at the mercy of whatever wind blew her way." Rese sagged. "I shouldn't have mentioned God."

Lance worked the tendons up under her skull. "You should be able to talk about your experience. I'd think Star would want to know." Was Star threatened by the revelation, or by imagining Rese vulnerable?

She wanted Rese to play the role she gave her. But why did people keep trying to box Rese in? He slid his fingers into her hair, wishing he could let her out completely.

"It's like talking to a cloud. Poof. She's gone."

And there was Rese, as present as a Sequoia redwood. "You never know what gets through."

"It appalled her that I might believe in God."

"Maybe she's afraid you'll change."

She turned. "People change. Can't I learn from adversity, grow in character? God forbid — have faith?"

"Of course you can."

"That's all I was trying to say. That maybe there was something, someone Star could trust too."

"You've come a long way."

She shook her head. "I don't know the half of it. Obviously."

But she'd put her trust where it mattered, and fear of the Lord was the beginning of wisdom. "Chaz'll help."

She frowned. "Why won't you?"

Because he didn't translate well from what he knew to what he did. "I don't think I'm the best example."

"You're the reason I believe at all."

Wouldn't Evvy like that? She'd scolded and nagged him to "speak the truth." And he had, but his actions hadn't matched.

Rese clenched her hands at her sides, exasperation sparking. "You made sense of it for me. You made it real."

"I lied to you." And it stood between them like a guard dog, keeping him out. Even if she was letting it go, how could he explain his fear of spoiling her faith by some faulty action, some missed cue? He might claim her heart, but Chaz was the one to safeguard her mind and spirit.

"Lance." She searched his face. "Can't we just . . . start over?"

His breath stopped. A do-over? He'd been hoping to make up for the hurt, to prove he could do better. But to start over with no regrets, no blame? That was more than he'd expected, more than he deserved. Yet . . .

He read her expression, hopeful and sincere. Rese meant what she said. He took her into his arms, pressing her head to his shoulder, breathing the clean scent of her. Or was it the fragrance of grace? Relief rushed in, and gratitude so deep it touched his soul.

Chapter Fifteen

The door opened and Rico came in. "Where's Star?"

Rese pulled out of Lance's arms as Rico tossed two DVDs on the table, then took a bottle of sparkling artesian water and organic cheese puffs from the paper bag he carried. They'd obviously planned another movie night, and while Rico was off getting their contraband, Star was running out on them all.

Lance said, "She got upset and left."

"Left for where?"

Rese shrugged. "She didn't say." She never did. It was part of the punishment to make them wonder, worry and wait.

Rico looked from her to Lance as it dawned that she hadn't simply stalked off to sulk.

"She does this, Rico." Lance hooked his thumbs in his jeans.

"What do you mean, does it? She hasn't done it at all."

Rese walked to the window and looked out. "She goes along fine for a while, then takes off."

"She didn't say where she was going?"

"She never does." Rese turned. Not where or why or with whom, but it was certain she'd find someone to commiserate with her. The first few times Star had disappeared, Rese had tried to find out where she'd been, tried to tell her it wasn't safe to go off alone. Star wouldn't hear it. Maybe it was danger she craved, or the worry it created for those who cared. There were never apologies or excuses. She neither explained nor acknowledged, only expected to be accepted back without question.

Rese had learned the pattern, but Rico hadn't. Looking at him, she regretted her part in it, but there was never any telling what would set Star off. "She might be back tonight." But not likely. Kissing Lance had been a parting shot. Star would let it sink in.

Anger stirred. What had she done? What had Rico done? Yet Star was off in New York City somewhere, had probably already picked someone up. She might say she'd had enough of old almighty men, but she sought the situation again and again.

Rico turned and headed for the door, pausing just long enough to tell Lance, "Call if she gets back."

Lance had to know Star wasn't likely to walk in any time soon. If she hadn't found a lift out of the neighborhood, Rico might cross her path, but not if she didn't want him to. Star was elusive in more ways than one. Even so, he handed over his cell phone. "Rico's keyed in."

She nodded as he went after his friend. Lance would share the exercise in futility. He had to. It was Rico.

She sat down and flipped open his phone, scrolling through hundreds of names to Rico's. Did Lance know everyone? She closed the phone and dropped her head back. What were the chances they'd go back to Sonoma if Star didn't turn up? In the next few days? Slim. After that? Possible. Depending on Rico's frame of mind.

Maybe he would realize she was too high maintenance. Sure she was dazzling, fearless, and fun. And she'd plugged right into his musical aspirations. Maybe they were even good together. But Star was . . . Star. Rico just hadn't seen it yet.

Rese flipped around on the TV channels. After about an hour the guys came back. No Star. They had combed the neighborhood, but there were not that many places to look at night.

"Where would she go?" Rico said, almost to himself.

"Is there somewhere you hung out that she might have gone?" Lance asked.

Rico spread his hands. "We've been all over, man."

Rese looked up. "The theater district?" She wasn't sure why it came to her, but Times Square was the kind of place Star would lose herself. She'd been there to sing with Rico at the Java Cabana. And she would recognize its potential for companions and camouflage.

Rico focused on her. "You think she went into the city?"

She could be halfway to Canada, but Rico didn't think in Star terms. He thought the magical nymph she played was the real thing. "She could have."

Rico swore. Manhattan was, after all, a big place, lots of people. There wasn't much chance he'd see Star if she didn't want him to, but he obviously wouldn't quit looking.

Lance pulled his leather jacket back on. "Let's go." There was only concern for Rico in his voice.

Why didn't she feel it for Star? "I'll come too." It was better than sitting there alone, and the guys must realize it was unnecessary to have someone stay home. Lance waved her out, then led the way down to his parents' apartment.

She waited in the living room with Rico as Lance borrowed his mother's Fiat. Rico's eyes darted everywhere, as if he might find Star sitting on a shelf like a figurine. Seeing his anxiety, she wished there was some way to change the reality, but he was probably far from Star's thoughts. She was making a point and didn't care who fell along the way. "Star won't realize she's hurt you, Rico."

He turned onyx eyes on her and grew perfectly still. "She will know, chiquita." Something cold passed through her. Had Star tapped the part of Rico that knew violence, the part Lance had tamed by sharing the blows? But then she realized it was bare hope she saw, Rico's heart uncloaked.

She looked away. It was hard to fathom Star's utter lack of conscience or compassion or whatever the hole inside her was. Maybe her mother's drugs had destroyed that capacity in utero; or abuse had driven it so deep she could no longer access those feelings. She was utterly self-absorbed. Rico hoped in vain.

Following Lance in, his mother came to Rico and caught his face in her hands. "You be careful." She must see the tension gripping him.

"Si, Mamacita."

"No trouble." Doria's concern was probably based on history, and it could get ugly if Rico found Star in any of the situations Rese imagined. He might even believe it the other guy's fault. Rese knew better.

They responded to what was offered.

"We'll be okay, Momma." Lance patted her arm and she released Rico, then gave Rese a look as though she alone might avert disaster. Rese drew herself up. She had no intention of doing something stupid.

Lance maneuvered the Fiat through the traffic in much the same way he handled Rico's bike or his Harley. It was now evident he drove like a New Yorker. Rese sat back to endure it. She had given Rico the passenger seat so that he and Lance could plan their strategy, and they discussed likely hot spots and possible low spots to look for Star. Though he had to realize how useless it was, Lance was there for Rico, engaged and determined.

Belmont had been dark and closed up, but the city that never sleeps was wide awake. Times Square dazzled the eye; white and multicolored lights everywhere, massive electronic billboards flashing females and fashion, teeming sidewalks, restaurants, theaters, stores. Rese shook her head, wishing she'd kept her mouth shut.

But it was definitely Star's kind of place. She stared out the window. Star could absorb this block alone for weeks, sucking energy from unsuspecting strangers instead of her friends for a change. Rese frowned. She was angrier than she'd realized.

The kiss hadn't mattered to Lance. It was what it said to her that counted. *You have nothing I can't spoil.* Or take, maybe. Or desecrate. Lance being the bearer of faith. Maybe it was Lance whom Star wanted to defile. But ultimately it was all to hurt her. She was the only person Star lashed out at, the only one she came back to again and again.

Relationships like the one she had with Maury followed the pattern to a point, but once she'd severed the tie, it stayed severed. Rese had learned long ago that Star lived life on her terms, but for some reason those terms included the one friend she could walk on again and again and again. Her rock.

"Let me out here," Rico said at the intersection, unable to sit still any longer. "You'll never park."

"I'll find something." Lance looked at his watch. "Meet us back at this corner in half an hour. We'll make a plan from there."

Rico climbed out as the taxi behind them blared its horn. Lance moved on. God didn't seem to owe him parking in this district. Rese kept her eyes sharp, but even so she missed the spot Lance darted into almost before it was vacated. Sighing, she got out and waited on the sidewalk.

Lance joined her. "Ready?"

"For what?"

He cocked his head, taking her measure. "It might be pointless, but it matters to Rico."

And at this moment Rico meant nothing to Star. Nobody did. She was the only thing shining in her sky. Rese seethed.

"Is it the kiss?"

She scowled. "It's pretty much everything."

He looked down the street, waiting for her to decide. Why had she come, anyway? Had she thought there'd be anything she could do that would matter?

She clenched her hands and said, "Star could be distraught. She could be in danger, dying in an alley. But she's not. She's off dancing, or acting, or making out in a corner, and if she knew we were here searching the streets for her? She'd laugh." Rese could not contain the bitterness. Where had it come from? Why did all her emotions suddenly emerge in the presence of Lance Michelli? "I'm tired of being what she needs. Giving and forgiving with nothing in return." When he didn't answer, she turned on him. "I'm wrong, aren't I?"

"No." He shook his head.

"Then what?"

"There's a name for what you give Star. Unconditional love."

Rese did not want to hear it. Anger so rarely had the chance to vent, it seemed to ooze from her very pores at the thought of Star's parting kiss. She groaned. "It was so absurd and spiteful."

"I know."

And selfish and overly dramatic. She wanted to swing a sledge hammer, the ring of steel on steel, the reverberation charging up her arms. She blew out her breath. "So where do you think she is?"

"I'd guess making out in a corner."

It broke the spine of her anger, and she dropped her head back with another groan. "We won't find her."

"Let's hope for Rico's sake that's true. And mine."

She faced him. "Don't do anything stupid."

His mouth pulled.

"I mean it, Lance. I will not write to you."

Laughing, he slipped his arm around her shoulders. "You're not so tough, Theresa."

It was true. She'd write, she'd visit, she'd bail him out. Unconditional love.

Rico wanted something to beat on; Lance could read it in his eyes. He hadn't anticipated Star's flight, hadn't known at the first provocation their idyll would end; no word of explanation, no consideration for him. Through the subway tunnels where goth and punked-up kids loitered, past homeless people and downtown suits, they searched. Rico prowled the bars and restaurants and theater hangouts, his own desertion issues growling inside him.

Fiercely loyal, he expected the same — in spite of all the people who had proved otherwise. He had no claim to Star, except that of consideration. Fear for her safety and emotional condition was foremost in his mind as they searched, but Lance knew there was also the sting of yet another potential rejection.

Momma opened her door in her nightgown when they came back sometime after three in the morning. He had intended to sneak by without disturbing her, but she had a second sense that woke her any time one of her offspring came in late. And she'd have been fitful at best.

"No luck?" The relief in her expression did not mean a lack of concern for Star, but an overabundance for him and Rico.

He shook his head. Rico was ready to ignite, but they'd seen not a shadow of Star. There would have been fireworks if they had.

Momma trained her gaze on Rese as the guardian angel who must have kept him and Rico from the fall. Rese showed none of the anger and hurt she'd expressed before giving in and looking for a friend who used her up and wanted more.

"Thanks." Lance dropped the car keys into her palm. Rico was already climbing the stairs.

"You want some milk?"

He leaned in and kissed her. "Go back to sleep, Momma. We're fine."

She turned to Rese. "When you get up, come down for coffee. We'll chat."

"Okay." Rese nodded. They climbed the stairs without speaking, but at the door, she said, "She means both of us, right?"

Rico had left the door touching but not closed. Lance pushed it open. "She means you." By the light of the single lamp inside, he glimpsed something close to horror on her face.

"I don't chat."

"Sure you do."

"Lance, you know . . . you've seen . . . ."

"That was with strangers. Momma's family." He stretched. Rico must have gone straight to bed. Chaz was probably home from work and sleeping already. Worrying about Nonna all day and Rico all evening, Lance had expended enough energy to sleep for a year, but not Rese. He reached for her hand. "Want to make out in a corner?"

She raised her jaw. "I don't appreciate the comparison."

So she was still stung. "How about the couch in the middle of the room?"

"Lance."

296

He took her into his arms, felt her stiffness. She was far from sleep, as he'd guessed. "Neck rub?"

"You need one?" She meant it as a taunt, reversing his offer, asserting her self-sufficiency.

But he tipped his head. "Sure." His answer took her by surprise, but he headed for the couch anyway. The cushions sighed as he sat sideways and waited.

Chaz's sonorous snores seeped through the closed door as Rese dropped reluctantly. "I won't be any good at it."

"Close your eyes." He closed his too. "Now grip my neck and feel the muscles."

Her hand was cold.

"Just work your thumb and fingers into what you feel." Her hands had carved beauty into wood, and he felt the strength of that now as she rubbed, not just his neck, but after a time moving down his back, using both hands. The fact that she would go beyond his instructions said a lot. He hadn't needed sore muscles rubbed, but he reveled in her touch.

So many times he'd worked out her knots and she'd never reciprocated. But her hands were ungrudging now, working up and down the long muscles of his back, her breath warming his neck as she rubbed his shoulders. Something wet struck his shoulder, and he turned.

She sniffed, angry at being discovered. "Is there such a thing as emotional anorexia?"

He half smiled. "Starved emotions?"

"More like refusing to feel until it's hard to know what to feel."

He rested his wrist on her shoulder. "There's nothing wrong with how you feel."

"But I don't, Lance. I care about Star, but I'm not worried. I'm sorry for Rico, but there's no . . . ache. Even when you left —"

"When you kicked me out."

"It hurt so much that I . . . felt nothing."

"That's how you cope. You had a lot of junk at a very young age, emotional expectations no child is equipped to handle."

"What if it's just broken?"

He cupped her face. "You're not broken. Why do you think there are tears in your eyes?"

"I don't know."

"Because you care."

She pulled away and slid back on the couch. "As we were looking for Star I kept imagining finding her in a really bad way. Killed, even. And Lance, I wondered how I would feel. I wondered."

"It's a protection. You shut yourself off."

She sat silent a long time, then turned.

"Why can't Star? Why would she keep putting herself in danger and degradation again and again when that's what messed her up in the first place?"

"Ever heard of cutting? Burning?"

Rese's brow pinched.

"Using physical pain to self-medicate emotional wounds."

"But . . ."

"Sofie could explain it better. She's got the science. But it's basically that injury triggers something in the brain that anesthetizes. You said Star doesn't use drugs, but she's finding a way to numb herself."

"So sex is a drug for her?"

He shrugged. "I'm guessing."

"Like stomping your toe when you've hammered your thumb."

He smiled. "Sure. If what you told her triggered memories, her reaction makes sense."

Rese shook her head. "But Rico . . ."

"Rico is safe, like you. She needed pain."

She leaned her head back. "How do you stop it all?"

"I don't know." He slid his arm around and nestled her into his shoulder. "Pain has a life of its own and comes out in ways you never expect. Even when you think it's over."

"Then what hope is there?"

He caressed her upper arm. "I keep

trying to find out."

"I can't do this." Rese paced the living room the next morning in the beige rayon shell and cargo shorts she had debated over far longer than her few choices required.

Lance showed no sympathy whatsoever. Perched on the arm of the couch, he looked annoyingly amused. "It's just Momma, Rese. She'll do all the talking anyway."

Chaz came out of the bathroom, shower fresh and smiling. She did not need his cheerfulness on top of Lance's assurances. If she hadn't been dazed at three in the morning, she might have said no, or at least made sure Lance was included. Why should she have to face his mother alone?

" 'This is the day the Lord has made.' " Chaz beamed. " 'Let us rejoice and be glad in it.' " He had obviously overheard their argument.

"She's waiting." Lance's tone was gentle but insistent. He was not going to get her out of it, or help in any way besides pushing her out the door.

Fine. She didn't need him. She stalked to the door and went out, then drew a long breath and went down to his parents' door. She knocked.

"It's open. Come in." Doria was dressed in a burgundy leotard and wrap skirt. "I'm

300

teaching in an hour."

Rese nodded. Should she apologize for being late? "What do you teach? I mean, what kind of dance?" Not that she would know one from another.

"Oh, some of everything. Except the break dancing. We have a man for that."

Rese nodded again. "Oh."

"Sit down. You want cream . . . sugar?" Doria set a cup before her with biscotti on the saucer.

"Yes. Thank you." Rese sat. The kitchen was cluttered with knickknacks, the refrigerator papered with photographs. Children and grandchildren, Rese guessed, recognizing many without being able to name them.

Noticing her gaze, Doria touched a photo. "This one's Lance."

A little boy with large brown eyes, an impish smile, and baseball mitt. Rese wanted to reach out and hold him. Something was happening to her, something she hadn't expected when Lance said they needed to "square things away with his grandmother."

"And this was his high school graduation." Doria picked up a photo on the windowsill next to an urn that Rese prayed didn't hold ashes but sure looked like it could.

"And his baby shoe." She picked up the bronzed shoe.

Did people do that? Rese nodded and smiled, then her eyes went once again to the kitchen ceiling. "Have you had that sag checked out?"

Doria looked from the shoe in her hand to the ceiling over her head. "I've been talking to Roman. He's got no time. Lance and the boys take care of things, but they're everywhere else these days. No one has time."

"I could look at it."

Doria waved her off. "A guest of my son's?" She shook her head.

"I have experience. It's what I do . . . did. Renovation. That looks like a leak. It could cause trouble."

"Roman will get to it." Doria sat down with a cup of her own. "Do you dance?"

"No."

"Lance was my born dancer."

Naturally.

"He wouldn't stay with it, though. Tony told him he wasn't big enough to dance like that without getting hit."

"Lance thought a lot of Tony."

"Everyone did." Doria stared into her cup. "But he was wrong about Lance. There's life in that boy that has to come out. Why shouldn't he dance?"

Rese sipped her coffee, then startled when Doria tucked a finger under her chin and raised her face.

302

"You have a good form. You just need to loosen." She moved the chin in circles. "Stand up."

"I really don't —"

"Shh, shh." Doria raised her to her feet and motioned for her to turn.

Rese did a jerky pirouette, arms clamped at her sides. *It's only Momma. She'll do all the talking anyway.*

"Come out with the elbows." Doria pulled until Rese's hands were on her hips. "Up with the chin." Again the finger positioning her. "Perfect for the cha-cha."

Rese snorted.

"Give me six weeks; I'll have you performing the two-sided break with a man wrap."

Rese shook her head. "No way."

"You have balance."

"Walking roofs."

"Good musculature."

"Swinging a hammer."

They laughed.

Doria turned. "You really know how to fix the ceiling?"

Rese stepped under the sag a short distance out from the sink and looked up. "Never came across one I couldn't handle. At least I could get in there and tell you what it needs."

Doria looked her over slowly, then spread her hands. "Ah well, things are different now. If a woman wants to be a plumber, why not?" She sat back down and dipped her biscotti. "What does Lance do at the inn?"

Rese rejoined her at the table. "We haven't worked it all out yet. Cook, of course. Maybe something with his music. He handles the customers." In other words, the whole operation. Without Lance there was no inn, even if she had faked breakfast a few weeks. Left to her, the business would collapse. But together . . . They should be back there, getting established before the grape harvest brought tourists in droves.

Doria frowned. "It's so far."

Rese paused with the cup near her lips. For the first time she considered how it would be for Doria if Lance moved across the country. This woman who didn't want her children scattered, who stayed in the old neighborhood just to keep them all close. "You could come any time. There's room."

Doria pressed a crumb with her fingertip. "When do you leave?"

They'd been there six days, and it looked as though they'd need a few more. But that wasn't what Doria was asking, so Rese told her, "When Lance is ready."

Chapter Sixteen

Life is a bowl of cherries to Rudy
Vallee. But he didn't pick them; he
didn't grow them. His love and labor
didn't sustain and nurture them. Ah, to
live and laugh at it all.

In the city of Toledo a crowd has blocked
the streets surrounding the city hall.
"What's happening?" I ask as Marco stops
in the street and steps up onto the running
board to see.

"Some sort of protest." He narrows his
eyes. "Don't think it's a labor strike. There
are women and children marching. Probably the residents of a hobo camp trying to
be heard."

I climb out and move with him through
the crowd to see the marchers. Some carry
signs; some carry children. Looking at their
faces, I don't feel so alone in my grief.

"How will this help?"

"It won't."

"Then why are they marching?"

He shrugs. "Can't think what else to do, I guess."

I shake my head. Passing through the industrial cities of the North, I've seen conditions far worse than any I imagined. "What happened, Marco? How did things get so bad?"

He explains, as Papa never would, the rampant speculation that led to overinflated stock values, and the government's idea that liquidation, regardless of the human cost, would correct the crashed market and encourage new investment. But looking at the marchers, I wonder how anyone can ignore the human cost and, worse, blame the unfortunate for their plight. These people are no more responsible than I for their situation, yet I see them spit on. It could be me. Any one of us. If I could lose everything in one night . . .

"What will happen to my home, Marco?"

"I don't know."

Catching a sob in my throat, I whisper, "I can't go back." I know this already, but it hurts when Marco agrees. I look back at the marchers. "I know how these people feel."

He reaches over and holds my hand.

I turn with eyes awash. "You think I'm ungrateful."

"No."

"You've done so much."

"Antonia . . ." His voice is soft, embarrassed.

"You've risked your life." I sniff. "Your job. Were you finished?"

"Don't worry about that."

"But were you?"

"Yes. Yes, it was finished."

I face him. "Then you would have left. If Papa hadn't . . ."

He squeezes my hand. "Don't."

"Were you going to say good-bye?"

He doesn't answer for too long. "I hadn't gotten that far. I didn't want to leave you."

"And now you have me for better or worse."

"I can protect you." He says it under his breath.

I fist my hands. "But why should you?"

"I want to." But there is something else in his eyes, quickly masked. "Look, let's find a way around this." He means the march, but I think also the subject. We walk back to the car, and he does find another way through. He is good at that.

I can't stop seeing the faces of the marchers; some angry, some bitter, most weary and beaten. "Why is there no aid?" We have stopped in the next town for the night, but it's as though the marchers have traveled with us.

"Tapped out." Marco says. "There are too many."

"But the children."

He nods.

"I didn't know it was so bad."

"You were pretty well situated."

"No thanks to the government and the awful Halstead Act. But it did prepare us. Papa and Nonno cursed its stupidity, agreeing on that much, but not what to do about it. Nonno was certain it would be repealed once the voices of reason were heard, and refused any talk of selling out. Instead, we tightened our belts and found ways to get by long before the crash." I picture my beloved home, blessing Nonno for refusing to sell, though what has it gained us now?

"Nonna Carina and I built up our garden until we had more than we could use. Livestock for meat and milk for cheeses. And we had Papa's income, which allowed us to keep the land." I'm surprised to say it without choking up, but seeing the marchers has stiffened my spine.

"You were lucky."

I don't feel lucky. As banks tumbled like dominos, Arthur Jackson's prospered — and Papa with him. It had to be by underhanded means. Bitterness fills my mouth, and I wish Papa had never set foot in that bank — even if it paid the taxes.

"Antonia." Marco takes my hands. The light in our small room is dim and unsteady. His face is craggy with shadows. "I don't regret our wedding. I hadn't planned on a wife. My business takes me away too much, and —"

"You'll have to sell me to the circus?"

He stares a moment, then throws back his head and laughs. Then he grabs me into his arms, more exuberant than I've ever seen him. "Can ya walk a tightrope?"

"I've never tried."

"Then I'll have to keep you." Looking into my face, he sobers. "What I'd really like is to kiss you."

My heart stills. "I suppose you can do pretty much what you like."

"I don't want to make it worse for you. I told you it was in name only."

I am suddenly aware of his scent, faint pomade, the fish we had for dinner, the soap he washed his hands with. My Arpège perfume is gone, and I taste of fish, as well, but I have already tipped up my face, and as my eyes close, our mouths blend.

When the kiss brings my tears, Marco holds me like a solicitous uncle, smoothing my hair and patting my back. Desire slides behind another face, and I wonder at this man who plays so many roles. I want to be what he wants, but my heart can't open and guard itself at once.

"I'm sorry." I sniff.

He shakes his head. "I shouldn't have asked."

"No. I'm . . . If I could just . . ." *Forget.*

"Maybe this wasn't the way." He lets go and paces the room.

He can't be unsure. It scares me how much I've come to depend on his knowing, his taking charge. I catch his arm as he passes. "Marco." My voice trembles. "If it's not in name only, what happens?" I didn't mean that the way it sounded. I meant what would our lives look like. I need the path before me.

But his face changes, and I think I am seeing the real Marco, the man inside. He wants to make me his wife. "I forget how sheltered you've been."

"Not so much."

He smiles. "So much compared to some dames."

I raise my chin. "I wasn't asking for instructions, only . . . *if* our license was for real, would you want that?" I move close again.

"Cara, don't." His voice is thick in a way I recognize.

I know my power. My fingertips touch his chest, and he clasps them roughly.

"Antonia." His roles are falling away. "There's time to undo that ceremony. Enough rules were broken to invalidate . . ."

I reach behind his neck, bring his face down.

His breath rasps. "Cara mia . . ."

I have made my choice, and he makes his. His mouth is firm, commanding. He will be my match. I feel safe and scared at once. But when he has made me his wife, he murmurs, *"La mia vita ed il mio amore."* *My life and my love.*

"Yes," I whisper. "Yes."

And so she was ready when Lance came for her. Bolstered by the memory of who Marco was, who she was, Antonia rode the wheelchair like a chariot. She might not be able to walk or speak right, but she was not going into the wretched bank like a broken old woman. If Lance wasn't allowed to make her wishes known, she would make them known herself.

But as they neared the doors her chest quaked. *Oh, Marco.* The EKG had shown a strong heart, but it felt like breaking now.

Lance swung her around backward and pushed the door open with his backside, then spun her forward into the bank's lobby. Roman had handled all her bills for so long she couldn't remember the last time she'd been inside. She felt queasy.

Marco, Marco, Marco.

The slender man Lance greeted came forward and shook his hand. He looked as though he would shake hers, too, then gave

311

her a little wave instead. She pinned him with a look that made him straighten his tie and square his shoulders. "So . . ." He indicated the office behind him. "Why don't we step in here."

Lance had explained her request by phone, but this man had to see for himself. This man expected an old woman to leave her sickbed to get something her own husband had left her in his own box. This *banker* could learn some respect.

Lance said, "Since the stroke, my grandmother finds it easier to speak Italian."

"No problem." The man swept his hand to the name plate on his desk. *Emmanuel S. Giordano.* "My grandmother does too."

Lance made a strange face. "Oh."

Why didn't he tell the man what they wanted and get done with it? She grunted.

Lance glanced down, but she didn't want any of his placating smiles. "Bah . . ."

He waved her down with a gentle hand motion. "Hold on, Nonna."

The banker sent an insipid smile. "I know this is a difficult time."

You know nothing, fool. Then she cringed. What was this spiteful spirit? Fear. It was fear.

Lance took out the key. "As I told you on the phone, she wants to open this safe deposit box."

"Yes, I've checked that hers is a valid signature. The original holder included her name with his and stipulated her access to the contents in his will. However, I have no record of her accessing the box upon his death or since."

"Well, she'd like to now." Lance held out her identification with the key.

"I'll need to make sure that is her intent, Mr. Michelli." Emmanuel Giordano turned to her. "Mrs. Michelli, how are you today?"

She said nothing. What did he think, she could discuss the weather?

Lance cleared his throat. "You'd better stick with yes or no questions."

The man nodded and spoke louder as though her hearing had suddenly worsened. "Mrs. Michelli, do you wish to access your safe deposit box?"

She answered.

The man raised his brows, rocked back on his heel, and turned slightly. He spoke through the side of his mouth. "Did she just say what I think she said?"

What? What did I say?

Lance answered, "It means yes. The stroke has jumbled her words a little, but she knows what she means." At the man's skeptical look, Lance said, "Ask her something obvious."

Mr. Giordano said, "Is this the Fourth

313

Federal Savings Bank?"

She had no idea what bank Lance had driven her to, but she answered.

Lance rubbed his mouth.

"I'm sorry, I can't tell anything by that. She's saying the same thing, but . . ."

"Ask her something false."

Antonia scowled. What was this? She had told him what she wanted.

"Is . . . this pen green?" He held up a shiny black and gold pen.

What did he think, she was stupid? "No."

Again the man's eyes widened. He turned to Lance.

"That one means no. It's like a code. She knows what she's saying; it's just different words."

What was he talking about, different words?

Mr. Giordano pocketed the pen and continued to question her. Was Frank Sinatra the president? Were there seven days in a week? On and on. She gave her answers more vehemently each time. *Let me into the box, idiot!*

Lance put a hand on her shoulder. "I think that's enough."

Mr. Giordano looked apologetic but firm. "I'm legally required to protect the integrity of that box and its contents. I need to question her without you, to make

314

sure there's no coercion."

Lance bent. "Is that okay, Nonna? I'll step out and you answer a few more questions?"

She didn't want him to leave. He was her strength, her joy. More so even than her son, her Roman. Lance was her heart. So like Marco. *Marco!*

"Just for a minute." He kissed her cheek. "A few more questions." He stepped away and went out.

Nonna returned her gaze to the banker. What did the S in his name stand for? Samuele? Salvatore? Sebastiani?

"Mrs. Michelli, are you being forced to open your box against your will?"

What did he think, her grandson was trash? "No. No."

The banker moistened his lips. "Do you want to access the contents of the box?"

"Yes, I told you, yes!"

The man's face twisted into a grimace.

She slapped her good hand on the armrest. "Yes. Yes!"

He drew himself up, formed a plastic sort of smile, and motioned Lance back into the office. "Although the vocabulary is . . . uncertain, I believe the intent is clear."

Oh, grazie. *A mule could have understood.*

He talked around her, but she didn't care. She needed to get out of the bank.

She closed her eyes and pictured Arthur Jackson, smug and suave, Papa like a shadow behind him. She hated banks, hated bankers. Even the smell of money conjured awful thoughts. Why had she come?

They entered a metal room with walls made out of drawers. The banker used one key and Lance gave him the other. What was in the box the banker took from its slot and carried to the small closet where he left her and Lance alone?

Lance put the box on the table and looked at her. "Are you sure?"

She closed her eyes. *Per piacere, Dio.* She opened them. "Yes." She knew the sounds coming out were not right. She didn't care. Lance knew her heart.

But he didn't open the box. He knelt beside her and clasped her hand. "Don't do this for me, Nonna."

What was he talking about? "O . . . pen." There. That had come out right.

He stood up, lifted the metal lid, and took out the only thing there: a bound set of pages. He looked at it a long moment, then set it in her lap. Her throat squeezed. The front page said only *La mia vita ed il mio amore.*

Chapter Seventeen

To understand the end, I must start at the beginning, the day it all began. It was warm and beautiful in Sonoma, with a clarity of sky I had seldom seen. The earth smelled rich and reminded me of the farms in the Bronx, north of Manhattan, though yours bore vines nestled in pale rolling hills with mounds of scrubby oak.

Birds sang as I approached the house that looked more Italian than its neighbors. It was old, but well tended at a time when paint was a luxury, and tin and cardboard roofed with burlap could be called a home, when people considered themselves lucky for the tenement room that sheltered their whole family, when hot water and a latrine meant a step up in the world.

The people who lived there were not among the quarter population without income or resources. But I already knew that. As I approached you, idling away your time on the swing, I remembered who I was supposed to be and spoke accordingly. "I'm looking for Vittorio Shepard. This the place?" I'd put a bit of swagger in my tone, and perhaps that explained the bite of your reply.

"Vittorio Shepard is my papa. What do you want from him?"

Those were your first words to me, and soon I would ask myself that very thing. I met your nonno, Quillan Shepard, there on the porch, but not your papa. Vittorio, I had come to know from watching and from the information I had regarding him. I told you none of that, because secrecy was my life; my purpose, deception.

In the closet at the bank, Antonia gasped. *Secrecy was my life; my purpose, deception.* More pain, fresh undiscovered wounds. How could there be more? What part of her was left unmarred?

"Nonna?"

She opened her eyes to Lance. He had not seen the page, did not know the words that had waited in that box since Marco's death. *My purpose, deception.*

Not Marco. Her head shook side to side.

"Are you okay?"

She couldn't answer. Something inside screamed, *"No!"*

"We can take the pages with us and put the box back. Mr. Giordano is waiting to lock it up."

Yes, yes, Mr. Giordano, important banker, keeper of secrets. She nodded to her grandson, doing his best for her as always. For a moment she wanted to lock the pages back up as well. But they held Marco's words. *Marco!* And she couldn't do it.

Lance closed the metal box and returned it to Mr. Giordano, then wheeled her out as she clutched the pages close that would surely break her heart.

Pop met them at the door. He must have come home for lunch and seen them from the window. Lance searched fast for a reason he might have taken Nonna out, but Pop didn't ask. As Lance took the packet from her lap, Pop lifted her from the wheelchair and started up the stairs.

Some buildings of the time had elevators, but not theirs. Lance had carried her down and planned to get her back upstairs without anyone the wiser, since his sisters and their kids had gone to the zoo. He couldn't help that the neighborhood, the Bronx, and the greater Manhattan area had probably all noted and remarked on their trip by now. But he'd planned to have her back in bed before the family was onto them.

He looked at the pages he held, but didn't read them. The words on the front page were for Nonna alone, though one look at her face as she'd read had scared him enough to get her out of there quick. He just had to trust they were doing the right thing.

He folded the unwieldy chair and leaned it against the wall, then followed Pop up the stairs. Nonna looked like a doll in Pop's arms, and she'd been almost weightless when Lance carried her down. He hadn't realized how frail she'd become. Somehow she'd grown old.

Lance slipped the pages behind the lamp on her nightstand as Pop tucked her into bed instead of seating her in the chair by the window. Their trip to the bank had exhausted her. He should have waited another day or two, but the moment he explained the situation, she'd wanted it over with. Once her mind was set, Nonna was never one to procrastinate.

Pop straightened, rubbing his neck. "You want a beer?"

Lance hid his surprise. "Don't you have to get back?"

"Momma's feeling lousy, so I stayed home today."

They'd been there the whole time. So much for getting one by the family.

"A headache?"

Pop nodded. Momma's migraines were one of the only things that kept Pop from work, even though he was past the age of retirement.

Lance didn't want to explain more than he had to. But maybe it wasn't right keeping them all in the dark. If he went back to Sonoma, the rest of them needed to know what was up with Nonna. "Sure, Pop. I'll have a beer."

They went down and his father took two cans of Bud from the refrigerator. They sat in the kitchen across from each other at the table with the yellow daisy cloth Lucy had embroidered in home economics. A half carafe of coffee soured on the hot plate since someone had forgotten to turn it off, and the miniature TV played mutely in the corner.

Pop fizzed open his beer and palmed the can. "You gonna marry that girl?"

"Haven't gotten that far." He had two strikes already but didn't need to go into that with Pop.

His father took a long draught, even though it was early in the day for beer and Pop was not a hard drinker. Maybe he needed bolstering to meet his youngest son across the table. He rested the can on the cloth. "You ought to think about it."

"Okay."

"Someone else can make you different, you know."

"Different how?" Lance opened his beer, and mist from the aluminum mouth whispered *smart, responsible, worthy.*

"When you got someone who believes in you, you believe in yourself."

Lance raised his eyes from the can. Pop's brow had cragged in the last few years; the hair had silvered at his temples and in the cleft of his unshaved chin. He still had the athletic build he'd passed on to Tony, big hands, hard and generous.

The brown eyes were neither hard nor generous, but at least they weren't blank. Pop looked straight at him. "It's time to grow up."

"I'm trying, Pop."

"There's no try. There's only do."

Lance took a swallow, and the biting malt flavor filled his mouth.

"You stop running now." Pop crowded the table. "It's time to stop."

Lance held the gaze with difficulty.

Pop's hand tightened on the can. "You can't bring Tony back."

Lance jerked away and closed his eyes. Pop's chair creaked as he sat back and waited. Finally Lance said, "What do you want, Pop?"

His father sighed, because what he wanted, he could never have again. "This is about you. Where you should be; what you should do."

Lance rubbed his chin in a slow arc, up and down with the ball of his thumb. Where he should be and what he should do was what this week in Belmont was all about. He'd brought Rese there as a catalyst between his past and his future. Already they'd spent more time than he'd expected. Even though the next week was free of reservations, he had thought they'd be back, getting their heads into business, not still entangled in the Michelli dramas that sucked him in as though he'd never stepped away.

He made his decision. "It won't be here."

"Where, then?"

"Sonoma. Nonna's place."

Pop's brow creased. "What place?"

So Lance told him. Conchessa, the villa, the cellar where he found Nonno Quillan, the letter. "Could Nonno Marco have been a federal agent? Undercover?"

"I don't know." Pop unclenched the can with a tinny bang. "He was . . ." He chewed his lower lip, then drained the rest of the beer and tossed the can to the wastebasket in the corner. It banged off the wall and dropped in. "Maybe he was undercover."

"But he was a cop, and everyone knew it. You're not undercover in an NYPD uniform."

"That was later. Before that — But you wouldn't know much before that."

"Much of what, Pop? Talk to me."

"Before you were born. When I was young he did something else, something that took him away for weeks at a time. Months. He'd maybe drop home for a night or two." Pop frowned. "And sometimes . . . sometimes it didn't seem even he knew who he was."

"I don't remember that."

"Momma said he had to travel for his job, but there was one time when she said he was in Chicago that I saw him outside the school watching. He was dressed like a bum, and he watched me all the way to the trolley."

Lance searched his pop's face. "Why would he watch? Why not talk to you, ride with you?"

"It was like he stood guard, but didn't want me to know he was there." Pop brought his thumb to his teeth, nipped off a hangnail, and spat it out. "I asked him about it later, and he made a joke. 'You think your pop's a bum?' Then he wrestled me down, and when we were done playing I wasn't sure I'd seen him at all."

Nonno might have wanted to be sure his son got safely to the trolley, but why the disguise? Unless he was involved in something that might have endangered his son, and he couldn't blow his cover by openly approaching him.

"Later I wondered if he went off on

binges, you know, drinking or something. But . . . that never seemed right either."

"Could he have been so deep under that even Nonna didn't know?"

Pop shrugged. "Those days, you crossed the wrong person and not only you but your whole family could end up in the river."

Pop was talking the stuff of movies, the Corleones and Scarface. But Lance thought of the dossiers collected in Vittorio's cellar. "You think Nonno infiltrated the mob?"

"Not the mob, you idiot."

And then it hit him. "Camorra? But that was his bunch."

Pop scowled. "That was never his bunch. Naples isn't Sicily. The Camorra served no one but themselves."

"So Nonno . . ."

Pop's fist opened flat on the table. "I don't know, okay? He could have gotten in with his connections."

Lance had known there were ties. Momma had joked about marrying into the "family." He couldn't imagine Nonno involved in Camorra business, but could he have lived a double life?

"Wouldn't that be worse if they found out?"

Pop shrugged. "Dead is dead. I guess they never found out."

So what did that have to do with Arthur

Jackson? Hands down he wasn't Camorra, though the bank could have been a front. Or it could have been completely unrelated.

"The question is . . ." Pop looked toward the ceiling as though he could see his mother upstairs. "Why did she take this to you?"

"Only one with nothing important to do." Why did he hang the bait out there like that?

But Pop didn't take it. He studied him a long moment, then said, "She trusts you."

Surprised, Lance sighed. "Don't know how she'll take my telling all this."

"She's a good one for secrets."

"I don't think she knew — about Nonno, I mean. She didn't take the news so good."

Pop's brow furrowed. "That's what set her off?"

Lance sagged. "I didn't think. I just told her what I'd found."

Muttering under his breath, Pop stood up and walked to the sink. He leaned heavily on his palms, head hanging, then said, "Stuff happens. You couldn't know."

Lance's throat tightened. Absolution? From Pop? "What do we do now?"

His father shook his head. "You think I'm God, or what?" There was enough of an edge to his words to show they were through. But it was more than they'd had in a long time.

Rese looked up from the trim piece along the floor when Lance came in. "Well?"

"We got in."

"And?"

"All that was in there was a letter or journal to Nonna. I don't know why Nonno didn't just give it to her."

Because that would be obvious and logical. It presumed people did what others expected them to. "What did it say?"

"I don't know. The front page had the phrase they used for each other and no one else. *La mia vita ed il mio amore.*"

The words sounded lovely coming out of his mouth, especially the way his voice softened, lilting as he pronounced them. But she didn't know what they meant.

"My life and my love," he answered before she asked. Then he looked down at what she was doing.

"It has a warp that's causing the detachment from the wall."

"You don't have to fix it."

Maybe not, but while he was off solving Nonna's problems, and Rico was out searching for Star, she had to do something. "I found some tools in your closet downstairs. Screws will hold better than the tacking nails, and with all these layers of paint, they'll embed. A little touch-up and they should all but disappear."

His mouth pulled. "Bored?"

She sat back on her heels. "Rico had a guess where Star might be."

Lance glanced out the open window forming the warm block of sunlight on the floor where she sat and allowing something like a breeze. "Did he say where?"

"No." Maybe she should have asked, but Rico hadn't looked open to questions. "He was strung pretty tight."

Lance frowned. "Did Chaz go with him?"

She shook her head. "He got called in to work."

Lance's brow tightened. "Does she usually stay close? Like in the neighborhood?"

"She could be anywhere. She's good at hiding." She'd mastered the art of deflection. "A regular escape artist." *Then why hadn't she gotten out before people came after her? Why did she slip away after the fact to cry on Rese's shoulder?* She shook her head. "Even if he has guessed where she went, I doubt he'll find her. Star's a free bird, Lance. There really is nothing holding her here."

Lance hung his thumbs in his jeans and pressed his shoulder blades together. "How long's Rico been gone?"

Rese checked her watch. "Almost an hour."

He let his breath out slowly. "What are the chances she's alone?"

Except for when she shut herself into her room to sleep or weep for days, Star hated being alone. "I'd guess she's with someone. But that's no crime."

"Yet. Rico's a street kid. He handles things his way."

She set down the screwdriver and rested her palms on her thighs. "He's not a criminal."

"Anyone can get there with the right provocation." Lance leaned a hip to the window frame. "I'm not sure what kind of hold Star has on him, but it isn't normal."

A shiver went through her. When Lance said things like that they were totally believable. And there was something about Star that entrapped and inflamed the guys she got involved with. Maury had been wrong to get violent, but Rese guessed the time with Star was scarring to him as well. And as Lance said, people could be pushed past their limits.

His head jerked back toward the open window at the sound of Rico's bike, unmistakable over the other traffic, not too close, but fast and angry. The roar of the poorly muffled engine was followed by a raw screech of brakes and scraping metal.

Lance braced himself across the glass to see the intersection, then launched off the frame and ran for the door.

Rese scrambled up and tried to see what he had, but people were gathering at the intersection. She hurried after Lance, down the stairs and out to the street. At the corner Lance crouched beside Rico, who was spitting blood and curses. Relief rushed in before the smell of burnt rubber and blood hit. Then the sight of Rico's arm paralyzed her with blurred images of another blood-soaked arm, Dad's screams and hers.

On his knees, holding Rico by the shoulders, Lance pulled his phone from his pocket and thrust it at her. "Call for help, Rese."

Rico swore. She didn't move.

"Rese."

Pulse pounding in her ears, she took the phone and forced herself to think. 9-1-1. Red and blue lights; Dad carrying her out. Red and blue lights; Dad bleeding in her arms. Bleeding to death.

"What is the nature of your emergency?"

"There's been an accident." The voice sounded firm and controlled. It took a moment to realize it was hers. She described the scene and Rico's condition as well as she could tell. Was he alert — yes. Moving — yes.

She searched the intersection and gave the street names. As she finished, the faces around her came into focus. Old and young, dark and light and in between. "They're coming," she told Lance, then squatted down, cradling the phone in her lap. "What happened?"

"Guy ran the stop. The bike's brakes were soft."

She closed her eyes, recalling too well Lance's speed on that same bike — with her. "Did he hit his head?" She'd have asked Rico but he was gritting his teeth in pain.

"He knew enough to ride it down."

"Ride it down?"

"An experienced biker never separates in a crash. That's where the head injuries happen, when the driver lets go and tumbles. Rico stayed with the bike to the ground."

And it looked like his arm made first contact. The air filled with a wailing siren. Her stomach rolled. Closer and louder. She forced her mind back to Rico. Friction from the pavement seemed to have cauterized the blood, or maybe that was how arms bled when the artery had not been severed. She gagged back the memory of her own slippery attempts to staunch arterial flow.

Louder. Closer.

Rese forced herself to look at Rico, to realize that his life was not pouring out onto the pavement, even if bone protruded from his arm and the pain must be awful. The scream of the siren set her teeth on edge. The squeal and sigh of the fire engine's brakes and the flashing lights registered, though she kept her face averted, tasting the exhaust that clung to the air.

Lance got out of the way as the emergency personnel took over. He drew her back against him while Rico argued about being laid flat on a backboard. More sirens. Rico turned to the police officers arriving on the scene and spoke in Spanish.

"What did he say?"

Lance said softly, "He wants them to find the jerk who ran him off the road, so he can slit his gullet."

Rese looked over her shoulder. Lance was not making it up. "He's okay, then."

"His arm looks bad."

It wasn't pretty, but the hand was still attached. As with Chaz's friend Ubaiah, it was all a matter of perspective.

Lance had wrapped her around the waist and held her against him as the officer continued his investigation. If Rico had made his own stop here at the intersection, his speed could not have been that high. But what she'd heard from the window hadn't sounded like deceleration. More likely they'd both ignored the stop sign.

More sirens. An ambulance had been called. Couldn't they just walk him to the hospital? Put him in a cruiser and drive the few blocks? But she knew they'd take no chances with a possible spine or neck injury. Red and blue light slashed across her vision. Lance's hold tightened, and maybe that was why it got hard to breathe. She couldn't avoid seeing the stretcher without ignoring Rico. So she made herself watch as they raised him up on the backboard to the gurney.

She could almost feel the mask pressed to her face as they strapped it over Rico's, smell the sweet oxygenated air he breathed. It could have been her getting closed into the ambulance. It could have been Lance. But she didn't go light in the head. Everything grew shockingly clear, thoughts linking like a chain being forged. Helpful adversity. If Star hadn't left, Rico would not have gone looking. If Rico hadn't crashed, she and Lance might have taken the bike out. Soft brakes. Soft . . . brakes.

Was there a reason for this accident that might be no accident at all? Was there a meaning and purpose behind every bad thing — no, behind *everything?*

Chapter Eighteen

Lance waited for Rese to lose it, but she didn't. As the ambulance took Rico to St. Barnabas, he loosened his hold. "Are you okay?"

She turned in his arms. "Yes."

He studied her face, then let her go as his own fear calmed. The professionals had charge of Rico, and there was only one immediate thing to do. From the officer in the intersection, Lance asked permission to get the bike out of the street.

The damage didn't seem irreparable, and Rico would want to try. He had done the original chopper modification — on a Kawasaki no less — stripping off everything extraneous. And he'd done all the repairs over the years that kept it running. Lance made no attempt to start it, though. If he even thought of driving the thing, Rese would have his head.

She came up beside him. "What are you doing?"

"Walking it back."

Her mouth dropped open. "You can't think Rico would drive that again."

He walked it around the parked cars. "Might not be possible." But Rico would give it his best shot.

"He could have been killed. We could have."

Not surprising she'd drawn that conclusion. He shouldn't have mentioned the brakes. Rico was probably gunning it, rolling or ignoring the stop — traffic signs being more suggestion than law in his right mind. Angry or disappointed, Rico got crazy, took chances. But pointing that out wouldn't help. Rese could easily attribute the same to him.

"We weren't killed, and neither was Rico." He'd saved a head injury, riding the skid, but his arm was bad. It would have been better to break a leg, both even. Rico's livelihood was in his arms, and more than that, his identity. If he couldn't drum . . . Lance shook his head. *No way, Lord.* No more grief for people he loved. Quota filled. When they reached the yard, he put the bike into the enclosure.

Rese pressed a hand between her eyebrows. "He could have brain damage."

"He wasn't hit. There was no collision."

"He made contact with the street!"

It was catching up to her. "He's all right, Rese." They would do a CT scan or MRI to be sure, but Rico would be fine. *He'll be fine, Lord.* Because Rico was like a brother, and Lance was not losing another brother. *No way. No way!*

It was catching up to him too.

"Promise you'll never drive it again."

Lance looked from her to the offensive machine. *It* being Rico's chopper, he said, "I promise," and before she could broaden the demand added, "We need to get to the hospital." That thought tightened his stomach like a cramp. "I'll find a car. Rico won't feel like walking home."

Did he really think they'd put on a Band-Aid, give him a sucker, and send him home? Best case: a cast and sling, and Rico immobile was a scary thought. He functioned in motion. He thought in rhythm. He breathed in beats.

They took Sofie's Neon to the hospital. Word had spread, and someone would have certainly called Rico's mother by now, but Lance didn't see her. Rico's older sister, Gabriella, came by, but no one else from his immediate family, and as the hours dragged on and Rico went from the emergency room into surgery, even Gabbie didn't stay. No matter. He'd have the rest of the neighborhood there if the hospital would let them in.

Rico could handle pain, but judging by his swearing before the adrenaline set in, his concern was the immediate and long-term effects of the injury. Losing use of his arm would be death to Rico. Lance felt a tightening inside, like the inner girding before a fight. *Not this time, Lord.*

But the first information they got was good. Sprains and contusions, but no internal head or spine injury. He'd bitten his tongue pretty bad, but no internal bleeding. So now they waited for word on the arm. Rico must have reached down to control the skid as they'd done dirt racing. But pavement was not as forgiving.

Lance kept a running conversation with God, some of it supplication. Rese had paged through everything from *Golf Digest* to *Sunset,* and she wasn't even a reader. Some trip this was turning out to be.

Momma came in with Sofie. "How bad is he?"

"You better start cooking."

She sank into a chair. "I thought he only broke his arm."

"It is his arm, but it's bad."

She shook her head. "And him with no insurance and no job."

Momma was a good one for pointing out the worst. "Rico has a job; it's just not nine-to-five. And it takes both arms to do it."

Momma pressed her palms to her cheeks as though it just occurred to her that Rico couldn't drum one-handed.

"And don't make this worse for Rico.

When he comes out, don't talk about money or the future. It's going to be hard enough not moving his arm for a while."

"All right. Okay. You think I don't know?"

She might know, but she always did it anyway. In case someone wasn't fully aware of the pit they were in, she described just how wide and deep and dark it was. But there was love and concern behind it; Rico knew that much.

After a while, Sofie stood up. "I need to eat something." The urgency in her voice was no doubt a hypoglycemic reaction to going too long without. If she'd been working or studying, she might not have eaten all day.

Momma jumped up. "I've got meatballs in the oven."

"Since when?" Lance winced.

"Since I put them there. You come in for a sandwich after."

He bobbed his chin. "Yeah, okay, Momma."

She turned. "Rese, you come home now."

He glanced to see if she'd caught the destination and realized the significance. Only family went home.

Rese met his glance but seemed more concerned about leaving him than going with Momma — another sign that their coffee chat must have gone better than

Rese let on. She'd come upstairs and stipulated right up front that she was not learning the two-sided break with a man wrap. But she hadn't been traumatized.

He squeezed her hand. "Go ahead. I'll stay with Rico awhile when he wakes up."

Not long after they left, he was admitted to the post-op recovery room. He hooked fingers with Rico's good hand. "How you doing, 'mano?"

Rico nodded, then looked down at the arm strapped in place across his chest. There was no cast, just bandages from the elbow to the wrist. A nurse brought in a cup of ice chips and spooned some into Rico's mouth, then gave Lance the cup. When she left, he said, "What say we make a break for it?"

Rico smiled, but it turned into a grimace, and he closed his eyes. Maybe not yet.

After a while, the surgeon appeared and explained the reconstruction; the wrist being the worst of it, pinned in several places, and the rod and screws to secure the fractured ulna he'd seen protruding from Rico's arm. That much metal was almost bionic. "Brunhilda's wand for you at the airports, buddy."

Rico cracked a grin, then faded back out. Maybe he'd be up for jokes tomorrow — or not. Lance left him to get settled into a room for the night, then met everyone at Momma's, where the main course was how much worse the accident could have been, served with sides of other close calls, especially his and even Tony's. Misfortune bred misfortune in Momma's kitchen until Lance was choking on it.

How could so many bad things happen to one family? Of course the refrain was, "It could have been worse. Could have been killed like poor Tony. Such a waste." And tears would salt the memory.

He had to get out of there. "Rico's gonna be fine," he said. Then came all the shoulder-patting, head-stroking assurances for Lance, who was taking it too hard.

Chaz would sprinkle it with glory. Must have had angels warding him off the car. What a miracle he didn't hit his head. But Chaz hadn't even heard yet, as far as Lance knew. He'd work late into the night at the fancy Manhattan restaurant that supported half of Jamaica through his long hours and come home none the wiser.

Chaz hadn't prayed through the surgery, hadn't beseeched God to guide the surgeon's hands, to bring order to Rico's bones, to sustain his spirit. Chaz was not in the forest when the tree fell. Which begged the question, where was God? Afar, removed and uncaring? Or hearing every word Lance said and weighing them according to his deeds.

Lance shook himself. What were these thoughts? The God he served, the God he loved was neither of those things. It was his own understanding that fell short. But his understanding had been falling short a long time now.

Bobby and Lou had gone to the ballpark. The kids had long before grown bored with the conversation and crowded the TV in the living room. Either choice did Rico as much good as hashing and rehashing life's misfortunes. He looked at Rese.

She'd been all but silent. She didn't know how to charge into the conversation on top of someone else if necessary, didn't know volume equaled relevance. But that wasn't her mode anyway. Brad said she didn't speak for weeks after her dad's accident. This wasn't anything near that bad, no death or dismemberment. And she was coping. But he had to get her out of there. He needed out of there.

He stood up, kissed Momma, Sofie, and Monica, Lucy's cheek damp with tears — she was the crier, nicknamed The Faucet in his less kind moments. Pop brooded at his end of the table, and Lance avoided it. The rest of them found comfort speaking Tony's name, keeping him present, keeping him real. Not Pop.

Lance laced fingers with Rese as they

climbed the stairs and entered the empty apartment. No Chaz, Rico, or Star. Only the two of them, a situation that would have excited him, spurred thoughts better not acted upon. Thankfully his mood was too dark for temptation, and Rese was surely craving solitude. He kissed her cheek as he would his sisters' and closed the bedroom door behind her.

They'd hardly talked in the hospital, said not a word at Momma's. He didn't know what she was thinking, what she was feeling, yet he seemed acutely aware of all the other pain in the world. Pop's loss throbbed in his heart. Momma's fears entangled his thoughts, her need to keep them close, as though she could stop any others from injury and death. Didn't she know they were pawns?

Job's entire family had been crushed in one blow so that God could watch what he would do. Lance gripped his head. *Stop it. Get out.* He'd felt darkness like this before. God's ways were above his. He couldn't ascribe human motivations to the Lord. And where did Rico's choices come in? Things got messy when people were involved.

Dressed in jersey pajamas, Rese came out of the bedroom and joined him on the couch, tucking her foot up under her. "Are you all right?"

All right? Now that was an expansive question. "Just thinking." He hadn't expected comfort. He'd thought her own fears and memories would occupy her, and guiltily avoided addressing them. Enough grief had been dredged for one night.

She drew her other knee up and held it with her arms. "If you could be anything in the world, what would it be?"

Of all the things she might have said, he hadn't expected that. But she'd turned her frank and darling face to him and obviously expected an answer. "Besides partners with you?"

"Anything."

"Shortstop for the Yankees."

She rolled her eyes. "Typical."

"I suppose you've got better?"

"A whale."

"What?" He laughed.

"Why not?" She rested her chin on her knee. "Think how peaceful it would be under all that water, how simple."

"Little stressed out?"

She shrugged.

"Rese Barrett a whale. Boggles the mind."

She straightened. "Mom and I pretended all kinds of animals."

"Ah yes, the earthworm."

"More often it was flying things. Or mermaids. Underwater creatures." She released a slow breath. "Those were good times."

He circled her in his arm. "I'm glad." He loved that she kept looking for the good in something that had hurt so much. As he should. As he used to.

She rested her head against him. "If Rico had died, would you still love God?"

His heart lurched. Thoughts of Rico unresponsive, unbreathing had filled his mind as he ran toward the corner. Gone in an instant. One wrong choice — or simply God's will. "I can't think about that."

She nodded. She would leave it alone, but then he said, "I don't think I'm capable of hating God. Some people get angry and turn away, but that would be like turning my back on Rico, or you. It's just not in me."

"So why do you hit the road when things get tough?"

He thought about it, wanting her to understand. "It seems like running, and I do need miles and speed and distance. But it's really searching, trying to get closer. It sounds dumb, I know."

"It's not dumb, Lance. It's how you are. You have to be close."

"Sometimes I need so much to know why, to see how, to understand *what* God's thinking! I want to climb inside His skin." He didn't expect her to get it. He hadn't found anyone who did. Not even Chaz experienced the desire to grab God by the ankle and wrestle.

Lance nestled Rese into his neck, wondering what she'd do if he kissed her as he wanted to. She yawned. In another moment she would get up and close the door between them. And so he seized the moment he had, and her mouth. Sweetness. Killer sweetness.

Lance kissed her as though he might never have the chance again, transferring his worry for Rico and everything else pent up inside onto her lips, and Rese responded with fervor. She'd intended comfort, distraction maybe. But now she understood his need for closeness, his desire to touch, to connect, to be one with another being. *Yes.*

It might not be her natural inclination, or maybe it was. Maybe it just took Lance to make *her* real. Desire surged. Time no longer mattered. She'd never felt this way before, so totally consumed.

Lanced owned her, but he pulled back, groaning. "Off the couch. Go to bed, Rese, or I'm not responsible."

The shock of it caught her cold until she saw the strain that once again sent a tremor to his hands. He looked up as she stood. "I'm sorry. But you're more than a number on my wall. I want to do this right."

She got the point, but even now she'd give in if he reached for her.

He stuck his fingers in his hair. "I shouldn't have started it. I'm sorry."

"We've been here before." The chemistry had set in immediately, fueling her initial animosity, but too soon becoming an adhesive no solvent she knew could break.

He nodded. "Take a shovel to my skull, will you?"

"I'm past that."

He smiled wryly and took her hand, studying it with his eyes and fingers. "I'm in a bad way here, Rese."

"Me too." She couldn't believe she'd admitted it, but he already knew.

He brought her knuckles to his lips. "Please go." But he didn't release her.

"That requires disconnection."

"I'm working up to it."

She drew a shaky breath. "You better work fast."

He groaned again and let her go. "And lock the door," he called when she reached her room.

She did, but she didn't lock the bathroom door, and she wondered if he'd try it and if she hoped he would.

Chapter Nineteen

Grief is a coat you put on and off, wearing it only until it has warmed the chill of loss, but not so long as to take the edge from memory.

I would write that in my diary if it had not been lost in the struggle. I would put it in ink to remind me of this time, this aching that is both sickness and life. Something inside me wants to hope, but how can I when everything I know is changed?

Standing beside the road, arms crossed, I wait. Marco's car has broken down again. It's the hard miles, he says, and I know it well. Marco appears unfazed, but if he were honest he might wish he'd never come to Sonoma. A man with important business, strapped with a wife people want to kill. I promise myself he won't regret it, but is that even possible?

He laughs. "You're going to worry a dent in your forehead." He climbs out from under the hood, sleeves rolled, hands dirty. He rubs them with a rag, then motions me over. His arms are the only sanity I know.

"What are we doing, Marco?"

"Climbing back in and praying this works."

Turning aside the larger question, he tosses the rag into the trunk.

He smells oily when we get in, and I know he's running out of patience. If the car doesn't start, will we stay there for good, building a hut from branches and leaves, begging from people passing by? Silly. But worlds of possibilities gape before me; things I'd never considered possible I've now seen with my own eyes. I could not have guessed I'd be here with Marco Michelli and no one else anywhere who matters.

I have lost my home, my family, my peace. Why not my mind? Is that any more unbelievable than Papa . . . No. I still can't think of it. And my Nonno, my dear, dear Nonno. It isn't right. It isn't just. God . . . isn't just.

And yet there is Marco. I tell my heart to make an end of grief and accept what good has come. Another thing I would write is that my heart does not listen very well.

Rese opened when Lance tapped her

door, but it was morning and he'd recovered — mostly. He pulled a side smile. "I've got bread and cheese and peppers and sausage."

She bunched her fingers into her hair and met his gaze with her sleepy face. "Are you bribing me?"

"Bribing would be *sfogliatelli* and *trota al vino rosso*."

"Oh." She yawned and stretched, adorably kittenish and totally unaware of her impact.

"Help yourself, okay? I've got to get Rico before the hospital charges another day."

"That was major surgery. They're discharging him already?"

"He's discharging himself." Rico had called at the crack of dawn, half-coherent but determined. Lance shrugged. "None of us is flush right now."

"But —"

He bent in and kissed her sleep-soft mouth. "I won't be long."

He borrowed Momma's Fiat and got to the hospital as the doctor was declining liability if Rico left her care prematurely.

"I absolve you, lady; now get me out of here." Rico sank weakly back against the pillows until the nurse brought the discharge papers. His left hand was as dexterous as his right had been, but his signature looked shaky as he signed the responsibility-for-payment forms, muttering curses under his breath. When all the bills were in it would be ugly, and he hadn't had anything big or steady since Lance broke up the band.

They had a sweet setup in their living arrangements, but none of them wanted to take advantage of Pop. And as soon as things were certain in Sonoma, Lance would be out altogether. Rico would have to do something, even if it was running sound for other bands. He'd done it before, and people knew he could. But it would eat him alive to watch someone else with the sticks.

Lance doubted Rico was thinking that far ahead as he made it to the living room chair and sank like a ship. Chaz had completed his second job's deliveries and met them at the bottom of the stairs. Now he walked around behind Rico, placing both hands on his head, eyes closed. Lance had prayed as they waited yesterday, but Rico took the laying on of hands better from Chaz. Lance could hug the man's neck, but anything super-spiritual . . . fageddabout-it. Rico knew all too well his warts and blemishes.

He sat down beside Rese on the couch, trying not to recall last night's electricity — easier done in the daytime with Chaz and Rico than alone with her in the night. They needed to get a handle on things, where they stood with each other and the rest of the world. But right now the rest of the world was pressing so close he could hardly breathe.

He wasn't sure yet that he was through with Nonna, and Rico would need help for the next few days at least. He looked across to Rico's bruised gaze. "Chopper needs some work."

Rico sank back and grinned. "Yeah."

Rese looked from one to the other and shook her head. She might never understand, but that was okay.

So what if she'd never heard of Bloomingdale's? Rese did not consider that a crisis, but Monica gaped. She had come down with brownies for Rico — some with finger holes where Nicky had tested their texture and durability — and one thing led to another until Rese had revealed her ignorance and Monica pounced.

Lance said not one word of protest when his sister recruited Lucy, left Doria with their cumulative kids, and shanghaied her onto the train. Maybe he wanted time with Rico — who was not in a good way — but she suspected he thought this beneficial to her general development.

Flanking her, the sisters talked over everyone else including the automated voice at each stop informing riders, *This is a Manhattan-bound two train. Stand clear of the closing doors.*

"So Monica says you do construction?"

Rese jumped.

Lucy flipped her coarse ponytail over her shoulder and caught Rese squarely in her myopic gaze. They must have exhausted the rundown of each kid, every lousy teacher, and all their husbands' gripes that she had successfully tuned out.

"Renovation. I tear it down first."

Lucy shared a glance with Monica. "And your pop got you into it?"

Obviously Monica had filled her in on the relevant details, so why did she need to hear it again? "I don't do it anymore. I sold the company." She paused while the commuters exited and took their seats. "The crew's not happy about that, but it's not my problem."

"You ran the business?" Lucy shifted on the slick blue plastic bench to make room for a pierced and braided man who outweighed her twice over. He plopped down and jived to the beat on his headphones.

"Technically, I was in charge of the crew, and Brad was in charge of the sites." It should have been the other way around. She had the technical expertise and gut instincts; Brad owned the guys. "He did answer to me, but he could act autonomously." The source of much friction.

"And you liked that work?"

Rese nodded. "I liked the work; I didn't always like the crew. They could be really obnoxious." Why was she telling them this? But the rapt looks on their faces led her on as she described the pranks, the insolence, Brad's competitive attitude. She told them more than even Star knew, but not what she'd told Lance, not the incident with Sam and Charlie.

Monica's face had taken on frank admiration, but Lucy said, "Why did you sell it?"

Rese looked away. "It was too hard after Dad died."

"Oh." Lucy squeezed her hand. "I'm sorry."

Rese marveled at the warmth in her tone. Had Star ever expressed honest regret for her without launching into some dramatic pathos? Yet here was Lance's sister, whom she hardly knew, hearing her and caring. She had no idea how to answer.

"Next stop's Penn Station." Monica gathered her purse. "Bloomingdale's has an entrance there." She stood up. "You're gonna love this."

Rese doubted that, but she'd make the best of it. "If we stay here much longer, I'll need a few things."

Both women looked at her as the train lurched to a stop. "Oh, honey," Monica said. "You don't buy from Bloomies. You only shop."

Rese looked from one to the other. What was the point of shopping if you didn't get what you needed? They burst into laughter at her expression, but even in English they were speaking a foreign language.

There is bliss in not knowing what can happen next, not seeing a trial until it's there. Then there is no chance to run.

I will suffocate in Manhattan. What were they thinking, cramming so many people into one place? How can Marco expect me to live, to breathe? His momma's house is no house at all; it is a tunnel of rooms crammed together with other people's rooms, too close and too flimsy. I can hear everything.

"That's life," Marco says and laughs when I whisper in our bedroom, four painted walls with no window and one photograph of Marco's dog and three circus clowns with hardly any teeth.

I pull back from his embrace. "I don't want them to hear."

"They'll think I'm not a good lover."

He laughs harder when I clamp his mouth with my hand. I have learned so much, but I can't imagine learning to live like this. We've been in the house two days, and I have not met his mother. Marco said she must be helping his aunt who has female trouble and was not well when he left.

We don't know for sure because there's no telephone in the tenement, as Marco calls it, since the original house was partitioned into separate dwellings. There is also one bathroom to each floor, and five or six families for each. His pop is laying brick someplace called the Bronx and only comes home on Sundays. He's a good craftsman, Marco says, but has to go where the work is. Times are hard even for those with jobs.

I feel like a sneak coming into a home when no one knows I'm here except the man who brought me. But he will not take it seriously, and some time later I wonder if we have conceived a child in the shadows of this room with his two-legged dog and the clowns looking on. . . .

Antonia opened her eyes to Lance. His face held such tenderness, she thought for a moment she was still in her dreams. His likeness to Marco, not just outside but inside as well, had made him special in a way he always knew but never flaunted. He leaned forward and kissed her cheek, his smile deep in his eyes. "Hey, Nonna."

She blinked and tried for a smile, knowing her words would not be right.

With the washcloth on the bed stand, he wiped the moisture from the side of her mouth. "What can I get you?"

Not "can I," but "*what* can I?" Expecting to serve.

"Macchiato and biscotti? Polenta besciamella?"

She laughed. It was a joke trying to make her needs known.

"I know. I'll surprise you." He squeezed her hand and started to stand.

"L . . . ance." Well, that was better than before. Sleep must have helped.

He eased back down. "What, Nonna?"

She nodded toward the papers.

His gaze softened. "You need something in you first."

"A . . . fter." *Madonna mia.* Her words were back!

Clearly hesitant, but for once obedient, he picked up the papers and held them out. When she shook her head, he raised his brows. "You want me to read?"

"Yes." Now there was the right word. If she'd waited just this long she could have told that banker. No matter. She had what she needed.

He looked at what he held, reluctant, it seemed, to search the secrets within. So much unsaid, but also unforgotten. He

356

frowned. "I think you should get your strength back first."

She waited. He would run out of arguments soon enough. Recalling what came before had prepared her for what would come next. Whatever Marco had to say would not change what had already been. She knew his heart. She knew.

Lance met and held her eyes, then sighing, flipped over the cover page. He read the beginning part that she had read in the bank, and his face mirrored her own initial reaction. "Are you sure?"

She nodded, and he continued aloud:

"My first impression of Vittorio Shepard was intelligence coupled with fundamental gullibility, too much conscience for an inner-circle man, but enough ambition to be useful in spite of it — the exact sort of fellow men like Arthur Jackson looked for.

"When I approached him secretly, Vittorio doubted neither my credentials nor my information. He'd come to suspect the operation already, and faced with the evidence, his concern was for you and for his pop. He would help me, he said, if I assured your safety. From my position, I owed him nothing; his own decisions had put you at risk. Yet I agreed, seeing an opportunity for cover.

"As a suitor, I could meet with Vittorio without raising suspicions. In return, the Bureau would assure your protection — an arrangement neither of us found ideal, but it was workable. He clearly stipulated the restrictions I tried to voice to you once, but neither of us had taken into account your spirit and fortitude. For my part, I was charmed and could only pray it would not interfere with my ability to do my job."

Lance looked up. Could he see her shaking? Even though she knew Marco's heart, she still could not hear his words without pain. The thought that he had deceived her from the start . . . And she felt so weak. *"Bene,"* she said. "I . . . 'll eat."

"Good." Lance set the pages aside, obviously relieved. He lifted and carried her down to the wheelchair, then rolled her into her restaurant and cooked for her. She had thought that he would take the place over, and watching him work in the big old kitchen she wished it still. But his heart was in Sonoma, at the villa she had once called home.

Chapter Twenty

Walking in, Rese smelled something wonderful. They'd grabbed pretzels on the street for lunch — all that Monica could stomach — but that was hardly enough to fuel their marathon of stores and bargain basements.

"Lance is cooking," Lucy said.

"How do you know it's Lance?" Rese followed her toward the inner restaurant entrance.

Lucy shrugged. "It smells good."

"Don't talk about smells." Monica clamped her hands over her mouth and hurried up the stairs.

Lucy pushed open the door for Rese, saying a little reluctantly, "I'll have to deliver Momma from the kids."

Rese went in and set her bags on a corner counter, then walked around the large walk-in refrigerator to find Lance assisting Antonia's fork to her mouth.

He looked over and smiled. "Have fun?"

"Actually . . . yes." Once she realized she didn't have to buy anything in the multilevel city block of a store, she'd merely marveled at the designer outfits, jewelry, perfume, and even allowed Lucy and Monica to have their fun, holding up dresses, whisking scarves around her neck, trying on hats, purses, shoes too spiky to walk in.

"Pull up a chair." Lance motioned toward the dining room.

She hadn't meant to interrupt, but she brought a chair close and gave Antonia a smile, surprised to receive a version of one in return. His grandmother was recovering; Lance must be so relieved.

"Hungry?" He nodded toward the stove.

"It smells great."

Normally he would have gotten up and served her, but his hands were full, and she was glad he didn't. The only time she'd helped herself to Lance's cooking before was when she'd reheated his lasagna for breakfast. That lasagna had been heaven. She went to the stove and lifted a lid.

A shrunken chicken, but the aroma delighted her. "What is it?"

"Quail braised in cognac with polenta besciamella."

Rese found a plate and helped herself to the tiny bird and cheesy cornmeal side dish. "I've never had quail."

"It's Nonna's favorite." He winked. "Got to fatten her up."

The delicate poultry didn't seem as good

a choice as his mother's gravitational spaghetti sauce, but she took a bite and sank into the flavor. "Lance, it's delicious."

He smiled. "I hoped you'd be back before someone claimed the rest."

"I hadn't expected to take so long."

"You don't know my sisters."

She did now. After seeing what they liked at Bloomingdale's, they'd scoured other stores for knockoffs and bargains, and if that didn't show all, Rese didn't know what would. She had gotten some things she needed if they had to stay longer, which was possible since she didn't have any immediate reservations in the next week either. After that it was touch and go. She'd have to get onto the site and see what days were already reserved. She could go back without Lance, but what good was that? She'd have his dog, but not his cooking.

"Have you checked with Michelle lately?"

He nodded. "Baxter's in love."

"The traitor." Every golden shaggy bit of him.

"That's what I said when he fell for you, but at least he's got good taste."

Rese tipped her head. "He groveled at Sybil's feet."

Lance winced. "Okay, he's a pushover."

She tried the polenta and found it a

good companion to the quail. Lance did with food what she strove for in renovation, integrating and complementing each element with another. "I'm glad you got through to Michelle. I haven't been able to do anything but leave messages. She must keep busy." It struck her how little she knew the woman who had heard her confession of faith on the back porch after Evvy's funeral and was now watching out for the inn and keeping Lance's dog.

Lance said, "I also talked to Pop."

Rese stopped chewing. "You did?"

"Yesterday after the bank."

And right before Rico's accident. No wonder he hadn't mentioned it.

He dabbed his grandmother's mouth. "What do you think of that, Nonna? Me and Pop, man to man."

She nodded, warmth filling her eyes.

Rese swallowed. "What did he say?"

"Basically . . . grow up." He set aside the finished plate and fixed his gaze on Antonia. "I told him about Sonoma."

Antonia stiffened.

Rese did too. "Lance . . ." It came out under her breath. Even she knew Antonia had kept all of that between the two of them alone. In a family that shared everything, she had kept the things Lance learned a secret — until now.

He took Antonia's hands. "When I leave,

they've got to know what you're dealing with. It's too much for you to handle alone."

Of course. He'd said the same thing to her, *"You can't face everything alone."* His nature was communal, his first reaction to share the burden. He didn't understand that some things could only be faced alone. And by the looks of it, Antonia didn't want to hear it any more than Rese had. Even if it was true.

They locked eyes and sat in stubborn silence, until Lance said in a soft voice, "Forgive me?"

Two devastating words. They demolished angry walls, brought down defensive fortifications. Impossible to resist, especially when Lance said them with all his heart.

Antonia struggled to speak, and finally came out with something that had to be wrong. "J . . . acob."

She didn't know his name?

Lance didn't realize or didn't care. He shrugged. "Pop needed to know."

Antonia's eyes flared. Rese held her breath. Hadn't he learned from the last time he upset her? How could he keep pressing people further than they wanted to go? But she saw the strain in his posture. He wasn't as sure of himself as he sounded when he continued, "Jacob might have been a rascal and a cheat, but God loved him anyway."

What was he talking about? But Antonia's mouth jerked. She raised a finger at him.

"I know." He smiled. "I deserve everything you want to say."

Rese had thought Antonia's anger would escalate, risking another stroke. But her face flushed with warmth — and humor? Lance responded, the joy in his eyes unmistakable, like the first rim of sun above the horizon. Between them passed a communication so fine-tuned, words were irrelevant.

Rese watched mutely. Her heart hammered. How would it be to love him that way? To be loved that way, by someone who cared so deeply that maybe your darkest fears and future really didn't matter? For a moment she glimpsed what God must see in Lance, and understood the choice. Tony might have been the world's version of a hero, but Lance was something more.

"So." He stood and angled the wheelchair away from the table. "Like your stew?"

Antonia slapped at his hand.

"Careful. You'll knock off my goatskin."

What on earth was he talking about? But Antonia laughed. Whatever it was, they were in it together.

Rese followed them to the base of the stairs, where he lifted Antonia into his arms. "Fold that chair, can you, Rese, so the kids don't play with it?"

He carried his grandmother up to her room and helped her into the chair by the window. He offered to stay, but she motioned them out. "L . . . ater."

As they crossed the hall to his apartment, Rese said, "Jacob?"

Lance looked amazingly pleased with himself. "She's called me that since I was a kid."

"Why?"

"It's kind of a joke." He peeked in at Rico, zonked out with painkillers, and closed the bedroom door. Chaz would have left for the restaurant hours ago.

"I don't think she was joking." Rese settled into the chair across from the couch. Her legs were as tired from shopping as if she'd walked roofs all day, but she wanted to know what had gone on between Lance and Antonia.

"It's from the Old Testament." He took his guitar from its stand and sat down on the couch. "There were these twins, Jacob and Esau. Esau was born first, but with Jacob holding on to his heel."

She did not want to picture that.

His fingers worked the strings softly as

he spoke. "Firstborn Esau got the inheritance and the right to lead the family when his father, Isaac, was gone. But he sold that birthright to Jacob for a pot of stew."

"Must have been some chef." Rese raised her brows. "Is that what Antonia meant?"

Lance laughed. "Not exactly. More that Jacob tended to get what he wanted."

"Oh."

"And not always by the right means."

"He lied?"

Lance looked down at his fingers picking, then out across the room. "Esau was a man's man, the mighty hunter sort, and his father's favorite. Jacob was at a disadvantage."

She suddenly saw how personal this story could become, and maybe why Antonia called him that.

"God had told their mother that the older would serve the younger. So Jacob thought he was in God's will when he did what he did."

"He thought God wanted him to deceive?"

"He didn't deceive Esau. His brother had willingly given up his birthright. But his father's blessing could have changed that. So Jacob tricked his father into blessing him by mistake."

"And what happened?"

"Jacob became Israel, father of the twelve tribes. Jesus was descended from him."

"It didn't matter that he lied and cheated?"

"It didn't change what God intended for him." His voice wavered. "But he paid for it."

"How?"

"Got tricked into marrying the wrong woman, for one thing."

She raised her eyebrows.

"Call it payback." He smiled sideways. "He had to work seven more years to get the one he wanted."

"What happened to the first?"

"She had most of his kids."

"He kept both wives?"

"And a couple handmaids." Lance winked.

She crossed her arms.

"The point is, even though Jacob screwed up, God knew his intentions were good."

"As Antonia knows yours."

Lance stopped strumming. "I'm talking about Jacob."

"Are you?"

He settled into a strum and sang the soft ballad of a man who had made too many choices to turn back time.

Antonia watched Sofie take off her

sweater and fold it over her arm, careful and quiet. She stood a moment with her fingertips against the base of her throat, held motionless by thoughts that would remain her own. Antonia never pressed her. Unlike Lance, who couldn't bear an unshared thought, Sofie had learned to tuck hers in.

Then she glanced over. "Oh, Nonna, I thought you were sleeping."

Sleeping, waking; it all seemed the same.

Sofie kissed her cheeks. She smelled of almonds. Her hair fell softly against Antonia's face. Antonia reached up to stroke it, but her hand jerked uselessly. She had forgotten.

Sofie caught the palm in hers and brought it to her head, sliding the hand through the cascade of hair in the simple gesture that used to require no thought, no effort. "Can I help you to bed now?"

"I . . . 'll s . . . tay." Sleeping by the window, the morning light would kiss her face when she awoke. How she missed the pure golden sunshine, the mist in the vines, the smell of soft earth and the sweetly pungent blossoms bursting with promise.

"What are you thinking, Nonna?"

Antonia fixed her focus on her granddaughter's face. Sofie knew it would take too long to answer, yet she asked. Such a soft and gentle heart. "S . . . un . . . sh . . . ine."

"Mmm." Closing her eyes, Sofie rubbed cheeks with her. "It's stormy tonight. But maybe it will blow over by morning."

Stormy. Morning would dawn gray and wet. A dull street below; a heavy sky above. She could feel it in her bones. The storm inside her had spread, affecting all the world.

Sofie pulled a chenille throw from the sofa and draped it over her. "Sure you don't want to lie down?"

Antonia shook her head. She must be vigilant, vigilant in the storm. *If trouble comes . . . trouble . . .*

Chapter Twenty-one

Lance woke with a splitting headache. Dinner with the aunts last night had become an endurance test between their sage proverbs, *"No matter how hard you beat a donkey it will never turn into a racehorse,"* and Zia Dina's homemade grappa, for which she seemed to think he had a steel stomach. No wonder Zio Benito's liver had given out.

Lance pressed his palms to his temples and pulled himself up by the head. Then he sat long enough to recover before his bladder drove him to his feet. There was no being quiet for Rico and Chaz on one side and Rese on the other. His stream was powerful and sustained, and the relief almost made up for the throbbing in his head. Zia Dina must have it out for him.

He turned on the shower, stripped, and climbed over the side of the tub, pulling the curtain across. An hour or so under the water might clear his pores. He opened his mouth to the spray to get the fuzz off his tongue, then let the hot water beat against his teeth and gums. Seriously soaped and rinsed, he shut off the now tepid spray and toweled dry.

Rese, thank God, had taken one sip of the killer brew and declined another. Zia would have been miffed and heartbroken if he'd done the same. It seemed he would recover though, and in Zia's own words: *A tutto c'e rimedio, fuorchè alla morte.* There is a cure for everything except death.

He shaved, combed his hair, and studied the diamond in his ear, then switched it out with his gold hoop. It was a casual kind of day. Dressed in jeans and a clean T-shirt, he slipped out to the drizzly street and bought a macchiato strong enough to kill the last of the grappa. Technically that should have waited until after communion. So he'd confess it.

After leaving the church, he chatted with a dozen shop owners setting up for the day, picked up some fresh trout just driven up from the docks, truffles and capers, a crusty loaf of bread. Days like this he wondered why he ever left.

Chaz was into his morning devotions when he got back. There was no sound of Rico or Rese, so he set about preparing the trout and making the truffle and caper sauce. He set two of the fish aside for Nonna and Rico, then started the other three frying. Sometimes he enjoyed the limiting experience of two hot plates and skillets.

Gauging the time remaining on the food, Lance tapped Rese's door. He tapped again, then opened and hung his head in. She raised up on one elbow, looking tousled and way too attractive.

"You'll want to get up for this one," he said.

She yawned, curling into herself, and he decided right there that if she turned down his third proposal he'd start planning his fourth.

"Five minutes." He closed the door before joining her seemed a better idea. Breathing with difficulty, he went back to the kitchenette.

Chaz glanced up. "Lead us not into temptation."

Lance turned the trout. "And deliver us from ourselves."

Chaz grinned. "At least you know where the trouble starts."

"It was my earliest cognitive thought."

Fortified with panfried trout in its succulent sauce; warm, crisp bread that couldn't have been baked but an hour before; and cool tomato slices sprinkled with fresh minced basil, Rese sighed. She'd never really thought of fish for breakfast, but told Lance, "I could get used to this."

Chaz smiled. "Ah, but complacency is the root of ingratitude."

She shook her head. "After what I've eaten in my life? No chance." She looked at Lance. He'd had to teach her it was okay to have preferences, to enjoy a meal and express that. But it was a lesson she'd learned well.

"The eyes eat before the stomach," his aunt Anna had said when Dina set out the lasagna last night. She and Lance had laughed about the proverbs all the way home, but that one had been especially apt.

"Well." Rese picked up her plate and stood. "I guess I better get to work."

Lance raised his brows. "Work?"

"Your mother's kitchen ceiling." She purposely hadn't told him since he would have taken it on himself.

"What about it?"

"It's got a sag over the sink."

"So?" He took her plate and stacked it with his.

"I think there's a leak."

Lance studied her face. "You told Momma something was wrong with her kitchen?"

"She knew. I just offered to fix it."

"And she agreed?"

Rese raised her chin. "Why wouldn't she?"

He opened his mouth and closed it, glanced at Chaz, then said, "It's not her normal mode, that's all." He set the plates in the little sink.

Rese shrugged. "She seemed normal enough — once she finished posing me for the cha-cha."

Lance smiled with his whole face. "Where's that hidden camera when you need it?"

She frowned, but he took her hand and drew her close. "Need help with the ceiling?"

"You're reading to Antonia." And the sooner he'd seen her through this one last thing, the sooner they'd go home. Though it didn't feel as imperative as it had. If it weren't for the inn she could almost imagine . . .

Chaz brought his plate to the sink and said, "I can lend a hand."

"Aren't you working?"

"Not until tonight."

"Okay." Rese nodded. "If I'm right, there's lathe and plaster up there, so it could be difficult getting through. I don't want to disturb more of it than I have to."

Chaz spread his hands. "Let's go have a look."

She glanced back at Lance, who seemed to feel left out, but it wasn't her fault he had other people needing him. And for this, frankly, she didn't.

The closet under the stairs had a surpris-

374

ingly good selection of tools, many of them dated but still sound, the collection of a family who took care of their own problems. She hung the elastic-banded safety goggles around her neck. It was possible the ceiling was constructed with wallboard, since the thirties was the transitional period. But she'd guess otherwise.

Dressed in a turquoise fitted top and black capris, Doria let them in. Her hair was tied up in a wide band, and large silver hoops hung from her ears. How could a woman her age look so good in everything? "I have coffee cake in the oven. Do you like tea or decaf? We ran out of regular coffee this morning."

Carrying the stepladder, Rese followed her to the kitchen. What could she say? *"I don't want anything; I came to work"?* She pulled the yellowed safety goggles onto her face. "It's going to get messy. Do you have a tarp to cover the sink and floor?"

Doria went out and came back with flowered bed sheets. Chaz set the caddy with her selected tools on the kitchen floor and accepted a cup of decaf while they waited for the cake to finish baking. Rese laid out the sheets, then placed the stepladder beneath the sag in the kitchen ceiling and climbed up. With a utility knife, she cut through the thick layers of paint and found what she'd expected.

While Chaz chatted with Doria, Rese took the chisel and sank it into the semi-crumbly, semi-soggy plaster covering the one-inch lathes. After scraping a hole about ten inches square, she examined a portion of wood lathe exposed. It was too soft and flexible, causing the bow that allowed the sag. Lathes could do that without a leak, but she suspected she'd find a bad pipe above. No flooding or even regular dripping, or the ceiling wouldn't have held. Maybe no more than oozing, but enough to create an environment of decay in the ceiling. She'd have to cut the lathes at the studs to make the plumbing repair, and then replace them with timber batten, new plaster, and paint.

She jumped when Doria touched her hip, holding up a plate of crumbly coffee cake. She had all but forgotten Lance's mom and Chaz were there. She wanted to get inside the ceiling and see what she was up against, but it was a good bet that refusing the coffee cake would insult Doria, and Lance would hear about it, and Monica and Lucy and the aunts and . . . it wasn't worth it.

She pulled the goggles up onto her head, climbed down, and took the plate with a smile. "Thanks." It was almost an hour since she'd finished the trout. And the coffee cake looked good.

It didn't taste as good. There was a sharp, chalky flavor that reminded her of powdered adhesive, and if she had to guess, she'd say something had been added twice or in the wrong amount. She had mistaken a tablespoon for a teaspoon on one of Lance's recipes, and come to think of it she recognized the taste as baking powder — the same mistake she'd made.

If Chaz noticed, he made no comment, so she took her cue from him. Besides, she'd eaten worse at her mother's hands. She accepted a cup of decaf, since it was already made, and got as much of both things in as quickly as she could. Then she thanked Doria and set her plate on the counter.

"You want another piece? It's a special recipe. Goes only to the bust and skips the hips." Doria made a dancing motion with her hips that was powerful and sensuous. No wonder Roman couldn't resist getting her alone.

Rese said, "No thanks." She'd barely gotten past the need to hide her shape in the baggiest shirts she could find. And she didn't need Chaz checking it out. But he seemed amused by Doria's antics and didn't inspect any deficiencies Rese might have in either area.

She replaced the goggles. "I won't have this completed today. I'll have to find timber batten and fixings."

Doria said, "They have it all at the hardware. Most of these buildings were built the same time, the same way."

It was possible a local hardware would stock the fixings, but batten had to be ordered and took about three days — unless the hardware store did keep some on hand especially for repairs to buildings in the area. "Well, let's see what we're up against." She climbed the ladder and used the pull saw to cut through the cleared lathes where they attached to the stud. Chunks of plaster crumbled off, and she was glad for the goggles, but a mask would have been nice to block the choking dust.

When she cut across the second lathe, still partly connected to the first by the plaster between, the loose edges dropped. Mice tumbled from the hole. She shrieked, batting them off her face and arms and shoulders. Her chest heaved. Her arms shook, and her only consolation was that Doria was screaming still, swinging a towel at the scurrying vermin like a Spanish bullfighter.

"I knew there were mice! I told him!"

She might have told her.

"But no. There's no mice in *this* building. Bah!" She slapped the towel at the corner, then screamed when the creature doubled back between her legs and escaped to the living room.

Rese looked down and realized Chaz had caught hold of her on the ladder. "You can let go." She glowered. "I'm not going to fall. I never fall." She never shrieked, either, but she had.

Chaz let go.

She hadn't expected it. If she'd been thinking, focusing instead of eating cake and . . . She expelled a hard breath. It didn't matter. She hadn't screamed as long or loudly as Doria, though she must have thrashed enough that Chaz thought she'd come off the ladder.

Still breathing hard, she looked into the gap, tensed now and ready should any more creatures decide to make their escape. She shook off the feel of their feet on her skin, their tails dragging. She could not believe she'd lost it. But then, it had been a while since she'd had to keep her guard up. She'd gotten careless in more ways than one.

Doria hollered into the phone, "I'm calling the exterminator." She turned and leaned against the counter, scouring the floor with her gaze. "Because there's mice like I told you! You don't hear no more."

She must have called Roman. "No, you won't shoot them with a BB gun! I'm calling a professional. There are babies in this house!"

Rese shot a glance at Chaz, who was patting Doria's shoulder and murmuring, "It's all right, Momma."

Then she noticed tears in Doria's eyes. Her family was endangered — even if it was just vermin — and she was fighting for them. The stark contrast to her own experience floored her. *Don't think about it.*

Rese looked back at the ceiling, assessing the extent of the portion to be removed. She knew too well what likely lay above the sag, and it wouldn't be good for Doria to see. Besides, she'd rather work alone now. The previous display of weakness was enough for one day. "Chaz."

He left Doria arguing with Roman on the phone. "Yes?"

"Take her out of here," she whispered. "This isn't going to be pretty."

He raised his brows suspiciously. If she was right, there'd be ratty nests full of pink babies, droppings, and more. She didn't relish the thought, but she could handle it. It was surprises coming at her she hated, not things she prepared for and faced head on.

Doria hung up the phone and stared at Rese methodically chiseling off the paint and plaster of the next lathe. "What are you doing?"

"Taking down the ceiling."

Doria stood mouth open for a long moment. "You're going to fix it?"

Rese looked at the hole she'd made already. "Can't leave it like this."

"Roman can do it! Roman and Lance."

Maybe they could, but Rese looked down at her and said, "You wanted a professional. You've got one."

Doria drew back her shoulders and assessed her, then nodded. "Good." She put her hands to her hips. "I'm warning the girls we've been invaded. And I'm calling an exterminator." She turned and stalked out.

Chaz leaned on the broom and smiled up. "You are girt about with strength and sturdy are your arms."

Rese looked up into the hole. "If I see one whisker, that varmint's sausage."

Lance had gone across the hall and found Nonna sitting by the window. She'd wanted him to read, but he had wooed her first with trout. When she saw the plate, she shook her head and called him Jacob, but he'd smiled and said, "I can live with that," and proceeded to feed her.

Now he took up the pages. Rese needed to get back — they both did — but this thing with Nonna wasn't finished. And he was part of it somehow. He looked at Nonno Marco's handwriting on the cover page. *What are you telling her, Nonno?*

381

And why couldn't you say it before?

If Nonno was a Fed, so deep undercover that even his family knew nothing, there had to have been a good reason. Many men were gone during the Depression and the years that followed, going where the work was or going to war. It seemed Nonno had fought a secret war, but he had been home often enough to father five children, to have the sort of love affair with Nonna that Lance recognized even as a child. Was that possible with so many secrets?

Nonna touched his hand, and Lance turned the page and read.

"Even without Vittorio's warning that you might see through our plan, I'd already accounted for your perception and spunk. It became a challenge — could I hold your interest without enticing your heart? If you refused to see me, it would have complicated our plans. Meetings with Vittorio would be scrutinized by Arthur Tremaine Jackson, a scrutiny I intended to avoid. But no one would question my interest in you, and therefore Vittorio's interest in me.

"I didn't know how much time our covert efforts would take. I never went in with expectations of that sort. My knack was reading the situation as it unfolded and reacting accordingly. So, though I hadn't planned the role of suitor, I slipped into it with no compunction whatever.

"As a special agent of the Bureau of Investigation, I used any means within the law to accomplish my ends. Out of about 650 operatives, I was one of the few who worked undercover. A natural mimic, Momma often said. And I put that to use, playing many roles to gain the trust of those I intended to bring down, spending whatever time it took to establish myself. It was what I did, what I was made for."

Antonia closed her eyes. *"Roles to gain the trust of those I intended to bring down."* Like Papa? Like her? No. . . . But at first maybe? Her mouth quivered. Arthur Jackson was his target, not Papa. *"Any means within the law." "No compunction."* Marco became her suitor to trap Arthur Jackson — and maybe Papa with him. And she had been his cover.

She moaned softly. Why was he telling her this now? Why not when her decisions were unmade? *"A natural mimic." "Playing roles."* She pictured his protean face, how even in those first days he'd seemed to change from one man to another, keeping her off balance yet intriguing her all the more. She wanted to think she'd seen through it, but it was only after Papa's death that she had questioned his identity; only then had she wondered who this man was. And by then, of course, it didn't matter.

They were on the run, Marco her only hope of safety, the man she came to trust and to love. Marco playing a role that had seemed so real. . . . Marco! Panic clawed inside her. What if her mind gave out from the strain?

She needed time to let his words find a place without resentment or fear. Her body had betrayed her twice, and she was afraid. Another shock might incapacitate her. She wasn't afraid to die, but she didn't want to live out her days like an eggplant, unable to do anything for herself.

Maybe that was pride. She would confess it.

But she knew her limits. She would not read alone, nor would she allow more to be read than she could bear. She would keep Lance beside her, not just a physical guardian, but spiritual as well. She knew what others missed, that he possessed an awareness beyond her so-called angel sight, as though God whispered directly in his ear.

Conchessa had seen it. The letter she

had written after Lance found her in Liguria was filled with wonder. Not only that she, Antonia, was alive, but also that she had produced such a grandson. And it was true. The boy had found his share of trouble, but it was rooted in his need to help, to drink the cup someone else had poured. Whatever it was, she wanted him beside her as she drank this goblet of tears Marco had served her from the grave.

Chapter Twenty-two

Rese saved as much of the original lathe and plaster as she could. She was still gagging from the rotten material and refuse she had removed, but as soon as she reached the part that was sound, she left it intact. It went against her grain to take out more of the original construction than necessary. Anywhere a place could hold its own, she gave it the chance.

Doria blew in with her daughters and their kids and the two old men from the back, and a few more faces she didn't recognize. They all wanted to see where the mice had come out on top of Rese. She was not interested in rehashing the experience, but Doria did it for her, with far more detail than necessary. Rese ignored them all as long as she could, then ordered them out. And why was Chaz grinning like a Cheshire cat?

With painstaking care, she'd gotten through the ceiling, and she was right; there was a corroded pipe over the sag, a cheap grade of steel, but at least it wasn't lead. Chaz cut the water supply, and she went to work on the pipe just as Lance came up with lunch — a crispy thin-crusted pizza with some kind of dark ham, grilled peppers, and bubbling cheese. She hadn't planned a break, but the aroma caught her right where Doria's coffee cake had left her wanting.

She climbed down the ladder. "Giovanni's?"

"Nah. Michelli's."

"Bribing isn't fair."

"A worker deserves her wage." He raised a slice and slid the paper-thin tip into her mouth.

Maybe there was something to partiality because it was the best pizza she'd ever tasted.

He laughed before she could say anything. "Gotcha."

"Now I know why Baxter likes you. It's all in the stomach."

"The stomach could fare worse than this." Chaz helped himself to a second slice.

"Eat up; I've got another one in the oven for Rico." Lance checked his watch.

"How's he doing?" She hadn't had time to worry, but he had not looked good last night.

"Better when he's incoherent on the meds. Soon as they wear off he starts growling." Lance glanced at the ceiling.

"How's this going?"

"In spite of incessant interruptions, I'm ready to cut out the bad pipe and go buy the replacement."

"Buy." Lance spread his hands. "What's to buy?" He looked up into the hole, then sent her an enigmatic smile and went out.

"We've done some plumbing repairs," Chaz said.

Lance came back with copper pipe and couplings, exactly what she would have insisted on. The Michellis obviously agreed their repairs should not only address the problem, but improve the property's condition — a thought that energized her. She crunched the last bite of crust and shooed them both out. Chaz had to get ready for work, and Lance had pizza in the oven. But most of all, she had a project to tackle.

She had all the damaged ceiling cut away, the old section of pipe removed, and was fitting the copper into place when Roman came home.

"What's all this?"

Rese pulled her head out of the hole and looked down. Doria had told him, hadn't she?

"What are you doing in my kitchen ceiling?"

"Restoration." Her throat tightened. She hadn't expected confrontation.

His mouth hung slack. "Who said?"

Then Doria flew in, hands in the air. "I told you we had mice!"

Roman turned. "What's a girl doing in my ceiling?"

"Girl? A professional!" Doria fixed her hands to her hips. "Did you fix the sag? Did you hear the mice? Did you listen to a word I said?"

He waved a hand behind him. "You got Lance's girlfriend in my pipes."

"Your pipes! Whose sink you think that is?"

While they debated ownership, Rese climbed back into the hole, inserted and tightened the final coupling. A minute later she felt a hand on her ankle. She looked down into Roman's face and understood the intimidation factor Lance had described. Her hackles rose. "You want a look?"

"Off the ladder, young lady."

Her spine stiffened. The last guy who called her *young lady* had pulled cleanup for a week. But it was his ladder, his ceiling, his kitchen. She climbed down, and he took her place. Doria still stood with her hands to her hips, but Rese didn't look her way. If Roman found fault with her work . . .

He climbed back down and eyed her. "You know how hard it is to patch this kind of ceiling?"

Nothing about her plumbing? "I've been repairing lathe and plaster since I was sixteen."

"And you're what now, eighteen?"

"Twenty-four," she said before she realized it wasn't his business. "And before I did the repairs I watched and learned from the best in the industry. And when I *was* eighteen I already had a reputation for excellence in carpentry. Your ceiling will be better than anything you or Lance or Chaz could do."

She'd seen him sullen, she'd seen him playful, but until that moment she hadn't seen him mad.

His big hands clenched as though he was ready for some physical communication. "You think so?"

"I know so." She drew herself up. She hadn't meant to insult him, but her kind of expertise didn't come cheap. "Be thankful I'm not presenting a bill."

He expelled his breath. Then stared at her as though she were an oddity in a zoo.

Doria came over and slipped her arm through his. "So before she closes it up, we get the exterminator."

"Sure. And he won't present a bill either." He glared. "Why don't you get this girl to chase away the mice?"

"I don't like mice. I hate mice." Rese raised her chin. "And after this morning

I'll have nightmares of mice."

Something flickered in Roman's eyes. Then it spread to his mouth, a sinking in of the corners. He planted his hands on his hips. "You gonna marry my son?"

She glanced at the ceiling. "Does it get me the job?"

Roman barked a laugh. "Sure. You fix this ceiling, marry Lance, and make us some tough babies. Too many whiners around here." He looked at his wife, who slapped his chest.

Rese released a slow breath. "I need to order the timber batten. Think you can spring for that much?"

Patience, kindness, a soft word. Are these driven out of people who live too close?

Those first days were a blessing I failed to appreciate. Then Momma Benigna came home.

Now it is Marco this and Marco that. How could I not know my husband walked on water? He'd seemed substantial enough until we moved in with Momma. *We* moved in, but Marco doesn't live here.

Marco does important things for important people, people with jack who send him all over the country. And while he is gone, I have Momma. There is nothing benign about Momma Benigna. All the things I don't know! How to keep house, how to sew — making too fine a work of it, when the clothes we mend are paid for by the piece. How to make meals, especially how to make meals. *"Where is the sauce?"* It must be smothered to be edible. How I long for the grateful glances I once received.

When I go out, the wolves in the street whistle. Momma thinks I invite it. Can I help it if I seem unattached? If Marco could walk on air, maybe he'd stay closer now and then. But he warned me his job would take him away. And I don't blame him. For his sake, I do the best I can. For his sake and for the one who flutters within. . . .

Antonia dragged herself back. Lance had come in to read, but she couldn't hear it yet, so she had told him about coming to New York. Her words were slow and torturous, but she described the tenement in Manhattan, Mulberry Bend, where Marco's people had lived for fifteen years like rats because they didn't know better. They couldn't speak the language, couldn't read the forms. Then after a time, they learned, but stayed there still because they'd made it their world.

"M . . . ine was a more gr . . . acious l . . . ife. You've s . . . een it." She closed her eyes and pictured the vine-covered hills rolling in the golden mist of an evening sunset.

"I've seen it, Nonna."

"S . . . uch beauty." Tears pooled and ran down her cheeks. She didn't know whom she cried for and it didn't matter. Sorrow needed no explanation.

After a time, Lance squeezed her hand. "Do you want me to read?"

"N . . . ot yet." A reluctance had settled on her like dread. Her former angel sight? Or simply an old woman's desire to hold on to what she had once believed?

After placing the order for the batten from a company she knew and trusted — since her reputation was on the line — Rese accessed the inn's Web site. Waiting for it to load up on Lance's aging system, she wondered what material things he actually valued. Guitars. And his Harley. She brushed a film of dust from the monitor as she waited for the dinosauric modem, then squeaked the chair around and studied the apartment. Each of the guys was represented there.

Rico's drums dominated the corner, autographed posters of bands on the walls behind, including one of the three of them in the club Lance had shown her. A silver cross from Jamaica hung in the kitchenette alongside a crude weaving made by a blind prophet woman Chaz had feared as a child but loved now. Over the door, a Yankees pennant for both Lance and Rico; respectively the irrepressible and the doomsday fan.

The framed paintings on the walls, they had acquired from street artists. So Star's painting had not been as novel to Lance as she'd thought. He understood the chance discovery of beauty — and valued it.

The most expensive items were the sound system components, Rico's drums, Lance's four guitars, and Chaz's sax, keyboard, xylophone, and an assortment of wooden flutes. She realized once again the part music had played in their lives, in a large way forming the glue of their friendship.

She returned to the screen and brought up the reservations on her site. She had blocked out the week she intended to be gone and kept the next empty as well — good thing, since they'd been away nine days already. If Lance was pictured on the Web site, and they were there answering phones, the inn would probably be full. But she was hoping for some leeway.

Her kitchen-ceiling project required at least a couple days once she got the batten up, time for the plaster to dry before the skim coat could go on, using up most of the second week. And that didn't begin to address the rest of it.

Rico was morose and agitated. She had checked on him when she came up, and agreed with Lance — he did growl. Immobilizing Rico's arm was like muzzling a lion. And he'd already been edgy over Star. And where was Star?

Rese picked up the envelope that had come in the mail. Judging by the return address, it was a money order from Star's trust. She must have given them this address, must have also switched her disbursement from quarterly to monthly. She had that option, just rarely took it, not wanting to use the money sensibly. Maybe she and Rico had made plans. No telling now how that would go. Rese frowned. How could she go back to Sonoma with Star wandering New York City? She knew it wasn't her responsibility, but then whose?

Rese rubbed her temples. Above all, there was Antonia. She might suspect the woman of manipulating Lance if she hadn't seen for herself the tender bond between them. Antonia had one more thing to face, and she wanted him there to help her. Rese understood that all too well.

As for Lance, he was so deeply a part of his family, he seemed to have forgotten their purpose was to settle matters and get back to the inn. If she reminded him, he'd probably send her back, but she didn't want to go back alone. It wasn't that she didn't trust him to return, but that . . . she didn't trust him to return. Too many people needed him, and too many things happened. It was almost a conspiracy.

She studied the situation. Most of their reservations were for later in the season. People came in droves as the summer drew on toward the grape harvest in the vineyards. But she had rooms reserved sporadically in the near weeks — four in the next, when they would have been back, but now might not be.

Sighing, she crafted a notice to the people who had reserved rooms in the next week, stating that reservations were temporarily suspended due to a family emergency. The family was Lance's, but the emergency was hers. She couldn't do it without him. She apologized for the inconvenience and credited back their payments. It was early enough in the season that Sonoma wasn't full. They'd find something else.

Letting personal concerns interfere with business ran against her grain, but the fact that each cancellation felt better than the last concerned her even more. She should be disappointed, concerned for her future, her plans. Had she lost her vision? Had she ever had it?

Rese closed out of the site. It wasn't as though she'd put years into the bed-and-breakfast industry. If her competition laughed her out of business, well . . . what? She'd been more concerned over Roman's opinion of her work. Something was wrong with that picture.

She turned off the computer, stood and stretched. Lance was with Antonia, so she went across the hall and tapped the door. Knowing he was freed up from the responsibilities of the inn would give him the chance to focus and accomplish whatever he was doing. Then they could decide what, if anything, they were doing.

Lance waited through Nonna's tears. They should forget it. Two, three paragraphs at a time exhausted her emotional stamina, and now she was avoiding Nonno's letter altogether. But she talked, telling him things he'd never heard before, the parts of her life she'd kept quiet but needed now to make known, as though she was afraid what Marco might say could tear apart the reality she was describing word by arduous word.

He didn't want this to hurt her. Even now he'd forget it, put Nonno's pages with the other things, the dossiers and Sybil's letter from Sonoma, things he'd put out of Nonna's sight. He would put it all away and let it go. He almost wished he could. Something wasn't right, and he was sure they both sensed it. For once he was on the front side of trouble, but Nonna wouldn't let him walk away.

He rose from her side at the tap on the door, surprised to find Rese.

She asked softly, "How is she?"

He glanced back over his shoulder. "It's hard." He ran a hand through his hair. "I'm sorry it's taking so long."

"I wanted to talk to you about that."

He leaned a shoulder to the jamb. "I know we need to get back."

"I canceled the reservations for next week."

"What?" He sagged as that load settled on him. "I wish you'd asked."

"It was my decision."

His, too, if they were partners, but frankly, the inn was far from his thoughts. He stepped outside the door, pulling it behind him, then rubbed his face. "I keep thinking we're getting close, and then . . ."

"Things happen." She didn't exactly sound like Pop, but he'd gotten that message there too.

He sighed. "Yeah."

"Maybe for a reason."

"Yeah?" That was a new twist for Rese.

She tapped her thumb on her thigh, a rare signal of unease. "Lance . . . when

Rico crashed, I had the thought that maybe it wasn't an accident."

"Someone meant to hit him?"

"No. Nothing like that. Just, like you said, a reason behind things, even things that seem bad."

She hadn't appeared to accept that the saving presence she'd encountered in her room could be the same divine being he'd described at Ground Zero, that God could choose to save — or not — even His own servants, His sons and daughters, people who had seemed blessed beyond measure. Now Rico's accident had opened her eyes, but she didn't resent the reality; she found hope in it.

She expelled a breath. "I know it sounds weird. But I thought the sight of the ambulance would paralyze me like before. Then when I saw it, when they put Rico inside, it hit me that it was all part of something bigger."

He knew it was. It all was. But sometimes he wanted things to be small, inconsequential. Haphazard. He was a walking contradiction; trying to get inside God's head, yet resisting the permeation of that Spirit in all aspects of his life. In Rese's fresh understanding he saw his reluctance.

"Maybe even that night with Mom was meant to happen."

His protective spirit rose up at the

thought, but he couldn't argue her conclusion. If there could be purpose behind Rico's crash, how much more in Rese's rescue?

She frowned. "If it hadn't, the next time might have worked."

His mind jumped to all the ways Rese could have died, a little girl alone with a mother she loved, but who could not be trusted. But why put her there in the first place? So the Lord could reveal himself? His first cynical reaction was countered by excitement. She was speaking the faith of new belief. It hadn't been battered yet, and he could still remember how it felt.

"Or Mom could have died. And I wouldn't have the chance to do something for her."

That purity of thought speared him. How had he grown so jaded? "You're amazing." He threaded their fingers together.

"You say that? After all the ways you're there for people, all the things you've done?"

Had he? Was he? "I guess that's what it's about." They might be pawns, but they were pawns with an irresistible drive to take that next step, marching into whatever lay ahead for the chance to make a difference. "So you think we're still here for a reason?"

"Does it feel finished to you?"

He shook his head. But he hadn't expected her to feel it. "I thought you were getting antsy, finding projects to keep from climbing the walls."

She shrugged a shoulder. "Some things I can't resist."

He raised his brows. "Oh yeah?"

"Old houses. Shaggy dogs."

"A man with an earring." He brought their entwined fingers to his lips.

"You'll need to talk to Michelle again. Baxter could be an issue."

Cool, practical Rese. Only he knew better. "The only issue with Baxter is if he'll ever settle for me again after all this female attention."

"Good point." She nodded toward Antonia's door. "Are you going to be a while?" There was just a hint of longing behind her question, so slight he could have missed it altogether.

He pushed the door open behind him. "Let me just tell Nonna good night." He went back in and found her sleeping. He hoped she'd rest well, and maybe tomorrow they could read. Or not. The story she'd told was compelling, and he wanted more. He had known her as his nonna, but now, through her labored words, he was getting to know the young woman she'd once been, and he considered that a privilege. He bent and brushed his lips over her forehead. "T'amo, Nonna."

"She knows." Sofie had slipped in behind him, and together they got Nonna to bed.

Chapter Twenty-three

Lance went across the hall, anticipation rising. Rese had come to him, interrupting as she never did. She had all but asked for him. This was good. This was real good. Their responsibilities had kept them apart all day, and it was time to change that. His step found an old, familiar bounce as he crossed the hall, anticipating time spent with a glass of wine, a beautiful woman. . . .

He opened the door. Rese and Rico were at the table with a deck of cards. So much for romance. He sat down and eyed Rico, holding his cards with the arm strapped to his chest, his unbuttoned shirt thrown over his shoulders.

"Playing it close to the vest?"

Rico glared.

Had he chosen this moment to regain sociability? Or had Rese realized the fire she'd stoked and remembered not to play with matches? Or had he imagined it all? "What's the game?"

"Five card draw. She has the wickedest deadpan I've ever seen."

Lance laughed out loud. "To say the least."

She laid a couple cards down. "Dealer takes two."

"From the top," Rico said.

She raised her eyes. "You think I cheat?"

"Just making sure."

"I've never cheated a hand in my life."

Lance leaned his chair back. "How many hands have you played?"

"A few. Brad and some of the guys came over sometimes. Dad's game was five card stud, but I prefer draw."

He shook his head. "Basketball and poker. What else don't I know?"

"You were going to call Michelle." Rese fit her new cards into her hand.

"It's three hours earlier Pacific time. Deal me in."

"Call Michelle. Then I'll deal you in."

The bossiness that had raised his hackles at first amused him now. He got up and took his phone from the charger. He'd programmed Michelle in when he left Baxter in her care. Funny, he thought, he'd entrusted his dog to her without even knowing her last name. Some people were like that; you just sensed it. And while Baxter was not very discerning, he hadn't complained much.

Lance leaned against the small sink in the kitchenette and waited through the rings to leave a message. "Hi, it's Lance. Things are still up in the air, but if Baxter's a problem —"

"Hi there." Michelle surprised him. "No, he's not a problem. In fact, he's been coming around with me to visit my homebound friends. He's a big hit."

"His spirits are good? No moping and sighing?"

Michelle laughed. "Hate to tell you, but he's pretty content."

Traitor. "Well, I appreciate it. I just don't know yet how much longer we'll be."

"Take care of business. Your dog's doing fine."

He hung up and sat down. At Rese's raised eyebrows he said, "He's changed his name to Benedict."

She rolled her eyes. "Funny how animals take after their masters."

"Ouch."

"Friendly, adaptable . . ." Rese set two stacks of chips before him. "Ante up."

He tossed a chip, then sat back as she shuffled and dealt him in from Rico's handicapped position. He picked up his cards. "You sure you're okay about the inn? You could go back."

"It doesn't make sense for me to go back alone. I can't take guests without you."

"You did before."

"I had Chaz and Rico and Star."

Rico stiffened. "Can we play?"

Lance opened with one chip.

Rese tossed in two. "See your bet and raise it one."

Lance and Rico shared a glance. Rico saw her bet, and Lance flipped another chip in and said, "Pot's good; I'll draw three."

Rico slid three cards off the deck with his index finger. "Rese?"

"I'll hold."

Rico raised his brows. "None?"

"Yep."

Lance sat back in his chair. She'd raised and drawn none. Hmm. He studied his pair of jacks, tossed in two chips. Rese saw it and raised him two. Rico hesitated long enough before matching that he might have something small and suspect a bluff, in which case the jacks were better than they looked.

Lance held two chips to call, rubbing them between his fingers and watching Rese for tells. Her face revealed nothing. No gloat, no overconfidence. No doubt. He set the two back on the stack, then lifted five. "I raise you three." Just to see if she'd break stride.

She had chips in her hand almost before his landed. "See your raise; raise you five." The chips clinked into the pot.

Rico tossed his cards down.

Lance pursed his lips. Five more chips on a pair of jacks. He'd already invested too much. If he folded now he wouldn't see her hand, but five chips was steep for curiosity's sake. Was she bluffing? If she wasn't, what would it say for him to call? If she was . . . what did *that* tell him? He toyed with the half stack of chips he had left. See her? Or fold. He eyed his jacks, but it wasn't about them. He laid his cards face down, then met Rese's gaze. "I believe you."

Still nothing more than a flicker in her eyes as she slid her cards together and set them on the deck for his deal. Then she scooped the pot in and methodically stacked the chips. Still nothing as he reached for the deck to shuffle. He hadn't paid to see. He had to cut and mix. No way. He fanned the top cards up and smacked them down, then rocked back and stared.

Even with his cheating she held her cool.

Rico ran his hand over his jaw. "You are in so deep, 'mano."

Lance laughed. "I never recommended poker with Rese Barrett. Parcheesi was cut-throat enough." And if he could spend the rest of his life and all eternity with her, that would be sufficient.

She raised her chin. "Your deal."

The door opened and Chaz came in, deposited his coins into the money bowl, and sat down, stretching his legs out with a low moan.

Lance hooked his arm over the back of the chair. "Long day?"

"Good day. Productive, rewarding." He looked around the table. "But why am I the only one who works?"

Lance shrugged. "The rest of us get by on our looks."

"I work," Rese said.

Rico got up and took a beer from the refrigerator. The conversation could tank if he took the subject too seriously.

But then someone knocked on the door. Chaz moved to rise, but Lance motioned him down. "Allow me, you who labor and are weary." He opened the door and braced himself.

Coiled in what looked like a magician's multicolored scarf, Star drifted past him with a puckish glance, then greeted Rese with a pirouette and air kisses. Before she could respond, Star moved past Chaz, dragging her fingers over his scalp, to Rico who stood in the corner like a dark pirate.

With a playful smile she flitted to him, then noticed his arm bound up to his chest beneath his draped shirt and gasped. " 'Affliction is enamoured of thy parts, and thou art wedded to calamity!' What happened to your poor arm?"

"I was looking for you, chiquita," he said. "But found a car instead."

She reached out her fingers. " 'O comfort-killing night —' "

Rico drew back. "Cut the crap."

There came the donkey ears.

Rese stood up. "We looked all over for you, Star."

Star spun. "Why follow the moon, knowing it will rise again tomorrow, brighter and fuller for having been dark."

Murder flashed in Rico's eyes. Star had cut deeper than she knew.

"Star . . ." Rese tried again.

But Star raised her hand. Tremulous and pale, she turned to Rico. "Speak your verdict upon me. Shall I stay or go?"

Lance closed his eyes.

"There's no place for you here."

"Rico." Lance and Chaz said it together, but Star spun with a glistened stare, then went straight for the door.

Rese jolted. "Wait! Star!"

But Star pulled it open and went through.

As Rese followed her into the hall, Lance turned to Rico. "I told you she had issues."

"Everyone's got issues, 'mano." Rico clunked his beer down on the counter and paced. "Maury choked her. Maury bruised her. And she would have gone back to him. I never touched her. If she can't see the difference, there is none." He glared. "No difference at all."

Lance took that in. He had tried to tell Rico to be careful, to keep his eyes open. Streetwise as he was, he'd been jacked over, and he hadn't seen it coming. Star didn't realize. Or maybe she did. Maybe it was her way of striking back.

Rico paced and spun, his free hand splayed. "You blame me?"

Lance shook his head. The situation spoke for itself. If she'd come back contrite, or even mindful of the hurt she'd caused, it would be different. But as Rese said, Star either didn't know or didn't care. And it was Rico's cut palm he'd pressed his own bleeding hand to, when they were just old enough to mean it. He didn't turn his back on blood.

"Star, come in and talk about it." Rese followed her down the hall.

"I am made tongue-tied by authority." Star's feet pattered down the stairs.

Rese hurried to keep up. "Rico's upset. You should have expected that. But we can —"

Star rounded the landing. "You heard him. There's no place for me."

"He's not the only one. We're all involved in this." If Star took off again, how would she get back to Sonoma? How would any of them? "Star, wait."

Star landed at the bottom. "The fates have spoken."

"There are no fates." Rese clambered after her. "And Rico isn't God. Just give him a chance to —"

"I gave him a chance." Her chest heaved. "And I don't do God." She stalked down the hall, jerked open the door, and went out into the night.

Rese stared after her. She had known better. There was no holding Star back. There never was. What peace she seemed to have found from Mom's words in the mental hospital, the joy she had with Rico, obviously wasn't enough. Or it had been stolen, as Lance said, by some stalking evil.

Whatever the case, Star was gone again. Rese went back up, amazed she could still care.

Lance motioned Rese onto the couch beside him when she came back alone. He wasn't surprised and doubted she was. But it could get touchy if Rico kept talking — and he did.

"She makes you want to help, then cuts when you're not looking."

Rese looked up at Rico. "You don't know where she's been."

"I know where I've been. Where we've

all been. It's what you do with it, chiquita." He slid his good arm into his shirt sleeve, left the rest dangling. "It's how you treat your friends, how you treat your enemies. She made the choice, not me." He strode to the door and went out.

Lance released a slow breath. Rese really couldn't argue. She'd expressed the same when Star took off before. And she had more experience with Star's behavior than Rico.

She pressed her palms to her forehead. "Why does she do this? It's like she's possessed."

Across the room, Chaz opened his eyes. He'd been in silent prayer, Lance knew, since the whole thing unfolded. Now his face drew tight.

"People do things for all kinds of reasons, Rese." Lance didn't like the way Chaz had fixed on those thrown-off words. She hadn't been serious, but Chaz came from a place of voodoo and violence. They'd contended with forces of darkness before, only not in this living room.

Circumstances on the island were clear, but this . . . How much was Star's recklessness, her choice? Human frailty. But Chaz started to speak, binding spirits, his voice soft yet vehement. Rese lowered her hands and stared. Slipping an arm around her, Lance tried to convey normality. But unexpectedly, his spirit ignited.

As Chaz spoke the spirits into submission, he saw them bound and flailing, a vision clearer than anything he'd experienced before. He no longer thought of Rese in his arm, or Chaz across the room. He hardly even thought of Star, so deep was his realization of God.

After a time, he realized Chaz had stopped speaking. His thoughts slowly coiled back, and his eyes unglued. Rese became solid under his arm. He straightened.

"Are you okay?" She scrutinized him.

Chaz grinned. "We lost you for a while, mon."

"I'm fine." Lance slid his fingers into the back of his hair. "But I think this fight is real."

Chaz locked his gaze. "A principality?" He wasn't really asking; he'd sensed it too.

Rese looked from one to the other. "You don't mean seriously . . . I was just talking." She slid back in the couch. "You bound evil spirits?"

She resisted, naturally, but he was not up to the battle. More than anything he wanted a quiet place to regroup. One didn't recover lightly from an encounter with the living God — which sounded bizarre even to himself.

Chaz said, "Through the same Spirit that raised Jesus from the dead, all fallen things are subject to us."

Lance swallowed. Though he'd referenced an actual evil, this was more than he'd gone into with Rese.

She turned on him. "You said the dead don't threaten the living."

"We're not talking about ghosts."

"Demonic spirits can harass us," Chaz said. "And sometimes they are invited in."

Rese stood up and paced. "So . . . the *thing* I felt in the tunnel was real?"

How had she jumped to that? Lance crossed his ankle over his knee. "It was fear, Rese. You can't ascribe everything a demonic nature."

Chaz said, "But it could have been real."

She spun. "Walter was real?"

Chaz had no reference for her question.

Lance shook his head. "Walter was part of your mother's illness. Someone who became real to you as a child alone with her."

She turned back. "I felt him down there."

Lance reached out a hand to her. "Something, maybe. But don't be too quick to name it." He drew her back down beside him.

She shook her head. "I don't believe this."

"The powers of darkness are real," Chaz

414

said. "But you can't look for them behind every bush."

"Or wine rack," Lance added.

She glared. "There was something down there, and it wasn't your great-grandfather's skeleton."

"Great-great-grandfather."

She glowered, then turned to Chaz. "Is Star possessed?"

"Possession is very rare." He spread his hands. "But her beliefs and actions are risky."

Rese closed her eyes. "I don't believe this."

Lance squeezed her hand. "We don't know," he said, though the vision clung to his mind. He hadn't anticipated anything like that, but something had shifted. He didn't know what or why, but he knew what Rese said was true. Things happened for a reason. And he could not doubt now that he was part of it.

Chapter Twenty-four

Two days later the walls echoed. The windows shook. Hair flying, skin dripping, Rico beat on his drums, wincing with every shift in position, his left arm doing the job of two — not pretty, but indomitable, working out his hurt and anger and maybe a little regret. Lance had seen him like this before, and there was only one way to communicate. He plugged in the electric guitar and matched Rico's rhythm, then laid down the lead and lyrics of one of the edgier songs he'd written in their dark phase.

"Scream. Plead. Bleed out your heart.
What does it matter? What does it gain?
It doesn't stop the pain.
When hope is escaping, where do you
  start?
How can you matter? What can you
  gain?
Nothing you do stops the p-a-i-n. . . ."

"Every degree the planet turns
Someone burns, someone burns.

Every heart that pumps with greed
Someone bleeds, someone bleeds.
But no one stops the pain. . . ."

Rico's voice joined, and for the first time in too long they found their harmony, he and Rico blending pitch and tone and dynamics. They sang the second verse and chorus, the third and fourth. Facing off, eyes locked, Lance absorbed the anger and frustration and hurt, adding verses he hadn't written yet, words that came as the music built.

"Have you looked into the eyes of
    hunger in a child
Crunch your crispy fries; like your chili
    hot or mild?
What does it matter? What does it gain?
Have you walked among the ghosts,
    hands out hoping for a dime?
Outta my way, outta my way;
Can't you see I don't have time?
Scream, plead, bleed out your heart.
What does it matter? What does it gain?
Can't, no, can't, no, can't stop the
    pain. . . ."

And when the words ran out, the instruments spoke on. Reverberations numbed his ears. His forearm screamed. Eight minutes. Ten. Fourteen. Playing until Rico slumped on the stool, chest heaving.

Winded himself, Lance waited. He'd known Rico to regenerate, but his hand dropped, dangled the stick, then let it fall. He spoke one word in Spanish that pretty much summed it up.

Lance took off the guitar. "You need a shower, 'mano."

Rico raised his arm and sniffed. Lance didn't need that proximity to know Rico had purged poisons. Another wave wafted as he got up and stripped his shirt, wiped his head with it, then walked stiffly to the bathroom.

While Rico showered, Lance heated oil in a skillet on the hot plate, fried the plantains he'd purchased that morning, warmed some rice and seasoned it with sofrito — a blend of cilantro, garlic, oregano, and minced peppers.

Rico emerged ravenous, as Lance had known he would, given the scents of his heritage and his exertion. He devoured the offering, then sat back and sighed. "You were right."

Lance rested his forearms on the table. "About what?"

"It wasn't really her. She was only going along."

"Still had a good thing, Rico. What did Saul say about your sound?"

Rico tipped his eyes up without raising

his face. "What does it matter?"

Lance let out a slow breath. He'd seen Rico do surgery on his heart before — the reason his father, Juan, had no place there. It had been two days since he'd cast Star out, and now he'd purged more than toxins on the drums. "What are you going to do?"

Rico shrugged, looking down at his arm, strapped tight to his chest. "We'll see, won't we?" Then he straightened. "Except you won't. You won't be here."

He was right. "Rico . . ."

"That's life, man. It comes at you, and if you don't get out of the way, it runs you right over."

As good an explanation as any.

"Where's Rese?" Rico looked around the room as though just realizing they were alone.

"She's fired up Pop to tackle every project he's let slip. I'm not sure if it's a competition or a buddy club. But they're building Dom a curio shelf while they wait on the plaster in the kitchen." He shook his head with a laugh. "Pop had to admit the job she did with the wood patch was better than any he'd seen."

Rico grinned. "So now she's not a girl."

Lance laughed. "Not sure he'll go that far. But he told me last night I should get my head on straight and marry her."

"Does he know it's against your religion?"

Lance rocked back in his chair. "I'm thinking of changing that."

Rico shook his head. "Right."

No surprise Rico didn't believe him. He'd seen the crash and burn of every other relationship, knew the moment Lance would turn and run. "It's different this time."

"It's no different, man." Rico's face took on a strange expression. "Love is for mortals."

Lance huffed. "And?"

"You're something . . . else."

"I think maybe you did hit your head."

Rico spread his hand. "Look in the mirror."

"Get outta here." Lance brought the legs of his chair down. "I'm going to sit with Nonna. Want to say hi?"

"I spent time with her yesterday. She slept, though. Don't think she knew I was there."

"She knew." If anyone could see in her sleep, it was Antonia Seraphina Michelli. And she wouldn't miss Rico in any event.

Though she knew he was the devil on her grandson's shoulder, she'd had a soft spot for the scrawny boy from the first day Lance brought him home. He was like an alley kitten, skittish and starved for affection. They'd found solace and shelter in her kitchen, brought her laughs and trinkets. She'd made Rico return his mother's jewelry, but kept all their bird's nests and marbles and drawings, displaying Rico's side by side with his.

Lance hadn't realized until he was older that their situation was unusual. He'd adopted Rico and assumed the rest would too. And they had, becoming Rico's family in every way that mattered. Momma stuffed him, and Pop got as much work from him as from his sons in return for cheap rent. Chaz helped, too, once he entered the picture, and now Rese was balancing the score.

Not really though. If Pop had ever collected what he could, he'd have retired long ago. But at sixty-three he was still setting the example. Work hard and give generously. Don't talk about it.

I am large with child when Marco tells me my sentence is over. His pop has laid brick for an apartment building in the Bronx. Its financier is on the point of ruin, and Gustavo Michelli is no fool. He has taken the building off the man's hands in payment for his work. All I hear is that we're leaving the tenement that has been my personal hell these last eight months. With a squeal, I encase Marco's neck. I don't even care if his mother scowls. Her

421

scowl is a permanent fixture. Her Marco, her prize, married without her knowledge to a Northern snob. The ball of my belly presses between us and the baby kicks. Marco laughs, then eases me back in deference to his momma.

"We're moving up, Momma."

Suddenly I can't breathe. She's coming too? But of course she is. The building is her husband's. I've seen Pop Michelli enough to know they're married, but I can't blame him for getting as far away as he does. Who would want to contend with the sour spirit I must face every day?

Like his pop, Marco is still gone too much, and my hearts aches without him, but when he comes back, I give him the best of me. What man wants to return to a shrew? He is mysterious about his job, but I don't press it. I'm just glad he's working.

It would crush me to see him in a breadline, to worry about him in a communist labor strike. I feel for those people, but I have no wish to join them. "When do we go?"

"The building isn't complete. A couple months yet."

I can't hide my dismay. I don't want this baby born here. "Oh." My voice gives me away.

Momma Benigna pounces. "Now she's complaining. Gustavo works himself toward an early grave to give us this, and she's complaining."

If anything puts him in an early grave it won't be me. How badly I want to say it aloud! But I've promised myself I won't put Marco in between as she is always doing. How she makes me regret that I ever wished for a momma. But I will not ruin the moment. Marco must know the gift he's given me with his news — hope.

Antonia realized she'd done it again, drifted off while Lance waited patiently beside her. *"Io Io fatto."* Her apology came effortlessly for once.

"Don't worry about it."

His eyes were gentle. She had seen them flash and seen them cry; seen them hungry and rebellious. She'd seen him full of righteous anger, but most often she'd seen him with the look he wore now. He had the letter ready, but waited for her, wondering if she could bear it. She had put him off long enough.

"R . . . ead."

He lifted the pages. "Sure?"

No, but clinging to the hope in her memory, she nodded.

Lance read.

"With Vittorio inside, my job was more field marshal than foot soldier. I'd worked it both ways and generally preferred the latter, but Vittorio was discreet, partly why Jackson had brought him in, no doubt. That worked both ways now.

"Though he knew from me the bank was dirty, and Jackson dirtier, Vittorio maintained his deference to the boss. He pulled it off better than I'd expected, and I thought if we got out of it intact, I'd recommend him to the Bureau. More than one agent had come out of similarly shady situations. They provided useful insights. And frankly, I liked the man, though I admit I was more favorably disposed to you and Quillan. It became a priority to insure all your welfare. In that I failed, though I didn't understand why.

"I'd kept the operation straightforward, learning early on that simplicity worked best — one reason I preferred a cover to clandestine meetings. Vittorio agreed. His part was to record what he witnessed without judging its usefulness. Dates, times, transactions, meetings. He would be my eyes, and I'd decipher what all he gave me. A simple plan that would have worked — if I'd received the information."

Lance looked up. "That must be the envelopes I found in the cellar."

Antonia pulled herself into the present. "En . . . ve . . . lopes?"

He winced. "Never mind."

"L . . . ance."

He shook his head. "If you don't remember, forget it."

She glared. "Tell m . . . e."

He sighed. "From the cellar with the money. I showed you. Then you got theatrical and made a scene."

Insolent! She swatted his hand. "Sh . . . ow me."

"Nonna."

She gave him the look that brooked no argument. It may have been a shock before, but now it was Marco, a part of him he'd never shared. And Papa too. All these years she'd judged him, hidden him away in her heart, ashamed of the love she still felt. All these years . . .

"Okay." Lance got up. "But if you scare me again, that's it. I'm burning it all."

Lance went into his apartment. Rico must have gone out, because it was empty and completely silent except for the ceiling fan rocking in its bracket as the blades moved the air around. He got the box he'd tucked away after Nonna's ministroke. He had sprung it on her the first time — stupidly — but now she was asking. Maybe she recognized the purpose that seemed to be driving it all, purpose even Rese had seen.

He got the box and held it for a moment before going back to Nonna. Rico's contention that he was anything other than painfully human was crazy, but as he stood with the box he almost felt outside himself, as though he wasn't quite solid. Something tugged inside . . . something undeniable. He wanted to resist but couldn't. Was that how Tony had felt, charging into the tower when every human sense must have screamed to turn back?

Closing his eyes he whispered, "Here I am. Such as I am."

The fan *click-click*ed as he stood unmoving. Whatever it was lasted only a moment; then he opened his eyes and wondered if he was imagining all of it.

He brought the box back to Nonna. It felt strangely heavy as he set it in her lap, or maybe that was his own fear weighing. He didn't want another setback.

The envelopes were at the bottom, so after helping her open the lid, he lifted out the items he'd shown her before, watching intently for any sign of strain as he handed each over. This time she seemed to take them like old friends, unafraid of what they might tell her. He should have waited on God's timing. When would he learn not to force his own will?

She seemed reluctant to let go of her diary, but set it aside at last and looked at the envelopes. She studied the names penned there. "Th . . . is is Papa's penm . . . anship." Her face tightened when she reached Arthur Jackson's file.

Lance knelt down beside her. "Are you upset, Nonna?"

She looked into his face. "You'll kn . . . ow when I'm u . . . pset."

He squeezed her hand. "Your pop might have been involved with something he shouldn't, but as soon as he knew, he did the right thing. He worked with Nonno."

She nodded. "Arthur J . . . ackson m . . . urdered Papa."

Lance shrugged. "Maybe. But it wasn't his idea."

Her brow pinched. Confusion filled her eyes.

He took out the letter he'd gotten from Sybil, the one she'd copied from her father's safe, a bit of family lore. The time her great-granddad hired a hit man — only the assassin had approached Arthur Jackson, informed him, offered his services.

Nonna read the letter, her face moving side to side as she read, a mute denial. She dragged her gaze from the page. "Wh . . . o?"

Lance shrugged. "The guy knew Nonno was a federal agent. He might have figured out your pop was the inside man, but it looks like it started with Nonno."

Definite strain in her forehead. The letter shook. He clasped her withered hand. "Stay with me, Nonna."

But her tears came. He slipped the letter free and put it with the envelopes into the box. He took it out of her lap, leaving her personal things beside her, though she seemed to have forgotten them altogether.

Her trembling lips worked, and she whispered, "Marco," with such confusion and despair it gripped his heart.

Why were they doing this? What was the point? Did God delight in bringing His creatures low? Angry, Lance jerked his chin up. *No more strokes, no more shocks, no more pain, Lord. Your burden is not light.* Couldn't He see it was crushing her? *I'm taking this yoke. Lay it on me and give Nonna peace.*

Again, he felt hollowed out, but this time he wrestled in his mind like Jacob with the angel. *It's between you and me, Lord.* And he was not letting go.

Chapter Twenty-five

Over the next three days, Rese watched the way Lance's family cared for Antonia, allowing her the dignity of things she could do for herself while providing what she needed. Couldn't she do that much for Mom? She might not know what the doctors and nurses knew, but if the new drugs provided some peace and clarity to Mom's troubled mind, she could give her a home again, a family, even if it was only the daughter she hadn't wanted to keep.

Though Antonia had slept almost constantly the past few days, between naps there was always someone checking in and children presenting drawings and stuffed animals and wounded fingers to be kissed. Rese knew all this because Lance now kept their door and Antonia's open. He wanted to be instantly available to read or sit or listen, though she seemed to have put him off again. Maybe they were done and Lance just hadn't realized. Or she was gearing herself up, as he said, getting back her emotional stamina.

Rese sighed. His patience was admirable,

but they were through the second week, and though she had cleared the next, she would need to give the three reservations in the last week of June enough notice to find alternate lodging if necessary. The inn might have been full if she hadn't suspended reservations, but she couldn't worry about that. Lance had to tie up his loose ends so he could focus on their business. She had to see that he didn't lose sight of that.

A passel of children scuffled through Antonia's door across the hall, hushing each other and giggling. Rese could now identify which ones went to which parents, and even knew their names. But when Nicky separated from the group, ran in and climbed into her lap, it sent a glow through her she couldn't hide.

Lance shook his head. "I've been replaced."

Rese smiled. "There are some things quarters can't buy." But she was as surprised as Lance.

Nicky snuggled in, sending waves of warmth right through her.

"Nice, ay, Nick?" He ruffled the toddler's hair. "I like that spot too."

New waves of warmth. "Don't you have something to do?"

He leaned back and cloaked her with his gaze, a slow smile.

Vinnie came and rapped a knuckle on the doorjamb, the scent of cigar smoke curling in around him.

Lance only tipped his chin. "Whatchu need, Vinnie?"

"Nothin'. I came to see your girl."

Lance raised his brows.

His girl. Rese turned her attention to Vinnie. "Yes?"

The old man shuffled over. "That shelf you did for Dom. What's the chance I get one too?"

She smiled. "Came out nice, didn't it?"

Lance crossed his arms, looking from her to Vinnie.

She could imagine what he was thinking. "I'll have to run it by Roman."

"Don't take no. I got more stuff than Dom, and better stuff too. His old trophies?" Vinnie blew through his lips. "I got a signed Sinatra doll."

Rese nodded. "I'll see what I can do."

"And three albums, all signed. Those shouldn't be in a box."

"Okay."

"Okay." He nodded. "I gotta go." He turned to Lance. "You oughtta marry that girl."

Lance shrugged. "I'm working on it."

"Working." Vinnie fanned both hands down at him. "What's to work on?"

"Only got one shot left." Lance flicked a

glance her way, causing just the reaction he intended, she was sure. "Can't waste it."

Vinnie flapped his hands again and walked out.

"Lance . . ." This was as good a chance as any to get a progress report, but Monica came to fetch Nicky, and then Jake, Tony and Gina's oldest son, arrived with a battered guitar case. As he set up to play with Lance, she guessed it was as much to soak in time with his uncle as for instruction. Watching them, she felt the rightness of Lance's influence.

Would he ever want to leave? Would they ever let him? If she felt torn, how must it be for him? But she should be running her business and making decisions for her mother's care. She had responsibilities too.

And she missed Baxter. She missed the way he flopped his head in her lap with a look that said, "Where have you been?" when she sat down beside him. She missed the super-soft fur between his ears, and the way his paws curled around her arm when she rubbed his belly. And though Michelle thought the dog was content without Lance, Rese knew something came alive in him for his master that none of them could touch.

It was the same thing that came alive in her. She watched him awhile with Jake, then stood up. "I'm going for a walk." Maybe she'd find Star, and when they came back Lance would be packed up and ready to leave. Antonia would wave good-bye, and all the others, too, with tearful hugs and kisses. Rese felt a pang. Would she actually miss them?

Outside, the trees were in full leaf, the ground patched with shade and sunshine, the air swirling past storefront restaurants scented with sauces, cheeses, and exhaust. People greeted her, and she laughed to think she'd once wondered if she needed Mace. Though the neighborhood bordered one of the worst parts of the city and things happened after dark that had to be ignored, on this golden afternoon it was an enclave of safety, of relationships, of life.

There was Carmine, nose healed, sitting in a plastic chair outside the candy store with another gent, chatting and watching the street. There were Joe Palese and Vinnie Avenzzana having clams on the half shell squeezed with lemon. There were the pasta shop owners washing their window and talking with the almost centenarian resident priest from the church across the street.

Near the corner, a stocky man in an apron smoked a cigarette and watched her approach. A stockier woman stepped out the shop door and smacked his arm. "What are you looking at, old man?"

"A woman is as old as she looks. A man isn't old until he stops looking." He winked as she passed.

In another life Rese might have taken offense, but these people were genuine. And crazily enough, she felt real too.

What if Lance wanted to stay? Could she make this place home? She passed the little shops stuffed with knickknacks, the religious bookstore, and a half dozen food purveyors. If Lance was with her, every single proprietor would have called out a greeting.

Yes, she could live there, but what about Mom? The inn? Star?

Across the street, she stopped outside the church and looked up. The architectural design drew the eyes and heart upward. But when she'd pointed that out, Lance had shrugged. "That's right, but Christ is also here on the street, sleeves rolled, laboring in the kingdom."

"Then why hasn't it worked?"

"Renovation," Lance had said. "A new way inside the old."

And Chaz had called it "a situation of weeds and wheat," necessary until the given time when their labor would bring in the harvest and the chaff would be burned. She was starting to see how faith was simply life.

As she stood there, distracted from the street kingdom by the beauty of the stained-glass window, Sofie came out of the church and paused, then came down to her. "Hi."

Rese returned the greeting. "I was just walking."

"Can I come?"

She shrugged. "Sure."

"Heard anything from Star?"

Rese shook her head. She hadn't expected to. "Sometimes she's gone for weeks, even months."

"So it's a pattern."

Rese watched a brown-striped finch hop along the sidewalk, then take wing. "Lance thinks she wants to hurt herself. That somehow it makes her feel better."

Sofie nodded. "That's a clinical condition that usually indicates deep-seated issues."

"She has issues." Didn't they all? Rico was right that it came down to what you did with it. Yet . . . what if Lance and Chaz were right? What if it was some evil that drove her? Like Walter whispering in Mom's head. Rese shuddered. "I should have stopped her."

Sofie touched her arm. "You couldn't."

Rese turned, surprised to find Sofie piercingly transparent.

"People set their course, and all the

loved ones in the world can't change it. It has to come from here." She pressed a hand to her heart, and two beats later said, "Six years ago I tried to take my life."

Rese stopped. Having survived a murder attempt, she could hardly imagine trying to take her own life. But when Sofie kept walking, she made her feet move.

Sofie crossed her arms. "Everyone knew the reason, but no one saw the hurt that was killing me. I kept face, you know, smiling at all the kisses and hugs and assurances. *'Time will heal.' 'You're better off.'* And some less than kind. *'If you spit in the sky, it comes back in your face.'* " She laughed, then sighed. "The thing is, you can't know Star's pain unless she shows you."

She had shown her, again and again all the years of their growing up. And Rese had held her and soothed her and told her it was all right. But it wasn't all right, or she wouldn't still be running from it, or to it, as Lance believed.

"I wish she'd come back. We can't stay much longer."

"So Lance is really leaving?"

Sofie knew about the inn; why would she ask? Rese nodded. "As soon as he's done here."

"He's the best of us," Sofie said.

"He thinks he's a screw-up."

She laughed. "I know. But he's special." She turned her face to Rese. "Do you love him?"

Rese swallowed the ache in her throat. She had tried to deny it, but how could she? Everyone he knew loved him. How had she thought she wouldn't?

Holding Celestina is touching heaven. This life, this wonder Marco and I have made! He took the night train to be here in time, and now here she is, and he is too.

Marco presses his lips to my cheek. "Are you all right, cara mia?"

"How can you ask? Look at her." But I'm touched that he's thinking of me when his daughter just came into the world. How Nonno would have smiled. And Papa. My tears catch in my throat, and Marco covers my mouth with his, loving away the loss, leaving room only for joy.

He is my strength. My love and my life. I can almost forget. Almost . . .

Antonia looked up as Rese and Sofie came in together. She received their kisses, Sofie as natural as breath and Rese who'd been so stiff before.

"Monsignor offered Mass for you," Sofie said.

"Buono." Antonia nodded. Who knew, maybe it mattered.

"Anna and Mary Elizabeth send their

prayers." Sofie sat in Lance's chair. Antonia had come to think of it that way during their journeys through her life. It was selfish to keep him so long. She should finish with Marco's pages and be done with it.

Sofie filled her in on people who had worshiped with her most of their lives. They all sent their prayers. She listened and smiled. But as soon as Sofie had finished, she turned to Rese, who stood back as unobtrusive as a post. "Get L . . . ance."

Rese nodded, then when she had left, Antonia turned to Sofie. "She h . . . as L . . . ance's heart."

"Maybe," Sofie said.

Lance paused in his instruction when Rese came in and told him, "Antonia wants you."

She seemed reluctant to interrupt, but he and Jake had spent some productive time already.

"Good." Jake shook his hand like a rag.

"You lost your calluses." He didn't need to say it. Jake's fingers spoke for themselves. His own were callused for life, but Jake's were tender enough to need reminding.

Jake frowned. "What's the point?"

Lance shoved his arm. "Whatchu mean what's the point?"

Jake pushed him back. "You're just gonna leave again."

"There's no guitar instructors in Manhattan?"

Jake shrugged.

"What's with this attitude? Where's your hunger?" He wanted more than adulation. He wanted Jake to grab something for himself.

"Why should I learn from some dork when you could —" Jake shook his head. "Never mind. Go see Nonna."

"When I could what?"

"It doesn't matter."

Lance set his guitar in the stand. "I could what, Jake?"

"Take me with you."

Lance rested his forearms on his knees and studied his nephew, Tony's son, already showing the blocky shoulders and large hands. Eyes way too old for his years, like all the kids of the victims, knowing the face of evil before they could grasp the concept.

"Your mom needs you, Jake."

He rolled his eyes.

"Come o-on. You know she does."

"Who cares." He glowered. "She's got that guy now."

Lance raised his brows. "What guy?"

"She's seen him twice. Some doctor she works with."

Lance glanced at Rese. She'd asked him how he'd feel if Gina moved on, if he would blame her. "Twice is hardly serious," he convinced them both. "Unless you're a Michelli." He grinned. "Then it's locked up."

Jake scowled. "Their mouths were locked up."

"You spied?"

Jake flounced back on the couch, letting the guitar slide flat on his lap. "They were right out on the porch."

"And your head was hanging out the window?"

Jake gripped his arms across his chest. "So what if I looked? She's my mom."

"So she deserves some respect. You don't spy on her."

"She shouldn't suck face on the porch."

"Well, maybe she didn't want to suck face in front of you."

"He's a dork."

"How do you know?"

"A doctor?" His tone dripped scorn.

Yeah, well, next to a cop . . . Next to Tony . . . "First, you don't know it's anything serious. Even if they're sucking face," he added when Jake started to argue. "And if it is, you still can't run away."

"You did."

Lance frowned. "Would Tony Michelli have run away?"

"Dad would've punched the guy's lights out."

True.

"But Dad's not here." Jake's voice cracked.

"So think like him."

"Punch him? Break his glasses?"

A doctor with glasses. Kissing Gina. "You can't punch him. Tony was fair. You gotta be fair."

Jake's chest rose and fell beneath his crossed arms. "I don't want a new dad."

"So tell your mom how you feel."

Jake looked away.

"What?"

The boy swallowed. "She's sad, you know? I don't want to make it worse."

There was the Jake he knew. "She'd want to know it's hard for you, Jake. Maybe you could work out a plan. Get to know the guy."

Jake pushed the guitar aside, scowling.

"Besides, if it's hard for you, it'll be hard on your brothers too. You need to think of that. Tony always looked out for me."

Jake was listening. He might not like what he was hearing, but he heard it. Lance stood up. "Now go see what your cousins are doing."

Jake had developed a walking speed of near inertia, but he obeyed. When he'd closed the door behind him, Lance joined

Rese, locked their fingers, and said, "Wanna suck face?"

She snorted, but he saw the pulse flutter in her neck and kissed it. Then he took hold of her mouth. Gina was moving on, and Rese had told him to live his life. Now seemed a good time to start.

"Antonia needs . . ."

"I know." But he had needs too. He slid his fingers into the soft layers of her hair and deepened his kiss. Didn't she know, didn't she care that life was too short? That one day you could be there, and the next you were gone?

When he said he loved her, he meant it, but she didn't want to hear it, so he wouldn't say it again. He would just — Desire slammed him so hard he staggered. Now. Why not? But he drew back, breathing hard, and it was almost anger that frayed his voice. "You're hard on the heart, Rese."

"Lance, I . . ."

He pressed his fingers to her lips, unwilling to hear her excuses. "I have to go." Because every fiber screamed to take her into his room and make her love him before it was too late. He walked out, using every scrap of strength he had.

Heart hammering, Rese stared after him. She was going to say she loved him until he stopped her. Now the words lodged in her throat. She couldn't remember the last time she'd used them. She wasn't even sure she had answered Mom that night; she'd been so afraid.

Dad neither required nor desired the words. Their companionship was on the job, the excellence they achieved together, the unique challenge of each project, the deep satisfaction of completion. Beyond that . . . there had really been nothing. Two people in their own worlds sharing the same space. He couldn't keep something like Mom secret and have any relationship with her at all. Or maybe he just wanted to be left alone.

Lance was always present. Even with his head down, guitar across his lap, pencil in his mouth, working out a melody and lyrics; even focused, he drew her in with a glance or a smile. When she was in her carving zone, she hardly acknowledged him, hardly realized he was there. It had become her way to shut out the world, to forget the guys and their resentment, or whatever she didn't want to think about.

Lance never shut out; he always included, laid himself open. They were opposites, yet they'd forged a pathway into each other's reality. Lance didn't resent her zone, though sometimes he destroyed it. She appreciated his ability to connect with everyone in even a small way, but it was a gift she lacked completely.

She laughed now at the idea of her running an inn. Renovating the villa? Piece of cake. Serving the guests? Forget it. She'd mastered the art of ignoring. Lance was the supreme connector. But together they would make it work — if they could just get back.

Chapter Twenty-six

"I promise you, carissima, I had no intention of sacrificing Vittorio. His death was my worst failure, and I have carried the burden of it. There was always risk; for myself I accepted that. Penetrating the operations of the ruthless men I intended to take down fulfilled me like nothing else. One slip, one word, and they would kill me. But those were the ones I stopped, darling Antonia, men like those who killed your papa. That was why I took my job, and why I kept it secret, even from you."

Lance swallowed. A legacy of concealment. No wonder he'd fallen so easily into the mode.

"The Bureau wanted your eyewitness testimony. But the quickest way to end an investigation was to eliminate the witness, in this case a girl who had seen and guessed too much. I had to get you away, keep you safe until we built our case.

"But Arthur Jackson moved with such efficiency, I realized his pockets were deeper than we'd thought. Neither the press nor the police reported the killing. Even the coroner's findings were revised. There was no investigation, though the house was searched by Jackson's cops; Vittorio's evidence, confiscated."

He had that wrong, Lance thought. It had been hidden in the cellar. If Nonno Marco had gone back to look there, he might have built a case after all.

"Without the record of transactions, our operation was a bust, but I knew Jackson would still try to silence you. Your father and grandfather were gone, but you were a messy detail, and Jackson didn't like things messy. You could have testified against him, but a glimpse in the dark with no corroborating materials was not worth enough for me to break my word. I had promised to keep you safe, and there was only one way I could see to do that. Play out the role I'd begun."

Lance glanced at Nonna. Nonno Marco had given her a new name, a new home, a new life — out of guilt and duty. He

446

frowned. Should Nonno have told the truth to a young woman in the depth of grief and shock, whom he was sworn to protect? In a lawless, ruthless world he knew too well?

"What if he'd told you, Nonna, that he was responsible? What if you knew he'd gotten your pop killed?"

She blanched. "I w . . . ould have h . . . ated him."

"Then it was better you didn't know."

She clenched her hands, her jaw working, saliva moistening the side of her mouth. Her gaze sharpened. "I bl . . . amed Papa."

Lance set the pages aside. "You wouldn't have gone with Nonno if you knew." No marriage for them, no life together. He wouldn't exist. She might not have even survived. Lance looked into her twisted face, seeing her struggle. Would she change it all, if she could?

Her voice was a rustle of brittle leaves. "Go a . . . way."

He leaned forward, concern churning. No way would he leave her alone. "Let me stay."

Tears poured from her eyes. Because of Nonno's silence she had believed Vittorio guilty and carried the shame of it. He could have told her otherwise, but all their years together, he never had. Nonno's whole life was deception, playing whatever role accomplished his ends — even his marriage to Nonna?

Lance got onto his knees and held her as she cried silently. Momma came up with soup, but left it and went out. He'd get an earful later, but for now he rested his head on Nonna's and shared her tears.

Why had Nonno left this deathbed confession? What good could it do to reveal it all now? That wasn't the man he'd known, the caring, laughing Nonno he'd known. Or was even that a part he'd played? Had the deceit eaten at him, the roles blending until he hardly knew who he was? Even Pop had said it. Were these pages Marco Michelli's true identity? A cry to be known? Truly known. Lance swallowed his indignation. Nonno had chosen a life of mirrors. But Nonna had failed to recognize the illusion.

Rese walked with Monica through the indoor market, breathing the scents of tobacco being rolled in the cigar booth at the front, blocks of cheese, barrels of olives, and a dry salted fish that looked like something she'd nail to the wall. In the corner butcher stall, a young man waved his cleaver. "Yeah? You're so desperate you call the operator, just so someone don't hang up on you."

The guy three stalls down called back, "You're so desperate you talk to the recording." The men working around them laughed. Rese shook her head. Men were basically men, but for some reason that amused instead of perturbed her.

"What can I get you, sweetie?" asked a robust, silver-templed man behind the meat case.

Rese shifted Nicky on her hip and looked for Monica. "I'm with her."

Monica stepped up and scrutinized the veal. "Got any fresher than this?"

Rese wandered as the two argued over the condition of the meat that had looked fine to her — not that she'd know what veal looked like, good or otherwise. The horrifying prospect of dinner with Monica had been diluted by other meals that had not become interrogations since Bobby and Monica preferred to talk about themselves. If Monica's various ailments were less than entertaining, Bobby's renditions of the ways people hung up on him were truly funny. Bobby liked the spotlight, and when he got rolling, it was stand-up comedy.

Their children had stories too; each seemed determined to impress her more than the last, a trait from their dad, she supposed. She shifted Nicky again as they shopped, trying to keep him from reaching for everything that looked good, and

449

some things that didn't.

"Bread we'll get at Terranova's." Monica shouldered her canvas carryall. "Addeo's is good, but too predictable. Terranova's gets a little burnt sometimes, and Bobby likes that better." For all their bickering, Monica knew and cared about Bobby's countless preferences. Either he was the pickiest man alive or Monica lived to please.

In contrast, Lucy's husband, Lou, hardly voiced an opinion. An insurance adjuster by day, league bowler by night, he was happy for whatever Lucy set before him. But then, she'd been right about Lucy's cooking. She didn't have Lance's flair, but she knew her way around a stove. She and Lou would add balance to tonight's experience, but their family nearly doubled the children.

At least she and Lance — She stopped. She'd been thinking at least they didn't add kids to the party, but was that a good thing? Nicky had snuggled his head into her neck, his little hand pressed to the opposite side, an unconscious hug of sleepy abandon. Before encountering Lance's family, she hadn't thought about children. Her focus had been so narrow, her identity staunchly defined, her feminine inclinations so fiercely controlled that she hardly knew what to do with the melting inside her now.

Monica was chattering about using the restaurant instead of her own kitchen. "We'll fit better around a table down there. Or use two. We can give the children their own and have grown-up conversation for a change."

Rese nodded. "It's handy having the restaurant."

Lance had used up a good deal of its inventory, depleting the shelves of canned tomatoes and olives, oils and vinegars, dried mushrooms and pasta. He had intended to make a plan with Antonia as to its future, but she wasn't sure how far that had gotten. Without Lance or Nonna, Lucy had said, the restaurant wouldn't be the same. Rese hadn't flinched. If Lance intended to take over Antonia's restaurant, he'd have said so.

But his whole focus was on Antonia, getting through the letter so they could leave. How could those few pages take so long to get through, and be so draining? Antonia was fragile and Lance desperate not to upset her, but if it was so bad, why read it at all?

Lance kept the content to himself, and that was fine. She didn't need to know people's secrets. Sofie's disclosure had shaken her, even without details. If someone so brilliant, so lovely, so loved could despair, what hope was there? She almost wished she didn't know, didn't have to realize that everyone struggled, that there was no way out of it. A little secrecy might be a good thing. She just didn't want things that mattered kept from her. Big things. Life-changing things.

"Now some ravioli for lunch." Monica headed for Borgatti's. "It's all the kids want." She shrugged. "So, hey. Give them what they want."

It was strange to think of children having that power. Between the bizarre combinations Mom had put together and the cans and packages Dad provided, Rese didn't think she'd ever had the chance to wonder what she actually wanted to eat — a source of difficulty for Lance when he'd arrived. How could she not have an opinion?

It was almost as hard now, since everything he made was so good. She would not back down on which wood was better for a banister, or what brick could be saved, but when it came to food, he had more experience than she had ideas. She had learned to express appreciation, though. Lance's exasperation had taught her that much.

She and Monica made their way back, chatting amiably in a way Rese could not have imagined when she first arrived. Monica was forceful, but fiercely caring underneath. As Lance said, she overnurtured, like Doria. Well, Rese thought, there were worse things.

She carried the dozy child all the way up for Monica and laid him in his bed, warmth growing inside as he scrunched into a ball and succumbed to sleep. It looked like Monica was ready to nap herself, so Rese headed back down, surprised to find the apartment door closed, though Antonia's was open. It wasn't locked, though. "Lance?" She stopped just inside.

He stood by the table over Star, who was huddled and shaking in a chair, her hair hacked off to the blond roots. Her head looked so pale and vulnerable it hit Rese low in the stomach. She closed the door and glanced around for the others.

"Rico's working. Chaz too."

She didn't stop to wonder what Rico was working at, or why he wasn't here to see what his rejection wrought. Lance cupped Star's shoulder when she shuddered. Her eye sockets were gray as rain, her lips cracked and bleeding.

Rese looked from her to Lance, searching his face for answers as she joined them.

"She's coming down from something," he said softly.

"No way. She wouldn't . . . she doesn't . . ." Rese crouched, taking the icy hand — fingernails chewed to the quick — between her own. "Hey, Star."

Star rocked. " 'Mercy but murders,

453

pardon . . . par . . .' " She started to shiver, gripping herself. "Pardoning . . ."

Lance grabbed the folded blanket from the couch and wrapped it over her shoulders, even though the room was overwarm. Rese drew it closed at the front, then gripped Star's hand again. "Do you need a doctor?" Maybe she'd contracted some deadly virus, some food poisoning.

" 'Mercy but murders . . .' "

"Star, look at me." A passing glance was all she got.

Star tried to stand, then dropped to the chair again, scratching at her skin. Rese pulled her hand away from the raw patches on her arms. She'd never seen her this way. Distraught, yes, inconsolable, but never incoherent.

"She's on the backside of it," Lance said.

He could not be right. "She wouldn't take drugs." She avoided preservatives! But what else could it be? She'd been gone five days, not long enough to look like this.

"The best thing you can do is get her out of here."

"Out?" Rese stared. He would make her leave?

"Take her home."

Rese stiffened. "To Sonoma?"

"She's obviously messed up. Odds are someone believes she owes him."

Star was a magnet for men of lousy character, but she had always avoided real trouble — until now? "What do you mean, owes?"

"Did she take her money order?"

Rese shook her head. "It's on the dresser."

"Well, using isn't free. There are always strings attached."

"She wouldn't use drugs." But her argument was starting to seem feeble. "Can't we keep her here?"

"What do you think the chances of that are?"

"I'll talk to Rico. He'll —"

"It's not Rico." Lance raised her up and stepped her aside. "You know how she is. She'll take off the minute it hurts. And even if Rico doesn't try, it'll hurt. They're both raw."

"I can't believe she'd —"

"Get her back to Sonoma. Keep her at the inn."

"Lance, I can't —"

"You have your return ticket. Use the money order for Star's."

"What if she won't sign it?"

"Put it on a credit card. I'll give you mine."

She shook her head. "No, I just . . ." *Don't want to leave without you.* "Won't Rico help her when he sees this?"

"Probably. But I won't let him."

455

She did not believe he'd said that, and her face must have shown it.

"You don't know what we're dealing with." He pulled her farther aside. "Suppose you're right, and Star didn't do this to herself."

Rese swallowed. "She wouldn't. Staying clean is her religion."

"Then read between the lines."

She shook her head.

"Come on, Rese."

But she really didn't know.

"Someone slipped her a mickey, then introduced a stronger cocktail. I'm guessing smack, but it could be meth or crack. And not in introductory doses."

Rese expelled her breath. "Why? It's not like Star resists. You said yourself sex is a drug to her."

"It's not about what she wants. There are predators and networks that eat women like Star alive. Addiction means control."

"You think she's addicted?"

"Not yet or she wouldn't be here. But what happens next time? And if Rico interferes he could get killed."

She closed her eyes, not wanting to believe it. Drugs were Star's taboo, tapping into all her issues since birth. If she'd broken it, or someone had made her, the backlash could be horrible.

Lance gripped her shoulder. "Take her home."

There was no choice, but it still stung. "What about you?"

"I'm close; I can feel it. As soon as I've done what I have to —"

"Or something else happens." Panic seized her.

"Don't." He raised her face and kissed her. "I love you. I want to be with you. Nothing's going to change that."

She clutched the sides of his shirt as though holding on could matter. "I love you too." The words were out before she thought, their impact radiating from him like daybreak.

He crushed her against him, kissing her neck, her jaw, her ear, breathing into her hair, "Now I don't want you to go."

"Can't have it both ways, bud." But she clung to him without reserve. She wanted him to take everything that was in her heart. He was her heart. But she looked at Star, kneading the blanket with her fingers and rocking. Reality descended. Star, her mother, other needs, other situations. She had no control over life. She could only do what was right, and trust.

Grindingly reluctant, Lance saw them to the airport. He had almost hoped there'd be nothing available, but by upgrading

Rese's ticket, for an outrageous amount, they'd gotten two first-class seats, the only thing available from LaGuardia to San Francisco — courtesy of Star's trust.

She was still agitated, and he wondered if that wouldn't trigger security concerns, but possibly by virtue of that first-class ticket, or the basic oddity of life, she passed through the first ID check in the line with no trouble. Rese had regained her composure, naturally. But he held her admission and its expression inside him like a torch.

He'd done it. He'd won. Rese loved him — and admitted it. He wanted to crow like Bobby, strut like Tony, dance and sing and tell the whole world Rese Barrett loved him. But on this triumphant pinnacle, he had to let her go. How else could he get Star out of trouble and keep Rico from worse?

And himself, since Rico's fights were his fights, and he had enough to deal with already. How long could it be before he finished with Nonna, brought her whatever peace they could find in it all, and joined Rese in Sonoma? He knew exactly the spot he wanted to use, the ill-fated picnic spot, site of their first disastrous date, the one that almost got him fired and had him eating dirt for weeks. He'd drive her out there on the Harley — an ache seized him at the thought of his own bike between his thighs, the Petaluma Road beneath his wheels, and Rese hanging on behind.

It had to be sunset. He imagined the hills dotted with cows and patchwork vineyards, the wind-bent tree where they'd spread their leathers and sit. Would the irony annoy her, or would she see the humor of it? Either way, she wouldn't resist. She couldn't.

Rese suddenly turned. "Lance! Monica expected us for dinner."

"I'll take care of it." Her concern touched him. His family was no longer a threat or a burden to her.

"And tell Rico."

"I will." But as Rese started toward the point he could no longer follow, he caught her arm. "Wait."

Passengers behind her stepped around as he closed her hands in his. "Just . . . one more time."

"What?"

"I want to hear it."

She rolled her eyes, but a smile tugged her lips. "I love you, Lance."

Power surged. He leaned to kiss her. "Hold that thought."

"That works both ways."

"You know it." He'd made it as clear as he could.

Their fingers slipped apart. She had to

go. It was the right thing. He'd withheld the probable details of Star's ordeal from Rese, things he suspected given her diminutive size and fragility. If Rese couldn't imagine someone drugging her, she didn't need to contemplate worse.

Thank God Star hadn't fought them about leaving. She must have been scared enough to let go. He and Chaz had contended with something the other night, something with teeth. He wasn't sure they were through, but for tonight, at least, he prayed it was enough.

Chapter Twenty-seven

Star had not spoken one word in the two days they'd been back. She had alternately slept and raged, but she would not say anything when Rese tried to talk it out. Now she sat shaking and silent in the Rain Forest room, sipping tea through a straw. She'd eaten three times in two days, gorging like a wolf, then losing it all.

Not even her terrible cooking could be blamed for that, Rese told herself as she set down a saucer of Minute rice that for once had not come out like glue. "Try this."

A metallic odor hovered over Star. She looked up with brittle eyes. "Thanks."

Surprised, Rese sat down on the bed across from her. She hadn't expected a response, but she could see by her heightened color that Star might talk and be better for it. She waited without prodding.

"He said I had 'it' — that thing that makes a star."

"Who said that?"

"Faust."

Right. "And who is Faust?"

Star's face pinched. "Someone I believed."

Rese sighed.

"He watched me sing and dance. He said I could be a star, and that's all I've ever wanted — to be . . . Star. You know? To really be Star." Her voice cracked.

Rese didn't know what to say. None of the things she'd told her in the past had made a lasting difference. And the one thing that might last had set her off. So she said, "I'm sorry."

Star rubbed the needle marks on her arm, frowning.

"Lance thinks he drugged you."

"With what?"

"He was guessing heroin."

Star emitted a whine and gripped the fragments of hair that looked as though they'd been hacked off with a handsaw.

"It's out of you now. It's all out." At least her tremors and hysteria, stomach issues and fatigue seemed to have subsided.

Rese stood and moved Star's hands, then smoothed the strands with gentle strokes. No more rosy spirals. "What happened to your hair?"

Star jumped up. "I thought there was something in it. I felt things crawling." She shuddered.

Hard to say whether she'd imagined or acquired something. Rese didn't want to think where Star had slept those five days she was gone.

"They kept crawling, and there was a knife, so I cut them out."

Thank God it was only hair she'd cut.

"Faust was incensed." Star gripped her throat. "He said my hair was his. That I'd cheated him."

Cheated him? *"Someone thinks she owes him."* Star had picked some winners, but Faust — or whatever his name was — must have topped the list.

"He charged at me, but I had the knife. I reached the door." She started to shake.

Lance was right. Someone like that might have come after her. Rese took her hands and sat her down on the bed.

Star curled up and moaned. "This most loathed life. Why can't it end?"

"Shh." Rese soothed her like a child.

"The worst thing —" Star sucked in a sob — "is they're gone."

"Who?"

"The fairies. The colors."

Her hand stilled on Star's head.

"I looked for them, Rese. I looked so hard. Maybe it was the drugs, I don't know." Tears were rushing, and her words poured out in gasps. "But I had to face it all without them."

Rese chilled. "Face what?"

"Everything they did to me, Faust and

the others." Star started to shake. "I looked and looked, but they didn't come, Rese. They weren't there."

Rese could hardly breathe as a thought took hold. "Is that why you do it, Star? To see the fairies?"

"I need to know they're there. To see the colors."

So Lance was wrong. It wasn't for the pain or for the sex, but to produce the effect, to trigger her imagination or . . . Her throat squeezed. She'd been willing to think maybe angels came, or some manifestation of the Lord taking a form Star recognized. But God wouldn't lure her into being used just to experience it.

A heaviness filled her limbs as she heard Chaz's voice binding spirits, saw Lance lost in prayer at such an intense level she'd been afraid for him. Had they blocked Star's "fairies"? Beings that "comforted" her when her body was abused, but made her seek the abuse to find them?

She squeezed Star's hand. "Maybe it's better."

Tears washed her eyes. "How can it be?"

Rese stroked the ragged tips that would curl as they grew but now stood out in peaks like a harvested field. "Because without them you're Star. You shine."

Star closed her eyes. Her shoulders rose and fell as she tottered on the brink of sobs. Then sleep descended. Rese took the rice down to the refrigerator, went to her own suite, and called Lance.

He had phoned the first night to tell her Rico was relieved and furious and melancholy. But she could hear his relief and guessed Rico would put it all behind him. Chaz sent his prayers and told her to stay on guard, whatever that meant.

The second night Lance had called to say Momma was in an uproar. How could he send her back alone? What was so important with Nonna, so mysterious that he risked his future and her grandbabies? He had imitated her scolding so accurately that Rese laughed aloud, then missed him so much it hurt.

Michelle had also brought Baxter home. And what a comfort it was to have Lance's dog, partly as surety for Lance, but mostly for Baxter's sweet self. As she pressed the buttons, she looked at Baxter lying inside on the small rug beside her bed and smiled. Guests were just going to have to deal with it.

Lance answered and she said, "Hi."

"No fair. I wanted to call you."

"It's an equal opportunity world."

He laughed. "I swear Lancelot had an easier time romancing Guinevere."

"And look where it got him."

"I was hoping you hadn't read the story."

"I saw the movie."

"Which version?"

"They all end pretty much the same."

"Okay, bad example."

She laughed.

"You can't be ready for bed this early."

"Thought I'd save you waiting until midnight."

"I like talking you to sleep, having you under my control."

"Tell me something I don't know."

"Okay. Pop offered me a job."

Her breath caught and refused to find any sort of rhythm.

"Someone's retiring, and Pop recommended me for the position. Rese?"

"He must believe you can do it. That's great, Lance." He'd wanted rings and a robe.

"I told him I had a position already, as soon as I finished with Nonna."

The air pushed out in a flood.

"You didn't think I'd take it, did you?" There was laughter in his voice.

"Lance Michelli . . ."

"Wish I could see your face."

"You'd be seeing my back."

"I'd be rubbing your back."

The rush that turned her to jelly was not fair. "Lance, I called you for a reason."

"You've replaced me with a Mexican maid?"

"Stop it."

"What's up?" His tone sobered.

She told him about Star. "It was you and Chaz, wasn't it."

"The power is God's, Rese. We only wielded it."

"But what do I do if — Lance, she's not happy they're gone."

"Listen to me. Satan wants you to doubt, but you can stand in the gap for Star."

"I don't know what you mean."

"Pray for her."

"She'll go ballistic."

"Pray silently. Lay hands when she's asleep. She's crying out for help, Rese, or she wouldn't have come back to you, knowing you believe."

Rese sank back against the pillows. "I don't think I can do that. I saw you."

"Forget about that."

Right. Like she could forget Lance beside her, gripped by something so deep he had to recover.

"Just keep praying for her protection."

"What will that do?"

"Keep them away."

"What if she goes looking for them?" Rese stroked Baxter, who'd brought his snout up to the bed.

"Pray even harder. If we keep them bound, she'll find no reward in the pain."

"Won't it hurt more?" Baxter brought

467

his front paws up on the bed and lowered his head between them. She rubbed his neck and shoulders.

"It has to hurt, or she'll keep looking for comfort there instead of finding it in people like you and Rico."

"Rico!"

Baxter raised his head and licked her hand.

"Rico didn't touch her, and believe me, that took an effort. He brought her into his music, his soul. He read her sonnets in the park!"

She hadn't thought of that. Maybe Lance was right. She remembered Rico's face the night they went looking, the stark hope in his eyes. Star had burned him. But was it all her fault?

She pressed a hand to her face, then startled when Baxter leaped onto the bed, snuggling up against her, plunking his shaggy head across her waist.

"What? What happened?"

She laughed. "You didn't tell me Baxter was a snuggler."

"What?"

"He just climbed into bed with me."

"No way."

"So I'm imagining this big shaggy thing sprawled up against me?"

Baxter licked her hand as real as anything.

"You have him in your room?"

"Quite."

"And he climbed into your bed."

"Leaped is more like it."

"He knows better than that. Put him on the phone."

She held the phone out to Baxter and heard Lance's, "Baxter, down."

Baxter whined, looking at her with soulful eyes. She stroked his head. "It's okay."

"Rese!"

She brought the phone back to her ear. "The damage is done. He likes it here."

"Tell him to get down."

"You're jealous." She heard his expelled breath and bit her lower lip.

"You're undoing my training."

"You'll have to get out here before he's completely spoiled."

"Rese."

"Go to sleep, Lance. I have a dog who needs attention."

He growled. Lance, not Baxter. She hung up the phone and snuggled down beside the animal. She hadn't dreamed of letting him into her bed, but took wicked pleasure in it now. "Yes." She rubbed Baxter's ears. "That Lance better get here soon, huh, buddy?" Baxter sighed hugely, and she laughed.

Alone on the anniversary of my wedding

469

to Marco, with our firstborn in my arms and a dose of self-pity, I think of Nonna Carina, of the violence she suffered, the baby she lost. Carina Maria DiGratia married Quillan Shepard in a mining camp in the Rocky Mountains. She married for protection a man she half feared, who, for fear, deserted her.

And I think of Nonno Quillan loving her until his dying breath, the regret of that early desertion torturing him, even though he'd loved her thoroughly all the years after.

A tear drops to Celestina's fingers coiled around my own. I draw them up and dry them on my cheek. She suckles in her dream, her lips sinking and puckering, the tiny chin bobbing up and down, content as I rock her back and forth, back and forth, her neck sweaty in the crook of my arm. "We are not deserted," I tell her. I tell myself.

Footsteps. I blink away my tears. Momma Michelli hands me a telegram, her face sending one of its own, judging my weakness to need and expect such extravagance from her son. She waits expectantly, but I outwait her, and she leaves. Awkwardly around the baby, I unseal and open it.

KNOW THIS DAY HOLDS MIXED

EMOTIONS. WISH I WAS THERE TO HOLD YOU. LA MIA VITA ED IL MIO AMORE. MARCO.

Eyes closed, I press his message to my heart. There is the grief of Papa's murder, of Nonno's death, and all my loss. The memory of a rushed and confused ceremony. There's also Marco and something more real than words. When my voice can break through the tears in my throat, I tell Celestina, "See, cara? Papa's here. . . ."

Bolstered by the memory, Antonia said, "I'm r . . . eady."

"Good." Lance flipped the pages, eager, she knew, to be done with it, now that Rese was back in Sonoma. She knew the ache of absence. She wouldn't keep him. He was right to find his own way, to follow his heart. He'd lived too much for other people and not enough for himself.

"The Bureau made our hasty wedding possible without papers, verifying for the judge my identity and the necessity of our union. They may have thought you would testify, or at least realized we owed you protection. For my part, the role became real. Hadn't planned on that, my girl. You had a way of turning the tables, and how."

There now. That was Marco. A smile played on her lips.

"Though I left you alone too often and too long, you were never far from my heart. It made everything I did more perilous, for now I had something to lose. With each child the burden grew, yet I knew I was doing what I had to, what I was born to. God had made me for it. To crush the violence, the decadence. To give my children a better life, and you a safer home.

"For that I took whatever assignment I was given. I won't tell you all the cases I handled, but the one that matters happened before I went to Sonoma. It followed me there and caused it all, though I didn't know."

Lance paused, reread the sentence to make sure. It fit with the letter from Sybil that what went wrong in Sonoma started with Nonno Marco, not Vittorio or Arthur Jackson. Someone had gone to Jackson, someone who sold his services as a hit man.

"And now it comes to why I am telling you what I've kept silent our whole life together."

Lance looked at Nonna, who had grown

frighteningly still. He would burst if they had to stop, but he'd stop if she needed to. She gave him a slow blink of assent.

"I'd blamed myself for Vittorio's death, but only tactically, for not getting there in time once I realized the trap was set. It puzzled me that Jackson had seen through us, and I could only think that Vittorio had slipped. But it wasn't Vittorio."

She closed her eyes, and pain creased her brow. He went on.

"One of my first assignments was to infiltrate the fledgling New York Camorra."

His breath escaped. He and Pop had guessed right.

"Being a *paesano* and, in fact, related to the family, I was an obvious candidate to penetrate the operation. I had no record to speak of that Don Agosto might discover. I was young enough to look hungry, bold enough to look useful. He took me on and put me to work accepting payoffs. You'll recall the incident with my two-legged dog."

He'd heard stories of the two-legged dog, but not in connection to any covert assignments.

"Not everyone appreciated the protection those payoffs bought them, and I took the brunt of their anger. But I was establishing myself. For two years I worked in the organization, gaining trust and responsibility, biding my time. I communicated what I had to, but kept most of what I saw and learned to myself. I trusted no one else, knowing we would have one chance only with someone like Agosto Borsellino."

Lance read how his nonno had taken down the Camorra don, sending him to prison, but that in prison the man had been killed by the rival Sicilians who'd been waiting their chance at the Camorra boss who'd invaded their territory. It was right out of the history books, or the movies.

"Bitter over his father's murder, Don Agosto's son Carlo followed me to Sonoma. He . . . killed your papa, but it was me he wanted."

He looked up, certain Nonna would make him stop. Her eyes had closed; her

474

brow pinched in. But she said nothing, so he continued.

"You were still Jackson's target; I had no doubt of that. But I didn't know until I shot Carlo in the gully that it was my actions, not Vittorio's, that had brought us down. More than ever it was my duty to protect you. You were so brave, so determined, and as God is my witness, I'd fallen in love with you. But, darling Antonia, I forgot the power of vendetta."

Vendetta. Lance had joked about it, teased Rese with the idea. Now he realized it was no joke.

Nonna said, "Read."

"Don Agosto's second son, Paolo, had disappeared following a highly publicized murder. That bought me a window of time to plan my strategy before his brother's death would bring him out of hiding. Though I knew him to be ruthless, I prayed other factors would work in my favor.

"And God was faithful. Paolo Borsellino had to battle for control when he returned. He had no time to take up a failed vendetta with his own power at stake. Don Agosto had not favored his second son, and revenge did not burn in Paolo as it had in Carlo.

"When I suggested a truce, he realized the advantage. I would not reveal what I knew of him or his dealings to the Bureau, and he would not threaten me or my family. It was in both our interests to keep our pact, and I was convinced he would. It rankled to see him establish his power, to know his means, but I did my job elsewhere, to the best of my ability.

"He raised his family, and I raised mine, children and grandchildren. The vendetta might have been buried forever — but for Don Paolo's arrest and imprisonment. Three months ago he was convicted and incarcerated. I had no part in it, though he must believe otherwise. Or perhaps it has simply lain too long between us. Vendetta has a power of its own. Once begun, it must be satisfied."

Lance's throat went dry. No . . . He shot a look at Nonna, whose gaze was fiercely set.

"Read . . ." she breathed.

"I've been away from the Bureau so long, not even a cop for years. I had almost forgotten how it was to sleep with

476

half my mind awake for any sound, any shift in the air. I'm an old man. I could die tomorrow. My thoughts are only for you.

"I kept my work secret, because to reveal any part would have opened your mind to questions, to what had really happened in Sonoma. I could not face your hurt. But when the phone call came this morning, I knew I'd been wrong to keep it from you."

Phone call? What phone call?

"How will you understand now, what I have to do?"

His throat closed. Nonno couldn't be saying what it seemed.
"L . . . ance." Nonna touched his arm.

"Antonia, those I love live under one roof, and as the caller explained, what a tragedy it would be if something destroyed that building and all of you within. I value nothing so much as the family I'd thought never to have until a promise opened my eyes. A family that will continue when I'm gone. So you see, cara, I have one final role to play."

Her hand seized hold. He wanted to

stop, but her grip compelled him.

"I've spent my life recognizing the evil that kills the innocent. I have imitated and opposed it. Today I go to meet it. For nothing stops evil except personal sacrifice. Know, dearest, that my time with you has been more than I ever expected. *La mia vita ed il mio amore.*"

Nonna cried out, meeting his eyes in an agony of realization. She hadn't seen it coming. Neither of them had. Nonno Marco's death was no accident. The knowledge sank into his bowels. *An evil that kills the innocent.* From the grave Nonno had named it: *Vendetta.*

Chapter Twenty-eight

What cruel ache in spleen and bone.
What breaking heart that weeps alone.

Nonno Quillan stays beside Nonna Carina until they put her body into the ground, his wrenching vigil a testament to his love. In my own childish grief I can hardly stand to see it. If that is love, how can anyone bear it?

Nonno takes my hand. "Nothing precious comes cheaply, Antonia. You must count the cost and choose. . . ." *Count and choose. . . .*

But how could she count what she didn't know? How could she choose when God wasn't just. He wasn't . . . just. Wasn't . . . She spiraled down. *Marco.* She hadn't known; how could she know? *Oh, Marco* . . . Killed like Papa. Killed. The weight of it crushed the breath from her lungs, the life from her spirit.

She had no strength for anger. No strength for anything. She stared at the wall, wishing she could climb back into the womb . . . or the tomb.

Marco . . .

Leery of God, she had put her trust in flesh, and he had sacrificed it on his altar of duty. For her, yes, and their children's children. Oh, the pain, the debt. *Count the cost.* Had Marco counted?

Deeper now, where it didn't hurt. No, even there pain found her. Where could she hide? The cost was too high. Too high.

"Nonna?" After crying out, she had withdrawn into a place he couldn't penetrate. It looked different from a stroke, but what did he know? "Nonna, talk to me!" No response. "Nonna." Panic choked him. She had wanted this kept between them, but it was way past that now. He grabbed the letter and went downstairs.

At the door, Momma saw his alarm and matched it. "What is it? What's happened?"

"Go check on Nonna. She might need a doctor."

Momma slapped her cheeks. *"Gesù, Maria, e Giuseppe."*

"I gotta see Pop."

She all but shoved him in where Pop sat watching TV. "Turn it off. Lance has something to say." Then she rushed out.

Pop thumbed the TV off with the remote and waited.

He hadn't thought until Pop looked up how it would be to tell him Nonno was murdered. Their one conversation hardly compared to the weeks Lance had searched piece by piece into the past, only now learning it all. And he hadn't guessed, hadn't known how it would hurt. How would Pop take it cold?

"You gonna talk or what?"

"Pop . . ."

But then Bobby and Monica barged in and Lucy and Lou with his cousin Martin from Jersey, all of them yammering, "What's happened? What's the fuss?" Momma must have spread the alarm.

Lance slipped the letter behind him, unwilling to toss its news to the wind. "Nonna's not doing too well." And it was more than he should have expected to talk it out alone with Pop.

"What's wrong with her?"

"Is it a stroke?"

"Did someone call an ambulance?"

Pop raised his hands. "Momma's with her. Now everybody get out." He fixed a glance on Lance that rooted him to the floor, and when the room had cleared, it seemed to echo around them.

Lance wished he hadn't left Nonna's side. But Momma would take care of her, and Pop had a right to know. Though Nonna hadn't seen it that way, as Marco's only son, shouldn't he decide what to do?

He jutted his chin. "Whatchu got?"

Lance handed him the letter. "From Nonno. He left it for Nonna in a safe deposit box, only, you know how she is with banks; she never picked it up until now."

Pop didn't seem sure what to do with it. Lance told him, "You need to know what it says." He'd already told him the Sonoma part of the story, but as Pop perused the first paragraphs, Lance said, "Nonno was murdered."

His father's jaw dropped as he looked up. "Whatchu talkin' about?"

"It's all in the letter. He's telling Nonna good-bye." He'd gone to meet the threat with intention and finality.

Pop frowned back down at the pages he held.

Lance forked his fingers into his hair. "It's the whole story, what I told you and more. Marco was a Fed and, Pop, it wasn't an accident."

His father's throat worked as he read through the first page, then the next and the next. Lance dropped to the footstool. Only then did it start to sink in. Nonno murdered. An old man. A grandpa. Why? His spine quivered as the hurt and confusion converted to anger.

Nonno, Vittorio, Quillan — Tony. It was too much. How could anyone take it sitting down? He clenched his hands, willing Pop through the pages, even though each paragraph brought him closer to the end, to the place of no return.

His throat tightened when Pop swiped a knuckle under his eye. Lance hadn't seen him cry since Tony. He should have prepared him somehow, not sprung it. He chewed his lip. Maybe he could have done it better, but however it came out, the message was the same. Nonno had sacrificed himself for them.

"What do we do?" Lance almost whispered.

Pop had reached the end but stared at the pages still, his jaw clenching and releasing. "Do?"

"About this." Lance slapped the pages with the back of his fingers.

"Nothing." Pop's voice grated.

"Pop, it's . . . true; it's gotta be. Nonno wouldn't make it up, wouldn't leave it for Nonna to read if it wasn't all true. He locked it in a safe deposit box. It's not a hoax."

Pop's head pivoted side to side. Lance could only imagine the emotions assaulting him. He'd lost his son to violence. Now Nonno too.

"Pop."

"Leave it alone." His voice was a graveyard, full of dead hopes.

That wasn't what he'd expected. Anger. Grief. Not this defeatist . . . "You know I can't." The one thing he couldn't do was leave it alone. Something was required.

"What do you think you can do? Change this?" Pop clenched the pages. "You think you can undo what happened twenty-two years ago?"

Lance shook his head. How had it come back to him? Wouldn't Pop . . . ? Shouldn't he . . . ? "Pop, I . . ."

Pop looked up, stark pain in his eyes. "Don't try to play the hero. You're not Tony."

He took it like a sucker punch. He'd let his guard down, and it caught him where it hurt. *"You're not Tony."*

Rese walked out to the garden Lance had made beautiful, plants blooming and verdant along the flagstone paths, but not overflowing as they'd been. The raised beds were aromatic with herbs he no doubt knew, though she simply appreciated the effect. The people coming this evening would too.

Michelle had planned to hold the potluck there before she and Star came back unexpectedly. In spite of Star's situation, she could hardly say no when Michelle had kept Baxter and watched out for the inn the whole time they were gone. But, even after two weeks with Lance's family, facing a fresh horde was intimidating.

She could hide upstairs with Star, but . . . that was weak. Lance would be disappointed. If he were here he'd provoke her into attending. She dropped her chin and smiled.

She had been insulated, first by Mom's antagonizing the neighbors, then living alone with Dad, working with the same handful of guys every day. She had dealt with homeowners and subcontractors, but not en masse. In school she had never roved with bands of girls through the halls, no slumber parties. She'd become a self-sufficient machine — there when Star needed her, but needing no one in return.

"In fact —" she looked down at Baxter — "being with Lance's family was the most intensive interaction I've ever had."

Baxter wagged his tail.

"I miss them." She missed him. She crouched down and hugged Baxter's neck, soaking up the scents of honeysuckle, roses, bougainvillea, and dog. What she really wanted was the scent of fresh-hewn wood, but Michelle and a few others would be there soon to set up. It would be rude to hole up in her workshop with a saw.

Before Lance, she wouldn't have cared.

Would not even have known. But now that he'd exposed her flaws, it didn't feel right to settle back in. She looked over at the carriage house Lance had restored, shoring up the original stone walls and adding the sky-lighted roof and glassed front, the interior divisions of bedroom and bath. She smiled, recalling their argument over fixtures, her resistance to cost overruns, and his flabbergasted replies. She'd been impossible. But there was something in Lance that brought out the worst in her — and the best.

He just made her . . . more.

She walked over, peered through the glass beside the door, and glimpsed the guitar leaning in the corner. How long before its strains rose up and his aftershave tinged the air? How long before they were back in business and her kitchen became his? She ached. How could hope hurt as much as grief?

Baxter pressed into her and whined. "I know." She crouched again and buried her face.

Michelle found her like that and laughed. "That dog gets more hugs than any human alive."

Rese looked up. Michelle's face was a broad plate with a wad of a nose, blunt eyebrows over eyes sunk too deep and narrowly, a generous mouth made incidental by a prominent cleft chin, and the whole, irresistibly warm and inviting. The face of a friend to walk beside.

"Mind if we set the food up in the kitchen; then folks can funnel out to the garden?"

"That's fine. However you want to do it." She had no doubt Michelle would handle things. That was another thing her face told you — competence, as well as compassion and companionship.

People arrived in twos and threes, and, like a frog in warming water, she handled the growing crowd with less discomfort than she'd expected. They brought the homey foods she remembered from Evvy's funeral. Nothing like Lance's cooking. But she hadn't had a good meal since they got back, so she helped herself without reservation.

So many people introduced themselves, she would have been lost if she hadn't just practiced on Lance's family. The children playing in the yard reminded her of Lucy's and Monica's gaggle, the cousins, nieces, and nephews. The quiet the last couple days had been incredible, but so were the little voices laughing and calling to one another — and her. She got tugged into a game of tag that actually seemed to be everyone just running around tagging one another.

After enough of that, she collapsed on a bench Lance had rescued from the surrounding vines and saw with surprise that Star had come down, looking like a wraith beside Michelle, who loaded up a plate for her. How long would it be before Michelle mentioned God, and Star took off? But another woman joined them, and as they all talked, Star finished her plate with no problem.

Rese didn't exactly mingle, but she talked to anyone who talked first. Nothing glib, but she managed.

"This is such a wonderful place," Michelle said after most of the people had gone. "A real welcoming feel to it."

Rese glanced around, trying to see the villa from an outsider's perspective instead of her intimate knowledge of so many details. Welcoming and wonderful. Why not?

"I just can't get over your doing it all yourself."

"Lance did the carriage house."

"And where is he?" She looked around as though he might be hidden somewhere.

Rese sighed. "Still working things out with Antonia." She'd explained the purpose of their trip before they left, but it didn't begin to address all the stuff that had happened since.

"Well." Michelle clapped her hands to her thighs. "It looks like we're just about wrapped up here."

Shouldn't she be relieved? As Michelle hauled a stack of serving dishes into the kitchen and filled the sink with suds, and several others scooped the remaining food into baggies and containers, she felt reluctant for them to leave.

"You two will use this, won't you?" Jackie asked, sticking the food into the refrigerator.

"Sure, thanks." Rese nodded. It appeared Star enjoyed their fare a lot more than hers. All that she could make with relative success were Lance's recipes, the five breakfasts she had mastered when she'd planned to do without him. "Would you all like a latte?" And now she was fairly certain something had taken over her body as she indicated Lance's fancy machine. "It's the only piece of equipment I really know how to use."

Jackie said she had to go. But the willowy, red-haired Karen, who had eaten with Star and Michelle, said, "Love one. Decaf, if you don't mind."

"Me too." Deb sat down with Karen.

Michelle got watery in the eyes. "Nice of you to ask."

Rese shrugged. It wasn't a big thing, but then again it was. It was probably the first overture she'd made to other women, the first gesture of friendship she'd made in a long time, maybe ever. Lance's sisters must have worn off.

There'd been too many surprises that evening for her to wonder that Star came in and sat with them, seemingly calm and attentive. From what she'd gleaned from the Internet on heroin withdrawal, Star's symptoms shouldn't be over yet, but after sleeping all day, she now led the conversation around Shakespeare and Monet, sonnets and impressionism, and her own style of painting that, amazingly, she'd shown Michelle in the carriage house.

Either it wasn't smack, as everything had seemed to indicate, or Star was having a miraculous recovery. Rese made a second round of frothy drinks, letting the others carry the discussion. It was eleven-thirty before they left and Star went upstairs, and midnight before she realized Lance hadn't called.

His thoughts spun like a gyroscope on a string, balanced by the centrifugal force of his rage. It was like the hours and days waiting for Tony to come out of the rubble. Somehow it would be wrong, there'd be a different outcome. In spite of impossible odds, they would find the people alive, all the people who'd vanished. But hour by hour hope had died, birthing rage instead. Rage that demanded an outlet.

He could smell the sick sweet breath of the war protestors as he'd pressed among them with their signs. He'd carried Tony's picture into their midst and ended up in a squad car. The emotion had been valid, but he had been fighting the wrong enemy.

He'd focused his anger on the tools, not the evil that drove them. Why had Tony been there, taking another man's place, covering a shift? It had seemed the supreme accident, but it wasn't. It was intentional, God allowing it. For His purpose.

"Don't try to play the hero. You're not Tony."

Not Tony. Not. Tony.

Pop was right. He wasn't the broad-shouldered, attention-grabbing, respect-commanding hero the world recognized. He was only a vessel. But God had removed Saul and chosen David, with only his sling — and his faith — to combat evil. Lance had no sling, but whatever he had . . .

He swallowed. He had snatched the letter back from Pop, gone upstairs, and climbed out to the fire escape. The stars had come and gone, and with the growing dawn his mind unraveled the facts and laid them out thread by thread.

Nonno had been murdered for doing his duty. Before and because of him, Vittorio, and, in effect, Quillan. Tony became a cop because of Nonno's example. And duty took him as well. Lance felt like Job with his family crushed around him. For what? Daring to stand against evil. To make a difference.

He clenched his jaw. Twenty-two years they'd thought it an accident. He'd been six years old when Nonno's car crashed, but he'd spent much of those six years at his grandfather's knee, youngest and oldest.

Then there were the stories. Nonno's generosity and the clever ways he'd helped people so it didn't look like charity. His big heart. His big laugh. A singing voice that could make a stone cry, but no tolerance for cruelty in any form.

He detested bullies and opposed anyone who preyed on the weak. He had loved the law, served it sacrificially. But he was also a product of the tyranny his family escaped in Naples. He knew there were times the authorities wouldn't or couldn't help, when a man stood up and said, enough. Those times were called vendetta.

Nonno — cop, federal agent, undercover operative — had acted in the only way he could. *Nothing stops evil except personal sacrifice.* But someone had planned the accident so convincingly his own family had never suspected. There'd been no investigation at all. Now, twenty-two years later

. . . what chance was there?

The sun gilded the windows. Stiff from the bricks against his back, the iron rail pressed into his shoulder, Lance raised his face. He had dared to grip God's ankle, sworn to hold on, and demanded the yoke be placed on him. The throbbing grew in his head until it seemed he could feel his skull bulging.

The common definition of vendetta was a blood feud. But it had another meaning — a curse returned.

Chapter Twenty-nine

Lance shifted when Rico opened the window beside him.

"Whatchu doing, 'mano?"

Lance looked over his shoulder. "You're up early."

Rico leaned on the sill. "Chaz was making deliveries. He called to say you were on the fire escape and I should find out why." He yawned.

Lance pulled away from the wall and stretched his spine. Could be difficult to explain why he did anything from here out. He rose stiffly and climbed back through the window.

Rico looked him over. "D'you sleep out there?"

"Didn't sleep."

Rico frowned at the rumpled letter. "From Rese?"

Lance looked down at the pages. "It's not to me." Though in a sense it was. Marco might have written it to Nonna, but the burden did not rest on her.

A vendetta, a curse on his family. Carlo Borsellino had started it. Too weak or

494

spineless to threaten the Mafioso who murdered Agosto, he'd turned his wrath to the man who'd sent his father up. Carlo died but the curse was set in motion. Through Nonna's marriage, Vittorio and Quillan were family. Only one had felt the bullets, but the curse had taken Quillan, as well, evil that would not be denied.

Maybe Nonno had been wrong to make peace with Paolo. Lives had been lost. Could he simply look away? Lance frowned. The Borsellinos had unleashed a destruction his family had watched in ignorance, taking the blows and not knowing why. Vittorio, Quillan, Marco, Tony. What would happen if he did nothing? Would it keep eating away at the Michellis?

Who was next — Jake, already tainted by Tony's death? Or himself. Or Rese. What if he brought it onto her, as Marco had carried it to Antonia? An ache seized him. How could he go back to Sonoma, knowing what he knew?

With Rico's stare ferreting into his thoughts, Lance drew himself up. "I'm late for church."

Rico didn't press it, but that wasn't the end, he knew. Lance just didn't know who to trust with his burden before he saw where it might go. He had told Pop, but Pop was choosing a path of nonresistance, a weary, trudged path he knew too well.

Lance felt in his gut that wasn't the way, but . . .

Vendetta. What did he know about feuds and curses? He'd had his share of fights, but they were face to face on the street. A simple problem; a simple solution. This was not simple, and he wasn't sure there was a solution. But as Rese had said, nothing happened by chance.

He dropped to the kneeler and spoke the responses, but his mind still spun. Every step he'd taken had brought him to this. He had felt it from the moment Nonna's finger on the envelope pointed him to Liguria, when Conchessa sent him to Sonoma, when he saw Rese's sign in the window and found Nonna's box in the attic. He'd attributed everything to the Lord.

Tony had died at the hands of terrorists driven by evil, but evil would have no power if it were not given by God. Tony: confident, capable, assured. Tony: black-and-white, bound by rules — only rules might no longer apply, and Tony wouldn't stand for that. It fell instead to the prodigal.

He stared at the crucifix. How could he refuse to see it through? He had demanded Nonna's burden before he knew what it was. But it wasn't only hers. It was all of theirs. They all bore Nonno's death upon them, those he died to keep safe and those

496

who would come from them — as long as the curse was unreturned.

Maybe he was confusing the spiritual battle he'd witnessed the other night with a purely human grudge. But then why had the Lord shown him? It had to be in preparation for the next level. He's reached the end of the board and become a knight, his responsibilities changed and magnified.

He left the church and started home, but stopped on the sidewalk. Stella sat in her plastic chair in a sky-blue floral shift, elastic stockings, and rubber-soled shoes. A ball of yarn rested against her ankle, the needles click-clicking dangerously in her knobby hands. *"Buon giorno,"* she said with a gappy smile on her liver-splotched face.

"Morning, Stella. Can I ask you a question?"

She paused her needles. "What question?"

"Are curses real?"

She squinted up at him. "As real as you."

He glanced along the street, watching a small black dog make certain all comers knew he'd been there first, then back to Stella. "Can they hurt people, lots of people for a long time?"

"You mean *mal occhio?* The envy?"

"Worse."

"La maledizione?"

"Vendetta."

Her eyes rounded to match her mouth. "The blood curse."

He nodded.

She made a sound deep in her throat, then, "Vengeance is mine sayeth the Lord, but sometimes it is mine, too, and yours." She pointed the needles at him.

Lance reached down to pet the little dog that sniffed his shoe and then jumped up on his leg displaying a tannish underbelly. His fur was wiry, not soft like Baxter's. "Does vendetta require vengeance?"

"Blood cries out from the ground to God."

Startled, the dog jumped and moved on down the sidewalk.

"Blood cries out." He'd heard the cries when he stood where Tony died. Unlike everyone who had sat at the table and mourned poor Tony — even Pop now — he couldn't let it go and move on as Rese said. Nonno Marco's blood was crying out as well, and Vittorio's and Quillan's. "How does it stop?"

"To end a curse that big takes a very big sacrifice."

Nothing stops evil except personal sacrifice. But Nonno's death hadn't ended it. The Borsellinos might have thought it was over, but the evil remained — because they had never paid. Anger surged. "What sacrifice?"

She shrugged. "Only you can know."

Chest squeezing, he stuffed his fingers into his jeans and started past, saying, *"Grazie."*

"Prego." Click, click, her needles went back to work.

When he didn't call the next night, Rese lifted the phone to call him. Maybe he was giving her the chance to initiate. She had claimed the right, and it was just like Lance to hold her to it. She touched in the first numbers, then paused.

What if something had happened? Her mind ran over all the possibilities. His life was hardly uneventful, neither of them immune to catastrophe. Something could have happened, something he didn't want to tell her.

Had Roman convinced him to take the job? She shook her head. No. He would have called. Had Antonia suffered another stroke? Rese lowered the phone. Was he at the hospital holding vigil? What if Antonia was dying? Rese pressed the phone off.

Dad's death had been the worst thing she'd ever gone through, worse than her mother's attempt on her life. After he bled to death in her arms, she had shut down completely. She didn't handle death well, not even Evvy's and Ralph's peaceful and timely passings. If Antonia . . .

Rese shook her head. If he wanted her, he'd call. But now her mind was churning. She climbed into her covers, resigned to fight for sleep — a fight she lost, of course, for most of the night.

Star was up before her the next morning, cooking crepes with Lance's recipe, still composed and obviously eager to eat again. Rese dragged herself into a chair. The scent of the buttery frying batter and the tart berry syrup filled her with nostalgic thoughts of Lance at the stove. The flagstones were cool beneath her bare feet, but somehow the kitchen always seemed warm, even on misty, overcast mornings such as this. Probably an illusion, but, hey, nothing wrong with that.

Rese turned on the espresso machine. "Want one?" She was not caffeine addicted, as Star liked to put it, but after a night like the last . . .

Star shook her head. "I'm not the one who wore a path in the floors last night."

Rese looked over her shoulder. "Did I disturb you?"

Star shrugged. "At least it wasn't the buffer."

Rese turned, surprised. "I thought you'd slept through that." Though she had hoped Lance couldn't. It was the first time he'd kissed her, and she had stomped upstairs to demand professional distance. Hah. Then she'd spent the night buffing the wood floors until she'd collapsed. "I thought you slept through anything."

" 'There's a lot you don't know about me,' " Star said with perfect Music Man inflection — another favorite. Star loved any story where impossible things happened. Rese had snorted when the few measly kids with instruments they couldn't play turned into the huge marching band, but Star had said, *"You don't get it, Rese. You just don't get it."*

She poured milk into the steamer carafe. "So tell me something I don't know." Because Star's life was pretty much an open book.

"I intentionally failed the biology midterm, because you'd been out late on the site all week with your dad."

Rese turned. That was the lowest score she'd ever gotten on a test, but Star's had been worse. Senior year, and she already knew she wasn't going to college and finishing high school was a formality. "Star, I didn't even care about grades."

"You'd have cared if mine was better."

Rese stared. "You don't really think that."

Star returned the stare.

Rese said, "I've never competed with you."

"Never thought you had to."

Rese expelled a hard breath. "What are you talking about?"

Star turned back to the stove. "It doesn't matter."

Rese left the milk and stopped beside her. "What are you saying? That you didn't do your best because you thought I had to be better?" *Compulsively competitive.* Had she made Star feel inferior — considered Star inferior?

" 'For nothing can seem foul to those that win.' "

"I've never tried to win against you. Never tried to make you feel . . . less."

Star giggled. "Like you had to try. That's the jest, don't you see?" She spun. "I let you win."

Anger washed over her. "Win at what?"

"Life."

Rese sagged against the counter. "Do not blame your problems on me, Star. I've been there for you, every time."

Star swallowed. "I know." She flipped the crepe. "Strong, steady Rese."

Impossible to tell if that was sarcasm.

Rese rubbed her face. If she had slept, she might have managed this conversation with some semblance of tact. Not having slept, however, she would no doubt hack it completely. "How have I offended you?"

"Did I say that?" Star slipped the crepe

onto a plate, spooned filling in a line down the middle, and rolled the edges over.

Rese couldn't help noticing how evenly golden and soft it was. "I think that's the basic message, here. That because of me you couldn't excel."

"Not couldn't, Rese." Star drizzled the deep red syrup. "Didn't."

"I've never held you back. I've supported every step."

Star tossed back her head and sang, "I have no strings to hold me down. There are no strings on me."

"So I'm Stromboli to your Pinocchio?"

Star put the plate before her, an offering Rese ignored. She had left Lance in New York to take care of Star, and this was her thanks?

Star walked back to the stove. "Michelle told me you've given your life to the Lord."

"I tried to tell you that too. You walked out." And kissed Lance on the way.

Star poured another crepe. "So maybe you'll see what it's like, being controlled."

Rese dropped into the chair, snatched up her fork and stabbed the crepe. "I've never controlled you, or even wanted to."

"But, Rese. Why else would you be my friend?"

Rese stared, every answer dying on her lips. Though Star sat down with her own crepe and proceeded to eat, whatever appetite the aroma of Lance's recipe had conjured was dead now. "If you think I only want to control you, why are you *my* friend? Or are you?" Because it was getting very hard to see.

"I guess it's what works for us." Star gobbled her crepe. "You the superstar and 'I have neither wit, nor words, nor worth.' "

Now that was too dramatic. Rese pushed her plate away. "What do you want from me, Star?" After seventeen years of giving what she had, she wondered.

Star dragged the plate over and cut into Rese's crepe. "Ah. It's what you want from me that puzzles."

Rese forced her tone to remain neutral. "I don't *want* anything."

"Nor expect nor require. It's as I thought."

"That's not what I meant." Rese planted her elbows on the table. "You're my friend. You have been for years. What do you expect me to say?"

Star ran her finger through the syrup and brought it to her lips. "I neither expect nor require."

Closing her eyes, Rese expelled her breath. "When did I become the enemy?"

When Star didn't answer, Rese opened her eyes.

Tears streaked Star's cheeks, and she wrapped herself in her arms and rocked. "I don't know. I just feel it."

Rese reached across and gripped her hand. "It's not true."

Star sniffed. "Can I stay?"

Rese almost screamed in frustration. "Of course. Nothing's changed."

"Good." Star stood up with a brilliant smile. "I'm going to paint." And she walked out. Rese dropped her face into her hands. Maybe the drugs weren't out of her system. Her prebirth addiction could have oversensitized her, or . . .

Was it the smack talking, or for the first time had Star really been honest? Did she resent the comfort she had always seemed to want? Rese tried to see it from her side, dropped her head back and forced a laugh. Would she never get it right?

The phone rang and she snatched it up, hoping for Lance's voice. But it was the mental health facility, and the quirky tones of Dr. Jonas. "I'm glad to reach you, Rese. I was hoping we could meet regarding your request to vacate the order and assume care for Elaine?"

Of course. She was certainly qualified to take on another dependent relationship. She handled them so well. Rese pushed the thought aside. "As soon as possible. Thanks."

She had started the process before leaving Sonoma, appealed to have Mom's condition reassessed, to be given not just decision-making power, but full custodial care. Dad had done what he had to with a child to protect, an occupation that demanded so much of his time, and with Mom's condition spiraling out of control. But Dr. Jonas was hopeful about her response to the new drugs. Anything was possible.

Rese closed her eyes and pictured her mother, disappointed that even the thought still churned emotional residue. This was the mother she loved, the one who'd tried to kill her, who'd let Walter into their lives. Lance had said he wanted to meet her, but he wasn't there. She sighed, picturing the mental health center and imagining her own possible future. She'd put things in motion to bring her mother home, but if she proved incompetent, would she be moving in with Mom?

Stella's words haunted him as Lance sat beside Nonna's bed. *"Blood cries out from the ground to God."* As Nonna had cried out when the realization struck? He had hoped the doctor would find something wrong so they could take her to the hospital and fix it. But since she'd suffered an emotional shock with no physical setback, there was nothing medically that could be done. The best they could do was keep her where she was, happy and comfortable — in her home with her family.

Momma had asked him to sit with Nonna while she taught her daytime classes. Momma said Monica and Lucy and Sofie all had things to do, but Lance saw through it. Pop had told her to keep him occupied, make sure he didn't do something stupid. That might have been a problem if he had any idea what to do.

He read and reread the letter. They had taken it in haltingly small pieces before, but now he went over each page as Nonno had written it until the flow and angst and sorrow of it filled him. Though aged, Nonno had been robust, full of life, full of goodness. What kind of spite cut such a man down?

There was no understanding it. But the question that got inside and twisted was how could Nonno's sacrifice not be enough? Lance clenched his hands. *"To end a curse that big takes a very big sacrifice."* Bigger than Nonno giving up his life? What could be bigger than dying sacrificially for those you loved? Lance shook his head. If he was supposed to act, he needed answers.

He reached for Nonna's Bible on the nightstand. From inside the cover, pictures of her children and grandchildren cascaded into his lap. He looked at the photos, most of which were taken at much younger ages than they were now. All the smiles, the combed hair, children posed and poised — well, his expression was a little rebellious — but they all stared up at him with expectation. Not just for the moment of time when they had to be thinking *Click the shutter!* but for all the years since and all those to come.

He closed his eyes as the depth of Nonno's love rushed him, and with it the loss. He grabbed hold of Nonna's hand and sank into her pain. What was she thinking; where had she gone? Into her memories, as before? Or were even her memories too painful now?

How did God think she could bear it? And why should she suffer for something she had not even known? A young woman full of promise and dreams until Marco's life touched hers. He hadn't known, but he'd brought death and loss to her. And now it tainted them all. *Lord . . .*

For some reason he thought of Gina, the weary grief that defined her face these days. It had been Tony struck down, but Gina was paying for it. A grim realization formed in his gut. Marco might have had no choice. Tony hadn't known before he married Gina, but . . .

Lance dropped his face to his hand, stifling a moan. If he hadn't dug into the past, hadn't unearthed the curse — but he had, and with that came responsibility. He didn't know how to settle the vendetta, but it had come to him to do it.

He stared down through his fingers. When he'd shifted to catch the slipping photos, the Bible had fallen open across his lap, and his gaze fell now on one verse as though illuminated. *"To this you were called, because Christ suffered for you, leaving you an example, that you should follow in his steps."*

Something gripped his heart like a fist. Short, hard breaths filled his lungs. Lance shook as God laid the burden on him, the burden he'd demanded. He must take the cross — as he'd known someday he would. He reached back and gripped his shoulder blade. *"To this you were called . . . that you should follow in his steps."*

Pain and ecstasy were hard to separate. He had yearned for purpose, even a purpose that caused him to suffer if it gave meaning and identity. And now, in the midst of Nonno's dark and desperate revelation, he heard the call, and his lips moved. "Here I am." He sank into the grasp of God, outside of time and place. *Here I am.*

At a touch on his shoulder he startled.

Rico stood harried and gray, cradling his unbound arm. Dragging himself back from the brink, Lance scoped the fresh swelling and bruising of Rico's hand and wrist. "What did you do?"

Rico shrugged in the "I screwed up" motion Lance knew so well.

"You used it? Rico, did you drum with it?" He'd heard the percussion across the hall, but thought Rico was doing the one-armed-bandit act. Obviously one hand wasn't enough. His pain was obvious. If Rico had rebroken the bones . . . What was he thinking?

"I had to try, 'mano. I had to know."

"It's too soon." How could he think a week or two . . . But Lance knew the restlessness, the impatience that kept Rico in perpetual motion, the beats and rhythms going through his head just as melodies and lyrics filled his own. "How bad is it?"

"Feels like something broke."

"Well, get down to the hospital."

Rico made the money sign with his other hand.

"Look, we'll rob a bank or something. Go get an X-ray."

Rico noticed the Bible in his lap. "Can't you multiply some fives and tens?"

"I'm still working on the water-walking part."

When Rico moved his arm, his face

screwed up in pain. Without thinking, Lance took the wrist and cupped it between his palms. He couldn't feel if damage had been done, if Rico had battered the fractures and tissues. But even more than throbbing nerves, he sensed the fear and frustration that had driven Rico to take hold of that drumstick and strike. *Lord* . . .

His clasp warmed. Rico's identity and future depended on those bones, and Lance imagined them knitting, filling in around the pins, the tendons strengthening — cartilage, ligaments, and muscles . . .

He opened his eyes, and Rico's expression caught him short. So they didn't usually hold hands, and Rico didn't go in for demonstrative prayer. Lance wasn't even sure he had prayed. But Rico drew his arm back and studied the offended area with a puzzled pinch in his brow.

"Better get a picture of it."

Rico's eyes came up to his. "Don't need one."

Lance sighed. "Rico, could you just once not be stubborn?"

"Pain's gone, 'mano." Rico stroked his arm with that queer look back in his eyes. He turned, paused, and then walked out.

Lance raised the Bible. If he was called to end this vendetta, he had to know what might be expected of him. What sacrifice could be demanded now that he'd accepted the call. As he searched, it sank in just how precarious his life had become.

Chapter Thirty

Moments of time, like drops of dew, glisten and are gone.

Marco laughs when I tell him he looks sharp in his uniform.

"I feel like I'm wearing a sign. 'Look at me, I'm a cop.' "

"Well, of course," I say. "What's wrong with that?"

He gives me a strange look, then pats my shoulder. "Nothing. Nothing at all."

I straighten his sleeve, note the veins standing up under the skin of his hand, the signs of age appearing there. He is old to be joining the police force, and his sudden career change amuses me. "Tired of handling rich people's jack?" I tease with his old line, though after all these years I still don't know what he did when he was away on business for his clients.

He takes me in his arms. "Tired of being away from you, my sweet." He kisses my nose. An old fool, but I love him. I won't know what to do with him home so many evenings. Now that the children are grown, the restaurant takes so much of my time. But I love what I've made, in spite of Momma Benigna's insults — though she eats there every day.

She is the cross I bear for the gift of her son, and in my better moments I'm grateful that she bore him. I'm mostly grateful that she gave him nothing of herself. I turn Marco around and straighten his collar at the back, under his fringe of silver hair. He is striking still, and my heart jumps at the thought.

"Marco."

He looks over his shoulder, and I say, "Why don't we go away somewhere, sometime?"

He turns fully. "Where would you like to go?"

"I don't know. You've been everywhere. Choose a place and take me there."

He laughs. "And what about your restaurant?"

"I'll hang a sign in the window like everyone else does: Gone on Vacation. A second honeymoon." I tighten his tie. "Since the first was . . . difficult." I wish I could undo those grief-filled days and be the happy bride Marco deserved.

He lifts my chin and kisses me. "Every time I come home it's a honeymoon."

Antonia stirred, aware of Lance beside her, and almost came out of the place where her memories lived. But she was determined to stay there, and settled back.

The first time I hold Lance, I know. This baby is my heart. How can that be, when I've held my own five to my breast, and seventeen other grandchildren? Yet this son of Roman's, Doria's child, takes hold of my soul. *Now I see, Nonno.* He had warned me, yet I cannot resist the tug of this infant in my arms. Yes, some loves attach to your very soul.

She had seen him take his first steps, not one but three at once. That was Lance, always reaching. While Doria taught other young feet jazz and ballet, Lance had developed his own listing weave and tumble. And Antonia had picked him up and set him right again.

I press the dollar into his hand for his First Holy Communion, but I know there's no gift that can replace what's inside him. The others, they take it in stride, but Lance is not like them. There is a glow in his face I can hardly bear. This child, who is my heart, loves God more. . . .

And because of him, she had made peace with the Deity who had tried her so terribly. She could not resent the One who'd put that child in her life. She couldn't trust, but she had not come between Lance and his Savior. She had sheltered and nurtured his faith, for his sake . . . and hers.

And what good had it done? She should have shaken her fist at heaven. Lance queried, "Nonna?" But the present was more painful than the past. She wouldn't hear him; she couldn't.

Lance ached. This thing was real. No way around it. He had a role to play, and like Nonna, he had to play it alone. He'd seen the haunted look on Gina's face, absorbed Nonna's many griefs. If he chose to do this thing, he could not bring it on Rese. His head felt like sludge, his limbs like planks. His insides were chewed up, thinking how it would seem to her, how it would feel.

But if he was the instrument, he had to subordinate all other desires, hopes, and dreams. *"If any one comes to me and does not hate his own father and mother, his wife and children, his brothers and sisters — yes, even his own life — he cannot be my disciple."*

He had always been sure Jesus didn't mean hate. It was a hyperbolic distinction between fervor for him and anything else that could get in the way. Now he realized the severing was as extreme as it seemed. A visceral longing seized him, but thinking of Rese distracted and weakened him.

He pressed his fingers to his brow. His motives must be pure, his conscience clear. The gauntlet had been thrown down, but he didn't know what that meant, only trusted the Lord would make it clear. In the meantime, he would learn the enemy. Even as God's instrument, he could operate only within the limitations of the physical world.

Unnerving even to think in those terms. Who did he think he was? He knew what Pop would say. But having glimpsed that other realm when Chaz prayed deliverance for Star, having twice been seized by the Spirit until all resistance melted away, he had to believe anything was possible.

He rubbed his face and looked at Nonna sleeping, her chest rising and falling in shallow breaths. She had brought this to him, because it was beyond her. And she waited now, suspended between the past and present, a past he had revealed and a present she couldn't face. He needed to act. But once he took up the gauntlet, there would be no turning back.

Rese followed the caseworker back downstairs. The residence assessment was obviously perfunctory, the woman scarcely impressed by the hard work and attention to detail that it had taken to create an environment so appealing and authentic. But the living arrangements of a woman with mental health issues moving in with her stable, business-owner daughter might not be high on the county's list of concerns — not that they would forego any part of the process to expedite things.

Rese led her out to the garden for a brief perusal of the property and carriage house. No stockpiled weapons, no meth lab. Not even a skeleton in the cellar anymore. Lance had taken care of that. But Rese chose not to mention the tunnel anyway. She didn't want to open and show it.

When the woman had gone, Rese wandered back inside and tried to decide what to do. Three days with no word from Lance? Something had happened — again. She didn't want to bother him, but four impending reservations had to be dealt with. Should she cancel and give them time to find something else, or confirm and assume he'd be there when she needed him?

She pressed her palms to her head. What if he didn't come and she had to handle it with Star? She had paced through the night imagining all kinds of things that might have happened, but she couldn't come up with a single reason for his not calling. Of course, she hadn't called either, but only because she was afraid she wouldn't know what to say. Lance had never in his life not known what to say. She expelled a breath. It was so much easier when he was simply there, sucking words from her with no effort at all.

Alone in the kitchen, she crossed her arms and pondered. With the early drizzle, Star had set up in the workshop to paint and stayed there even after the sun broke through and slid westward. Rese could have carved while Star painted, but though they had made a flimsy truce, she didn't want to crowd her. Baxter was sacked out in front of the stove, and other than the looming reservations, nothing demanded her time or attention.

She sighed. What if he was waiting for her to call? He'd made his feelings known, and she'd been the one dragging her feet. Now that they were apart, he could be hoping — Oh, what did she know about any of that? She headed for the phone, and just as she reached, it rang. Hah!

She picked up the phone, relief rushing over her at the sound of Lance's voice. "Are you all right?" She curled her arm around herself. "I was getting worried." Apprehensive, panicked, obsessed.

"Rese . . ." His voice clogged. "Honey, sit down so we can talk."

Honey? Her legs buckled. She slid down the wall and waited, but he said nothing for so long her heart started pounding like a drum in a tin room. "What's wrong?"

He sighed. "I don't know where to start."

Her limbs went numb; her head filled with fog. From a distance she heard his ragged breathing, and hers felt just the same. "You're not coming." She gripped the cool receiver. "Is that what you're telling me?"

"There's something I have to do. If there was another way, I'd take it. But everything has led to this, Rese, and it's bigger than me."

"Lance, *what* are you talking about?"

"It's better if you don't know."

Better . . . ? How could he even say that, knowing all the things that had been kept from her, things that mattered, big things? "So you're coming when it's done?"

"When it's done . . . things might not be the same."

For someone who could make himself so clear, that was incredibly obscure. "What things?"

He released a slow breath. "Everything."

She pressed a hand to her belly, wondering when she'd been punched. And he was right. Sometimes not knowing was better. She hadn't imagined this, that he was through, that he would dump her like . . . "Did you count me on your wall?"

He groaned. "It's not like that."

"I see." Clear as concrete.

"Rese, God —"

"Don't even go there." Anger had slithered in like a snake, swallowing fear and sympathy whole. "If you've changed your mind, fine, but at least take responsibility for it."

His voice came raw and weary. "You're right. I'm sorry."

Rage boiled up. "No problem. I don't want to run an inn anyway." If she had guests there now, she'd boot them out. These last months had been nothing but a huge mistake.

Lance said nothing to that. The man of many words had none.

She hung up and looked at her watch, then glanced outside where a shaft of evening light slanted through the garden. Even if he still stayed late on the jobsite, by the time she got to Sausalito, he'd be home. She went out, started her truck with a roar, and peeled out. Thankfully the drive cooled the anger to a slow burn, easily controlled, and by the time she got there she was composed.

Brad opened his door with a look of surprise and an exhale of smoke.

She waved it off. "I thought you quit."

He looked down at the butt between his thumb and forefinger, flicked it out to the driveway, and shrugged. "Does a month count?"

"Thirty days' worth."

His smile creased his suntanned skin. "What are you doing here, Rese?"

"I wanted to follow up on something you said."

"Uh-oh." With a laugh, he waved her in. "Want a drink? Beer, soda, tequila with lime?"

She shook her head, then looked around, walking through the living room into the kitchen that flowed through to the entertaining area. "You've done a nice job in here." It wasn't a large house, but he'd opened it up and made it feel right, more contemporary than she'd have gone, but Dad had spoiled her with historic places before she could form her own tastes.

Brad followed her through the rooms. "Works for me. I wouldn't want to knock around in something bigger."

No, big old villas should not be lived in alone. She turned. "Brad . . ." Words clogged her throat. There was so much history between them, and a lot of it ugly — her fault as much as his. *Compulsively competitive.* She pressed her palms to the kitchen counter, spread her fingers over the smooth Corian surface and wondered how responsible she'd been for everything she had blamed on him and the others.

He leaned on his elbows and looked into her face. "What's up?"

She could not do it. Why had she thought she could come here and . . . She drew herself up. "When we talked last, you said something interesting."

"I try not to bore people all the time."

She looked into his face, green eyes well-set beside his knobbed nose.

The lines along his mouth had deepened and pulled now with amusement. "I have never seen you flustered. I didn't know you had it in you." His face softened.

She raised her chin. "I am not flustered."

"Tongue-tied, then."

She threw out her hands. "What is it with men thinking they know what's in my head?"

The kitchen light caught the silver patches at his temples. "I wouldn't attempt to know what's in your head. I couldn't know if I tried. I have never figured you out from day one. But that's okay. Cuz if you came to take my offer, great."

"Which offer, Brad?"

His brow puckered. "Which . . . ?"

She leaned in and kissed his mouth. He drew back only inches, his lips parted with surprise, his gaze traveling from her hairline to her chin and up. He caught her elbow and drew her around the counter to his side. "I didn't expect that."

"Did you like it?"

"What do you think?"

Anger surged. "I'm not very good at judging."

He bent and took her mouth. He was taller than Lance, brawnier, and when his arms came around, it tipped her neck back farther, and he tasted of smoke, and she remembered every argument and battle.

He pulled back. "What is this, Rese?"

Dad had trusted this man with all the things he wouldn't tell her. He'd spent more time with Brad than any other person. They'd actually talked. Halfway between her age and Dad's, Brad had been part of their lives since she was twelve. "Remember what you said when I asked if there were other secrets I didn't know?"

"Umm . . ."

"You said you'd had a crush on me."

"Well, sure." He swallowed. "You're hard as nails, but that doesn't make you unattractive." He ducked his chin to the side. "Quite the opposite."

Pain and anger bolstered her as she kissed him again.

"Like taking charge, don't you?"

She controlled the urge to run. "Interested?"

He pulled her in and kissed her hard. "You're not the boss here."

"Fine." Let him have it his way. What

did she care? His arms and mouth gave grim satisfaction. She was not unattractive, undesirable. But that wasn't the point.

Brad gripped her shoulders. "What are you expecting?"

"You're in charge."

His chest heaved. "Well, you've taken me by surprise. I don't know . . ."

She didn't help him. He'd wanted to win for so long, and she had to be sure.

He drew a deep breath. "You drive me crazier than any woman I know. Even my ex."

Her eyes shot wide. "Ex? Ex . . . wife?"

"Brief and early. Before I went to work with your dad."

Weren't they a pair with their secrets?

"But that's not the point." His grip softened. "Rese, I don't know what you're doing." He fixed her with a quizzical stare. "I could take this the direction it seems to be going . . . but I can't." He dropped his hands, catching his thumbs in the waist of his jeans.

She waited.

"I won't say I haven't thought about it. But . . ." He looked away, then back. "You're Vernon Barrett's daughter."

A wash of relief.

"He's gone and you're a woman now, but . . ." He shook his head. "That's how it is."

She smiled. "Then I'm ready to discuss our partnership."

He cocked his brow. "Business?"

"Strictly." At his incredulity, she shrugged. "You'd made that comment and . . ." She would never consider a partnership on any other terms again.

His shoulders sagged. "This was a test?"

"Well . . ."

"You couldn't ask?" His hands went to his hips.

"Would you have known for sure?" And would she have believed anything he said without seeing for herself?

He clamped his mouth shut. "Okay, I might've wondered."

"Now we've settled that, let's talk terms."

"Mind if I get my heart rate down?" He went to the refrigerator and took out a beer, then held one up to her.

"Okay," she said. They'd talk as Brad and Dad had, man to man.

As he rejoined her, she stilled the rush of taking control of her life. "First of all, I'm not selling the villa." She had to live somewhere, and she'd done a bang-up job on it. "But I do have some assets to convert."

Lance banged the phone in his palm on his knee. For the last couple hours he'd resisted the urge to redial and tell her every-

526

thing, to try to make her see. *I didn't mean to hurt you. I didn't see this coming.* Or had he? Hadn't he felt the purpose driving him from the start? Yes, but he couldn't know it would come down to this.

He'd sent her home intending to follow within days. He'd thought to finish the letter, give Nonna closure and peace; he hadn't guessed the ending. Should he have warned Rese, prepared her? Maybe he had, by letting her see and hear and know his failures, his dismal record. That's what she'd thought it was. Another mark on his wall.

His heart squeezed. He hadn't led Rese on. He'd wanted a life with her, wanted it still. He'd drawn her inside him, and plucking her out hurt like the knife slicing between his ribs. But he didn't know what was coming, what risks he'd take, or what he might be required to do.

All through the night he'd brooded on Nonno's life, on the man committed to justice and order, a man given to kindliness with a penchant for humor. The senselessness of that murder had overwhelmed him.

Like the people doing their jobs when maniacal evil burst into the towers — what explanation could there be? Nonno had lived with integrity, his only fault the truce he'd made with the devil. A truce — Lance clenched the phone in his hand — violated by a man as underhanded and reprehensible as terrorists incinerating the innocent.

Yes, he would fight this war, though his battle might not end in glory. He knew well enough that pieces were sacrificed, and if it came to that he'd face it. But he wouldn't endanger Rese. She had no cultural basis for vendetta, while even as a child he had taken matters into his own fists. How could he expect her to understand? He couldn't.

That was why he didn't tell her, that and the fear that she'd change his mind. Groaning, he looked at the phone in his hand. He wanted so much just to tell her he loved her. Why hadn't he said that much? He shook his head. She wouldn't believe it. It was better to give her a clean break, but though he'd barely eaten for days, the ache in his stomach was not hunger. Slowly he set the phone down, words damming up inside that couldn't be spoken.

She had put it simply. *"If you've changed your mind, fine, but at least take responsibility for it."* What difference did it make if it was God's plan or his? It looked the same to Rese. As much as it hurt, he couldn't change that. He wished he had Rico's ability to surgically sever his feelings, but he could only gut it out.

He went into Nonna's room and sat. She

was awake but didn't answer his greeting. She seemed to be fading, Nonno's murder the final blow she couldn't deflect. Would she live to see the end? Anger leaching, the loss overwhelmed him. "Nonna." He took her hand. "I'll settle this vendetta for the Michellis, end the curse. Whatever it takes."

Her hand quivered in his, but she didn't speak, didn't look at him. She had gone somewhere in her thoughts that he couldn't reach. But it wasn't about her anymore. God had used her to get his attention, but this was between them now. *"If any man would come after me, let him deny himself and take up his cross and follow me."* He was hard-pressed to think of a more painful way to deny himself than what he'd just done. But it was only the beginning.

Chapter Thirty-one

"Have I told you lately what I think of my father?" Rico leaned against the chain-link fence of the handball court, scowling. It wasn't easy for him to return to where he came from, and Lance appreciated the sacrifice he'd made. It was a long shot that Juan would know any Borsellinos, but having done time and being entrenched in drug and fencing operations, Lance thought it a possibility.

He hooked his fingers on the fence between them, sweat cooling on his chest where the sleeveless T-shirt clung. "Did he know anything?"

"*Nada.* Squat."

Lance clutched the ball. "Not even a contact?"

Rico shrugged. "He's not saying, man."

Twenty-two years was a long time. Though he'd found several in the phone book, the Borsellinos might not be in business in the city anymore, and the one directly responsible for Nonno's death might not even be alive. He didn't know what he'd do when he learned who that was, but at this rate . . . He shook his head.

"Sorry, 'mano." Rico hadn't asked why, had just taken the inquiry to Juan.

"Yeah." Lance sighed. Nonno's pages had given him too little. If he expected someone to return the vendetta, to fight back, why had he not left something to go on? He'd been thorough in everything else.

"Are we playing or what?" Bobby called.

Lance glanced back at his brother-in-law. He wasn't sure, but he'd guess Bobby had been enlisted to get him outside, to stop his brooding. He wasn't brooding, though. He was thinking and praying, mostly praying when the hurt and longing seized hold, when fear and frustration choked him.

Exercise had been a bad idea. He could feel his system crashing, from fasting, maybe, or heartache. He'd ended enough relationships that he ought to know the drill. But this wound wasn't closing.

"Hey." Bobby spread his hands.

"I gotta go." Lance waved him off and went through the gate to Rico. It had taken a week for Juan to say he knew nothing. A week of worry for Nonna, for Rese, for what he was supposed to do. There had to be something to go on. *Lord* . . .

And then he had a thought, a memory: Tony carrying a box when he and Gina moved out. A box. Lance's breath arrested.

Maybe . . . He swallowed.

"What's the race?" Rico hurried beside him.

"I need something."

Rico cocked his head. "You got that look, man."

"I need to see Gina."

Rico slanted him a stare.

"Not like that." Rico had made up for Star's leaving with a series of encounters, but scratching a physical itch was not on Lance's mind. And if it was, his dead brother's wife would not be the means. What was Rico thinking?

When he reached the train stairs, Rico was still there. He paused.

Rico half turned. "What?"

"Don't you have somewhere to go?"

"Yeah, man. We're going to see Gina."

Lance weighed the situation, then released a breath and climbed the stairs. Though he prayed it would yield something, this part shouldn't jeopardize Rico, and he wouldn't mind a companion for the ride into the city.

Last he knew, Gina didn't work Sundays, so there was a good chance she'd be home. When they arrived at her row house, she opened the door, looking fresh and pretty in navy capris and a yellow-and-navy striped blouse. Her hair was pulled into a ponytail, and even though there were a few strands of gray, she looked girlish.

"Hey, Gina." He bent and kissed her cheeks.

Someone moved up behind her, and Lance looked into the lean, spectacled face of her doctor friend. "Hi." Lance held out his hand. "Lance Michelli." He knew why Jake wanted to punch the guy, though there was nothing officious about him. He just didn't belong there.

"This is Darryl Boyle," Gina said, omitting the doctor part. "My brother-in-law, and his friend Rico." She turned back. "What are you doing here?"

"Besides checking on Tony's family?" The discomfort and sadness that flashed across her face chastened him. "I wondered if you still had that box of Nonno Marco's stuff."

She frowned. "His old department things?"

Lance nodded.

She shrugged, waving them in. "I haven't tossed it, so if . . . Tony didn't, it should be here."

"Tony wouldn't toss it." He'd loved going through Nonno's medals and photos, trying on the hat until it fit. He must have memorized every article in the scrapbook, but Lance couldn't remember if there was anything in there that applied to the vendetta.

Gina scrunched her fingers into her hair,

533

messing up the smooth strands pulled into the elastic band. "I guess the storage closet."

"I doubt it."

She glanced over her shoulder.

"Let's try his office."

"Lance . . ."

He was already at the door when he realized she'd changed Tony's office into a game room for the kids. It shouldn't hurt. It was going on four years. The kids needed the space more than . . . Tony.

He followed her to the storage closet.

She turned on the light. "I hope you'll recognize it."

But he'd already seen it on a back shelf. He pressed through sleeping bags and sports gear and other boxes, then had it in his hands.

"I was kind of keeping it for Jake." Her tone was mild, but she meant it. Tony was Pop's firstborn son, and Jake was his. All heirloom paraphernalia belonged in the line of succession.

"I'm looking for something specific." Though he didn't know what. "I might need it for a while, but I'll bring it back." He could hear Rico chatting with Darryl.

She smiled. "Okay. Sure. You want to bring it out?"

He shook his head, settled down on a rolled sleeping bag with the box across his lap. "I'll put it back on the shelf when I'm done."

"Want some sweet tea? Darryl's taught me how to make it Georgia-style."

"No thanks." He lifted the lid off the box, pleased that he had held back his comment. Gina didn't need any more of his sarcasm.

As much as he would have liked to walk down memory lane, he was putting a crimp in Gina's date, so he skipped the photos and awards and meritorious medals and went straight to the scrapbook. It held articles about Nonno and others on the force, but nothing about the FBI or the Borsellinos.

Gripping the thick, separating binder, he set it on the floor and worked his way to the bottom of the box. Heart pounding, he removed an envelope that he didn't recall. Tony had probably not considered it newsworthy for a kid brother when they'd looked through the box together, but Lance drew it out with anticipation rising. It could be insignificant. But he didn't believe Nonno would give them nothing to go on. If he went to the trouble of leaving Nonna the letter, he must have expected some sort of action. Otherwise, why not keep his secret to the grave?

Lance pinched the metal closure and pulled open the flap. He saw no more than the top inch of writing on the first page next to the photo before his fingers started shaking so badly he could hardly close it up again. He set the envelope on the floor, repacked the box, and replaced it on the shelf.

Rico looked like a pup with a bladder issue by the time Lance came out, envelope in hand. He jumped right up and headed for the door.

Gina looked up from her tea. "Found it?" She was dying to ask, he knew, but was more eager to end the awkwardness.

Lance kissed her cheek. "Thanks. I'll get it back to you."

She patted his cheek in return. "You okay?" Concern washed her eyes.

"Sure."

She held him a moment too long in her gaze. "Okay. Stop in anytime. Jake'll be sad he missed you."

But happy to avoid Darryl, no doubt. Had Gina set it up that way? No matter. Their business.

They went out to the sidewalk, and before he realized it was coming, Rico snatched the envelope.

"What's this?"

"Don't open it."

"Why not?"

Lance held out his hand. "It's my problem."

Rico frowned. "There's no 'my' with us."

"There is this time." Lance reached for the envelope, but Rico stepped back.

Even with his arm strapped to his chest, he looked fierce. "You're not doing this alone, 'mano."

"Doing what?"

"You think I'm blind? I haven't seen you agonizing, starving yourself?"

"I'm not starving."

Rico clutched the envelope.

Lance sighed. "It's not your fight, Rico. It might not end well." Messing with a crime family usually didn't.

"However it ends, it ends."

His chest clenched. "Rico . . ."

But he opened the envelope and took the papers out.

Rese was alone in the workshop when the pain blindsided her. She'd expected it earlier, but it hadn't hit. In the nine days since Lance had called she'd worked non-stop, advancing the plan she and Brad had agreed on, voiding the plan she and Lance had made.

All reservations were cancelled, money returned, Web site discontinued. She didn't know enough to deal with the wine yet, but the silver certificates had netted nearly five times their face value, more than enough to set up the rival company — Plocken and Barrett, Renovation Specialists. She might have sold her blue sky with Barrett Renovations, but she didn't doubt they'd win it back. Brad hadn't pushed it, but they'd listed her name second to limit the obvious effect on their competition. Having Barrett there would open doors, but she didn't want to be sued.

After hammering out the agreement, they had talked about Vernon Barrett, her dad and hero. Brad's too, in a lot of ways. They were both products of his uncompromising standards, his drive for excellence, his frugal but fair praise. They'd shaken hands at the end of the night, and she'd gone home, convinced she could take on the world.

But in the quiet of the workshop, doing what she loved, the pain had come. Why hadn't she seen it coming? She could have prepared, could have looked it squarely in the eye. But no. Waves of hurt rolled over her.

Hurt and anger and confusion. What had she missed? Was it all about conquest? Maybe it was enough that she'd fallen in love. That had to have been one of his harder battles, if Sybil was any indication. She'd been all over him from day one, and was obviously not the first to find him irresistible.

She couldn't pretend ignorance. How many people had given it to her straight? Even Lance. Maybe he'd tried to be different, but when it came down to it, he'd ducked out before he could fail. The thought infuriated and devastated her. And the most unfair part was that in and around and through her pain was the awful feeling that something wasn't right.

Ridiculous, but . . . the feeling persisted, a concern so terrible she could not be imagining it, as though Walter had Lance trapped in the dark, breathing poisoned air.

"Rese?"

The chisel wavered in her hand. She looked up to Michelle, who stood framed in the doorway.

"Star said you were in here." Michelle held up a leash hopefully. "Can I borrow Baxter?"

Rese looked down at the dog lying at her feet, his tail wagging at the prospect, though he stayed put. Lance hadn't said a word about who got custody, but possession was nine-tenths of the law. "Sure. He'd like to get out."

She'd been finishing up a scrollwork design for a cabinet and hadn't noticed the hours passing. Baxter must be tired of lying at her feet, though he hadn't protested. Michelle would take him along as she took toilet paper and toothpaste, or diapers or soup to the needy just outside the esteemed Sonoma city limits. He seemed to like their trips, and everyone liked him — what wasn't to like?

Rese patted his head. "Go on."

He scrambled up. She was actually surprised he hadn't jumped up to greet Michelle immediately, but he seemed to sense the sorrow that had descended on her like a pall. Maybe he felt his master's desertion as acutely as she did, but lacked the ability to transform it to anger or action.

"Are you all right?" Michelle's brow puckered.

Rese sidestepped. "Michelle, how do you get along with people so easily?" Maybe it was something she'd done and hadn't even realized that drove him away.

Michelle straightened from attaching the leash and shrugged. "I see Jesus in them." Her face softened. " 'Whatever you do for the least of these, you do it for me.' Simple as that."

Simple. "You look for the best in people?"

Michelle laughed. "Now, that's harder. With the ornery ones especially. No, I just see whatever they want to show me and love them right there."

"And if they don't love you back?" Her voice had almost broken, but she caught it without showing the pain behind the words.

Michelle shrugged. "Some people are so holed up inside they can't reach out."

Rese studied her face, but if she'd meant that personally, it didn't show.

"Others are searching so hard they can't see what's in front of them. But we're all just doing the best we can."

Rese nodded. "Right." She'd spent all her energy doing the best, being the best. But it obviously wasn't enough, and now she wondered if it ever had been.

"Lord love you, Rese. I'll be back with Baxter." Michelle waved the leash.

And Lord love you, too, Michelle, because someday when you're not looking someone might just let you down so far you won't be able to love them no matter how hard you try.

The file held a meticulous account of Paolo Borsellino, his sons, Leon and Matteo, several cousins, a nephew, and two cohorts. The crimes and dirty dealings were detailed and dated, though probably past the statute of limitations since the information was over twenty-two years old and none concerned murder.

The one murder he knew of, Nonno had not recorded. Hard to do when you're the victim.

Lance sat with Rico on the fire escape, shielding the pages from the slight breeze with his body. The sound of a Harley several blocks away brought Rico's head up, but not even that broke Lance's focus. With the information in the envelope, Nonno could have put them all away, but he'd kept the truce. Why? His family connection? Some sense of honor, or guilt for betraying Don Agosto to his death? Possible, given the guilt he'd carried over Vittorio's. He and Nonno were alike in that, bearing the weight of other people's choices.

If Nonno had turned this information over and revealed the threat against his family, surely something could have been done. Or had he believed the risk too great? How could he protect them all, and for how long? Knowing his enemy too thoroughly, Nonno had assessed the risk and sacrificed himself to protect the ones he loved.

But he had left this so that justice could be served if the crime was committed. He must have expected someone to bring it to the authorities. Nonna's letter would have spurred a search, and maybe the folder had been easily accessible until someone boxed it up with Nonno's other things.

Tony — had Tony read the file? He was NYPD. Without the letter, he would not have connected it to Nonno's accident, but even a rookie cop would recognize evidence of crimes. Lance didn't know how long it had been in the box, but Tony had never shown him. Had Nonno told him the Borsellinos were hands off? Could Tony have known?

Rico's stomach growled. "Want to get some food?"

Lance shook his head. Nonno might have expected Tony to put it all together. How could he know his grandson would be dead before the letter was found? Twenty-two years ago, they might have investigated, built a case. But what chance was there now of proving anything? He sighed. Hopeless as it seemed, he had to start somewhere. He gathered the papers into the envelope and stood up. "I'm taking this to the cops. You can't come with me, Rico. I don't want them knowing you're involved."

Rico didn't argue. Going to the NYPD with anything was not for him. Tony, sure, who hadn't loved Tony? And Rico knew Juan deserved each trip he took, but beyond that, he had a basic distrust of the system.

"I don't see them taking you seriously. What can they do with that?" Rico nodded at the envelope.

"Maybe nothing. Probably nothing. But I

have to try." Lance climbed in through the window and left Rico shaking his head.

He could have gone somewhere in the Bronx precinct, but he took the train into the city to Tony's old station. He approached the officer at the desk and asked for Tony's former partner, Seabass.

The officer raised his brows at his use of the nickname and directed him to Sebastian Gamet's office. Lance knuckled the doorframe and walked in.

"Michelli!"

"You made detective."

"Last year." The man stood up from behind the desk and gripped his hand. Half a hoagie piled with onions ripened the air between them. "How are ya? Stayin' out of trouble?"

Right. "I try."

Gamet's ginger brows pinched together beneath the comb-over that was truly scary. "Sure miss ribbing Tony about his felonious kid brother."

"Not felonious. I was never charged."

Gamet cocked his head. "You doing okay? You look a little . . . gaunt."

Where did he begin to answer? "I'm fine. But I want to show you something." He held out the Borsellino file and the last page of Nonno's letter as well.

Gamet read it over carefully. "Marco Michelli's a relative of yours?"

"My grandfather."

"That's right. Tony told me that. He was with the force."

"Later on. FBI to start with. Worked undercover through some tough times."

Gamet nodded. "All times are tough undercover."

"He infiltrated the Borsellino Camorra family. Sent the don up the river, where the Mafia took him out."

"That happens."

Lance sat on the edge of the desk. "The Borsellinos made it a vendetta against Marco. One of the sons, Carlo, followed him to Sonoma, killed his contact, and tried to kill him. Marco shot Carlo in self-defense."

Gamet swigged his Diet Coke, listening, but not necessarily buying it.

"The next son, Paolo, made a truce with Marco. They'd leave each other and their families alone. Paolo needed to establish himself, and Marco had seen that they would kill."

Gamet took a bite and chewed thoughtfully.

"Years later Paolo got fingered and convicted. As it says in the letter, he must have thought Marco was part of it and ordered the hit from his cell in Ryker."

Gamet frowned. "We got a file on that killing?"

Lance shook his head. "We thought it was a car accident. It looked like an accident."

Gamet studied him. "But now you think your grandpa was offed in this vendetta."

Lance nodded. "The letter was written the day Marco died. Read the page. He received a threat in a phone call and went to meet it."

Gamet pursed his lips as he ran his gaze over Marco's letter. "That is a possible scenario. It's also possible his car crashed before he got there, or that he had his meeting, settled things, and crashed on the way home. Believe me, these kinds of ironic things happen."

Lance hadn't thought in those terms and didn't believe it, but gave the detective his due.

Gamet set the papers down, came around the desk, and gripped his shoulder. "If it's true, you've wrongly lost two people who mattered. You know Tony mattered to me. He wasn't even on shift that morning, just doing a favor for one of the guys."

It had tormented him to think of the man who should have been in that place at that time. But now he didn't believe that either. God knew what had to be. "Is there anything you can do with this?"

"I won't dismiss it right off. But it's pretty slim."

"But you'll look? Search out Marco's record, anything he might have left in the files or . . . anything?"

"I'll look, Lance. No investigation on the accident?"

He sighed. "I don't think so."

"And it was twenty . . ."

"Twenty-two years ago."

"And no record of a crime. Not even a cold case."

Lance shook his head.

"That'll be pulling a rabbit out of a hat. What am I supposed to use for evidence?"

Lance sagged. "I know. It's just . . ." *A vendetta*. His head spun, and he pressed his fingers to his eyes.

"Are you okay?"

He swallowed. "Guess I need to eat something."

"Well, here." Gamet reached behind him for the half hoagie.

Lance waved him off as his stomach turned over. "Thanks, no."

Gamet set the sandwich back down. "Lance, we lost some good men, but you have to stop looking in the shadows to cast blame."

"I didn't look for this." It was given to him. He turned toward the door. "Let me know what you come up with."

Gamet eased back down in his chair and picked up the sandwich. "I will."

But Lance could tell by his tone there wouldn't be anything. "Look up the Borsellinos, will you?"

He rocked back in his chair. "And what?"

"Just see if they're still in business."

"Police files are not public domain."

"And tell Sara hi for me."

Gamet cocked his head with a sigh. "Get outta here."

Chapter Thirty-two

"I'm very excited," Dr. Jonas said. "Her failure to respond to Thorazine and other treatments made controlling Elaine's psychotic breaks nearly impossible. But the Clozapine has shown marked effectiveness. It's beautiful to see."

Rese looked into Dr. Jonas's Santa Claus eyes, still unnerved by the bottlebrush brows that topped them. "So she's doing better?"

"She's doing remarkably."

"Does she want to see me?"

His bristly mustache stood out when he smiled. "I'm sure she does. Sometimes her negative symptoms — that is, her inappropriate expressions — make it hard to determine her desire for things. We have to look at the whole picture, agitation, sleep patterns, how well she eats and communicates. She was much calmer whenever Vernon visited. After his death, her delusions reappeared until we adjusted her dosage. It's not an exact science, but you learn what to look for."

"But she is communicating?"

"Some days she's quite talkative and moderately lucid." He laced his fingers across his chest. "And the important thing is that, in the absence of delusions, I don't believe she is dangerous to herself or to you — as long as she stays on the medication."

Rese digested that. It was what she'd been hoping to hear, wasn't it?

He leaned forward. "Her condition is not healed, but controlled. You understand the difference?"

She nodded. Walter was blocked by the drugs, as Star's fairies had been blocked by prayer. "So if I maintain her medication, she could come home with me?"

"It's probable. You have to decide if it's feasible. It would be a major life change."

She almost laughed. As though anything in her life was the way she had wanted it. "The only thing is, I'm working now. When I started this process, I thought I'd be there, at the inn. But I'm back in renovation. I work at home for some of it, but most is on site."

He lifted his hands from his chest. "She'll need someone with her. If not immediately attending, at least on the premises. The insurance benefit could provide home care, or —"

"I have a friend there. She mostly paints in the garden. Mom could sit with her."

He nodded. "She'd like that."

"I'll talk to Star."

"Good. Have you heard from the county?"

"I had the home study, and they checked my credit and determined I have no criminal record. Now they have to make sure I'm not drumming up dependents so I can defraud the state or rip off the insurance company."

He laughed. "Establishing your competency as guardian."

Her throat tightened briefly. "Am I competent?"

His eyes softened so much that fifteen years ago she'd have climbed into his lap. "I think you're extremely competent."

The words almost brought tears, but she was conditioned to block them.

He said, "I've put that into my report, though these next few years might show us something."

She didn't need the reminder. "I guess I'll deal with that as it comes."

"You have a good deal of your father in you."

She smiled bleakly. "The best of both of them?"

He reached across the desk and closed her hands into his. "I do believe that."

Her throat had closed, but she forced her voice through it. "So I'll wait to be approved, then . . ." A thought suddenly occurred. "Should I ask Mom if she wants to live with me? She's been here so long it might be hard to . . ."

"Let's go see, shall we?"

They walked together to the visiting room, and Rese looked up when the nurse brought Mom in from another door. She tried not to hope for too much. The nurse seated her mother, while Dr. Jonas stood near. Rese drew a breath and sat down. "Hi, Mom."

She looked up. "Because it's a very bad feeling, a very bad feeling."

The doctor nodded his encouragement, so Rese reached across the table and touched her hand. "Mom? It might be possible for you to live with me in Sonoma. Would you like that?"

She turned until her eyes found Dr. Jonas. "Do I know this one?"

It felt like something had sat on her chest.

"What do you think, Elaine? Do you recognize this girl of yours?"

Rese could barely stand the gaze that came back and scrutinized her, then slid away. "I told the truth. I told. But he's gone, gone, gone."

Tears stung. Okay, she was human. It hurt that Mom didn't know her, but she had to get past that. Maybe in time . . .

"What have you done with my little girl? They put her somewhere I can't find, and the feeling is very strong now; it's very strong, and if you wait, you'll see, they'll take you too."

"I'm right here, Mom. It's Rese." At least she knew she had a daughter.

"Theresa?"

It was like sunshine to her soul — and what better gift for her twenty-fifth birthday? "That's right." She could hardly be expected to recognize her after so few visits. But they would change that. "Do you want to come live with me?"

"Yes."

The word was clear and unencumbered by nonsense. Even though it might be no more than something pulled out of the air, she wanted to sink to the floor and lay her head in her mother's lap.

"Well, if you keep doing so well, and I pass everyone's scrutiny, we'll do it, okay?"

Mom's finger had not ceased its flicking motion since she sat down. She didn't answer. Twice would be asking too much. Rese looked up at the doctor, then back. "I'll see you soon, Mom."

She thanked the doctor and drove home, hardly containing her emotion. It wouldn't be easy, but it was happening. She swallowed back the tears. Fifteen years of loss being restored one day at a time.

Star was in the attic assembling a jigsaw puzzle on the floor. The design was a heap of multihued snails almost identical in size and shape with only shade variations to distinguish them.

An effective torture, Rese thought as she stopped above her. "Star, it looks like I might be able to bring Mom home."

In the past that would have been enough to send Star spiraling out of sight for days, but Rese was hoping the connection she'd witnessed between them at the center might make a difference. Star had projected a lot of her own issues onto Mom, but when she saw her again after all the years in between, they had shared a moment of understanding and recognition.

Star looked up. "You mean here?"

Rese nodded. "Her medication has made a big difference. Dr. Jonas thinks she's no longer dangerous." *To a little girl with no defense but the mysterious presence who wouldn't let her die.* "She said she'd like to live with us, and . . . I hoped we could give it a try."

Star blinked. " 'Then 'twere well it were done quickly.' "

She seemed to mean it, but that wasn't the biggest thing. Rese knelt. "Now that I'm working, I can't be here all the time. Would you be up for watching her, just being with her when I'm not?"

Star blinked. "You're asking me to take responsibility for Elaine?"

Rese swallowed. "It's a lot to ask, I know. But I thought —"

"Yes. I'll watch your mother when you work."

Rese sat back on her heels. "You will? You don't mind?"

Star shook her head. "I'm here anyway." She hadn't left the property since they'd come back.

Rese pressed her palms to her thighs. "That's great. I mean, you can say no. . . ."

"I said yes." Star picked up a piece. "What color would you say this is?"

Rese considered the puzzle piece. "Mostly blue."

Star stared across the length of the attic. "Elaine saw the colors."

Rese nodded. "Yes."

"I wonder what she'll see now."

"She'll see you, Star."

Star set the piece with a dozen others of similar hue.

Rese watched for any sign of resentment. Her throat tightened. "And here's the other thing. If I start having psychotic episodes, you're in charge of us both."

Star looked up. Rese braced herself for a flippant or caustic remark, but Star said, "Why did you go back to work?"

She hadn't expected that, but it must be

her day to feel everything. It had been three weeks since they'd talked, but it might have been that morning. "Because Lance isn't coming."

"So we're not running an inn?"

She shook her head. "More like a shelter for misfits."

Star's face flashed with acute delight, then she tossed her head back and laughed. Rese laughed with her, and it caught them both up until they were holding their stomachs and lying on the floor. When they had nearly recovered, Star rolled her head to the side and their gazes met. "Do you hate him?"

"I don't know. Right now it just hurts."

"I didn't know."

"Now you do."

In the month and a half since they'd finished the letter, Nonna's room had become a shrine of flowers and cards, prayers and novenas. People came by, leaving small tokens of love and respect, and though Nonna paid no attention, Lance found each face sweeter, purer than he'd seen it before. As they came to sit or say a few words, to bathe or feed or change her clothes or bedding, he observed an essence in each person that had never seemed so bright.

Even Pop, when he held Nonna's hand

and kissed her fingers, showed no toughness, just a gentle "How are you, Momma?" He didn't pray out loud, but Lance felt his prayers. They didn't talk, but he sensed Pop reassessing him. He'd expected him to give it up already, but that wasn't possible.

He'd brought up the job once, but Lance had earned his portion of the rent by soloing two parties, playing a wedding with Chaz, and finding odd jobs in the neighborhood. Most of his free time he'd spent with Nonna, though it seemed there was less and less he could do for her.

Physiologically, there was no reason for her to be failing. She ate and drank what she was given, moved with assistance, but spoke no word and showed no interest. A visiting nurse had checked her over and found nothing to warrant this slide. It was shock and heartsickness that had drained her spirit of life. He had never known her to give up, but she was giving up now.

In the chair beside her bed, Lance clenched his jaw. He had fasted and prayed for her to find strength, and for Detective Gamet to find answers. Neither had happened. Gamet had returned the file with an apology. "I can't commit the resources. We have too many cold cases as it is."

"What about the Borsellinos?"

Gamet had not liked the question. "Get

outta here, Lance. Do something with your life." But when he'd stood there still, Gamet had placed his fists on the desk. "I'll tell you this much. Paolo Borsellino? He's in Ryker's, serving life for racketeering, conspiracy, and murder."

Not for conspiring to murder Nonno, and the one who'd committed it might still walk free. The curse was unreturned until the vendetta was settled, but no one seemed to realize what was at stake. Lance had left there bleak and angry. Every time he turned to some other authority, it came back to him.

He hadn't gone to Nonna's room when he got back. He'd gone to work, searching public records and tangential leads to locate the men identified in the file. Two were dead, one besides Paolo incarcerated, but of the others, all but one still lived in the area. So he'd started his own detailed account of each.

Over the next week he'd located homes and offices and recreational spots; cars, boats, schools, and churches — significant places in the life of the Borsellino family. Mostly alone, but sometimes with Rico, he had moved through uptown Manhattan, swank Chelsea and Long Island neighborhoods. Though he had no training, surveillance had come naturally — imagine that.

In a sense, he now worked undercover

for Nonno, his eyes, as Vittorio had been. After the first week of locating, he'd started in to learn his enemy. And for that Sofie's Neon was a no-can-do. He'd hit up Saul Samuels. In return for playing his niece's bat mitzvah — Rico air-brushing the toms and cymbals — he got use of Saul's silver Mercedes. Saul didn't drive it much anyway.

Now he sat with Rico outside a Chelsea townhouse. At first, he'd expected crack houses and gang lords. But though the family had begun that way and undoubtedly profited still from illicit operations, the Borsellinos had risen to decadent opulence and bought themselves respectability.

He had to laugh at his own family, still tucked away in their four-story building, his aunts and uncles thinking they'd made good, moving north to the suburbs. But behind his laugh he seethed, not that these people had more, but that they'd built it on his family's blood. "It's obscene, Rico."

"Yeah. The wages of sin." He formed a crooked grin. "If Juan wasn't so stupid, I'd have grown up here."

"If you'd grown up here, you'd be one of them."

Rico sobered. "I didn't mean it, 'mano."

Lance turned back to the townhouse where a woman, the second wife of Ricky Borsellino Jr., stepped outside to catch a cab. He might have followed the cab, but he knew she was picking up their daughter from karate.

The problem with surveillance was that people became real. He now had faces to the names, faces for the wives and ex-wives, kids and stepkids and grandkids. Like Nonno, he'd entered their world, gone to church with them, shaken hands at the sign of peace. They had no idea who he was.

Chapter Thirty-three

Star's hair formed a soft bonnet of curls around her head where it rested on Rese's thigh. The late-August garden was splendid in the evening light, clumps of aster and daisies, mums and fuchsia — names she'd learned from Star. Around the workshop, goldenrod and penstemon stretched proudly to the slanting rays. She had laughed when Star spread the blanket and ordered her to sit, but now she was glad to be dragged from the workshop where she'd been diligently productive.

Star held the book open against her knees. " 'Some are born great, some achieve greatness, and some have greatness thrust upon 'em.' "

And some couldn't see their greatness when it hit them between the eyes, Rese thought with a familiar wrench. She pushed the thought aside with something close to violence and forced her focus another direction. How could it take so long to get a hearing to vacate a stupid court order that was no longer relevant so she could bring Mom home? She'd completed her part weeks ago.

"You're not listening." Star tipped her head up.

"I was thinking about Mom and if we'll ever get through the bureaucratic sludge." Though most of the time Mom wasn't even aware that her situation could change. Rese sighed. "Sorry."

Star settled the book on her chest and closed her eyes. "Hear that?"

She listened. Birds twittering. The tap of Baxter's nails and the pad of his feet as he crossed to them, licked her neck and chin, and then settled with a *wumph* across her other thigh. Rese stroked him automatically. "What am I supposed to be hearing?"

"Life passing."

"Hmm."

Star opened her eyes. "I finished something. I'd like you to see it."

Had to be some kind of record. When they were growing up Star was afraid to call any piece of art finished, and actually left most of her paintings incomplete. As she didn't want anyone to see something before it was done, Rese had caught only glimpses. But since the painting she'd made for Lance, Star had completed six canvases and let her see them all.

Something in her tone seemed different this time, though. "Is it in the attic?" Star had taken that space over as her indoor studio, even though it must have memories of afternoon jams with Lance and Chaz and Rico, of her taking the mic and finding her voice. Maybe because it did.

Star got up. "Yes, but don't move."

Good thing, since Baxter had scrunched in with his paws until his whole head, neck, and shoulders were on her. "You are a glutton," she told the dog as they waited for Star, and he accepted her opinion without remorse.

In a few minutes, Star carried out a midsize canvas and held it before her. Rese studied the collage of musical instruments framed by an inference of subway tunnel walls. As she looked, her eye picked out Rico's hair and face formed from the shadows and lines of the various drum images on the upper right. The face would appear to anyone who looked long enough, but Star had to know she would recognize Rico. "It's great, Star."

"I'm sending it to him."

Rese looked up from the painting to Star's face. "Really?"

"He doesn't have to keep it." A slight tremor betrayed her.

Rese said, "He'd be crazy not to." Though he'd been a little crazy; the whole thing had, but she and Star were doing fine now. Why would she want to stir the pot?

★ ★ ★

After studying the Borsellinos until he could tell where they'd be at noon on Wednesday, who they'd be with, what they'd order for lunch, it had come clear that some of the respectability was an illusion. Lance had guessed which members actively controlled the family "businesses," who were used as muscle, and who seemed to be uninvolved.

But he didn't know who had killed Nonno. And he wasn't likely to learn about it without getting inside the operations as Nonno had. He wasn't stupid enough to think he could pull that off.

If the hit had been a power play, then he'd assume Paolo's son Leon or his cousin Gerard. They had the biggest houses, the best toys, the meanest tempers. But those were guesses and didn't mean either had personally sabotaged Nonno's car.

He had watched, rage growing inside, but what good had it done? He had no answers, no direction. If God had called him to this, why didn't He make himself clear? Lance clenched his fists. He had followed Nonno's example, watching and waiting. He had gathered current information, nothing that would necessarily incriminate or be accepted by Seabass or anyone else as evidential.

But he was looking at an operation that

had profited by Nonno's silence, then stabbed him in the back. Lance shook as a new thought seized him. Vendetta did not require direct retaliation. As they had all suffered from the vendetta against them, so the Borsellinos would suffer whatever blow he struck. He had told Rese when one part of the body suffers, the whole body suffers. But he hadn't meant it this way. He'd never meant it this way.

His hands broke out with sweat. How could he even think it? *"Vengeance is mine sayeth the Lord — but sometimes it's mine, too, and yours."* Was this what it had come to? A justice outside the law? A personal vengeance? He gripped his head.

He'd fought in self-defense, fought to defend the weak. If he'd been given a shot at the terrorists en route to the towers, he'd have taken it — without regret. But that wasn't the same, or was it? He reeled.

Could he target someone and take him out? He knew which men still ran the rackets, which ones had probably killed, if not Nonno, then others. He knew who cheated on their wives, who beat on their kids. He could choose the worst of them and do the world a favor. Not only for his family, but all those who were still being hurt by the drugs and pornography and worse.

Others had been called before him to

end evil and accomplish God's will. Moses had struck the ground with his staff, closing the sea over Pharaoh's army, drowning men and beasts. Real men. Men whose eyes he'd looked into.

Joshua wrought destruction on Jericho. Peter spoke the Lord's edict on Ananias and Sapphira. Even Jesus had cursed the unproductive fig tree, metaphorically damning those who failed to respond to the Lord's desire. Unfaithful servants, afraid of a hard master who shrank from God's will, were slain.

He wasn't afraid to die. He would give his life as Tony, as Nonno, even Quillan and Vittorio, had done, but that sacrifice wasn't enough to end this blood feud. Dread sucked him down as he realized what might be required.

Would God make him lower than the low, despised, reviled? A murderer? His years in the Peace Corps, with Habitat, and on the mission to Jamaica like nothing. His daily offerings, millions of graces, prayers and praise — dust and ashes.

He would become his enemy. Like those who killed Tony, who killed Nonno. His spirit writhed. *No, Lord.* Call it pride, call it arrogance. He was not the evil he hated. He wasn't! Fists clenched, he shook his head in fierce denial, rejecting even the possibility.

Then he grew still, empty. He hardly breathed, hardly dared show his face . . . because he knew he had it in him. No loss had hurt so much as being laid bare.

Chaz had seen Lance's fervor. It was one of the things that had drawn them together, that had caused a friendship in spite of their natural differences. For Lance there was no halfway. He'd spent himself on the streets of Jamaica, in parts of Kingston that were more like hell, giving succor to the weary and downtrodden — sometimes at personal risk.

Chaz had carried him back one night, bruised and bleeding from interfering in a gang rape. Lance hadn't known the woman he'd defended, hadn't seen the color of her skin or counted those against her. But he'd taken the violence meant for her into his body as she escaped. That he hadn't died, Chaz considered a miracle. Lance had powerful angels.

Chaz had seen him burn with indignation, weep with compassion. He'd marveled at the joy that came over him when the last nail was driven and one family would no longer sleep in the street. When he put a bowl of soup into the hands of a child, it was almost a sacrament.

So he wasn't entirely surprised when Momma knocked on the door, beside herself. "He won't eat; he won't talk." Momma waved her hands. "I ask him to sit with his grandmother, and I find him in a trance. Not even Joshua's trumpet could get through. I should call the priest."

"Let me see." Chaz followed her across the hall to where Lance sat with Nonna's Bible in his lap. It wasn't a trance, but a fierce concentration. He didn't want to be hassled out of whatever he'd fixed on. "Don't worry, Momma. He's okay."

"He's okay?" She threw up her hands. "It's okay not to answer your mother when she's talking?" She shrugged. "Fine. I'll go." It was no wonder she'd worried. She knew the face he presented at home. She hadn't seen him out in the world, serving the wretched with zeal and thoroughness, hadn't witnessed the moments when something ignited inside him.

Chaz didn't know what was burning in Lance now, but when Momma had gone, he crouched down. "Look at me, mon."

Lance raised his eyes from the Bible in his lap.

"You want to tell me about it?"

"You know what Abraham said when God asked him to kill his son Isaac? I'm ready." Lance swallowed. "He said, I'm ready."

Chaz nodded, seeing behind the words. What did Lance think God had asked of him?

Lance sat back in the chair. "God told him, take this child you love, the one you prayed and waited for, the son my promise depends on. Take him like an animal and slaughter him. Make a holocaust of your heart."

Chaz said, "God had to know there was nothing between them, not the beloved son, not even the promise He himself had made. God had to know Abraham would do anything to serve him."

"Even something that seems so wrong?"

"What's the matter, mon?"

His gaze pierced. "Since I was a kid, I've looked for God's will, searched out the possibilities, the opportunities, all the little things. But inside, I wanted something big, something radical."

Chaz nodded. He knew that. Lance wore the hunger on his face.

"But now . . ." Lance looked away. "What if I can't do it?"

"What is it you have to do?"

Lance didn't answer.

Chaz frowned. "What is it, mon?"

Lance shook his head. "It's all been laid out, everything that's happened, even Tony . . ."

"He works all things for good." He was glad Lance could finally see that.

But Lance closed his eyes, pain pinching his brow. "I think I know what God intends. But I don't know how I'll do it."

Chaz clutched his shoulder. "His grace is sufficient, his power made perfect in weakness."

The breath escaped Lance slowly, and he nodded. "Thank you."

Chaz stood up. Lance held nothing back. His zeal for God was not feigned. Even so, passion could be dangerous.

Rese parked the truck beside the villa, hope swelling inside her. Mom had said nothing on the drive; whether out of terror or dismay or even happiness, it was hard to tell. As a child she had learned to read every nuance of Mom's expression, trying to gauge what was coming next. But now the medication or the progression of her condition had made that almost impossible. Or she just had to learn to see again.

"Mom? We're home."

Her mother stared out the window as Rese ducked under the branches of the scarlet-tinged maple. The vineyard owners had waited out the last golden days, then rushed into the highlight of the year, harvesting the grapes. If things hadn't changed, that would have meant a full inn, booked solid from Labor Day through mid-October, at the least. Throat tight, she went around and helped Mom climb out. How had she thought she could tuck her into a guest room with all the other guests? Thank God, she'd come to her senses.

As they approached, Star opened the front door and stood there in a blue dress, peacock-feather earrings, and an iridescent green scarf in a band around her head. Mom's gait had gotten awkward, Rese noticed as she helped her up the porch steps.

Star smiled beatifically and swung the door open. "Welcome home, Mom."

Rese startled. Star didn't even call her own mother Mom.

As they went into the house, Rese sensed Mom's confusion. "You won't remember it," she said. "It's a new house I fixed up as Dad taught me." Even if Mom didn't grasp that Dad had died, there was no point avoiding the subject. Too many things had gone unspoken for too many years.

She walked Mom through the front sitting room and into the dining room, but within minutes her eyes darted and her brow creased, her fingers flicking frantically.

"One, two, three, four. Now there aren't any more. One, two. One . . ."

It must be overwhelming her. Rese had thought she'd feel less confined if she'd seen it all, but maybe a single new room was enough to start with. "Come on upstairs. I'll show you your room."

"Rose Trellis," Star reminded as they climbed. She had declared the creams and pinks of that room healing, and Rese doubted Mom would voice an objection. If at some point she seemed to prefer one of the other rooms, they were certainly available.

Mom counted the stairs to the top, then looked as though she'd turn around and go back down. Did she want out already?

"This is your room." Rese led her into the one at the end of the hall. The canopy bed frame was wreathed in pink silk rose vines and creamy organza. It was the most feminine of the rooms, and now that she thought about it, that should suit Mom's personality. Unless her tastes had changed. Could she even think in those terms?

Rese eased her into the chair by the window so she could look out over the olive tree to the garden. Then she stepped back, surprised when Star knelt beside her with an expectant look in her eyes. Did she hope Mom would still see the colors? Call her the fairy child; bring them back?

Rese didn't want Star disappointed, but she had kept praying as Lance told her, and under her breath she whispered, *Lord, protect her.* If Mom saw something now . . .

But though not one word had passed between them on the drive, and only nonsense since they'd come in, her mother raised her hand to Star's fragile curls and said, "You don't need the black one either."

Star gasped, almost choking, and gripped Mom's knee. Her breath quickened, then quieted. Her pinched brow smoothed, and staring into Elaine Barrett's eyes, she smiled. Rese had no idea what had just happened, but something had. She looked from one to the other, part of it herself without even knowing how.

Star stood up. "I'll brew some tea. Green tea with peppermint." She swept by with a glancing stroke to Rese's arm.

When Star had gone, Rese smoothed her mother's loose white hair, freshly clipped below the ears. It was almost the color of Star's pale tousle, and she imagined them all in a photograph. Mother, Rese, and little sister. Not how she'd thought it would look, but okay. More than okay.

"I hope you'll be happy here." She didn't expect an answer. Happy was not something her mother could gauge. Emotions passed through her without causative connection. But that was okay too. She stood beside her mother until Star came up with the tea, three mugs in one hand like a barmaid.

Rese took one and let Star serve Mom's. With a quirky smile, she held out her mug to Star's. "Here's to us Looney Tunes."

Star giggled and clinked mugs. "The excellent foppery."

Foppery maybe. Excellent for sure. She sipped, then checked her watch. "Brad's expecting me."

"Then off you go. We'll read sonnets and bless your horny hands of toil."

Rese laughed. "Good. I can use the blessing, working with Brad and the rest of them. They think it's a great joke that they've roped me back in." The strangest thing was glimpsing the affection behind it.

"Ah, the damsel's woes."

"Yeah. Damsel." Rese glanced at her mother, almost asked if they'd be all right, then stuffed it. "I'll be back by dark."

Chapter Thirty-four

Chaz carried the large flat package into the apartment. Rico sat on his drum throne, but he wasn't drumming. His stare jumped, and he'd obviously been deep in thought. "Something for you, mon." Chaz set the box on edge and balanced it. He didn't say where it was from or Rico might kick it to pieces or set it on fire before he saw what was inside.

For some time now, Rico and Lance had been like cats in a lightning storm, all raised fur and tight nerves. Something was brewing, something that troubled Chaz's spirit, but between his jobs and volunteering at church and a Bronx youth center, he hadn't figured out what.

"Want me to open it?"

Rico's brow puckered. "Okay."

His arm had healed better than anyone expected, but he was behind the drums and it was just as easy for Chaz to cut open the edge of the shipping box and bubble wrap, releasing the scent of oil paint. Holding the bottom edge of the box between his shoes, he reached in and slid the canvas out, studying the design and star-shaped signature before he turned it to Rico.

Mercurial reactions raced over his features as Rico took it in. He muttered something under his breath, but his gaze remained riveted. Then he stood and came around the drums. He took the canvas and studied it up close. "So this is what she does now."

"It's what she did before."

"I didn't remember." Rico frowned.

"She had something like it in the carriage house."

Rico narrowed his eyes. "A garden scene."

"Yes." With Lance worked into the foliage, but Chaz didn't remind him.

Rico shook his head. "She's crazy, man."

"Maybe we're all a little crazy."

Rico laughed. "Maybe we are." He started for their bedroom with the painting. It would either be hanging there when Chaz went to bed or meet some destructive end.

"Where's Lance?" Chaz called just before he passed through the doorway.

Rico answered without turning. "In the restaurant."

"Cooking?" A leap of hope in his chest.

"Doesn't mean he'll eat it." Rico disappeared into the bedroom.

Chaz smelled the savory broth all the way down the hall, but like Rico, he doubted Lance would eat much if any of it. It was odd for someone who'd considered food a mission to suddenly reject it. He had said nothing, hoping whatever Lance was struggling with would pass, but if anything, it had gotten more extreme since their conversation.

Lance turned at the stove. "Not working?"

"Tonight I will wait on tables at an extravagantly expensive restaurant, wielding my island charm to elicit big fat tips."

Lance smiled, but it was strained. He turned back to the pot, rubbed a small dry leaf to powder with his fingers, letting it drift into the mix, then stirred. As he set the spoon aside, his hand shook. How long had it been since he'd eaten anything to speak of? Something was devouring him, and the easy companionship between them as well.

Where once Lance had been painfully open, showing everything he thought and felt, it shocked Chaz now to see him hidden. What was it he thought the Lord had laid on him? Or was it also from God he hid?

"You want to talk about it?"

Lance pulled out of his thoughts as though he'd already forgotten he wasn't alone. His throat worked, but he shook his head. "There's nothing to say."

Knowing what was required of him, Lance had set the next step in motion. It would be harder, in a way, than what he'd first imagined, but there was no uncertainty. In that, he felt relieved.

He went first to Nonna's room and stopped beside her bed. Her eyes were closed. The broth he'd made sat half eaten on her bedside table. She wasn't doing much better than he, these days. Momma had threatened to spoon-feed him if he didn't quit with the not eating, but it was difficult to take much of anything in. Most of the time anything more than bread and broth seemed obscene.

Maybe that would change when this was done. He raised Nonna's hand, but of course she didn't respond. Her eyes were closed, and maybe she slept, maybe not. He pressed his lips to her papery skin and the web of veins that mapped the years of her life. "Even if you can't hear me, Nonna, I want you to know it's as much for you as for me that I'm doing this. It's for all of us."

Her eyelids flickered, but didn't open. He didn't need her acknowledgment. His own doubt had been cured by fire, and a brilliant glaze of trust replaced it. He knew what he had to do, and didn't waver a couple hours later as he emptied his pockets and was searched. He would not only do what was demanded, he would embrace it. The thought fortified him for the moment he sat face-to-face with a bullet-proof barrier between himself and Paolo Borsellino.

The man was shriveled, white-haired, and scarred, with the look of someone who'd learned life the hard way. "You're Michelli?"

Lance nodded. "Marco's grandson."

The man's throat worked. "He sent you here?"

"We both know that's impossible." Though in a way he had.

Paolo's eyes shifted away. "Whatchu want?"

Lance looked around the dismal room, the shabby chairs, the clouded glass dividing the free from the not free. "Do you hear from your family much, letters, maybe visits?" He named every one of the Borsellinos who had been mentioned in the report, then added wives and children he'd found and followed. Did the old man wonder which one he would hit?

As Lance looked into Paolo's face, his breath suddenly seized. Not going to be easy, not easy at all. He thought of Nonna slipping away, the knowledge of Marco's murder stealing her hope, her strength, her very life. All the years he'd lost with Nonno, hardly knowing the man he'd revered. And it hurt.

"You took something valuable from me, something that can't be replaced. The life of Marco Michelli, my nonno."

"You can't prove nothin'."

Battling through the sudden rage, he said, "I don't have to. I can return the vendetta."

"Yeah, well, Jojo's dead. You're too late. Nine years too late."

Lance took that in with hardly a blink. The answer to all his searching, and it meant nothing. "We're talking vendetta. Doesn't matter who did your dirty work. I have addresses, phone numbers, schedules. I can make it look like an accident." He'd thought of a hundred scenarios. Or he could just borrow theirs.

Paolo sat silent and staring, one eyelid twitching.

And now it came to it. *Lord.* "I could return the curse." He swallowed the bile rising in his throat and emptied himself, because if he didn't, he'd see the planes crashing into the towers and Tony inside, imagine Nonno's car skidding and burning, Nonno Vittorio's body ripped apart by bullets, Nonno Quillan's heart stopping in the tunnel. The evil pitted against his family, instead of the hand of Jesus calling him out onto the waves. "But I came here to forgive you."

Paolo jerked back in his chair as though punched. He shook his head with a half laugh that stilled as the smile fell from his mouth. Then he pressed his trembling lips together. "Some things . . . you regret."

Lance closed his eyes as both the truth of it and the pain overwhelmed him.

Paolo said, "I didn't show him the respect he gave me."

Nonno could never have respected the man. But he'd kept his part of their bargain. Lance opened his eyes, stayed silent.

"I dishonored him."

You murdered him.

"You still mean what you said?"

With a strength beyond his own, Lance nodded. "For my family and myself, I forgive you."

Paolo stretched a shaking hand to the glass, and Lance pressed his to it. Paolo fought the sobs, but they took hold anyway. "Pray for me to God. He don't hear me so good."

Sure, heap it on, Lord. "He hears you."

"Yeah?"

"How else would I be here?" As likely as not, it was this man's prayers that had brought it all to light. No matter what he'd done or who he'd been. They were all nothing before the Lord. And everything.

Paolo sat back, raggedly pulling himself together. He said nothing more, and neither did Lance as he stood to go. They shared one last glance, then he left the Ryker's Island Prison and went home, tears streaming, with an emptiness he could hardly bear.

How empty it was without the memories. Was she dead? Maybe that was hell, to remember no one. No face, no voice. No scene played out in her mind. All gone.

She had blocked her heart, shaken her fist at heaven, and all that was good and beautiful, all that had brought her joy had faded to black. She was more alone than she'd ever been.

Weary. So weary. Yet she must be alive to know the effort of every thought. Not hell, then, but a blackness of soul. A vale of tears. The valley of death.

Yea, though I walk through the valley of the shadow of death . . . How well she knew that shadow. How it haunted her, tested her.

I will fear no evil, for thou art with me. A long moment her mind contemplated that; then in her desolation she recognized what she had failed to see before, how she had been protected. God had never left her.

Thy rod and thy staff they comfort me.

582

Even in her distrust, He had kept her from wandering.

Thou preparest a table before me in the presence of mine enemies. Thou anointest my head with oil; my cup runneth over. She had not only survived but prospered.

Surely goodness and mercy shall follow me all the days of my life. Goodness and mercy. Mercy? Yes. Mercy, joy, and love. Gifts she hadn't earned, didn't deserve. There was nothing owed to her, nothing she had the right to claim except her place before the throne, worshiping the One she now missed with all her heart.

And I will dwell in the house of the Lord forever. Where was the dread? The anger? Where was the need? Through it all, He'd been sufficient.

Antonia heard someone come in, felt him stop beside the bed and stand there. She opened her eyes and looked into his face. How had he gotten so gaunt, so haggard? "L . . . ance?"

He wasn't sure which of them was more surprised. He'd given up hoping for a response, and here she was talking. With his luck he'd put her right back over the edge, but he took hold of her hand and sat down beside her. "It's done, Nonna."

She searched his face, not comprehending until he told her word by word

583

what he'd gone through while she fought her way back to them. He could almost read her thoughts: *You forgave him, the man who ordered Nonno's death?* He expected anger, but it seemed all burned out of her. Into her eyes came acquiescence and even acceptance.

"Yes. All right." She motioned him to come close, kissed his cheeks and cradled his head. They stayed that way a long time; then she raised his face.

He tried not to show what it had cost him, but when could he ever hide from her?

"Lance," she whispered. "I w . . . ant to s . . . ee your inn."

The blood left his head. She must not understand. "It's not mine." His brow pinched with what he'd lost.

She did not relent. "I w . . . ant . . ."

"Nonna . . ." He groaned. "I can't. It's not fair to Rese. And you're not strong enough to go anywhere." They'd both been through fire. But then, fire could temper steel, and he saw the look he knew too well.

"I'll get strong." She squeezed his hand. "Take m . . . e home."

He drew a shaky breath. And he'd thought the worst was over.

Chapter Thirty-five

Rese stuffed the diagrams and a case of new chisels under her arm and climbed out of the truck. She laughed when Baxter bounded over and planted his paws on her belly, panting his warm dog breath right into her face. He'd only recently started jumping up like that, and she really should make him quit, but it was so like a hug that she loved up his head instead. "Hello, boy. Miss me?" She bent to nuzzle his face, and he stroked her chin with his velvety tongue.

The evening light slanted through the bare lacy trees, the raised beds of the garden still dimly fragrant with pale green and dry russet sprigs. The vines around the carriage house had borne grapes, but they'd been tough-skinned and too tart for eating — a wine variety, she'd guessed, so hadn't picked them. Neither she nor Star had any interest in making wine or jam or whatever else.

Easing Baxter down, she locked the truck door, then froze when a taxi turned into the driveway. Panic rushed her. Had she forgotten to cancel a reservation? Had she taken any after the new year? Who visited wine country in January? But her panic morphed to fury when the car stopped in front of the villa and she saw who it was that climbed out.

Of course there'd been no call; she would have saved him the trip. Well, she'd save him the trouble of unloading now . . . except he went around and opened the door for Nonna Antonia. Rese sagged when the old woman pulled herself up to cling to her walker. While she might have ordered Lance back into the cab, she could hardly do that to his dying grandmother.

Shielded by the truck, she was out of Lance's direct view, but Baxter heard, sensed, or smelled his master. As Lance paid the driver who had taken their bags from the trunk, Baxter bounded over. Lance turned at the dog's joyful yips, knelt and took the animal into his arms.

Pure rage, not ennobled by understanding what he must feel, choked her.

After a long time communing with his dog, Lance stood up. He pulled the wool coat around Antonia's thin shoulders, left the luggage in the driveway, and assisted her slow progress toward the door. Baxter led them on, the traitor, as though she hadn't been the one rubbing his head and soothing his forlorn sighs these last months.

Antonia's condition had obviously improved, but with both his leather jacket and his jeans hanging loose, Lance looked as though he'd been eaten out from the inside, and maybe that was what kept her from heaving the chisels at his head. But she stalked over, leaving him no question how she felt about his surprise appearance.

A poignant expression had taken over Antonia's features as she stared up at the house, but Lance turned with a look she couldn't begin to contemplate. "What are you doing here?" Because she would relinquish the Harley and good riddance, but Baxter was leaving over her cold, dead body.

"I should have called."

She was beyond response.

The slight, chill wind lifted the front of his hair as he raised a hand toward the house. "Nonna wanted to see the place, to . . ." He swayed. "Can she just . . ." His legs buckled, and he went down.

Baxter darted back, nudged and licked his head, but Lance didn't move. Rese stared at him lying face down in the white gravel driveway, his hand outstretched, as though he'd crawled through a desert to get there. Torn between concern and fury, she looked from him to Antonia.

"What's wrong with him?"

Antonia pulled her eyes from the house,

seeming only then to realize he'd collapsed.

Rese crouched and gripped his shoulder. "Lance?" Nothing. "Is he sick? He looks wasted."

"N . . . ot sick." Antonia shook her head. "Used up by God."

What? Rese glared, then rubbed a hand over her face, feeling used up herself. Life didn't have to be as complicated as Lance made it. She shook him again, but he didn't respond even when another puff of wind lifted the hair from the back of his neck.

Since she could hardly leave him lying in the driveway, she put down her load, reached under his arms and rolled him to his back. No return to consciousness. She considered slapping him, but as on that day at the shore, she couldn't quite do it. Clenching her teeth, she hoisted him up against her thighs and dragged him to the porch, amazed at how light he seemed. Maybe he *had* been used up.

"O mischief!" Star hurried down and caught his ankles, but Rese noted the glance that darted to Antonia and past her to the empty driveway, looking . . . for Rico? Rese huffed. One delinquent appearing was quite enough.

With Star's help, Rese got Lance through the door and into her own bed, which was the only one that didn't require hauling him upstairs. He didn't move, not even to blink his eyes, but he breathed, so she left him there and went back out for Antonia.

The old woman's eyes had grown misty, and Rese wanted to gather her in and re-assure her that whatever insanity Lance was perpetrating on her, she would make it right. What was he thinking dragging her all the way out here? But then, it was Lance. He didn't think.

She scooped her things up from the driveway and helped Nonna climb the steps of the porch while Star came behind with her walker. Lance had been light, but Antonia was almost weightless. At the top, Antonia searched the porch as though missing something, maybe a swing or piece of furniture that must have held memories. Rese had sensed a lot of history in this old place when she bought it. She had never guessed she would get to know so much of it, or the people who had lived it.

Star placed the walker in front, and Rese helped her get hold of it; then Antonia focused her gaze through the open door, and her arms shook.

Please, please don't have a stroke.

Rese could hardly imagine how this must be for her, forced out as a girl and not seeing her home once in all these years. Not to mention the grief and violence that happened to her family inside these walls.

Though Rese had mistaken old wine corks popping in the cellar for ghostly gunshots, Antonia might very well remember the real thing.

But then, if she expected things to be as she recalled, Antonia had another blow coming. To soften it, Rese said, "It might not look the same. It was badly damaged, and I took some liberties." A few walls removed, new floors, new shelves, new moldings, paint, and carpets, but always with a tenacious replication of the original style and materials.

Antonia nodded as she stepped inside, tears streaking the soft powder on her cheeks. Rese's anger drained at the sight. Certainly she could not blame Antonia. Even if, as Lance said, she had wanted to see the place. Wanting and doing . . . well, Lance did have a problem saying no to her.

Antonia raised her face. "Lance?" Her main concern, even in these first moments home. He sure knew how to steal the scene.

"This way." She led her down the hall into the kitchen, where the old woman paused once again, gulping. Anger rose at the poor woman's predicament — Lance dragging her there, then passing out and leaving her to face the shock of it alone. Not alone, Rese vowed. She'd do whatever it took to ease Antonia's stress. "He's in here."

Antonia looked through the door. "N . . . onno's room." Her mouth trembled.

With Star hovering, Rese ushered Antonia through the narrow passage and into the room, which, judging by the look on her face, was also steeped in memories.

Lance lay as they'd put him, his eyes sunken, his breathing shallow. A surge of concern tugged her. "Does he need a doctor?"

Antonia shuffled to the edge of the bed, her hand on the walker reminiscent of Evvy's, though without the crabapple knuckles. She looked down at Lance, her face flushed.

Rese swallowed hard. She did not need this. She had found her equilibrium.

Antonia shook her head. "Let him rest. M . . . aybe now he'll eat."

Eat? But unbelievable as it was, he didn't appear to have eaten in ages. Lance — for whom sharing a meal had eternal significance. "Does he have something awful?"

"Yes." Nonna nodded. "The w . . . orst I've seen."

Fear tore through her. If Lance had come there to die, she'd never forgive him.

Antonia swayed, the edges blurring again.

Rushing into Nonno's room, I shake him awake. "Come, Nonno. Hurry. There's trouble. We have to hide."

Arthur Jackson's face, match-lit in the driveway; another man hidden by shadows — Carlo Borsellino. Stealthy footsteps, gunshots! Fear fills my lungs. The tunnel. We must hide in the cellar. Hurry, Nonno! But . . .

Was the tunnel still there? Yes, Lance had found Nonno, buried him. Time overlapped, and she struggled to keep it straight. Did they have to hide? Where was Papa?

A hand touched her shoulder. "Let me pull the chair up for you."

Rese. Lance's Rese. And it was Lance in the bed, not Nonno. The fear was past, but she sank into the chair, overwhelmed. How had she come here after all these years? And then she looked at Lance, lying where Nonno had lain. Ah. It wasn't over. Not yet.

It would help if Star stopped laughing. Having settled Antonia into the wing chair in Lance's room — formerly her own, but seemingly not to be for a while since neither Lance nor Antonia could manage the stairs — she stalked out to the yard before doing something she'd regret. She had worked hard on the walls and didn't plan on repairing punch holes.

"I'll need to rig up a cot in the office for

Antonia until Lance can get out of my bed," she told Star, then stopped halfway down the flagstone path. "Or maybe I should put them both in the carriage house."

"She's awfully old, Rese."

"He's not."

Star caught up. "He doesn't look up to helping her if she falls or something."

"It's an excuse for showing up without a word."

"And what, pray, could he have said?" Amusement danced in her eyes.

"This isn't funny, Star! I wish I could —"

"Did you see Antonia's face?"

Rese sighed. "Yes."

"Such rapturous sorrow."

"I know. It must be awful and wonderful." Her chest squeezed. Maybe it really had been Antonia who needed to come. Maybe that was what Lance had tried to say: *Don't think this was my idea; I only came for Nonna's sake.*

"Call Michelle and see if she has a cot, and tell her it needs good cushioning." All those bedrooms with their top-quality beds were inaccessible for a ninety-something stroke victim. She should have put in an elevator. Maybe she'd build the shaft tonight. It was a sure bet she wouldn't sleep.

"I'm going to tell Mom they're here so she doesn't think she's seeing things." Rese went upstairs where Mom was watching the only TV in the house. It had been in her own room, but she gave it up. Maybe she should have seen that as prophetic.

"Mom, we have visitors."

Her mother nodded. But that could have been an involuntary motion.

Just in case, she added, "It's a man and his grandmother."

Mom didn't turn from the nature show on the TV, just started nodding again, her fingers flicking away. "All they have is water. Water's all they have."

"Okay, then. You doing okay?"

Nodding and flicking. "Fine. Fine. I'm fine."

Rese went out, stood against the wall, and dropped her head back against it hard enough to hear the *thunk*. What was happening? Having Lance in the house was some nightmare deja vu. She hadn't wanted him there the first time, but he'd talked his way around all her objections. Now he didn't even bother to talk; just fell at her feet.

No one else could have pulled that off. And she didn't believe there was nothing wrong either. He looked worse than Star had when she brought her home. Or Mom for that matter. How many ailing souls was she expected to care for?

The whole thing had her so worked up

that when Michelle came with the cot and an extra foam topper, she hugged her.

Michelle raised her eyebrows. "So what's up?"

Rese glared. "Unexpected guests. Lance and his grandmother."

"Oh." Michelle's face brightened. "Where is he? I've got some Baxter stories."

She thought about asking Michelle to hide the dog, but didn't. "Sorry. He passed out in the driveway and isn't awake yet."

Michelle squashed the foam pad under her chin. "Passed out?"

Rese pulled the cot out of Michelle's car. "Antonia said he's used up by God. Whatever that means."

"Well, howdy. That's why I've had such a burden for that man."

Rese stared. "You have?" With all the people Michelle cared for daily, she'd been worried about a man three thousand miles away whom she hardly knew?

"It just seemed he was under fire."

Rese vividly recalled too many nights, waking up gasping, aching for him in a way that was deeper than her own loss. Feelings that now intensified her anger.

Michelle looked toward the house. "Can I see him?"

Rese frowned, feeling incongruously protective. "I guess. But he's pretty wiped out."

She carried the cot into the office portion of her suite, where Antonia would sleep. Star took the foam pad from Michelle, and then they went into the bedroom, where Antonia was already sitting. Lance had not moved a hair. She had never seen him sleep but doubted this dead faint was normal, even for Lance. Her heart clutched up inside her. With four women gaping at him, shouldn't he show some sign of life?

Michelle put a hand on his head, silent for a few moments, then nodded and released him. She bent and patted Baxter's head, but the dog wasn't budging from beside the bed. Rese found a sliver of consolation in that he hadn't climbed in. A matter of training, not preference, she knew. Even unconscious, Lance had better control of him than she did. So why had he deserted the animal, and her, and their plans, and . . .

She crouched beside his grandma, breathing a scent like winter roses. "Antonia, what's really wrong with him? He told me there was something he had to do, but he looks . . ." How did he look? Not sick, really, but gaunt and certainly exhausted. A pang shot through. Lance kept intruding on her life with no warning and no explanation. And anger and hurt made her vulnerable. She had to keep a clear head.

Antonia seemed to pull herself back from somewhere, cognizance dawning in her eyes. "It s . . . tarted here. In this r . . . oom." She spoke slowly, but much more clearly than when Rese had last seen her, sometimes searching for words, but doggedly continuing. A lot of the story Rese knew, but not what had happened after she and Star left New York.

Antonia barely held her emotions in as she told them Marco had been murdered, but when she said Lance believed God had called him to settle the vendetta, Rese almost lost it. How could he think that? But she'd seen the anger simmering, the unresolved grief and his need to prove himself.

Was it really surprising he would retaliate? Her throat closed. And now? Was that why he hadn't told her he was coming, why he'd said everything would be different? She rasped, "Did he settle it?"

Antonia nodded. Rese looked from Star to Michelle, whose faces reflected her concern. Even if he might believe she would shelter him, he couldn't expect them to.

Antonia drew a breath, and her mouth worked hard to find the words. "H . . . e prayed and f . . . asted. And when he knew God's h . . . eart, he forgave Paolo Borsellino."

Star made the connection first. "He settled the vendetta with forgiveness?"

Antonia nodded again. "He w . . . ent to the prison and f . . . orgave Paolo."

Comprehension rushed in. Relief and fury. Rese turned and stared at him. Lance had done the right thing, even a great thing. He'd found God's will — that big all-encompassing purpose — and had discarded her to accomplish it.

Waking with a jolt, Antonia sat up in the cot and searched her surroundings in the eerie half glow of a nightlight in the bathroom. Strange furniture filled Nonno's study, his writing desk gone and a computer in its place. Her cot had been tucked between that and a hodgepodge of things stored against the wall. She studied the shadowy stacks until a glint caught her eye near the corner. Something . . . familiar.

Drawn almost in spite of herself, she sat up and slid her feet into her shoes, then braced herself up and stood a moment to find balance. Her walker was folded against the wall, and her eyeglasses were near, she supposed. But she took three sliding steps toward the corner, reaching through the clutter, her fingers pulled toward the object.

Though her vision was foggy, the light only a dim glow, as soon as her fingers touched, she knew it. With fierce concentration, she slid it out and fondled the silver head Nonno's hand had held as he found support from the walnut shaft for his own leg crippled in his prime.

Ah, Nonno. She knew all about limbs that no longer held their own. But using the cane with her stronger arm, she crept past Lance, sleeping in the bed not unlike Nonno's, into the kitchen that hadn't changed so much. Memories rushed in: Papa at the table, Nonna Carina teasing Nonno with a spoonful of sauce. Friends and relatives. Even Momma was there, planting a kiss on Papa's lips, leaving a lipstick stain and laughing as she tried to smudge it off, Papa taking hold of her long strings of pearls and drawing her back for more.

She couldn't remember anyone being unhappy in the kitchen. Except once.

Heart squeezing, she stared a long minute at the pantry door. *Oh, Nonno.* She swallowed painfully. *Papa.* Slowly she passed the door and went outside in the dark. The velvet sky was studded with stars, the air a cold hand that gripped. Everything seemed too close. A shed that didn't belong. The house next door. Hedges and fences. No fields lush with vines. What few vines were left had not been harvested. That especially hurt.

The motion light from the back door

guided her to them. These vines were over a hundred years old. The grapes they had borne would have yielded a rare vintage. Heart pounding, she touched the gnarled wood, crisp leaves and tendrils, the shriveled fruit. These vines against the garage had worked hard to survive — as she had.

She gripped Nonno's cane, reliving the effort it had taken to get on her feet again. Lance had resisted, afraid the trip would be too much for her . . . and simply afraid. It was hard to want something so much. She knew, and yet . . . life was in the wanting, and in cherishing what you had.

She turned around and studied the old house she had left with such regret. Change was inevitable. Back in Belmont she had children and grandchildren and great-grandchildren, her friends and neighbors, her church. She knew every crack in the walls, every sound that came through her window. Here, where she had once known the breeze in the vines, the stones in the floor, the pace and pulse of each day, here it was all different.

She stared up at the window from which she'd heard the night sounds that had alerted her to danger. She might have died that night, but she hadn't. She had lived and raised her family and run her restaurant and grown old. And now here she was, ancient and crippled, her days numbered by God.

Ay . . . maybe it was time to learn something new.

Dragging down the stairs in jeans and turtleneck with a flannel shirt thrown over, Rese tried for serene, but it wasn't in her repertoire. Star had gotten Mom up, and Rese could hear them in the kitchen.

"Sausage biscuits, Mom?" Like Star didn't know the answer to that.

In her strange monotone, Mom said, "Sausage biscuits for the queen."

Rese joined them as Star took the plastic-wrapped sausage-stuffed biscuits from the freezer to stick in the microwave. Having discovered the gap in Lance's kitchen setup, Star had purchased the microwave to cook most of what they ate.

Rese glanced toward the door to her suite. "Any sign of them?"

Star beeped the cooking time on the touch pad. "I heard voices."

"Not you too."

Star turned with a giggle. " 'O, what a noble mind is here o'erthrown.' "

Rese turned as the door opened behind her and Antonia came out, braced by her walker.

Star plunked a plate down for Mom, then sucked her finger. " 'Tis an ill cook

601

that cannot lick her own fingers."

"An ill cook in . . . deed." Antonia smiled.

"Breakfast for the queen," Mom said, secure in her role.

"He's awake." Antonia patted Rese's arm in passing, guessing she wanted a word with the man in her bed.

She went through the door into the hall she had once forbidden to Lance. Funny how things changed. She tapped, then opened the bedroom door. He was up on one elbow, so he'd lived through the night. He looked a little better, though rumpled and contrite.

He said, "I didn't mean to take your bed," but his eyes were saying so much more.

She refused to acknowledge his regrets. "I wasn't about to drag you up the stairs."

Lance pulled up in the bed to sit, his torso hollow beneath his T-shirt. She hated the worry that took hold. Who did he think he was, jerking her emotions around?

She crossed her arms. "Exactly what do you expect to happen here?"

His throat worked. "I don't expect anything."

Right. Like he even knew what that meant. She went fully into the room. "You just show up with no explanation, not even a call. I would have told you the place is

602

not open to the public anymore."

He took "public" like a punch.

She softened her tone, but the next part of her message would hit even harder. "I'm not running an inn. I'm in business with Brad. I used the silver certificates to fund our partnership." Why did it not feel good to tear away his illusions?

He nodded mutely, no condemnation, even though technically that money could have been considered his.

She expelled a breath. "I can see this matters to Antonia, and there's obviously room." Although it was hers. "We have our routine, but . . ." She planted her hands on her hips. "You can stay. For a while, anyway."

He looked out from eyes only slightly less hollow than his voice. "There's nothing for me to do."

She scowled. "You're in no condition to do anything. Starving yourself might be very religious, but it's obviously not very healthy."

His brow pinched. What good did it do to berate him? His faith had always been radical. He'd just taken it to the next level. So what if he looked like John the Baptist with an earring? She suddenly wanted to cry.

"Star's warming sausage biscuits. Do you —" She turned as someone brushed against her arm. "Oh. Mom, this is Lance." She'd forgotten to mention that part.

His astonishment slid from her to her mother. He brought his legs over and stood, a little unsteadily. Then he took Mom's hand between his own. "It's great to meet you, Elaine. I've waited a long time."

The sincerity in his face actually hurt. Rese turned away. "Come on, Mom. Let Lance get ready for breakfast."

Chapter Thirty-six

A great impression he was making. Fainting on the doorstep; usurping her room. Not that it mattered. He'd had his chance and lost it. They could stay — awhile — but then they'd have to leave. He released his breath. Why had Nonna asked this?

As he headed for Rese's bathroom, he noticed a cot made up in the office. It must have been Nonna's bed last night. He sighed. He'd expected it to be rocky, but hadn't planned on complete humiliation. Fainting at Rese's feet? *Come on, Lord.*

He closed the bathroom door and leaned against it, light-headed. Frozen sausage biscuits. He got into the shower, hoping he didn't pass out in there. He wasn't as ripe as he might've been, but he had slept in his clothes.

The shower felt good to his joints, and the exhaustion was not as deep in his muscles. What hurt most was seeing Rese trying to be so tough again. He toweled off, brushed his teeth, and finger-combed his hair. Then he got into his jeans and sweatshirt that had been stacked on top of the dresser. Maybe Nonna had unpacked them there.

He slipped his bare feet into his Top-Siders and went out. The aroma of frozen sausage biscuits all but gagged him. He prayed he could manage it. Just one. And not look like a fool. *You owe me that much.* Though he knew it wasn't true.

Nonna was at the table with Star and Rese's mother, and he joined them in the only remaining chair. Star slid a plate toward him. Rese wasn't there.

"She's gone to work," Star offered.

Ah. With Brad. Her partner. He lifted the biscuit, eyed the brownish grease leaching into the stiff, floury encasement. He brought it to his mouth, gathered himself, and bit. If he didn't want to be a burden. . . . He chewed, swallowed, and kept it down.

As soon as he finished, Star asked, "Want another? There's one left in the package."

One too many already. "Do you have any fruit?"

"Peach?"

"Sure."

Star fetched a peach from a bowl and set it before him. He struggled with the thought of picking it up whole and biting in, the whole-mouth experience of savaging

606

even a piece of fruit. Star slid a paring knife onto his plate. He didn't know if she'd seen his struggle, and didn't want to know. He cut a thin slice and tore it from the pit, releasing the aroma. He gave it a moment to register, without attempting to eat, giving himself time. Pathetic, but necessary, like reintroducing foods to an invalid. *God.*

"Rese doesn't know how to take you being here," Star said.

He nodded. That was apparent and predictable. He'd done it to her again, maybe on purpose. He could have called and asked to bring Nonna, but he hadn't because if he did things right and it didn't work, what excuse was there? He could be empty and broken before God, but with Rese? He was all Italian-American male. Except for the fainting part. That was pure Lance Michelli.

"She's gone," her mother said. "Gone, gone."

The words sank into the hollow of his stomach. He had said he was willing to fail with her, but he hadn't believed he would, and even now his pride kept him from admitting it. But he was flint to her steel, setting her off just being there. He'd expected the thrashing this morning when she barreled into the room. But she wasn't quite as hard as she used to be. He raised the strip of peach and bit. The tangy juices filled his mouth. Intense, but easier than the sausage overload.

"Gone, gone," Elaine said. "The green is with the green. The blue is with the blue. But the brown . . ." She looked up. "Do you know?"

He smiled at the woman who looked so much like Rese. "I wish I did." Then he turned to Star. "I don't want to keep Rese from her bed. Is anyone using the carriage house?"

"No, but . . ." She looked at Nonna.

He turned. "Do you mind if we stay out there, Nonna, so Rese can have her room?"

She shrugged. "Fine. Bene." Her color was good this morning; her countenance peaceful. He had meant to watch her carefully, to be sure the strain of seeing the place wasn't too much. But he'd passed out instead.

Star cut a slice from his peach and ate it.

He left the rest for her and went to the window. "Nonna can have the bedroom out there. I'll move the cot into the other room."

Star shrugged. "If you want to."

He had to. He couldn't take another night in Rese's room, and if he stayed out of her way, maybe it wouldn't be so hard for her either. He suspected Nonna intended more than her own healing here, but she didn't know how utterly autonomous Rese could be.

Rese climbed the ladder to the roof of the project they had bid on and won over their main competition. It still gave her a shock to think of Barrett Renovation as something outside herself, and it was a good lesson in not making decisions during a state of crisis. No Barrett was represented by that outfit anymore, though Dad's reputation carried them.

She would have no problem with that if they even tried to live up to his standards, but the things Brad had told her, and what she'd seen herself in the two public buildings they'd renovated, justified her offering the real thing — Plocken and Barrett. Brad may as well be a Barrett for all he'd learned from Dad and his adherence to it. She respected him more than she'd realized. And vice versa.

But when he looked up from his knees on the roof, she wished he hadn't known her so long, because his "What's up?" held more than she wanted to go into. Maybe it was the strap around his hips or the pitch of the tile roof, but she had flashed back to the time Lance climbed up to save her from the turkey buzzards. And now she didn't remember the question that had brought her up there.

"Rese?"

"What?"

"I'm guessing you came up here for something." He was in a zone of his own, and she'd interrupted him.

"Umm . . ."

"Are you okay?"

"Of course." She stood on the ridgepole and thought of Lance screwing up the courage to let go of the chimney. She had been downright insulting. What had he ever seen in her? But he'd had his own agenda, and then she gasped. The villa.

He and Antonia out there together. Had he decided to fight her for it? Take back what Antonia had lost? He didn't look up to a fight, but he'd fooled her before. Maybe it was all an act to make her let him in. She couldn't claim possession if they were all on the premises, both parties having a deed. But that didn't feel right. Not that she knew what to feel.

Brad caught her elbow. "Hello?"

"I'm . . ." She shivered.

"Admiring the view?"

"No, I . . . I'm . . ."

"In my way?"

"Oh. Sorry."

Brad seemed oblivious to the chill kicking up as he tapped a cigarette from

610

the pack in his jacket pocket. "What's on your mind?"

"Nothing."

"Second thoughts?"

"No. It's nothing to do with you or the business. I should get back to work."

He still held her elbow, and even that made her think of Lance.

"Brad, why did your marriage break up?"

He pulled his brows together. "Besides her being unreasonable and pesky?"

Rese winced. He could be describing her.

He shrugged. "Not a good match, I guess. We drove each other nuts."

"And you haven't found a better one?"

He put the cigarette to his lips and flicked his lighter. "Haven't looked."

"Why not?"

"Because . . . it wouldn't compare."

She stared at him. "You're still in love with her."

He pulled a drag, long and slow. "Sometimes it's like that."

"Is she married?"

"She was for a while. Number two was even shorter. Got me out of alimony, though." He stared at the cigarette in his hand. "Not that it stops her asking whenever she runs short."

Rese studied his face. "Do you give it to her?"

He slid his gaze her way. "I've got enough. Just didn't like a court telling me I had to."

Rese planted her hands on her hips. "How did I not know this?"

"You weren't exactly approachable." He exhaled smoke through his nose. "Vernon thought you might grow out of it, but . . ."

"Grow out of what?"

"Your need to control, take on the world, whatever."

Her jaw dropped. "He said that?"

Brad raised a hand. "Don't get worked up."

Worked up. Dad had thought her a control freak, and Brad said don't get worked up? "What else did he think of me?"

"Best natural craftsman — craftsperson — he'd ever seen."

That part she'd known, though not in those terms.

"He was awfully proud of you, Rese. We all were."

Her throat grew tight. "Right."

"Oh, there were a few who couldn't stand you." He took a drag. "But you were like our mascot. On the one hand you're embarrassed to admit it's cute, and on the other you'd do anything to protect it."

She narrowed her eyes. "Protect? What about all those pranks?"

"All you had to do was show that it

612

bothered you. But you were one tough cookie. Best challenge the guys had going." He laughed.

She clenched her jaw. "You'd think grown men might be over picking on little girls."

"When you had it out for them? Making them look bad to Vernon Barrett, the most exacting taskmaster on the planet?"

"I didn't . . ." But she supposed she had exposed every flaw she found. Could she help it if she had a good eye?

He sobered. "I'd have fired Sam and Charlie, though."

Fire rushed to her face. He'd known?

"Problem was you kept it from your dad. Wasn't my business to tell if you'd handled it otherwise. But I did make sure Vernon took them on his crew when you got the other."

She gaped. He had looked out for her when she scored the position he wanted?

"Vernon could be pretty blind."

Tears stung. No way would she let them fall.

"No clue I'd taken a shine to you right about the time you turned eighteen." He flicked the ash from the end.

She chewed her lip. "Why?"

"Got a weakness for difficult women, I guess."

She glared.

"My wife had just remarried and . . . ." He stubbed his cigarette butt on the tile, then sent it tumbling down into the gutter. "Oh, I don't know."

Rese shook her head. "It's like we all lived in different worlds. No one communicating anything that mattered."

He nodded. "So are you going to tell me what this is all about?"

She almost choked. She'd set herself up completely. "It's not — Lance came back."

"The guy with the shovel?"

Lance had been working in the yard, maybe with a shovel, the time Brad came. She nodded. "I'm not sure what to do with it."

"What do you want?"

"I don't know." She squirmed under his scrutiny.

"Well, that's what you need to figure out."

She huffed. "That from the man who loves his ex-wife and won't do anything about it?"

"Too much water under my bridge."

"Chicken."

His mouth pulled sideways. "I don't need advice from a squirt."

She crossed her arms. "Even when I'm right?"

"Are you ever wrong?"

She swallowed. "Maybe. Sometimes."

"Wish I'd had that on record a few times."

She jutted her chin. "You were obstinately inflexible."

"I suppose you're silly putty?"

She held up her hands. "Okay. Truce. I'm going down. You've wasted enough time already."

He chuckled. "Right."

As she reached the ladder she thought of her question and hollered it up to him. He called the answer back, and she swung onto the ladder, recalling the ragged aluminum that had gouged her side when she'd tried to show Lance her mettle. She rolled her eyes. She wasn't half as tough as she'd pretended.

The crew left at five-thirty. Brad approached her an hour or so later. "Let's call it a day."

But she'd found peace with the wood, if no answers, and couldn't stop yet.

"I don't like you on the site alone." He didn't say it, but she knew he was thinking accidents happened.

If she let her mind go with that, she'd have a panic attack, but she would not let her mind go. "I'll be careful." She slipped her safety goggles back into place. "You don't have to protect me." Their mascot. It rankled, and yet . . .

He shrugged, knowing argument was futile. "See you in the morning."

She nodded, already lining up the next board.

A long time later, she drove the hour and a half home. The house was silent, and she crept in, careful not to walk into anything in the dark. She would just check on them, then go to sleep. She made her way through the kitchen, surprised that the door to her suite was open. But then she found both rooms empty. The shock of it was as painful as his arrival. She pressed a fist to her throat. He was the cruelest, most thoughtless man she'd ever known.

Just because she'd said things weren't the same didn't mean — Why had she stayed so late on the site? To prove she didn't care? She released her fists. Okay, so he was gone. He had probably called a cab to take his grandmother to the airport, then driven his Harley with no helmet all the way across the country with his dog. His dog!

The house seemed painfully empty. No Baxter tapping across the kitchen floor; no Baxter bumping her legs; no Baxter curling up on her bed. She dropped to it, despondent. No Baxter; no Lance. She had driven him off, laying it out that way; her partnership with Brad, the end of the inn.

"There's nothing for me to do." His face had shown it all.

616

When doing was how Lance mattered. She'd shown him that he didn't. Had he waited, hoping she'd get home so he could say good-bye? She hadn't even given him that.

She dropped her face to her hands. Hadn't he thought Antonia might want more time? She closed her eyes. Maybe he just couldn't take any more. Neither could she. Brad had said to figure out what she wanted. Now it didn't matter.

She curled into the bed without even changing and realized the sheets had been laundered. There was no scent of Lance, only Summer Breeze. He or Star had washed away all trace of him. And now she cried, soaking the pillow with tears and silent sobs.

Chapter Thirty-seven

Lance left Nonna sleeping in the carriage house and went with Baxter into the stone kitchen in the old villa where he'd once planned to be a part of something special. Those plans had changed without him, but he was still compelled to do something. Though it might disrupt their routine, he hoped they wouldn't mind too much if he cooked. Eating had become difficult, but preparing food for others always seemed right and good.

The pantry was still stocked with most of the imperishables he'd ordered. He took out flour and baking powder and checked the refrigerator for eggs — enough for the popover batter. He'd caramelize peaches for a filling. Whipping cream would have been nice.

He could go get some, but the Harley was loud. He had driven it yesterday, surprised it started, until Star told him she'd fired it up a few times to keep it lubed. Rese either hadn't thought of it or had hoped the thing would die a slow and painful death. Once he'd heard its purr, he'd strapped the guitar to his back, whistled Baxter aboard, and taken off. But no matter how many miles they'd covered, how many hours they'd sat on the cold knoll while he composed a new ballad for this stage in his life, his heart had called him back.

He passed a hand over his eyes, knowing he could lose. Nonna had told Rese everything, and it didn't make any difference. She'd had enough of his kind of trouble. But he was just reckless enough to keep trying.

When he heard the shower in her suite, he cooked and filled her pastry and set it out on the table. Then with Baxter glued to his side, he walked through the brisk, misty morning to see if Nonna was awake. She came out of the bedroom as he entered, one button skipped on her cardigan, but otherwise dressed and groomed.

The long silver braid hung down her back. Momma would have coiled it up, but he didn't think it mattered. "Good morning, Nonna." He kissed her cheeks.

She looked him straight in the eye. "Take m . . . e down."

"Down?"

She walked over to the trapdoor leading into the tunnel and cellar below. Was she serious? They had stopped at Nonno's grave on the way in, the meter running in the taxi while he showed her where he'd laid Quillan Shepard to rest, where others had buried her father. She had thanked him with glistening eyes but had not broken down, and he'd sensed her relief and the peace of completion.

Underneath them now was where Nonno Quillan had fallen, where she'd last seen him alive the night she'd been forced from her home. Why would she want to relive that? But her expression brooked no argument. He said, "We'd need a light."

"In th . . . ere." She motioned toward the bedroom.

He sighed and got the flashlight he'd swiped from Rese's workshop all those months ago and kept in the carriage house to light the tunnel without her knowing. Nonna didn't miss a trick. He brought it out and handed it to her. "You sure?"

She nodded.

Crouching down, he squeezed the release, then lifted the four-square block of paving stones and looked in. That black hole had caused them both a lot of trouble, but if Nonna wanted to go down, he'd take her down. She would never manage the stairs, almost as steep as a ladder, and he was not exactly at the top of his strength, but he'd try. Good thing she was little.

With extreme care, he carried her to the bottom and set her on her feet.

She turned and looked up. "I w . . . as carried on those stairs the l . . . ast time."

"Nonno Marco?"

She nodded. "When I w . . . ouldn't leave, he h . . . oisted me up and hauled me off."

"Best way to deal with obstinate women."

She chuckled.

Baxter whined from the opening. While his great-great-grandfather had lain in the tunnel he hadn't allowed the dog down, not wanting the bones disturbed. Now he gave a soft whistle and Baxter clambered down. Lance went back up for Nonna's walker, then made sure her grip was secure.

She stared into the tunnel, levity fading when he pointed the light; then slowly she started forward. They reached the gate and went through. She stopped at the spot where he'd found Quillan's skeleton. The lamp still sat against the wall, dry and useless, having burned its fuel and died. She bowed her head, and he couldn't see her expression, but imagined it.

"You okay?"

"So . . . senseless," she murmured. "Poor N . . . onno."

"He had you with him at the end."

She sighed. "Papa had no one."

"He had the Lord. He died to keep you safe."

She nodded. "They kn . . . ew he would come."

"He had to." Because when it came down to it, a person had to do what was required. No matter the cost.

The wine was still there, though Rese had used the money hidden under one of the racks. He didn't care. He'd learned surrender. And it might not be over yet.

Rese stopped at the table, flummoxed. The rich, peachy aroma of the filling inside the crisp, buttery shell seized her like a fist. How could it be there unless . . .

She jerked her gaze to the window. No sign of life in the carriage house. Had he carried Antonia upstairs? She hurried up and looked, but the only rooms in use were Star's and Mom's, and they were both sleeping soundly. So Star hadn't cooked it, even if she might have used Lance's recipe — only he hadn't given them that one.

She went back down to the kitchen. Did she imagine it? Was this the first psychotic break? In her misery, she could have crossed some line, passed through a barrier and made her own reality where Lance still cooked wonderful things and left them like gifts for her to find. Would she actually taste it? Would that cement the illusion?

She looked at the pastry with distrust, as though its being there was a test. If she resisted, would it vanish? Could she make Lance go away before he got entrenched like Walter? What if Mom had not kept inviting her invisible friend? What if she'd listened to her control-freak daughter and refused to play? Maybe they could all have lived happily together.

Rese backed away from the table, one step, two. "I will not eat it. I will not believe it's there." Another step, and the pantry door opened behind her. She turned with a shriek, but it was Antonia looking a little weepy, with Lance closing the back wall panel she had once banged in terror from the pitch darkness on the other side.

She'd all but blocked the tunnel from her mind, and as the memory of that awful passage rushed in, she scowled. Antonia emerged from the pantry, leaning heavily on the metal walker. Good support, but not to walk through a black cellar where anything might lurk. Rese shuddered.

Though her face demanded an explanation, Lance looked past her. "You didn't eat your breakfast."

"No, I . . ." She glanced back at the pastry cooling innocently on the table, then glared. "Where were you?"

He stated the obvious. "We came through the tunnel from the carriage house."

"You slept over there?"

"Didn't Star tell you?"

"I haven't seen her." She put her hands on her hips. "Don't you think it's dangerous taking Antonia through the tunnel?"

"It's m . . . y fault. I asked." Antonia settled into the chair and started in on the peach-stuffed pastry.

Lance closed the pantry door.

Rese crossed her arms. "You're obviously recovered." On his feet at least, though he'd knocked hers out from under her.

"I don't know why I passed out. The flight or something."

"Or something."

He looked away, not wanting to fight. And why was she? She'd spent the whole night mourning his departure. Now he was there, and all she could do was scold him. "I thought you were gone."

"You said we could stay." He frowned, glancing at Antonia.

Rese looked too, but Antonia was carefully feeding herself, bite by bite. A marked improvement. She could obviously put her mind to something and accomplish it. But what was it she meant to accomplish?

Lance moved to the stove. "I'll make you another."

Rese almost snapped for him not to bother, but his hand shook when he reached for the bowl. What had he done to himself? Other people served God, people like Chaz and Michelle, without physical and emotional damage. But Lance? Lance had to make it painful.

Rese's anger was palpable, though she wouldn't show it. Her expression was utterly stoic. He wished she'd hurl something, scream, shout, even pinch his sides and cry, but no, she would ice him.

He put the hot, crisp popover on a warmed plate and filled it with caramelized peaches, dusted it with confectioner's sugar, and prayed. Rese thanked him when he set it before her, and the chill spread.

He glanced down at Baxter, who sympathized but was not risking his own favored status. Planted at Rese's knee, his eyes said, "You'll have to dig out of this one yourself."

It was for her sake he'd broken it off. How could he know what God intended? It might have gone another way and endangered her. He had done what he had to, but it occurred to him the Bible was silent on the women's reactions to the men's deeds. How had Sarah responded when Abraham told her he was going to run on up the mountain and sacrifice their son? *"Okay, honey, be home for dinner?"* And they'd had a century of marriage to fall back on. He had two rejected proposals and a lot more time in the doghouse than out.

Rese had made a clean break all right; new partner, new direction, no inn — no need for him at all. So why couldn't he let it go? In the moments before he'd passed out at her feet, he had known God was not done with him. But Rese might be.

Star gave him a wry smile when he served her pastry. She was not missing a thing and seemed to find his predicament amusing. They had talked yesterday, and she'd told him about Rese getting custody and how Elaine had settled in and even improved since coming to live with them. Elaine had wandered around the house, now and then interjecting her own comments.

Rese had accomplished that, too, making a home for her mother. Did that bode well for him? If Rese could forgive Elaine — Better not presume. Rese drew a clear distinction between her mother's limitations and the rest of the world's. His in particular.

When Star asked, he'd told her Rico had the painting in his room, that he woke to it each day and spent a good deal of time comtemplating its composition . . . or something. She didn't pursue it, just said, "Thanks for getting me out of New York. I know it wasn't pretty." But she seemed to have put it all behind her. And she seemed happy. Was Rese? Not at the moment.

He served Elaine's pastry, then sat down with his own. He willed himself to eat it without looking ridiculous, but before he'd made a dent, Rese finished hers and brought her plate to the sink.

"I'll get that," he said, but she washed it herself. No comment, of course, on the food. That would imply approval. Within moments she was out the door. He dropped his head back and closed his eyes.

" 'What freezings have I felt, what dark days seen,' " Star murmured.

"And no thaw in sight," he answered.

"A . . . ll in good time." Nonna nodded knowingly.

But Elaine said, "She's gone, gone, gone."

Try as she might, Rese could not make herself stay past the end of the day. Brad even asked if she'd be there late, and that was her chance to say yes. But she went home and crept inside to the heavenly scents of something that brought a Baxter-like response to her mouth. Lance and Antonia worked together at the stove she guessed by the conversation emanating from the kitchen over the music. Star had pulled tables together in the dining room and decorated with silk roses and candles.

627

It was like walking into *House Beautiful*.

Slipping past without a word, Rese changed and washed up, then bolstered herself and joined them all in the kitchen. Because of the opera playing on the Bose sound system Star had purchased with money from her trust fund, Lance hadn't heard her come in. Comfortably invisible, Rese watched him give Mom a piece of cheese from a pile he had handy when she jammed her hand at him.

She put it into her mouth and walked to the wall where she stood with one arm in the air. "The pattern is very important. If you don't understand. Always put the green with the green. The green with the green."

Lance held a sprig of something for Nonna to smell. She nodded, and he rubbed it over whatever was in the saucepan. Once again everything seemed centered around him, and before that could seem right, Rese tried to slip back to her suite. But Lance turned and saw her there. Why did his feelings have to be so apparent? And what was she supposed to do about it?

A knock at the kitchen door broke the thread of their gaze. Rese pulled it open, and Michelle gave her a hug — she could only blame herself for starting that the last time Michelle was over. Baxter bounded over ready to spring, but Lance spoke his name in a tone that made him sit and wag instead.

"Doesn't it smell good in here?" Michelle advanced to the stove and made too much of the glorious aroma.

Just what Lance needed, someone else drooling. He deferred the praise to Nonna, but Rese knew how he sopped up any appreciation for the food he prepared. Whatever his difficulty eating, it had obviously not kept him from providing. She didn't know what to think about any of that, and it wasn't her problem, anyway. Why did people keep thinking she was any kind of problem solver?

"I can set another place," Star said.

What? Rese crossed her arms. Did she have a say in anything? She'd worked hard. She was tired.

"How can I refuse with two professional chefs working together?"

Oh, not professional. There was the little matter of certification.

Michelle turned to her. "Long day?"

Yes, I actually worked. How nice of you to notice. Rese bit her tongue and nodded.

"I came by to ask you something. A favor of sorts."

Great. Rese waited.

"What favor?" Star said.

"Well, I've got a little gal in a tight spot.

She doesn't speak much English, and I'm not too sure about her green card. But I thought of you with all these rooms. It wouldn't be permanent. Just until she had the baby, or found something else."

Baby? "You're kidding, right?" The words were out before she could stop them.

Star giggled.

Rese drew a breath and collected herself. "I mean . . ." What did she mean?

Michelle took her comment in stride. "We could do a little something from the sharing fund to help with food and diapers."

"Food and diapers," Mom said from her spot on the wall.

Rese frowned. "Diapers come after babies, or with. I mean, when she'd be finding something else."

Star giggled again.

Mom left her spot and jerked out her hand for another piece of cheese. Lance handed it over and turned back to the stove. Star and Antonia watched her reclaim her wall space. No one seemed to be reacting to Michelle's favor of sorts. Were they all waiting for her to speak the obvious? *We're not set up for a baby, or strangers, or . . .*

Rese sagged against the table. "We'd need to talk about it."

"Oh, sure." Michelle waved her hands. "I know I'm springing it on you, but she's in kind of a hovel, and it can't be healthy for the baby, you know?"

The weight descended. She could not take on another need. "I'm not sure . . ." She looked from Mom to Star to Antonia to Lance's back and wished she could pass out for a day or two.

"Let's eat," Lance said.

The roasted pork with saffron rice in a light, savory sauce, crisp green beans, and some kind of flatbread were fabulous, but she had as hard a time getting it down as Lance. Even though she had two cooks and three filled guest rooms, she wanted to holler, "I'm not running an inn!"

"The best I can figure," Michelle said, "Maria came up with the migrant workers, but some of them didn't move on. Anyway there's seven living in one room, six guys and her, and she's a little hazy about the father."

Rese closed her eyes. She understood Michelle's concern, but she had concerns of her own. What was happening to the plan she'd made? Work with Brad, take care of Mom, have a place for Star as long as she wanted it.

"And since she's only sixteen —"

"Sixteen!" Rese met Star's gaze across the table. She'd been waiting for her to flip out, but instead she'd grown quietly intense. Rese read the message there. How much could a pregnant sixteen-year-old eat?

But that wasn't the point. There would be a baby, and how could Maria work and pay child care? And then there was Mom. What if she got stressed out? And what if Star left? Rese had to work or there'd be no income.

She had avoided Lance the whole meal, but like Baxter biting a wound, she looked at him now and asked, "What do you think?" When she should have cut out her tongue before giving him the idea his situation was anything but temporary and his opinion mattered.

He tried to read her, but when she gave him nothing to go on, he shrugged. "Nonna likes babies."

Antonia nodded, her mouth pulling into a slanted smile.

Rese turned to Michelle. "Maria could be deported."

"She'll probably have the baby first. She's close."

"How close?"

"I'd guess within the month."

Rese dropped her jaw.

"Pretty short notice," Michelle acknowledged.

Why did all her reasons start seeming

like excuses? They were valid. "I'm not here much. It would be on you, Star."

"Oft the means to do good deeds, makes good deeds done."

"It might be hard to get anything done, like painting."

Star spread her arms. "Such is the fickle fabric of fate."

Well, against such fickle fabric, what choice did she have? "What about a doctor, and all the baby stuff?"

"A midwife at the church has taken over her care. A labor of love."

Meaning free of charge, she supposed, and if others were being generous, what kind of hardhearted lout was she?

Star pointed with her fork. "You could make the prettiest cradle, Rese, with that burly wood in the workshop."

"That burly wood is spoken for." But she might have some left over, and there were other nice pieces. She could not believe she was getting excited about a design that sprang to mind.

She hadn't even met Maria. But then, she'd been willing to open her home to strangers before. On a temporary, economically advantageous basis, with Lance handling it all. Lance. She groaned.

"We'll get back to you," he said, taking the pressure off, easing her situation.

Rese seethed, but didn't argue.

"Yes, great. Just let me know." Michelle was all smiles, knowing what the answer would be, so why not just say so?

But Rese kept quiet. There were too many variables. Antonia might like babies, but how long would she be there? And what if Michelle found uses for the other guest rooms? Taking Maria would send a message, set a precedent, make saying no that much harder the next time. She used to be good at no. She'd honed the skill of refusal. She could say no right now. But she didn't.

After Michelle left and Lance helped Antonia back to the carriage house, Rese took Mom up to bed. It was their time together, since Star had responsibility during the day. Sometimes she wanted to talk, but tonight Mom walked over and turned on the TV, a sign that she wanted to be alone.

Rese didn't take it personally. She understood alone. And it might become a rare commodity. She went downstairs. Lance and Star were cleaning up, Star whisking between the table and the sink, Lance up to his elbows in suds. What was he doing at her sink, and why hadn't they gotten a dishwasher? Oh, yeah; she'd nixed it.

The opera had been replaced by classic rock, and Star moved to the beat as she put a rose between her teeth and spun around the kitchen. Lance sent a sideways glance Rese returned before she could stop herself. She did not want to start the communication of glances again. It led to other nonverbal communication.

Clenching her jaw, Rese grabbed a dish towel and accepted the rinsed plate he held out. The muscles and tendons stood out in his forearms as he worked and made her think of Rico, but she didn't ask until Star had blown them kisses and gone upstairs.

"He's pretty well healed." Lance handed her the last dish. "If he doesn't overdo it."

"Is that possible? For Rico not to overdo it?"

Lance cocked his head. "Remotely."

She pressed her hands dry, then folded the towel over the rack and turned into his chest. He had her fenced in against the counter, and the look in his face hammered her. "Don't even think about it."

"Not remotely possible." His gaze went to her mouth.

"Lance." If he kissed her, she'd deck him. Then she'd deck herself for wanting it.

His throat worked. His chest rose and fell. But he backed away, and she moved out.

"I was going to ask if you thought you might stay until Maria had her baby and found someplace else."

"Then you're taking her?"

Rese blew an exasperated breath. "It's kind of hard to say no."

"I think you've got it down."

She ignored that. "Especially after Michelle's labor-of-love speech."

"You'd do it anyway." His gaze warmed her. "It's how you are."

Rese turned away, hurt replacing the rage. "There's a word for it — doormat."

"You're no doormat."

His hand closed over her elbow, and she felt the shock of it all the way up her arm. He drew her in.

"Lance, I swear if you kiss me, you'll regret it."

"I'll take that chance."

She huffed. "I don't believe you! How can you think I'd want —" Her voice played the traitor. She clenched her fists. "Would you even be here if Antonia hadn't forced it?"

"Rese . . ."

"Answer me."

"I didn't want to make it worse."

She snorted. "Since it was so good?"

Baxter looked up from the floor, sensing the combative strain and feeling for them. Lance slid his hands around her waist. "Rese, listen . . ."

No way would she let him talk. "Let go."

His throat worked. "Okay." But it was

three tense seconds before he did.

Rese drew herself up. "You can consider yourself hired. Antonia stays for free." She might not be schizophrenic, but she'd just proven herself certifiable.

Chapter Thirty-eight

Maria was about Star's height and so big in the belly she looked ready to burst. She stood in sweat pants and a ragged sweater stretched to lacy thinness, legs spread to bear the weight. Lance didn't say it out loud, but he doubted it would be any month before she went. He'd seen enough pregnant teens to recognize the imminence.

"Well, this is Maria." Michelle nudged her forward in the driveway.

He and Rese had gone out alone in the crisp, gray morning to meet them, since Elaine would take some explaining and Star didn't want to overwhelm the girl.

Jacketless, Rese wrapped herself in her arms. "Hi, Maria. I'm Rese and this is Lance." Clear and simple and more than she'd managed with previous guests. She no longer needed his glib intervention.

Maria didn't look up and barely moved her lips to pronounce a strongly accented, "Hello."

Rese rubbed her arms. "I've made up a room for you. I hope you don't mind stairs."

Maria's face washed with confusion, and without thinking, Lance translated. Rese turned in surprise.

"Less English than we thought." He couldn't help smiling. His prayer last night had bordered on desperate, and now they were. Switching back to Spanish, he asked Maria if she'd like to go inside.

She nodded.

Michelle spread her hands. "Well, I'll leave you all to get acquainted."

Rese looked a little panicked. "Do you think she'll want you here for a while? Until she gets comfortable?"

"She doesn't know me much better than you. And you've got a translator." Michelle smiled his way.

He shrugged. "Had to know what Rico was calling me." He turned to Maria and said gently, *"Vamanos."*

"I don't believe this," Rese muttered under her breath as she followed them into the house.

He'd awakened close to despair that first morning, realizing Rese had no need for him. He'd been through fire, but all she could see was the burned-out husk. And she'd moved on. This language thing was small, but significant? The Lord giving him one stepping stone in the torrent? He couldn't ask for more. He knew better.

Maria's eyes widened when they brought

639

her into the Jasmine Garden, all done in white with a slender-framed canopy bed twined with gauzy veils. She looked utterly confused and a little terrified.

"Tell her this is her room." Rese spoke softly, as though she might overhear.

Lance told Maria what Rese said, but she still didn't understand, so he explained she could sleep there and use the desk and the adjoining bathroom. He would have mentioned the closet, but she hadn't brought any other clothes.

When he had finished, she dropped her gaze to the floor and asked in Spanish, "What do I have to do?"

Lord. He drew a slow breath and said in words she knew and understood, "Have a strong, healthy baby."

She still wouldn't look up, but she nodded.

"Tienes hambre?" It didn't look like she could fit food in, but he knew from Lucy and Monica that didn't stop their being hungry.

She shook her head.

He told her the kitchen was downstairs, that she would eat with them, but she could also help herself to whatever she wanted. *"Comprendes?"*

"Si," she murmured almost too softly to hear.

He caught Rese's elbow. "Let's give her

a while to settle in."

Rese followed him out, leaving the door open behind her. Maria hadn't moved, but they didn't want her to feel locked up. They went downstairs.

Rese sank into a chair in the sitting room. "What did you tell her?"

He repeated it.

"What did she say?"

"She wanted to know what she had to do." He guessed she meant what would be done to her. This was one hurting world. "I told her to have a healthy baby."

Rese nodded, but he couldn't tell what she was thinking. She'd closed him out again.

"I guess it's good you're here."

A more lukewarm commendation he'd never heard. But what did he expect? He was once again the hired help.

She huffed. "I know enough Spanish to tell a worker to do it over, to make it straight, to please clean up the mess. Don't think that'll help much."

"Maybe she understands more than we know."

Rese shook her head. "She must be terrified."

"Yeah." And Rese knew all about fear and situations one couldn't control. It was no accident the girl had come to them.

Rese pushed herself up from the chair. "I

have to get to work."

He hated those words. Not that she was working at something she loved and was good at, or even that she did it with Brad, but that it gave such finality to the death of their dream. He tried not to show it. Failed.

She got her keys and went out without saying good-bye. He'd pushed her limits last night. She wouldn't want to leave him an opening. He joined Nonna, Star, and Elaine in the kitchen and explained their guest's language barrier. But even though none of them spoke Spanish, it hardly compared to his obstructed communication with Rese.

"Is it something about me?" Rese shoved her hands into her jacket pockets. "Do I look stupid or gullible?"

"Hardly." Brad laughed.

"One word of English, Brad. And she had to work for that."

Crouched atop the roof, he braced himself against a gust of wind. "Well, your guy's got the Spanish thing covered. I'd be more concerned about the liability of her condition."

"Liability?"

He shrugged. "She could be a con job, for all you know."

"She's sixteen, Brad."

"Says who?" He tossed a broken tile into the box of shards.

She would say she trusted Michelle, but Michelle had admitted that she hardly knew Maria herself. What if it was a scam to plant her there, then blame them for . . . what? Rese frowned. "You have a suspicious mind."

"So sue me."

She took a deep breath and let it out slowly. "I came up here to feel better, not worse."

"I just think you should be careful letting all kinds of people move in with you. What would Vernon think?"

Rese tried to imagine Dad at the villa. Not only could she not picture it, but she had a hard time feeling bad about that. "You know what? It doesn't matter what he'd think. I miss him. I'm sad he's gone." She felt the pang even now. "But it's my life; it's what I think that matters." It shocked her that she believed it.

Brad hunkered down onto his heels and studied her. His hands were stained with tar paper, and one of the knees of his jeans was ragged. His sweatshirt was thick, but even so he must be feeling the chill that had kicked up. "Well, honey, you're all grown up, then."

She scowled. "I didn't come up to hear that either."

His phone beeped, and he spoke to one of the guys inside. Rese shivered in the brisk wind and fastened the top snap of her flannel-lined jacket. Brad slid the phone back into his pocket and rested on his haunches.

Rese frowned. "Are you afraid?"

He cocked his head. "Of what?"

"Giving your marriage another chance."

He braced his forearms on his knees. "I'm regretting telling you that."

"Well?"

He looked away, then back. "Yeah. I'm afraid if we tried again, and it didn't work . . ."

"Does it scare you to think it might, and you'd never know?" She closed her arms around herself and shivered.

His nose had reddened in the wind. He sniffed. "Yeah. It does."

And what had she gained by that line of questioning? Why did she think there was a lesson in Brad's life for her? He was satisfied with his choices. Wasn't he?

She went back down and ended up staying after dark because she had to finish the cabinets so the electrician could wire the recessed lighting, and she wasn't satisfied with the finish on a portion of the banister, and . . . When she could find nothing else that couldn't wait, she drove home with something close to dread.

She'd had it mostly under control with Mom and Star. Even with Mom's special needs, it was the least complicated her life had been in a while. Then Lance sent her reeling, and now Maria. What had she been thinking? Maybe Brad was right. Maybe she should think more like Dad. He would not be in this predicament. But then . . . did she really miss those solitary evenings in front of the TV?

A gust of sleet ticked across the windshield like tossed rice. Her wipers thumped back and forth. Brad had finished up the roof just in time. She wouldn't want him up there with ice on the tiles, and they both hated delays — except when it kept her from facing a situation she'd rather walk naked through the sleet than face.

She parked the truck, and though the cab had been toasty, the blast that struck when she opened the door sent a chill to her bones. She wrestled the door shut, gripped her jacket around her throat, and ran for the kitchen door. It opened before she could reach out, and Lance pulled her inside. Removing her wrist from his grip, she brushed the freezing rain from her hair and sleeves.

"Take it off and hang it over the chair." Lance foamed a mug of milk he had obviously held ready and, when she'd shed her jacket, pressed a vanilla steamer into her hands, covering them with his own.

Not exactly employee behavior. She'd think of him as a houseboy. Or a slave. She almost giggled into her milk, and that terrified her worse than anything. Was she running a fever?

"I held your dinner."

"I ate."

His disappointment was tangible.

She didn't think it was spite that had made her grab a drive-thru burger. More like self-preservation. His food was already working on her, and she needed some defense. So what excuse did she have for slurping down the steamer until it coated her upper lip with warm, fragrant comfort?

Instinct. What cold, tired animal wouldn't do as much? But Lance was making more of it than that. Any minute he'd reach out and pull her close, and she was not in a place to resist because resisting Lance had been skipped in her skill set.

She brought up her chin. "How's Maria?"

"I'm not sure." He took the empty mug and set it on the counter. "She hasn't eaten, hasn't left her room. Star and I checked on her a couple times, but she doesn't say much."

Rese snorted.

"I think she might be further along than Michelle guessed."

"You mean any day?"

He shrugged. "I'm no expert, but I've seen my sisters and cousins and quite a few girls in the neighborhood. They get that unfocused look, and she's spread out like the baby's dropped."

Rese stared. "Dropped?"

"Into the birth canal."

She planted her hands on her hips. "I thought you weren't an expert."

"It's life, Rese. I've lived it close."

That sent shock waves that made her look away. *Don't think about his life.* About the people who'd taken her into their home, into their hearts, real people, real family, even those unrelated by blood. She'd lived his life up close as well. "Should I check on her?"

"If you want. She's probably in bed."

Rese nodded. What could she say, anyway? She didn't speak her language, didn't speak anyone's.

He took her hands and warmed them against his mouth. "Anything else I can get you?"

She shook her head.

"Anything at all I can do?" His voice rasped.

"Lance . . ." This was not going to work if he insisted on getting up close and per-

647

sonal every time —

"I love you."

Tears stung. "You said that before."

His brow pinched. "I meant it."

She closed her eyes and shook her head.

His breath was hot on her fingers. "I know I hurt you."

"I'm not hurt."

"And I'm sorry, Rese, but I did what I had to."

"Had to?" She glared.

"I didn't know what God expected. But you know I had to do it."

"But whatever it was, I was expendable. Our plans were expendable."

"I'm sorry." He pulled her in and took her face between his hands. "I didn't plan it this way. If it was up to me a whole lot of things would be different. And maybe I still don't get it right most of the time, but I'm trying."

The kitchen light glinted off the diamond in his ear. Where was the disdain she'd managed at that first glimpse? How had he swept aside her defense and common sense? She *knew* better.

His eyes darkened. "I'm trying to make it right."

Only Lance would think he could.

"However long it takes, whatever you require." He drew a ragged breath. "If you can't believe it now, give me time. Let me show you. Let me prove . . . faithful."

The thought of his faithfulness swelled her throat. Wasn't that his very core? Hadn't faithfulness driven him to serve Antonia and, more encompassing, God? Was he offering her anything close to the fire that had hollowed him? The thought ensnared and terrified.

His hands encased her face with a fiery embrace. "I love you. And I'm going to kiss you."

Her heart kicked her ribs. "It won't change anything."

"Maybe not." But he found her mouth and made her a liar. And a fool because everything in her wanted to respond, and then she'd be kissing him back, and he'd think he'd won, and he'd be right.

She wasn't ready to concede. She'd felt the agony that matched the ecstasy. But his kiss deepened, and his arms enclosed her, and she knew where she belonged if she was willing to take the risk.

But with a strength Vernon Barrett would have applauded, she pulled back and said, "Thanks for the steamer."

He swallowed. "You're welcome."

She felt his gaze on her back all the way through the door. Heart aching, she changed out of her clothes, showered, and pulled on her flannel pants and soft forest green top. With a Herculean effort, she turned her thoughts to the girl upstairs with her belly so distended and the baby dropped into the birth canal. Perspective.

Maybe tomorrow she'd start working on the cradle. She sighed. How had it gotten to this? Oh yeah. Unconditional love. Wasn't that, after all, what Lance wanted?

She woke with a jolt when Star nearly shook her teeth loose. "Rese, she had the baby!"

She shook the fog away. "Having? She's having it?"

"Had. And she's screaming her head off."

She bolted up. Didn't the screaming come before the baby? "Go get Lance. I mean Antonia. Get them both. And call the midwife." Though what good it would do now, she didn't know.

As Star took off for the carriage house, Rese mounted the stairs at a sprint, then stopped dead at the top. The smell of blood gagged and paralyzed her. Maria was screaming, but the baby made no sound. No way it was sleeping. It must be dead.

Lord. She sank against the wall, shudders dissolving her legs. Her head spun. Star rushed up from behind, then Lance with Antonia in his arms. He must have scooped her out of bed in her nightgown, but she was calmly telling him they'd need string and scissors and warm towels. They disappeared into the room.

And then Rese heard the baby cry.

The fog cleared in her head. She staggered to the doorway. Blood streaked Maria's thighs. The baby lay all clutched up and wailing on the soggy sheet, its tiny limbs shaking and a gaping crevice between its nose and mouth.

Braced by the bedpost, Antonia took hold of Maria's jaw and bore into her with a look that silenced the screams. In T-shirt and drawstring pants, with sleep-tousled hair and shadowed jaw, Lance dropped to the bed and lifted the baby, still dangling a tubelike cord and bloody mass. He curled it into his chest. His features twisted. The tendons in his neck stood out as he covered the baby's face with his hand, tipped back his head, and groaned, "Lord Jesus."

The moment hung, Maria gaping, the baby gasping, Star and Antonia silent. Rese stood like stone, and she must have seen wrong from the doorway, because when Lance took his hand away there was no gap. The baby resumed its rusty-hinge cries. Finding her legs, Rese ran downstairs for scissors and string, then back up, already rationalizing. Her angle, blood on the face, her own light-headed stress and trauma.

"Tie it tight and cl . . . ose, but n . . . ot

651

too close," Antonia instructed her.

Lance held the baby's tummy up as she fumbled the string around the spongy umbilical cord and pulled it tight. She looked into his face, saw the immediacy of the situation, concern, and probably adrenaline making his hands shake.

"N . . . ow cut."

Rese freed the baby boy from the cord and placenta. Star grabbed a fluffy white towel from the bathroom, and Lance swaddled the little guy so that only his unmarred face showed. Then he put the baby into Maria's arms.

Lance shook as he carried Nonna back to the carriage house, but not from fatigue. The midwife had arrived, cleaned and diapered the baby, and instructed Maria in his feeding. Star and Rese were there for anything else she might need. Elaine had slept through it all.

"Let me sit," Nonna told him as he carried her into the carriage house bedroom.

He sat her up in the bed Rese had built, and stuffed pillows behind her.

"Now you." She pointed to the foot.

He sat down and faced her. The shaking intensified.

"Don't be afraid of it." Her voice was stern.

"Nonna . . ." It was way beyond fear.

He'd felt something with Rico, but nothing like . . .

"If God sees fit to use your hands, then use them He will."

He knew whose power it was. But he couldn't get his mind around it.

"Since you were born, God's had a love affair with you."

Lance shook his head. No way. Not the way he'd struggled and rebelled. But rooted in the struggle, hadn't there always been a longing, a yearning so deep it groaned inside him? *Use me, Lord. Pour me out in this hurting world.*

"So now it shows." She shrugged. "So what?"

"So what!" He spread his hands, then looked down at them in consternation. "I don't even know it's coming." Because all he'd felt was Maria's revulsion and a harrowing sadness for the disfigured infant.

"And it may never happen again. He chooses." Her eyes took on a faraway look he'd seen on her before, the look that saw beyond. "Then again —" she shrugged — "it may."

He swallowed painfully. "But, Nonna, how can it . . . work, when I'm such a screw-up?"

She laughed, clutched her hands together at her chest, and laughed some more.

He spread his hands. "Wha-at."

"That" — she pointed straight at him — "is how it works."

Thankfully Carla, the midwife, had brought diapers and things for Maria and the baby, since they'd had no time to prepare. Rese provided clean sheets and blankets, waited until Maria was nestled in with her newborn son, then showed Carla out. Now in the near dawn, she headed to her room with Star on her heels. No surprise that Star climbed into the other side of the bed. They were both unsettled, to say the least.

Rese stared at the ceiling, letting the whole scene play out in her mind. One thing was certain, she should never be in a position of authority where blood was involved.

Star rolled to her side. "Rese?"

"Yeah?"

"What happened up there?"

Rese rolled her head to face her, a thousand possible answers and none that she could voice. "I don't know."

They lay in silence for a while, then Star said, "I'll tell you." She took her hand and threaded their fingers. "Something was wrong, and then it wasn't."

Rese's heart hammered as she lay there, seeing it all again. The red waxy baby curled like a caterpillar in Lance's hands, the expression on his face she'd never forget, the baby's own face . . . So she hadn't been mistaken. But that meant . . .

"If I had to guess, I'd say it was your capricious God." Star pulled Rese's hand to her cheek and snuggled in as she had when they were little girls, sisters in all but DNA. "I hope Lance cooks breakfast," she said drowsily. "I'm hungry already."

Chapter Thirty-nine

Rese opened the oven the next morning and breathed the aroma of the golden, bubbling asparagus frittata. Baxter got up from under the table and clicked across the floor to bump her legs. Rese closed the oven and took his head between her hands. "Good morning." She rubbed and stroked his fuzzy muzzle, face, and ears. It was a good morning. Though it was only a few hours after last night's drama, she had slept as deeply as a baby herself.

Star was still in her bed; all the house was silent. She hadn't heard a sound from the kitchen, and she could almost believe Lance had conjured the aromatic frittata from thin air. But that thought brought last night back in vivid detail, Lance with his hand over the baby's face, crying out, then drawing his hand away, stunned himself by what he saw. Had God brought Maria to them through Michelle just in time for Lance . . .

She pressed a hand to her forehead. If something was wrong and then it wasn't, what did that mean? And was that the same man who'd kissed her last night? *"Let me prove faithful."*

She slid her fingers down to rest against her mouth. Did he even see the way God used him to change lives? *"Maybe I still don't get it right most of the time."* The Lord didn't seem to share that opinion. Or maybe it wasn't about getting it right. Maybe it was all about trying, about wanting, about getting inside God's skin and seeing and feeling and loving.

Releasing a slow breath, Rese looked around the kitchen, trying to recall her first intentions. She laughed softly. Plans changed. Lives connected. Miracles happened.

Baxter's tongue warmed her hand. Smiling down, she opened the door to let him outside and saw Lance, face uplifted to the sky, eyes closed, cheeks glistening with tears. His skin had a glow like gold dust from the sun. *"I did what I had to."* He was telling the truth.

He'd been willing to give her up, to do anything for the God he loved. But she stepped out, and even though it was January, the warmth of the sun cloaked her from the crown of her hair down her arms and shoulders, to her bare feet on the rough flagstones. She moved toward him.

When at last Lance turned, he didn't wipe his tears. He probably didn't even know they were there. His eyes held plea and promise as he reached out his hand, and with an ache of recognition, she stepped forward to take it. Someone had to keep him connected to earth.

About the Author

Kristen Heitzmann is the bestselling author of fourteen novels, including *Secrets* and the 2003 Christy Award finalist, *The Tender Vine*. An artist and music minister, Kristen lives in Colorado with her husband and four children.